Extraordinary Praise for
The Invention of Ana

"Mikkel Rosengaard's intriguing first novel . . . weaves story upon story to explore . . . the bond between writer and muse."

—*New York Times Book Review*

"This strange story about strange stories, told with intelligence and humor, lingers in the mind like a dream." —*Kirkus Reviews*

"[Rosengaard] charts the emotional distance between Bucharest under Ceaușescu's despotic rule and present-day hipster Brooklyn, resulting in a striking, auspicious debut."

—*Publishers Weekly*

"[A] stirring debut. . . . Rosengaard's novel is a swift and memorable meditation on how storytellers struggle to separate the tangible from the contrived." —*Booklist*

"Surprising, suspenseful, and deeply affecting, *The Invention of Ana* is written in prose as elegant and precise as a mathematical proof. With Sebaldian layering and unflinching self-reflection, the narrator at the heart of Rosengaard's wonderful debut novel guides us through the story of artist Ana Ivan's parents' plagued existence under Ceaușescu's authoritarian rule, her tortured birth and the time-traveling curse that pursues her into adulthood, and the narrator's reckoning with his own relationships and desires. A meditation on time, mortality, and politics—from Romania in the 1970s to the New York art world in the 2010s—Rosengaard takes us into the darkness that haunts every honest examination of self, and helps bring us out again, with art and with artfulness. A beautiful and enlarging read, *The Invention of Ana* made me feel as if my own life had gained a bit of extra time." —Alena Graedon, author of *The Word Exchange*

"More intriguing still are the moments where the story pauses to reveal its philosophical import, moving across time and place, from arty Brooklyn to communist Bucharest to the streets of Rabat." —*Bomb Magazine*

"Fascinating. . . . Ana's stories are Rosengaard's great achievement." —*AM New York*

The
Invention
of Ana

The

Invention

of

Ana

MIKKEL
ROSENGAARD

Translated by Caroline Waight

P.S.™ is a trademark of HarperCollins Publishers.

THE INVENTION OF ANA. Copyright © 2016 by Mikkel Rosengaard and Gyldendal, Copenhagen. English translation copyright © 2018 by Caroline Waight. All rights reserved. Printed in the United States of America. No part of this book may be used or reproduced in any manner whatsoever without written permission except in the case of brief quotations embodied in critical articles and reviews. For information, address HarperCollins Publishers, 195 Broadway, New York, NY 10007.

HarperCollins books may be purchased for educational, business, or sales promotional use. For information, please email the Special Markets Department at SPsales@harpercollins.com.

Originally published as *Forestillinger om Ana Ivan* in Denmark in 2016 by Gyldendal.

A hardcover edition of this book was published in 2017 by Custom House, an imprint of William Morrow.

FIRST CUSTOM HOUSE PAPERBACK EDITION PUBLISHED 2018.

Clock illustration by Lunatictm/Shutterstock, Inc.

The Library of Congress has catalogued a previous edition as follows:

Names: Rosengaard, Mikkel, 1987– author. | Waight, Caroline, translator.
Title: The invention of Ana : a novel / Mikkel Rosengaard ; translated by Caroline Waight.
Other titles: Forestillinger om Ana Ivan. English
Description: First edition. | New York, NY : Custom House, 2018.
Identifiers: LCCN 2017036753 (print) | LCCN 2017044738 (ebook) | ISBN 9780062679093 (ebook) | ISBN 0062679090 (ebook) | ISBN 9780062679079 (hardback) | ISBN 0062679074 (hardcover)
Subjects: | BISAC: FICTION / Literary. | FICTION / Coming of Age. | FICTION / Urban Life.
Classification: LCC PT8177.28.O84 (ebook) | LCC PT8177.28.O84 F6713 2018 (print) | DDC 839.813/8—dc23
LC record available at https://lccn.loc.gov/2017036753

ISBN 978-0-06-267908-6 (pbk.)

18 19 20 21 22   LSC   10 9 8 7 6 5 4 3 2 1

I

I heard the first of her stories one spring evening on a Brooklyn rooftop. I was interning at an art festival back then, newly arrived and hungry for the city, fancying I belonged in the art world, and because I was keen to rub shoulders with artists, I found myself on the roof of the exhibition space that evening, listening to her tell me she had a quarter in her shoe. She'd made up her mind to walk around with the coin until she dreamed about it. It had been in there two weeks, she explained. She wanted America beneath her skin, but all she'd gotten were a few ugly blisters, and she hadn't even dreamed about the coin yet.

I wished her luck with the project, we clinked glasses, and she introduced herself as Ana Ivan. When I asked where she was from, she said Bucharest, telling me about where she grew up and about Ceaușescu's rationing in the eighties, when only every fifth streetlamp was lit and the television broadcast programs for just two hours a day.

Oh sure, Romania, I said. Things were pretty bad back then?

Ana shrugged. They never went hungry, but there was no electricity, and she remembered the long, dark evenings in the apartment, the afternoons when there was so little to do that she was reduced to padding out the hours with daydreams. Sometimes she sat in front of the blank television and imagined the cartoons she'd seen, rearranging them into new combinations. Other times she played a game with her father: They put a blank piece of paper on the table, shut their eyes, and let a pen fall on the sheet at random. A dot here and a dot there, until there were a few handfuls of them. Then they sat together and stared at the dots, looking for figures or patterns, or patterns that looked like figures, and when they'd agreed on one they joined up the dots to make a picture emerge. They drew lines between the dots to make an elephant or a flower or a snail's shell, and sooner or later her father always threw open his arms and said, Ah, Ana, just imagine! This is how the world hangs together, everything we see just a few tiny flecks in space. He said it every time—not, in that sense, an inventive man. What d'you make of that, then? he would say. Most of what we see is nothing but empty space. It's just the distance between atoms, sheer nothingness. And then Ana would pick up the pen and ask, So is this nothing? and her father would say, No, sweetheart, that's atoms *and* nothing, and it was all true, a nice edifying game they continued to play until one day Ana went on a school trip. She was in the second or third year, she told me—it must have been in the mid-eighties, because Ceaușescu's palace was still a forest of scaffolding growing out of the hillside into the center of town—and the teacher was shepherding the children toward the building site, pointing at the cranes and diggers and asking, So, can anybody tell me what that is? Yes, said Ana, It's nothing. Nothing, said the schoolteacher, what do you mean by that? That's what my dad says. It's sheer nothingness. Ana's father was summoned for a conversation. He had to explain and smooth things over, and if Ana was to be believed, he was lucky not to lose his job or his front teeth, because after that episode all the family's letters were steamed open, the Securitate kept coming to visit, and the neighbors listened in on the telephone line.

Join up the dots, said Ana, when she'd finished her story. Know what I mean?

I nodded as if I'd seen or construed or guessed what she meant, because back then everything was simpler. Ana talked and I listened, and what did it matter to me whether she talked about her father or her school trips? Ana was an artist, and in my eyes that made her worth listening to.

As I remember it, it was the first warm day of spring. I'd gotten there early to set up tables, leaning against the banister as I watched the guests come up the stairs, some of them pausing a moment and blinking as they emerged into the sunlight and the scent of the river that hung above the city that day, as if they'd forgotten why they were hurrying or what came after the short, endless days of winter. A train clattered over the Manhattan Bridge above us, down from the street came the bleating of a truck's horn, and around me the guests were chattering away. I wanted to hear what they were saying, but I didn't know them, and wasn't sure how to introduce myself. So I went to the bar instead, got a glass of wine, and stared at the island across the river, where thousands of people were swarming out of the towers onto the streets, full of thoughts and dreams I knew nothing about but which would soon be opened to me. That's the way I thought back then. I'd be dissolved into the city, and with a lightness in my chest I stared at the shiny panes of glass and the people behind them, people who'd soon be sharing in my memories, when a woman stepped away from the bar and gave me her hand.

She was pale and short, very short, with a black dress and dark hair gathered in a bun, about five or ten years older than me. She had a peculiar face, her eyes brown and inquisitive, and a smile on her lips as if my whole existence was a joke and she was waiting for the punch line.

Are you working at the festival? she asked.

Yes, I said. My brother's one of the organizers.

I asked if she was an artist, and what work she had in the show. Ana must have misunderstood me, or perhaps she just ignored my question, because she launched into the anecdote about the coin in her shoe, and after telling me the story of the school trip and the game with the dots she asked why I'd moved to New York.

Well, my brother works for the festival, I said. And he got me—

Yeah, you said that. But why are you *really* here?

What do you mean?

I mean you didn't travel all the way across the Atlantic to be an intern. You want something—to get rich or hunt bison or whatever.

I laughed. Well, I'm definitely not here to hunt bison.

Judging by that moth-eaten shirt, she said, I'd guess you want to be an intellectual of some kind. An academic or a poet or something.

None of the above, I said. Well, sort of—I write sometimes. Stories, I guess you'd call them. Short fiction and articles and stuff like that.

So you're a writer?

I wouldn't put it quite like that. I haven't published much.

Yeah, well, that's publishing, she sighed. It's not for kids.

Then we clinked glasses and she told me about a friend who was an editor at an imprint or literary magazine or self-publishing group; I don't remember exactly because at that moment I lifted my eyes and caught sight of my brother. Surrounded by a ring of well-dressed people, he was explaining the concept behind the exhibition. I could see it in the way he moved his hands, brandishing them in swelling gestures like a priest or a shaman or a witch doctor, summoning the spirits of the festival. Ana paused, as if she could tell my attention had shifted.

Sorry, I said, smiling. Back in a minute.

When I reached my brother he'd finished his monologue, and there was a chorus of laughter.

I see you've met our Romanian friend, he said with a nod toward Ana. Great, isn't she?

Absolutely, I said. She seems—she's quite something.

Mm, he said. Otherwise she wouldn't be here.

Around us the party atmosphere was gradually beginning to wane. The cheerful voices and the buzz of free alcohol were devolving into drunken, whiny drivel. It had reached that point in the evening when all the dull clichés began to surface: an artist's hand creeping up an intern's thigh, the gallerist pedantically bossing the caterers about. I remember that my brother took his time pointing out a few of the guests—an Egyptian curator, a German

journalist—and before we disappeared into the night I had one
last glimpse of Ana. She was bending over her watch with an expression of concentration, but I can't remember if we said goodbye.

And what if we did?

Back then it made no difference. Ana was just a woman I met
at a reception, one artist out of hundreds, nothing more. I didn't
even glance over my shoulder.

A week went by before I saw her again. The following Thursday
I was walking down the corridor after a lecture, going to deposit
the money we'd taken at the door, and as I passed through the
cavernous exhibition space I noticed the lights were on in the
office. It was late, about eleven or twelve at night, and I'd expected
to find the building in darkness, but coming from the back room I
could hear an almost childish laugh and detect the faint aroma of
fresh pastries, and when I turned the corner I saw Ana sitting at
the desk, bathed in the blue light of the computer screen. She was
video-chatting, wearing the same dress as she had at the launch
party, or one exactly like it, but this time she had no makeup on
and her face was somehow softer.

Oddly enough, it made me shy. Or not shy, exactly, but hesitant,
and for a moment I stood by the doorframe, wondering whether
to leave. I don't know what came over me. I didn't want to intrude,
I guess, didn't want to be pushy, or maybe my hesitation was more
intuitive, as if something inside me knew I should keep my distance. I'd only met Ana once, and although I was charmed by
the coin in her shoe and the little stories she told, I felt there was
something about her I couldn't trust. I wasn't able to put my finger

on what it was, but there was something in the air around her, something disquieting that I didn't understand. Then again, I'd just arrived in town and there were lots of things I didn't understand, so I continued into the room, nodding to Ana and locking the cashbox into the cabinet.

Well, if it isn't the intern, she said, closing the computer. What are you doing here so late?

I've just come from the lecture, I answered.

Oh right, the lecture. Of course.

What about you?

She tapped the black notebook that lay open on the table in front of her. I was going to make an entry in my logbook, she said. But then my mom called.

A logbook? I said. What's that all about?

You know, notes and coordinates and stuff like that.

She gave a brief smile but changed the subject, asking if I knew anywhere to get a decent pair of jeans. I recommended a few stores, but they were closed, of course, at this hour. Ana wasn't pleased.

Isn't this supposed to be the city that never sleeps? Even Bucharest has more going on than here.

I smiled. Can't it wait until tomorrow? They'll probably be open at ten.

Ten, she snorted. I'll only just have gone to bed.

No, no—ten in the morning.

Yeah. I'll only just have gone to bed.

I looked at her, unable to tell whether she was joking or had misunderstood me. Or maybe she was working on a schedule all her own. I asked: So you always work really late at night?

Yeah, you know, because of the time-traveling.

She said it completely naturally, as if she were talking about laundry or picking up a child from school.

Time-traveling?

Yeah. You haven't heard about that?

No, I mean—what? You travel through time?

Sure. I can show you another time, but right now I'm dying for something to eat. Want to get breakfast?

I could have said no. I could have told her I was busy, that it was too late, that I was tired and half-dead on my feet, but those would have been lies. The truth was I was brimming with energy, and even though there was something disquieting about Ana, she was also clever and funny, and I hadn't come to New York to turn down invitations for midnight snacks. I told her I'd be happy to, so we packed up our things, locked the door, and walked out into the city together. We ended up at a diner not far from the exhibition space, where we sat and talked about the service in America, so much better than in Europe, friendly yet ill-mannered in its own extravagant way. Ana told me about the restaurant-less part of Bucharest she'd grown up in, and I told her about my girlfriend Lærke, who waitressed at an all-night restaurant in Copenhagen and was going to move over here as soon as she'd finished her degree.

That's so sweet, said Ana. So sweet and young and innocent. I'm amazed you dared go out with someone like me.

What do you mean?

Didn't your mother ever tell you not to go out with Eastern Europeans? To toss a pinch of salt over your shoulder when there are Romanians around?

No, I said with a smile. I haven't heard that one.

Ah, well, we bring bad luck, you see. We're like a litter of black cats.

To illustrate her point, she told me about the apartment she was living in. She'd inherited it from an old friend of her father's, Paul Pintea, a Romanian mathematician who'd been a professor at Cluj university until the late nineties. When the reforms were implemented he was sacked, and to make matters worse his wife was diagnosed with a serious kidney disorder. In desperation, unable to afford dialysis or find a new job, the professor had entered the Green Card Lottery, and ended up winning, of course. As soon as the paperwork came through, he packed his bags and traveled to New York, but if the venerable mathematician had thought that jobs hung on trees here he'd been very much mistaken. He had to settle for work as a cleaner, plus a menial job on the side as a night attendant at a laundromat out in Sunnyside. The pittance he sent home was barely enough to cover the cost of his wife's dialysis, and soon he took to drink, falling into a deep depression. Oh, nothing but pain and drudgery all around, and after they'd been stewing in their misery for a few years, the wife succumbed to her illness. Six months later it was the mathematician's turn: he keeled over on the downtown R train, struck down by a blood clot in the lung or somewhere.

So there you go, said Ana. I'm living in the ruins of someone else's life.

Sounds like a horror movie, I said. Aren't you afraid he'll come back?

Come back?

Yeah. Paul, I mean. Aren't you afraid he'll return and start haunting you?

She had a lovely laugh, bubbly and forthright. I wish he would, she said, so I can give him a good slap.

At that moment the waitress arrived to take our order. I only had enough money for coffee, but Ana ordered pancakes, and before long we were talking about ready-made cake mix and Dr. Oetker. We talked about Dr. Oetker the individual, August Oetker Junior, who was apparently a big art collector, and about Dr. Oetker's product packaging, which darkened the farther south you got in Europe: cream in Denmark, yellow in Germany, scarlet in Serbia, and a sort of coffee-brown in Spain. Ana chatted and chatted, just nipping at the food, so I ate the rest while she talked. Slowly she cleared the table in front of her. First she moved the plate, then the coffee cup and sugar dispenser, the napkins and the bottle of ketchup. It was like she wanted space to talk. Her hands worked as she told me about her unlucky countrymen, about the accidents that struck both friends and relatives, and about the two minutes she'd been dead.

Sorry, what? I said. The two minutes you what?

Mm, were dead.

I didn't know what to say. Must be some kind of joke, I thought, but Ana seemed serious enough, and I remember very clearly her reaching for the coffee cup, kneading it between her hands, her eyes fixed on the bottom as if reading the grounds. Ana sat there and told me about 1989, the terrible year that had changed her life in so many ways. It had begun innocently on New Year's morning, as she stood on a milk crate and read aloud from Ceaușescu's speech. The other kids had cheered and yelled hurrah, and the local grocer smiled nervously as he watched Ana ape the Great Winter Shoemaker's gestures. She spoke with the same drawling rhythms and made the same spastic motions with her hands as the People's President, and when Ana's father realized what was going on he dragged her straight up to the apartment, where the family had to keep a low profile for weeks on end.

And that's what Ana was like in those days, I guess. A close-cropped mischief-maker who hated dresses and spat long gobbets of spit and refused to accept that she couldn't stand up and pee with the boys, so that her mother was always having to wash her spattered pants. She was small for her age, but that didn't hold her back. Ana was the one bossing the boys around in the parking lot outside the apartment block, and the neighborhood housewives laughed when they saw the little girl ordering pudgy Gabriel Mitu to climb so far up the chestnut tree that he had to be brought down with a ladder like a cat. If you believe Ana, she tyrannized the whole district—but a fall from the giddy heights of power was just around the corner. When she got back after the Christmas break, Violeta Mincic was standing in the schoolyard. The new girl.

Violeta, who wasn't a tomboy like Ana.

Violeta, who had hair that fell down to her butt.

Violeta, who somehow made her Pioneers scarf swell in broad, full waves across her chest, who altered and sewed and modified her school uniform just enough that she always stood out from the rest.

Yes, she was beautiful, but at first it didn't scare Ana. They made friends that day in the schoolyard, and Violeta was enlisted into Ana's regiment, assigned roles and tasks in games of Ana's devising. But although Violeta was allowed to be Nadia Comăneci when they played The Olympics, although Violeta was allowed first choice when they played Among Mountains and Valleys, she was always just that little bit absent, or aloof, or whatever you'd call it in a nine-year-old.

Violeta's true intentions emerged after a few weeks. As soon as she'd picked up how it all worked—who decided what, when, and why—she struck. At recess one day, when Ana wanted to play Rainforest and was splitting up her classmates into insects, carnivores, and herbivores, Violeta sprang her surprise.

That game, she said. You know it's just for babies.

No, it isn't, said Ana.

Okay, fine. If you want to play Ana's game, said Violeta, then play it. I'm just a bit too old.

So what do you want to play, then? asked Gabriel Mitu, who could sense which way the wind was blowing: another day as the hippopotamus.

Well, I actually do know a game my big brother plays, said Violeta, giving her disingenuously bashful smile, the same one she'd smile for sixteen years, until the day her boyfriend fell asleep at the wheel and crashed into a bus shelter.

If you want, she said, I can show you what to do.

During the next recess Ana stayed in the classroom while the other kids chased after Violeta's pigtails. Sulky and offended, she sat drawing Violeta as a cow with two udders. But if Ana thought her first day playing second violin was bad, things grew far worse when the mutiny really picked up steam. Violeta was the type to divide and rule. She split up her classmates into winners and losers, swapping best friends like the rest of us swap trash bags. One day she gave Ana a friendship ring, but the very next Monday, in front of the entire class, Violeta threw her ring into the wastepaper basket and terminated the friendship without explanation. Every single recess, Violeta played the same card: Ana plays games for babies, Ana's just a little kid, Ana can't figure out how to tie her shoes, Ana's got to stand on a chair to reach the shelf. Ana still wears diapers at night, she lied, I saw it with my own eyes on an outing with the Pioneers.

When Ana heard that story she was sitting on the jungle gym, swinging her legs. Is it true you still need diapers? someone asked. Yeah, Violeta says you still wear diapers at night, said another. Ana was trapped on the jungle gym; she couldn't get away. And how are you supposed to answer a question like that anyway? She sat where she was and felt the helplessness wash over her, the tears welling up. It was her word against Violeta's, and sniveling wouldn't do much for her credibility. Look, the baby's boo-hooing, someone yelled, and Ana tumbled off the jungle gym and ran home to the apartment block as fast as her sausage-dog legs could carry her. She lay down on the sofa and cried, quietly at first, snifflingly, but soon louder, until at last her father stuck his head out from his office and glanced around. Ah, Ana, he said, as if he'd found a natural explanation. It was just a branch against the windowpane, it was just the cat rummaging around under the bed.

Ah, Ana, he said, it's just you.

Many years later, when she and Violeta had both ended up, in their separate ways, as outcasts, Ana felt a peculiar blend of hatred and tenderness whenever she saw Violeta hunched around a cigarette behind the gas station, or on Lipscani with some drug dealer by her side. In moments of teenage gloom, Ana imagined the two of them somehow shared a fate, she and Violeta: like two accelerating bodies, they'd collided with each other, and were now free-falling into the abyss.

It was probably an exaggeration, the free fall, but that was how Ana felt. And not without reason, because that year all Ana's friends abandoned her, and before the month was out she'd briefly lost her life.

It began the morning their teacher gathered the girls together and explained that the Danube of Thought was turning fifty, and in celebration there was to be much pomp and circumstance: congratulatory speeches and festive fireworks, fluttering doves, tens of thousands of pennant-waving children, Romania's daughters shouldering five-foot rifles on a parade ground lit by the first gleam of day. All Romania was paying tribute to the Female Symbol of Creation, the Scientific Elena, and the epic leadership of her Hero Husband, Nicolae Ceaușescu. Ana's class had been given the particular honor of supplying the girl who would stand on the podium and receive a kiss on the cheek from Ceaușescu himself, and that same afternoon two officials trooped up to the school, and all the girls were lined up in the schoolyard so they could stand to attention while the bureaucrats went from child to child and scribbled down notes. Ana didn't stand a chance, of course. She stood there with her chubby, babyish cheeks, a whole head shorter than her classmates, and it came as no surprise when Violeta won the contest. Two days later, the President's chief medical officer knocked on the classroom door, and Ana seethed with envy as Violeta bustled off to be examined. We're talking the full change-of-ownership inspection here: After all, the Genius of the Carpathians mustn't be allowed to get cooties. Violeta was vaccinated for typhus and infectious hepatitis, she was tested for colds, mumps, and whooping cough, for meningitis, tuberculosis, measles, diphtheria, and scarlet fever, and the next day at recess she showed off all her punctures to her classmates.

Yeah, well, so what, said Ana. They're just a few stupid marks.

They're not just marks, said Violeta. Now I can never get sick.

Yes, you can, said Ana, as Violeta pulled up her skirt to show the bruise on her buttock.

See that there? That's a *presidential* swelling.

Now, I don't know if she was embellishing as she went along, but Ana often talked about the gymnastics display for Ceaușescu's birthday. The way they practiced formations for hours in freezing weather at the parade ground; the wind that swept among the empty bleachers; the chattering teeth; the classmates who passed out with cold and had to be wrapped in blankets warmed on the stove. Ana hated the cold and the rehearsals. Her coordination was bad and she was constantly dropping the pennant, so the coach downgraded her to walking at the back of the procession and waving a flag. Now, it was one thing to dance around and humiliate herself for Ceaușescu, but to do all that with Violeta on the podium—no, Ana couldn't bear the thought. Envy picked and tugged at her, she couldn't sleep at night, and the day before the dress rehearsal she played the only card a frustrated schoolgirl has to play, taking to her bed with a nasty case of malingeritis.

Nonsense, said Ana's mother when she felt her cool forehead. I want you out of bed right now.

And if Ana hadn't been the daughter of a father who'd grown up in the deepest recesses of Oltenia's darkest mountains, that would probably have been that, and Ana would probably never have died. But Ana's father was born in the kind of village that tall

tales and quacks come from, one far, far away, where the tumble-
weed blows and sprained ankles are treated with distilled spirits.
He may have been a man of science, but he was also something of a
hypochondriac, and he was just as hysterically afraid of inflamed
appendixes as the rest of Bucharest's impoverished population.
Was he slow to react when his daughter suddenly complained of
stomach pains? He was not. He put his hand southwest of her belly
button and asked: Is this where it hurts?

Mm-hm, said Ana, nodding, frightened of the earnestness in
his voice.

So Ana was whisked off to the hospital by the only person in the
neighborhood with a driver's license and put in a room with two
coughing boys, and there she lay, writhing in the bleached sheets,
not knowing what she was most afraid of, the birthday parade or
this mess. Her little lie was skidding out of control, but before she
could yank the emergency brake the doctor was standing over her
bed, pressing his hand against her belly.

Yes, she said again. It hurts right there.

Now her mother was worried too, standing whey-faced in the
hallway and peering guiltily at Ana. She wanted so much to come
clean. But her mother was pacing the corridor like a caged pan-
ther while her father was busy answering the anesthesiologist's
questions. Is she allergic to opiates? Taking any medication? I see
she's in Year Three—she's nine years old? The anesthesiologist was
checking against the table for age and weight, jotting down figures, and nodding to the orderly.

And all of a sudden it was too late.

The next thing Ana remembers is three doctors yelling in her face. What's your birthday, what's your name, who's the president, how old are you?

I don't know, she gasped, frightened. And then she began to cry.

Ana's heart had stopped. She'd been dead for nearly two minutes. The idiots hadn't weighed her before pumping her with anesthetic, going on the average weight of a nine-year-old instead. Mid-operation her pulse had disappeared, the nurses screamed and shouted, and the surgeon fumbled with the defibrillator until the anesthesiologist leaped up and massaged her heart back into action. He emerged a hero, that incompetent anesthesiologist, receiving the Order of the Star of Romania even though he was the one who'd overmedicated her, and even though it was obvious Ana's weight was more like a seven-year-old's than a nine-year-old's, and a weedy one at that.

Back at the diner, I asked Ana what it felt like to be dead. Did she see her life flash before her eyes, a tunnel of dazzling light, what? But Ana shrugged. She had no memory of hovering ten or fifteen feet above her lifeless body. All she remembered was an extraordinary sense of relief that she wasn't at the freezing parade ground, staring into Violeta's lovely, ugly face. And she remembered her father standing at the end of the bed with a glass jar, in which a lump of meat was floating in a yellowish liquid. He'd bribed the surgeons with a hefty share of his Christmas bonus so that Ana could take home her healthy appendix. She still has it today. It's sitting on top of her chest of drawers in Bucharest like a relic, in a place of pride beside her father's old pipe.

·   ·   ·

This was the story Ana told me as we sat in the diner that night, staring at me with those narrow eyes. We were the last ones in there. The waitress idled on the barstool, doing a crossword or Sudoku or maybe drawing mustaches on politicians, and Ana took her wallet out of her canvas bag. In the wallet she found a photograph she laid on the table.

That's me in Year Three, she said, sliding it across. A few days before I died.

I picked up the photo and examined it, searching for the self-assured woman who sat in front of me, but all I saw were the glazed eyes of a schoolgirl. I looked up at Ana and she smiled at me, and I laughed, because it was a peculiar anecdote.

What are you laughing at, she said. Don't you believe me?

Yeah, yeah, of course.

Why aren't you writing it down, then? Didn't you say you write stories?

Yeah, I do.

So why aren't you writing it down? Isn't it a story you can use?

Maybe. Bit short, don't you think?

But it was just the intro, it was only the first chapter. Wait till you hear the rest, then you'll be *begging* me to let you write it.

You think so?

Ana nodded. Before we're done with each other, she said, I guarantee you'll be writing my life story. Ana Ivan's journey through time, the whole true tale.

I laughed. Sounds like a thriller.

Yeah, you can practically hear it, right? Here, take the picture. Use it as inspiration.

You mean that?

Yeah, sure. But if it's a bestseller I'll sue you and run off with all the money. Might as well tell you that straightaway. That's what we Romanians are like. Unreliable.

I took the picture, smiling.

As long as I'm the one writing it, there's probably no need to worry about bestsellers.

Oh, come on. You seem talented enough.

You don't know that. You haven't read anything I've written.

No, but I could. Why don't you write a story for me?

A story?

Yeah, write a short story for me. A short story about my appendix. It's got real drama, don't you think?

I laughed again, but Ana wasn't smiling. And was there really anything to laugh about? She'd lost her appendix, she'd died because of medical incompetence, and by the time she got out of the hospital in February 1989 her world had come apart. That month all her friends defected, and suddenly there was no one to hang out with in the parking lot, not a soul who wanted to go home and play games. When the thaw shambled into Bucharest, trampling the parks to sludge, she was already an outcast, sitting all by herself in the schoolyard and walking home alone when the bell rang. All her old subjects took part in the uprising, and soon she was on a level with the Romani kids who picked up trash behind the marketplace. No, she was below that now. She was on a level with the handicapped girl, the one with the wheelchair and the crooked arm, or at least on a level with fat Dorin Puscas, who always had his fingers in his mouth or up his nose or somewhere worse.

Ana told me more than once about those dismal months in Year Three, about the sameness, the routines run on autopilot.

Getting dragged out of bed at five thirty every morning to stand in lines outside stores. Going to sleep every evening hoping she wouldn't wake until the summer. I heard her describe so many times getting up in the dark without electricity or gas or warmth, how breakfast was nothing but a hunk of dry, untoasted bread, how her father dressed her in four layers of clothing for a long day in an unheated school—so much clothing she could barely move, her hands gloved as she took dictation, scribbling texts about the Genius of the Carpathians, Elena, the Renowned Scientist—how she'd go home again through the cold and sit in front of the oven for the two hours they had gas and electricity, eating soup and doing homework, before the dark came back and all the layers of clothing had to be removed and replaced with new ones, two pairs of woolen socks, two sets of pajamas, and piles of blankets that held her pinned against the slats all night, until there it was again: morning.

Sounds pathetic, I know, but I guess that's what it was like in Romania in those days, just grindingly miserable. Not that I was there to see it, of course, I'd only just been born, and I know nothing of dictatorship and hunger, never having had a taste of it, not even speaking Romanian. But Ana was there, sitting on the floor in front of her father's office every day after school, waiting for him to come out. She wasn't welcome in the parking lot with the other kids, she didn't dare venture into the kitchen and trouble her mother, and she didn't want to knock on the office door and disturb her father in the middle of his thesis. Her world had shrunk to twenty-one square meters. It ran down the corridor from her bedroom and up to the living room, and from her spot outside the office Ana could hear all the small sounds inside: a match being struck, drawers shifting in their wooden frames, a pencil tracing rough paths across notepaper.

As she sat there, she guessed what her father might be doing. She imagined the scene. The small fat candles melted almost to the plate, the heavy reek of stearin, the drawing board flecked with paint, two or three sheets of paper, and the book of geometric figures, the ones with funny names. Möbius strips and tori, rhombuses and trapezoids. The theorem about the hairy ball, that one was funny. She liked it when her father talked about those things, but he rarely did. He'd sit hunched over his thesis for hours, absolutely still, and when finally he got up he'd say: Oh, Ana, are you sitting there? Shouldn't you go outside and play?

But Ana didn't go outside and play. Going outside sounded about as good as running into the arms of a hoard of angry miners, a band of hysterical farmers with machetes, or any other frothing mob she could come up with. Glue-sniffing child soldiers, a pack of drunken hooligans. Every day after school, Ana sat outside the office and fiddled with her homework and her crayons, and at some point during the spring it dawned on her family that she'd become a homebody, a timid child who'd inherited neither the go-getting energy of her mother's side of the family nor the earthy practicality and work ethic of which her father's side was so proud.

Why don't you have any friends? asked her cousins.

Yes, where are your playmates? said her aunts, as they stroked her hair and debated her flaws as though she were a sick cow or a mare gone lame.

Goodness, she still wets the bed, said one. Isn't she starting Year Four after the vacation?

You should give her St. John's wort before bedtime, said another.

Like hell you should, said the third. What she needs is a good kick up the backside. The girl's bone idle.

It can't have been easy, and if Ana had grown up in any other home, her parents might have helped. But the best her mother could offer was a piece or two of good advice.

If you get off your butt and run outside, she said, you might find yourself a few friends.

And when she was in a more philosophical mood: If you only knew what we went through so you could have it this good.

And Ana's father? He'd been something of a loner in his younger days too, and couldn't see why Ana pottering around by herself was such a problem. It was healthy; boredom was for idiots, and his daughter was certainly no idiot. In March he finally submitted his thesis to Babeş-Bolyai University at Cluj, and when he came home from the post office that afternoon he told Ana the big news.

So are we moving to Cluj? she asked excitedly.

Ah, well, we'll have to see, he said. Let's take things one step at a time.

Then he kissed her, put on his best jacket, went into town, and came home with a chicken. God knows where he got it from, but that evening the apartment smelled like bay leaves and fat, the pálinka and cherry juice emerged from their hiding holes, and Ana's father told old tales from the Romanian Academy that made Ana's mother laugh until she coughed.

To twelve years' work, he said, raising his glass.

To a hundred years' peace and quiet, said Ana's mother, her cheeks warm and flushed.

While Ana's father waited for the evaluation committee in Cluj to make a decision, he suddenly had time to spare. Time to take Ana to the Geological and Technical Museums, or to drag her all the way out to Bellu Cemetery, where they paid homage to the poet-mathematician Ion Barbu and laid a protractor on his grave.

It's about emotional understanding, he said, as they stood in front of the stone. Do you understand that, sweetheart, do you *feel* it?

At a café behind the university he taught Ana to play chess, and when she got back from school one day, to her surprise, the door to his office stood open. There was a geometry problem ready for her on the desk, and when her father came home they sat down together and went through her work.

Okay, Ana, said her father, when she handed over problem set number twelve. I think we'd better call a halt here. You should go out and get a little color in your cheeks.

No, she said. One more, then I'll run outside and play.

Alright, alright, he said, tousling the hair behind her head. He got to his feet and let his fingers glide across the spines of his books, his collections of formulae and the major works of topology, packed so tightly together the shelves bent under their weight.

You know, they say knowledge is a threat to the powerful, he said, his fingers coming to rest on the Russian dictionary. If there's a revolution tomorrow, we'll probably be the first ones they come for.

The next week he signed Ana up for the chess club, and every Sunday they'd hop onto a bus or a tram and go lurching off to a museum or nuclear power plant or bridge made of pre-stressed concrete. He talked and she listened. She learned it was a privilege to study mathematics, that back home in his village her father had been beaten because he always had his nose buried in a book. She learned he'd fled a drunken, illiterate father and lived in a basement at the Institute for Mathematics at the Romanian Academy, surviving thanks to the potatoes his sisters sent him on the train. In return, Ana told him about the bullying and Violeta Mincic, who ruled the schoolyard with an iron fist, and she asked: Dad, how old do I have to be before I can start at the high school with you?

How old? he said, and laughed. Oh, love, age is just something people have invented. Time's imaginary anyway. Quantum mechanics proved that ages ago.

They spent the rest of the spring wallowing in quadratic functions and going to town on combinatorics. Ana said it was like a veil had been lifted from her eyes. Not particularly original, true, but that was the metaphor Ana used. It was like a veil being lifted from my eyes, she said to me, and suddenly she saw math all over the place. Geometry in pine cones, wave functions when she threw a stone into the pond, topology in the belt she folded and put on a shelf in her wardrobe. Ana saw order and predictability everywhere. Everything in the world could be explained by mathematics, everything operated according to fixed rules that no one could alter, and although she didn't understand all or even half of what her father said, it filled her with enough peace and purpose to pad the longest, empty afternoons.

One evening in early April, when Ana had settled down with a system of coordinates, her father came into the room. He wore a scarf and hat, at least three sweaters and a jacket, or two coats, a couple of pullovers. It looked like he'd swelled up, as if he'd been fermenting, like grape juice left too long on the windowsill in the sun.

Put some clothes on, he said. You'll freeze in that.

What are we doing?

Well now. If I told you that, it wouldn't be a surprise. Come on, up you get.

The chill of night was settling as they emerged onto the street, and through the open kitchen windows they could hear the hum of the apartment block and the clinking of dishes and coffee sets. It was April 9, 1989, and Ana's father didn't know he had less than a year to live. Ana didn't know that either, which was just as well. Cutting a slanting path across the road to the bus stop, they took the first bus to Gara Nord. They were headed to the Institute for Mathematics at the Romanian Academy under cover of darkness.

I know this building like my own body, he said forty minutes later, as they picked their way among the trash and construction waste that surrounded the Institute. This was where I met your mother, did you know that?

Ana shook her head. It's all dirty, she said.

Don't be silly, he said, taking out a key, but the door was already open. Inside, candles lit the way upstairs, and dusty bits of paper floated along the corridors. A chair had been caved in, and a typewriter chucked onto the landing, scattering the letters of the keyboard down the steps. The staircase curved up through the building, and on the top floor a ladder led up to the roof. Ana climbed up with her father's arms around her, smelling the evening air as it drifted through the trapdoor, and when she stuck her head out the other side she saw the lights of the city.

Just take a look at that, said her father, but before Ana could admire the whole view, she heard the sound of men gathered noisily around a telescope. It was identical to the one she'd studied at the Technical Museum, and she gazed nervously at the instrument as the men hailed her father, before the lights beneath them all went out. Darkness swept like a wave across the city as the power was cut, from Otopeni in the north to Titan in the south, and the men clapped and cheered. The whole city twinkled as if the lights and lamps were putting up a fight, but the men didn't care about electricity. Uninterested in the cheap falsity of bulbs, they were pointing at the night sky, adjusting the telescope and jostling to peer through.

Do you see that? asked her father, crouching down on his haunches. He pointed to a big star in the west, and said, Can you tell me what that is?

Ana looked up at the sky. She thought it over.

Well, is the answer coming or not? Get washed away by cherry soda, did it?

I don't know, she said at last. What is it?

You've got to guess, he said. If you want to be a mathematician, you've got to be willing to hazard an opinion. Come on—is it a comet or a satellite or what? A galaxy?

But Ana didn't say anything; she knew nothing about astronomy.

Yes, no, short, long, don't know? Rather be a plumber, would you? Come on, just guess.

A satellite, she said. I think it's a satellite.

Are you bonkers? Satellites aren't that big. Try again.

A plane?

No, no, no. It's Jupiter. It's the biggest planet in our solar system. What d'you think of that, then? Isn't it fantastic how clearly you can see it?

Is it Jupiter? she asked. Are you sure it isn't a plane?

It's *definitely* Jupiter, he assured her. Jupiter was so big you could fit all the other planets in the solar system inside it, he said, and he explained the difference between gas planets and terrestrial planets. He explained how time worked up there, and how long it took Jupiter to turn on its axis. Everything weighed two and a half times as much, and a single day on Jupiter was only nine point eight hours long.

If you lived on Jupiter, he said, it would take eight hundred ninety-four days for you to get a year older. Isn't that funny?

Ana nodded, trying to keep up.

Yes, it might sound strange, he continued, but it's true. Time is a relative concept, love. You can't take it for granted. And I don't want you thinking it's just about rotation periods, because it isn't. It's also about mass—and I haven't even mentioned what happens when we get to huge extremes, I mean, Jupiter's nothing. Time passes at a different speed on a very large star than here on Earth, which is small. You've got to understand, time is determined by the objects around it. So if there were no mass, there would be no time or space either. See? Picture it like a stage at the theater. The props we put on stage define time and space. Before that, the stage didn't even exist. If there are no props, there's no stage either. Isn't that utterly insane, and wonderful?

But Ana didn't understand a word. It was confusing, all that stuff about time, and difficult to concentrate while the lights of the city were glinting on and off beneath her as if signaling in Morse code, as if the whole city were trying to send her a message; it wasn't, but that was how it looked. A twinkling, signaling city, and above it: a gas planet.

Don't you believe me? he continued. I'm not making this stuff up, you know. It's not a joke, it's not science fiction. It happens in laboratories.

He chattered on and on while the remaining lights were put out. The bulbs flashed their last for that night, and around them it grew dark. Jupiter and the stars brightened, and it was like the night sky tucked itself around them, the dusk lying heavily over them like a snowdrift after a storm, so dark it nearly made her shiver, and oh, how nice it felt to stand there in the dark with her father's stubble scratching at her cheek, so sweet it almost made her cry, yes, soundlessly at first, but suddenly it was impossible to curb, it rolled out and through her, made her whole body quiver.

Hey, my little sweetheart, he said. What's wrong?

But Ana couldn't answer that question. She couldn't do anything but cry and feel her arms and legs and the world around her, so big and beautiful and full of love it was unbearable.

Oh, sweetheart, he said, putting his arms around her. I shouldn't be asking so many stupid questions, I'm sorry. No more of that nonsense now.

It's okay, she sniffled between gasps.

No, it's too much to ask, he said, kissing her. There now, sweetheart, it's true. I just forget sometimes. It's not easy being the daughter of a father.

I don't think Ana told me all that, not with all those details. Still, that's how I remember it, and I can't tell how many gaps I've filled or how much of it's in Ana's own words. I've got the broad strokes, though; this was the story she told me at the diner, and when I got back to Greenpoint late that night, to the studio apartment nestled above the screeching door of an industrial garage, I jotted it down in a notebook. I brushed my teeth and drew the curtains, sat on the edge of my bed and stared at the phone charger, its cord sticking out from under the mattress, but I didn't feel tired enough to sleep. A kind of tension was vibrating inside me, the evening's chatter had evaporated and left an urge to hear Lærke's voice. It had already been a day or two since we'd last spoken, and I pictured Lærke in the Copenhagen dawn, Lærke's unconscious face resting against the pillow after a late night at the restaurant, her mouth slightly open and her fingers quivering through a dream about elderflower preserves or hares or Mexican poets. I envisioned sitting on the edge of the bed, waking her with a cup of coffee while I told her about my night, and how she'd laugh at my stories from Romania and I'd feel my nerves dispel with her laughter. When I couldn't bear imagining any longer I got up and opened my computer, clicked on her name and stared at the picture that emerged. It was morning in Copenhagen. Lærke was bathed in white light on her green sofa, her hair wasn't tangled at all, her eyes not the least foggy with sleep. The downstairs neighbor had woken her up early, she said, and when I asked which downstairs neighbor she told me about a man who'd just moved in, a new divorcee with a stereo system. The evening of the move he'd thrown a housewarming party with a disco theme, or what Lærke thought was a housewarming party, but the following night the lush strains of a violin had once again whined up from his apartment, and an organ bleated through the papier-mâché floors. She knew she could kiss sleep goodbye, so she'd put on her dressing gown and gone down to knock, but before she got that far the neighbor opened the door and invited her inside, like he'd been waiting for her all evening. Over his shoulder, Lærke could see the apartment, deserted apart from a table covered with empty cans, and the sound system, of course, its speakers blaring flügelhorns and keyboards and rhythm guitar, and Lærke asked if he could turn the music down, but he didn't understand her, or maybe he couldn't hear her over the synthesizer and the syncopated bass, because he offered her a beer, and Lærke said, No thanks, but could you keep it down a little, and then he offered a cup of coffee or maybe tea— Lærke couldn't hear over the high-hat and layered vocals—and she felt sorry for him, unearthing his fossilized youth all alone like that, so she went inside and drank the beer while she tried to piece together his sentences, his sentences cleaved by the beat of Chic and The Supremes and Sylvester James's soaring vocals, and it was only during a lengthy outro that Lærke managed to explain that her visit was about the noise level, about the disco he'd forgotten or hadn't noticed, and which he'd gladly switch off, no problem.

I laughed and said it was good she was nearly done with that apartment, and then I told her about my evening with Ana, about the nighttime breakfast and the tale of the appendix. Lærke wanted to know more. Why was Ana at the office so late, why did she go shopping in the middle of the night? Her I've got to meet, said Lærke, springing up from the sofa. She'd just gotten her passport back from the American embassy—she wanted to show me her visa with the photo where she looked like her mom—and she flicked through the pages of red and blue stamps while she told me about a border crossing in the Balkans and a transnational bridge in Central America, and about the time she'd fallen asleep on a tropical beach, from which you could see or imagine the

stippled line of a border stretching out across an azure sea, a hyp-
notically blue sea with waves that sloshed so lazily against the coast
that soon she'd fallen asleep. She'd only been wearing SPF fifteen,
so it could have been disastrous, she said, but luckily she was woken by a hungry coati, a curious coati rummaging through her
bag and saving her from burning and sunstroke and malignant
melanoma, a heroic coati she fed out of her hand and followed
deep into the jungle, the jungle that sat astride the border, which
the cosmopolitan coati probably crossed each day, and I laughed
and promised to take Lærke to the zoo as soon as she came over,
so she could show me the animal herself.

Lærke nodded enthusiastically and asked how my job at the festival was going, and I told her about Ana's work, about the coin
she wore in her shoe and how she was trying to shape her dreams,
and about the task she'd set me.

Why do you think she asked me to write that story?

No idea, said Lærke. Does there have to be a reason?

Maybe she's just lonely.

Yeah, maybe.

She probably wants attention, somebody to talk to.

Sure, we all want that.

Or maybe it's part of some kind of art project, some sort of
performance.

Yeah, maybe. But honestly, that coin thing is moronic.

I agreed it was a silly thing to do, but it was precisely its moronic-
ness that made it so fantastic. In any case, it was no mean feat,
invading your dreams with a coin like that, transferring the real
and the concrete into the virtual and the imagined. Ana had to
keep a logbook, Ana had to be methodical about writing down her

dreams. There was something almost scientific about her practice that was impossible to ignore.

I can ignore it just fine, said Lærke, cupping her hands over her ears, and she began to sing *Hear the Little Starling*. It sounded lovely, and I told her to keep going, so she sang *I Know Where Lies a Lovely Garden*, and she sang, *How Fair Smiles the Danish Coast*, and then she took her dress off, and I took my pants off, and we lay naked, masturbating in sync, swathed in electromagnetic waves or whatever it was that transmitted our pixelated bodies across Zealand's grace and Jutland's might, through rain and wind and the foaming swells of the Atlantic Ocean, and above the columns of vehicles shuffling inchmeal into Copenhagen and New York.

At some point we must have fallen asleep. I forgot to set my alarm clock and when I finally woke I was already forty-five minutes late to work. I had to rush out the door without breakfast or a shower, but when I stood in DUMBO on the block of former factories and gazed drowsily at the island, wondering how Manhattan held the weight of all those towers without sinking into the harbor, I was pleasantly confused about everything that had happened over the last few days. I was glad Ana had taken me to the diner, flattered she'd asked me to write a short story, but I didn't know how to interpret it. I'd just arrived from Denmark, I'd never met anyone like Ana, and as time went by our evening reminded me increasingly of a scene in a book or a movie, some story I'd once heard that lived on in my mind. The whole setup seemed implausible; how often, after all, do you meet a random woman and end up being asked to write her life story? No, surely Ana must have meant it ironically, the atmosphere must have run away with her, and I convinced myself she'd forgotten all about it.

But then again. It was possible she'd been serious, so why not give it a chance? It's not like I had anything better to write about. Certainly my own experiences weren't short-story worthy. I was just an intern—white and male and middle class to boot—so when Ana served up a curious anecdote about her appendix, it seemed the obvious thing to give it a try.

That evening I got down to work. Around midnight, as the one remaining light in the building opposite mine was switched off, I stayed up, because the story wasn't half bad. In fact, the tale of the appendix was clever and bristling with conflict, just as I'd read good stories should be. There was something at stake between Ana and her father, something tender I didn't understand, and the next few evenings I wrote late into the night, sitting at my computer or standing by the kettle in the kitchen, watching myself from the outside: A young man bent over his desk in the dusty glow of a lamp, poor and sleepless, as though living only for the text. A stereotypical image, of course, but one that made me dash back and write another page, filled with a shining or youthful or idiotic light that burned in the middle of my chest.

It lasted four or five days. For a little under a week I tried to imagine Ana's childhood voice. I envisioned her dead body on the operating table; pictured the parade of children marching through the frozen stadium while I stood eating pierogis in McGolrick or Transmitter Park, staring at the lewd monument to the beefcake seamen of the Civil War as the Brooklyn dusk pressed up against the river like it was jealous of the ever-glowing skyline of Manhattan. That week I wrote as if possessed, but when I biked home from the exhibition space the following Saturday, all the shine was gone. I'd just printed out the story to read it through, and I was

biking up Vinegar Hill in the late afternoon, weighed down by
the rough draft in my bag, clumsy and heavy and dull, without so
much as a hint of Ana's strange voice. This isn't going anywhere,
I thought. I've heard nothing from Ana for a week, she's probably
forgotten all about her suggestion. As I passed the Brooklyn Navy
Yard and turned in along the shadow of the Williamsburg Bridge,
my phone rang. I expected to see Lærke's name on the screen, but
when I fumbled it out of my pocket I found Ana's three letters
shining in my hand.

Ana, I said, surprised. What's up?

Good morning, she said. Am I disturbing you?

No, not at all. I'm just on my way home.

So, yeah. Are you busy?

No, not really.

Good. Want to come time-traveling with me?

Sure, sounds fun.

Maybe, although it's not as much fun as it sounds. But if you
don't have anything better to do, meet me at the gallery in an hour.
Then you can come travel back in time.

By the time we hung up I'd gotten off the bike and was walking
under the elevated tracks of the JMZ line, the trains shrieking as
they bore down on Brooklyn from the bridge. I was in a totally different mood than before her call. There was a lightness tickling in
my legs as I pushed the bike east, imagining what Ana might have
meant by time travel. Was she dressing up in clothes from another
era, perhaps, or reenacting one of her ancestors' lives, following
a grandmother's diary like a manuscript? Like a ghost invited
into her body, I thought, as I sauntered along to the sounds of
the bachata or merengue, the smells of fried plantains or whatever

was coming out of the bodegas, and on Montrose Avenue I saw an image of my swelled idealized self reflected in the window of a car: a young writer walking through the big city on his way to meet an artist friend, open and curious, headed for new adventures.

I made good time to the gallery, but once I was standing outside the entrance I got cold feet. Not wanting to seem too eager, I preferred to arrive a little late. So I took a walk to pass the time, standing on a street corner for a few minutes and watching the trucks hurtle down the avenue and the wind twitching at the cherry trees until the petals sifted down like snow or ash or confetti, I couldn't find the right simile. Maybe they were just like petals, flowers content to be flowers, not wanting to be anything else. Once I was suitably late, I went back and entered the gallery. I couldn't see Ana anywhere, but in the corner stood a wooden structure with a little sign: *Ana Ivan, The Time Traveler (2010)*. The installation was square, measuring two or three yards on each side. Through an opening I could make out the interior walls, which were covered in posters and hand-drawn sketches, and a TV playing a video. Squeezing through the opening, I put the headphones on and listened to the man on the screen, who was explaining something about photons and quantum mechanics in a thick accent, about Zeno's paradox, time, and gravitation. I must have been engrossed, because when I suddenly felt a hand on my shoulder I spun around with a jolt.

Oh, it's just you, I said, when I saw Ana behind me with a skewed smile and dark hair slanting over her forehead.

Did I scare you? she said. Sorry.

Ana took a step closer, standing almost underneath me, her face inches from mine, and suddenly I could smell her scent. A bit like crêpes or pancakes, or it could have been Belgian waffles. It was the moisturizer she used, smelling of sweet dough against a warm pan.

So. Welcome to my time machine, she said. Have you figured out how it all works?

No, not really.

Okay, then here goes, she said, pointing at the calendar on the nearest wall, a calendar that was more like a notice board, all the days covered with notes and calculations, and I smiled as Ana explained that she was researching the discrepancy between human and astronomical timekeeping, that for three months she was going to live on precise astronomical time. It seemed the Gregorian calendar didn't fit the Earth's passage around the sun. We calculate a year as three hundred sixty-five days, but in fact it takes three hundred sixty-five days, five hours, forty-eight minutes, and forty-six seconds for the Earth to complete its orbit. On leap days our time is brought back into correspondence with reality, but during the four years between each leap day it gets dislocated, and our perception slips further and further away from astronomically correct time.

See what I mean? she said. You're practically living in the future.

And you aren't?

No, I've traveled back to the present, I'm living on the correct time. So, for you there are only six hours left of today, but I've still got more than sixteen. It's only a couple of hours since I got up.

Then she showed me a poster densely scribbled with times and dates and numbers of hours, and a drawing of the Earth's path around the sun. She'd worked it all out with the Romanian astrophysicist in the video, and she told me that our time right now was ten hours and seventeen minutes ahead of the real, the actual, the true time, the time that wasn't plucked out of thin air but determined by the only factor that really meant anything, the Earth's position with respect to the sun, the star we orbited and depended on for everything, the single-celled bacteria in the seas, the plankton living off them, the fish and squid and reefs of coral that stretched deep into the oceans, the fruits of the orchards and the grain in the fields, the star that had brought us out of our caves and into civilization, the sun, that's what mattered, not some idiotic calendar a pope had chosen.

Okay, okay, the sun, I said, smiling. You're really into this stuff, aren't you?

Of course I'm into it, she said. It's about my life, it's my work.

I nodded, and Ana went up to the wall and leafed through a calendar.

And what about you? she said. What about your work? Did you bring me a story?

Um, no, I said, not exactly. I mean, I've written a draft. But I didn't know if you were serious. If you really meant it.

Ana narrowed her eyes and let go of the calendar.

So, she said, you're telling me you don't take me seriously?

No, no, I didn't mean it like that.

Okay, then where's the story? Send it to me.

Well, I've actually got it here in my bag. But it's not the final version. It's just a draft, it's really not finished yet.

That's fine, but I'm your reader, right? And it's good to get feedback from readers. Agreed?

Agreed.

Good, so hand it over. I'll read it while we have a cup of coffee.

I couldn't say no to her. An hour earlier I'd been ready to chuck the whole thing into the garbage, and now I was biking over the Greenpoint Avenue Bridge, excited and confused, with Ana by my side. At the apex of the bridge, Ana braked. It was seven in the evening—nine in the morning by astrological time—and she said it was exactly the right moment to enjoy the view. For several minutes we stood on the platform and gazed across at the island, at the skyscrapers and the spaces between them, the sunlight transitioning slowly into the glare of many thousands of lamps. It never really got dark, but for a moment the two lights met, the natural and the artificial, and the city and sky dissolved together. The next it was over, only electricity was left, and we tramped farther up the hill, past the cemetery and the lurid Sunnyside arch beneath the train tracks, and I arrived for the first time in Woodside. It was a motley kind of area. Victorian terraced houses stood cheek by jowl with garages and repair shops, apartment blocks with faux-timber-framed buildings, and as we biked through the warm evening we were lit by neon signs in Spanish and Filipino, and sparks from the trains that clattered along the overhead tracks. Ana pointed to the building where she lived and we turned down a side street, where we parked our bikes and sat down underneath a restaurant's paper lanterns.

Ana ordered coffee, I ordered beer, and while we waited for our drinks Ana got out my story and read it in silence. I tried to sneak a glance over the pages and catch a wrinkled forehead or a jeering smile, but I couldn't interpret her reaction. Just as she was putting down the final piece of paper, the waitress came over with the drinks, and Ana spent a few minutes asking me one question

after the next, as though playing for time or dodging the issue, I
thought, because she felt awkward about my clumsy story.

Remind me, she asked, you said you've been published before?

Only a few small things, I said. And only back in Denmark, it
doesn't mean anything.

So you *have* been published.

I guess you can call it that.

And how does it work, do you have a publisher or what?

Nothing permanent.

You're a free man.

Free as a bird. Or as the unemployed.

And the form, what about that? Short stories, or what—novels,
short prose, serials?

Well, I don't know. Depends on the story.

So you're not fussy.

No, don't think so.

Basically you don't care who I send it to?

What do you mean?

I mean your short story. Aren't you intending to publish it? I've
got a friend who's an editor at a literary magazine. And I have
another friend who works for an agency, so who would you prefer?

You mean you like it?

Stop playing dumb. I'm not going to send crap to my friends,
am I?

Then she tucked the pages into her canvas bag, and I remember
sitting mutely, clinging to my glass of beer, while Ana talked about
her friend who'd started the literary magazine in the eighties out
of boredom or a lost bet or a game of Truth or Dare. Nobody'd

given the magazine more than a volume or two, but now it had been in print for close to thirty years, its archives were included in Columbia University's manuscript collection, and it had fancy offices down in Fort Greene.

Wow, I said, that all sounds pretty great.

So I'm sending it to her, then?

Of course, I exclaimed. I mean, thanks a lot, that would be awesome.

Ana nodded and slurped her coffee, and I thought I should thank her or hug her, or at least buy something we could toast with, but I didn't want to seem like a rube, so instead I told her it was a lovely, mild evening, that we never or almost never had evenings like this in Scandinavia, and that the breeze smelled like holidays in southern Europe.

Ana snickered. She'd never been on a vacation like that, she said, but if this was how they smelled then that was just as well.

The only vacations I've ever taken, she told me, were at chess camp, as a kid. Plus trips out to the cabin, of course, the ones I told you about.

What? I said. What cabin?

Didn't I tell you about that?

I don't think so, I said, and she put the cup down, leaned across the table as if about to share a secret, whispering or muttering or humming through the twilight, and I leaned across the table too, trying to catch what she was telling me, some story about a cabin her grandpa had started building sixty years ago, a one-room hut, at first, but later extended, growing at pace with the family, acquiring extra bedrooms and bathrooms so rapidly that the floors warped and the walls creaked when there were storms. That evening underneath the paper lanterns, Ana told me how the cabin coiled through the brushwood like one of the slowworms her father found beneath the leaves, how if she put a marble at the foot of her bunk bed she could follow its path through the rooms of the house, watch it hop down the splintery stairs and past the shelves of books so old and damp that tiny mushrooms sprouted between the pages.

It was the summer of 1989, a summer so overfull with rationing and power outages that family came from near and far to escape the heat of the cities and the stores' empty shelves. Ana had been looking forward to the trip, filling her blue suitcase with pencils and notebooks, rulers and compasses, and on arriving at the cabin she settled down in the study, took out her pocket calculator, sorted her sheets of logarithmic paper, tugged at her father's sleeve, and asked him to come and help.

Ana's father said: Not right now, sweetheart.

Ana's mother said: Don't start pestering your father.

Ana's grandma said: Why don't you put down that malarkey.

They were still waiting for the evaluation committee at Cluj to make a decision, but for the last few months things hadn't been the same. Ana didn't understand what was going on. From the study she could see her mother on the terrace, a women's magazine unread in front of her, and several times she saw her in the kitchen, coming to a halt while peeling potatoes, setting one down half-peeled and standing there for thirty minutes at a time, gnawing at the skin around her thumbnail until it grew frayed and bloody and had to be soaked in soapy water for hours.

And her father? He got up early every morning and brewed coffee. Then he went into the woods, and Ana saw his checked shirt vanish among the trees. She wanted to go with him, but she never woke until the door slammed shut, and the one morning she leaped out of bed and tried to run after him she didn't get farther than the edge of the woods, because the trees were full of gnats and cobwebs, and ticks hung from the branches, the kind her father picked off his inner thighs each evening.

Ana gave up math problems. She roamed the house and tore up nettles, went to the beach and threw stones at the gulls. Days passed, but one morning, when Ana was poking at a nettle cluster, her Uncle Simion and Cousin Stefan came driving up the path. They'd been in town to buy butter and eggs, and now they were maneuvering a Ping-Pong table off the truck.

Got it from the gypsies, said Simion, patting it in satisfaction. Musta fell off the back of a truck.

Ana didn't think the table looked like it had fallen anywhere. It was lovely. The Romani always had so many fine things, and Simion and Stefan often did business with them. They bought televisions and stereo systems to repair, took old bikes apart and remade them into new ones. Now they were unpacking the Ping-Pong table, adjusting the legs and washing the surface clean, and Ana wanted to ask her father whether they too could go and buy things from the Romani, whether they too could build Frankenstein bikes, so she went over to the edge of the woods and shouted to him.

What now? he said, emerging from behind a thicket. Stop yelling. Come over here, I've got something to show you.

Ana walked through the high grass, and he took her hand and pulled her through the trees until they reached a clearing, where an enormous anthill loomed in the shadow of a pine tree.

What do you make of that, then? he said. It's a big one, isn't it?

Gosh, said Ana, as she admired the mountain of reddish pine needles vibrating like a living thing before her.

They certainly know how to build, the little brutes, he said, crouching down and pointing at the swarm of insects. But it's not the ants I'm interested in today. It's their nemesis.

Ana turned back and gazed down the path. From the other side of the house she could hear Stefan shouting with excitement, and she imagined the table-tennis ball's rhythmic smack against the table.

Dad, she said.

Have you ever seen an ant lion? he asked.

Ana shook her head.

No, of course you haven't. I haven't either. Nor has Simion. But unlike Simion, I don't give up that easily. I know they're here. They're lurking somewhere, I'm sure of it. Just got to keep looking.

Still sitting on his haunches, he nudged the leaves and twigs aside with one hand, then peered thoughtfully in the direction of the beach. Perhaps we'd be better off a little closer to the water. Yes, that might do the trick.

The next day Simion and Stefan played table tennis, and Ana watched from a tree stump. Simion said Stefan had to learn to smash, and smashing was the same as hitting the ball really hard. It looked difficult. When Stefan smashed, Simion said things like *Don't bend your wrist* or *Hit the ball to the side of your body*, and Simion showed him how to swing the paddle at the right angle. They let Ana have a go, too. But when she smashed, Simion didn't show her any angles, and every time she hit the ball he said, Good, you've got it, even when it missed the table completely.

When Simion and Stefan started forehand smashing, Ana went back to the anthill. Her father wasn't there. But a little farther away, up by the gravel track that separated the woods from the beach, she could see his checked shirt. As she battled her way through bushes and trees, she tried not to think about the ticks hanging from the leaves, lying in wait for fresh little-girl leg.

Dad, said Ana, reaching the gravel track. How long will you be looking for ants?

Ant lions, sweetheart.

Ana crouched down and stared at her father's fingers, which were pushing heather aside and exploring the sand.

Do you know what sort of fellow an ant lion is?

Ana shook her head, but he couldn't have seen her, because his own head was buried deep in the undergrowth.

Ant lions live here in Romania, but they're very difficult to find. The larvae dig pits and hide underground, having a grand old time and waiting for an ant to fall into their trap. Then, bam! The ant lion sucks the life out of it.

But Dad, said Ana.

If I'm lucky enough to find an ant lion pit, you'll have quite a drama in store for you. Once you've found it, all that's left to do is lie down on your belly and wait. And if you get impatient and you're sufficiently heartless, you can always give an ant a little prod in the right direction. There's something rather fascinating about witnessing the misfortune of others.

But Dad—

No buts, sweetheart. Nature *is* cruel. It's not like in your cartoons. Life isn't fair.

But—

I'm telling you it isn't! You might as well forget it.

Ana was silent a moment. Then she screwed up her courage and asked, But when you've found the ant lion, can we play table tennis?

Table tennis? he said, peering at her in astonishment. You want to play table tennis? Like your pea-brained Uncle Simion?

Ana stared down at the ground, scraping at the sand with her foot.

Yes, well. Her father brushed the dirt off his hands. We can, of course. Shall we say after lunch? After lunch we'll play a game of table tennis.

Ana used the time to study Simion's stroke, and later her mother called them in to lunch: soup and mămăligă but no Ciprian. After the meal, Simion took out an old kite from the cupboard; one wing was broken, but he patched it up with tape and the rod from an old New Year's firework.

So, said Simion. Anybody want to come down to the beach and fly this thing?

Ana shook her head and picked up the table-tennis paddle.

I'm playing with my dad.

Suit yourself, said Simion, and he and Stefan went down to the beach together.

Ana stood by the game table and swung the paddle in the air like Simion said you were supposed to: horizontally, and without bending your wrist. She hit at least fifty, maybe a hundred smashes. But then her arm got tired, and she sat back down on the tree stump and picked at the coating on the paddle. She stared into the woods. Not a shirt in sight, not even the sound of her father talking to himself. She closed her eyes to listen better, sitting like that a good long while, so long that at last she thought she could hear the birds and the dragonflies, the rushes swaying in the breeze, a kite fluttering in the wind, and Stefan's laughter being carried up from somewhere on the beach.

It wasn't until many hours later, after Simion and Stefan had come home and dinner was ready on the table, that her father came walking out of the woods. His eyes were red, his pants black with dirt.

Aha, said Simion. The big-game hunter returns.

Ana's father sat down heavily in a chair and rubbed his eyes. Simion poured him a palinká, and her father shook his head pensively.

I know they're out there, those goddamn ant lions.

Simion laughed loudly and clapped him on the shoulder.

You never give up, eh?

Ana's father clinked glasses with Simion.

No, I don't give up, he said, smiling. It's like I always say. They can force a scientist out of his laboratory, but the lab coat in your mind—that you never lose.

Early the next morning, Ana's father got up and brewed coffee before disappearing back into the forest. But, for once, Ana's mother didn't sit out on the terrace with her cigarettes. From first light she was in the kitchen with Ana's grandma, gutting fish and slicing vegetables.

What's going on? asked Ana.

Ana, I've told you a thousand times. We've got visitors coming from Paris. Can't you make yourself useful and run down to the farm for some cream?

Ana could. On the long way there she threw stones at the birds and lashed at the nettles, and when she got back to the cabin there was a car in the driveway. Ana had never seen a car like it before. It was big and shiny, its shapes rounded and soft, and through the kitchen she could hear her mother laughing shrilly. Ana went inside the house and out the French doors, where she found her mother and grandmother on the terrace, clinking glasses with a strange couple. Ana hardly recognized her mother dressed to the nines. She'd put on a long gown, her hair was piled seductively high, and her lips gleamed with a lipstick she never used.

Putting down the cream, Ana shook hands with the strangers, two tall people in loose shirts, and her mother poured more wine.

You just sit down, she said, and I'll bring out the meal.

Ana asked whether she should go and find her father, but her mother shook her head. He'll be here soon, she said. We're going to eat now.

Three courses and wine—she'd killed the fatted calf that night—but by the time the last blob of dessert had been eaten and the tall couple began to glance at their watches, her father's chair was still empty, his plate touched only by the flies.

Well, said the woman, I think it's getting time to make a move.

But Ana's mother must not have heard, because she got up and said: Goodness, I forgot all about the bottle we salvaged from the shed.

She laughed a peculiar laugh, which sounded to Ana like one of the girls from her class, and then her mother went into the kitchen and brought out another bottle of red.

I'm sure you can stay for one more glass, can't you?

Ana's mother stood in the doorframe and looked at her guests. The tall couple exchanged glances, and the woman smiled and said: Alright then, just one more.

But one glass became two and then three, because Ana's mother had some preserves they absolutely *had* to taste, and then they had to see the clippings about a mutual friend, who'd appeared on the front page of the weekly paper because she'd given birth with her arms in plaster casts. But at last the tall couple really couldn't put it off any longer, and they got up and asked Ana to help them find the way back onto the main road. They were in a rush, they had no time to get lost among the cabins, and Ana nodded and sat in the passenger seat beside the man, who ground his teeth and kneaded the gearshift. On the main road he stopped the car and said thank you. Ana nodded. And then the blonde woman leaned forward and put a hand on her shoulder.

You'll see, she said. It'll all work out.

She gave her a little squeeze, and Ana nodded again. Then she opened the door and got out of the car, standing and watching the taillights until they vanished among the trees.

The cabin was completely silent when she got back. Opening the front door, she paused and listened. It was a strange, humming silence. Maybe it was the flies hovering around the dirty pots and pans in kitchen, or maybe it was the breeze drifting in from the beach at this time of night. Through the French doors Ana could see her mother sitting on the terrace, a lit cigarette in hand. She was elegant as she sat there. It was as though she'd suddenly shrunk a size or two, the cigarette hanging loosely between her fingers. Ana took a step into the house, but stopped short. There was something in her mother's stoop, some eeriness about it. Like a sight recognized but never experienced, remembered from a dream or from the kind of mediocre film that's soon forgotten. Ana backed noiselessly out of the house and closed the front door behind her, continuing down the path toward the beach, and maybe she imagined it, because the sea fog made the foliage rustle and there were walls and doors between them, but the whole way down to the dunes she thought she heard her mother cry.

That night Ana lay awake. She listened to the noises of the cabin: the timbers that creaked and the floors that groaned, the arguments that floated from her parents' bedroom and down the many halls, that died away and started up again. When Ana was certain they'd fallen asleep, she got up and put on her clothes. She pulled on a long-sleeved sweater and tucked her pants into her socks. In the shed she found a spade and a flashlight. For a while she stood by the edge of the trees, trying to remember the right path, because it's not easy finding a clearing in a darkened wood. But she must have been lucky, because it didn't take her long to reach the ant-hill. It stood on a patch of higher ground, majestic in the flash-light's beam. Coming nearer, Ana switched off the light and tried to get used to the dark. Then she picked up the spade with both hands and swung it as hard as she could. Four or five sturdy blows, a final deep twist, and then she ran. She ran back down the path, branches whipping at her face, away from the ants that crawled up her leg.

Next morning she was awoken by her father yanking back the covers, grabbing her arm, and jerking her upright in bed.

Clothes on, he said.

Ana had made up her mind to be stoic. She'd planned to sit on the edge of the bed and stare, as indifferent to him as he was to her and her mother. But somehow it didn't quite work. He was already standing on the terrace, spade in hand.

Come on, he shouted, his voice ringing through the rooms.

They followed the tracks through the woods, and Ana didn't stop until they were standing on top of the dry pine needles. The anthill was half gone—she was surprised how much she'd destroyed. She could hear her father's steps continuing through the undergrowth, and when he was a little farther down the path, he yelled: Come on, Ana, move along.

For a moment she hesitated in the clearing. Then, curious, she followed him through the woods and down to the beach, where he thrust the spade into the sand and pointed at the dunes.

You see that dune?

Which one?

That dune.

That one there, you mean? The one with grass on the top?

Yes, that one. You're going to move it six feet to the left. You understand?

He tugged the spade out of the sand and held it out to Ana. She eyed him quizzically.

You're moving the dune six feet to the left, he said. Is that so hard to understand?

Then he turned and went back toward the woods.

I'll come back at lunchtime and see how you're getting on, he said over his shoulder. By then you might understand what you've destroyed.

For the first hour Ana threw stones at the gulls. She didn't feel like listening to her idiotic father and his idiotic lectures. But she knew he wouldn't give up until she'd moved the stupid dune. So, at last, she got to her feet, picked up the spade, and started to dig.

It was noon when her father came along with sandwiches.

You're making progress, he said, putting down the tray. Then he left again.

For the next three days, Ana worked from morning till night. She got blisters on her hands, and swimmers stopped on their way down to the water to ask whether she realized this was a protected beach, while their kids stared sheepishly at her. Ana didn't reply. She just dug and dug, and it was no worse than slashing nettles or throwing stones at gulls. Better, maybe. Because the dune really did move. It was hard to tell if you were a passing beachgoer, or the one ranger who drove by in his jeep, but Ana moved the dune. And on the fourth day, when her father picked her up for dinner, they stood together and inspected her work.

Well, look at that. I think you've done it, he said.

She nodded, and her father drained his beer. It's turned into a proper first-rate beach, he said. A good old-fashioned dune beach.

He laid his hand on the back of Ana's neck and shook her gently. Then he nodded in contentment.

At the beginning of September, when the family got back to Bucharest—returning, as though from a trip made at the speed of light, to find the neighbors aged years and the stray dogs shrunk to skin and bone—her father got word from Cluj. It was a gray morning with dusty light, and Ana was kneeling in the living room watching her father: the way he changed his shirt and tie; the way he paced up and down the hall, making the candles flicker each time he spun on his heel. It was half past seven in the morning. Her mother was having a bath, and Ana'd been up most of the night with her ear pressed against the wall, listening to them fight. First they'd fought about the bearskin rug her father's mathematician friend, Paul Pintea, wanted to give them. He'd inherited it from his parents but couldn't be bothered to lug it all the way home to Cluj, and it was kind of him, thought Ana's father, but Ana's mother wouldn't hear of it. It brought bad luck, having dead animals on the floor.

Can't we just sell it? Ana's father had asked.

But no, Ana's mother wouldn't touch it with a barge pole, and the argument flowed back and forth. He said: You know we need the money. And she said: What don't you understand? I don't want that bear, just get that through your head. And he yelled: You're acting like some farmer's wife, coming out with all this superstitious claptrap, just stop it. And she hissed: Go and sleep on the sofa, then, if you don't want to be here.

Early the next morning, things took another wrong turn.

Ana's father kicked things off: I don't know if I can take a visit from that guy. I get so—I can hardly be in the same room. But Ana's mother interrupted: Oh, just *stop* it. You've simply *got* to stop being such a sore loser. And he snarled: Sore loser, am I? And she said: Well you are, just listen to yourself. Such a bitter old man. When did you get so wretched? She paused for a moment, and then Ana heard the way she laughed. A little bit cold, a little bit nasty. God, she gasped between the laughter, you've become such a pathetic little man.

Pathetic, he shouted. Don't talk to me about being pathetic, you're the one who dragged us through this nightmare.

By now Ana was peering at her father through the crack in the door. She saw him jump when the doorbell rang, saw him fumble with the handle and embrace Paul, saw them shake each other and go into the kitchen and take out the bottle of pálinka.

That evening they took a cab into the city to eat dinner. Ana came too, sitting squashed between the dark paneling and the heavy wooden furniture, eyeing the grown-ups. Ana's father squirmed in his chair as he read the menu, and her mother also looked a little anxious.

They've raised their prices, she said. God, we don't have the money for that.

But Paul shook his head, holding out a hand like some latter-day Caesar. Don't you worry about that, he said, I'll pay. And then he ordered six appetizers and four main courses, two plates of sausage, a basket of bread, two pitchers of beer, a glass of red wine for the lady and a whole cake for dessert. Ana couldn't remember the last time she ate so well. There were meatballs and roast potatoes, stuffed peppers and creamed mushrooms, almost more food than she could comprehend. She shoveled down the courses while Paul told stories about the universities at Cluj. Something about a female research assistant, something about the students getting worse year after year. Ana's father said nothing. He picked at his food, downing the occasional pint.

You're certainly knocking that back, said Ana's mother, as he emptied another glass.

Yes, drink up, said Paul. Go for it, we're not here to shell shrimp.

And then he lifted the pitcher and nodded to the bartender: Another one, old man!

Paul! said Ana's mother irritably. Half the city was starving, not a decent head of cabbage to be had, and there they were, filling their faces. It must cost a fortune, surely, and where was he getting the money from? Was it dirty money, eh? Had he robbed a bank? Was it an inheritance? What was going on?

You hit the nail on the head, laughed Paul. Then there's my salary to top it up—I was promoted last August. So don't you worry about that. You just eat your fill.

But now Ana's father could contain himself no longer, and he leaned so far over the table that his elbow ended up in a puddle of gravy. But Paul, he said, you must know something about my thesis. You said it yourself, dammit, they've just promoted you.

Paul shook his head. He shoveled a piece of pork chop into his mouth. It's not my department, he said, smacking his lips. I don't know anything about it.

Come on, Paul, said her father. It's been six months since I sent it in. Can't you get anyone to take a look at it?

Paul wriggled a little in his chair, ill at ease, washing down the pork chop with a mouthful of beer. Oh, you know how it is, you know the bureaucracy. It's a damn—well, you know what it's like.

There was silence for a few seconds. Ana looked at her father, at the gravy stain on his shirtsleeve.

But for Christ's sake, he tried. There must be something we can do. Goddammit, you're a lecturer, aren't you, can't you try and get them to read it? Come on, Paul, help me out here, for fuck's sake.

Ana's mother was smiling nervously now, and she said, Darling, why don't we—

Maria, he said calmly. I'm just having a chat with my friend, okay? I'm having a nice little chat with my friend. With my best friend. Isn't that right, Paul?

Paul nodded. He was mopping up gravy with the last piece of meat.

For old times' sake, Paul, come on. You know how many times I've saved your ass. Can't you make them read it properly, just *once*?

Paul looked up from his plate, and for a brief moment the two men's eyes met. Then he put down his cutlery.

Maestro, please. This thesis—yes, of course I've read it. Look, how long is it you've been out of the university? Coming on fifteen years? And your thesis, well, it's—he sighed and took a pause. I'm really sorry about this. But it's simply not good enough.

The next day Paul took the train back to Cluj. Things changed rapidly. First, Ana's father stopped spending all his time at home, and Ana's geometry problems began to pile up on his desk. Days would go by before she saw him, and when she finally did—late in the evening, when he kissed her goodnight—he smelled so sharp it scorched her nose. When December came, Ana's grandma arrived to celebrate Christmas, and Ana's father started barricading himself in his office. He locked the door in the morning and re-emerged late at night, and silence fell across the apartment, across the whole block, a cave-like stillness that wrung the parks empty, drove the children up to their apartments and the traders from the market. When Ana went to borrow a ruler from her father a few days before Christmas, the door to his office was locked. The light was out, no sound came from inside, and even the aroma of tobacco was gone; it was as though the person working behind it had vanished, as indeed he almost had. He emerged only to go to the toilet, or to get a glass of water from the kitchen.

You'd best leave your father be, said her grandma from the living room.

But I want to go in and get a ruler, said Ana, tugging at the handle.

Oh, be *quiet*, snarled her mother. Go outside, if you have to be noisy.

Yes, sweetheart, said her grandma. We'll be listening to the speech in a minute.

But where's Dad? asked Ana. If he's in there, I've got to use his ruler.

Come here, said her grandma soothingly. Sit down next to me.

No, I don't want to, said Ana, and she went outside and slammed the door. She could hear the sound of televisions echoing in the stairwell, of residents waiting tensely in living rooms throughout the block. Nicolae Ceaușescu was going to give a speech, the Dear Winter Shoemaker would placate the demonstrators and bring the people to reason. Thousands had been summoned, bussed into the square from far and wide. Meanwhile Ana sat on the steps and moped, ignorant of politics. She imagined where her father might be: at the chess club or on the roof of the Institute, maybe in Piața Palatului with all the people on TV. He wasn't there for dinner, and late that night Ana woke to explosions, volleying shots ringing between the buildings. Through the gap in the door she saw her grandma muttering a prayer on her knees, and she felt her mother's warm hand on her forehead.

You mustn't be afraid, sweetheart, she whispered. They say they've caught them. You'll see, everything will be much better now.

And it was true: On Christmas Day the whole family gathered in front of the television to watch the Ceauşescus' drumhead trial. Even her father materialized, coming out of his office and flinging himself onto the sofa to witness the presidential couple's final minutes. The Scientific Elena cursed and screamed on screen, while her Hero Husband seemed bewildered as they bound his hands behind his back. They were led into a yard where the firing squad was waiting, and nobody covered Ana's eyes as the gunsmoke rose into the air and the cameras zoomed in on the dead bodies.

Ah yes, it was beginning to look a lot like Christmas!

On the streets the demonstrators set half the city alight, but at home in her apartment Ana's mother wept with happiness. She sashayed around with the phone under her arm, getting tangled up in the cord. She called friends and acquaintances, relatives near and far. *Now* the family would return to its former glory, the villa in Dorobanti, the tile factory, the confiscated forest. From time to time they heard a crash, the sound of a helicopter, but Ana never saw the soldiers or the tanks. She sat on the floor outside her father's office, drawing. She put her ear to the door, but heard nothing besides the occasional cough and the chair creaking as he rose. Sometimes she tried a cautious knock, but he didn't hear it, or pretended he didn't hear it, and Ana wondered. Where was the shuffle of books being drawn off the shelf? Where was the flick of a pencil swept along a ruler? Once, when she knocked, he opened up and stared at her with tired, red eyes.

Sweetheart, what do you want?

Nothing, she said.

Alright, then stop knocking.

But Dad, you promised to play the game with the dots. We always do that at Christmas.

He gazed at her.

Ana, he said, do we really do that?

Yes, we always do.

Well, okay. Let's give it a try.

Then he slouched back into the office and collapsed on a chair, and Ana grabbed the stool, she found the pad and pen, and she closed her eyes and let the pen drop onto the paper. A dot here and a dot there, more and more dots, until she was satisfied and put the pen down.

What do you think? she asked her father. What do you think it looks like?

But he couldn't have heard her, because he stared at the pen without any expression, so Ana held the paper in front of the lamp and examined the dots.

See, that looks like an apple tree, she said, and that there, that looks like a little crab. And that one, that's a whale. A whale at the bottom of the ocean, don't you see it? A little crab and a whale, and there's an apple tree too.

Her father drained his coffee cup, put it on the table and swallowed the last sip.

Humbug, he whispered.

What?

Humbug, humbug.

What is? said Ana, and she looked at him, and for a moment he caught her eye and lifted his fingers, nodding slightly, as though he meant the drawing or Ana, the family in the living room, the window or the rain that beat against it, the water puddling in the streets, the tanks rolling down the avenues, or the snipers on the rooftops, lying drenched and vigilant above the whole god-forsaken city.

Three weeks later, Ana started school again. After her last class, walking home among the tower blocks, she couldn't see much sign of revolution. The kiosk looked its normal self, the drunks sat on the same benches as always, the grocer still complained about the power cuts, and she continued across the parking lot and up the staircase. A heavy silence lay over the block, gray light falling through the frosted panes of glass, and when she let herself into the dark apartment there was nothing to be heard but her shoes dragging across the floor. In the kitchen she lit a candle and walked down the hall to the living room. A faint scent of something burnt; and, through the glimmer of the candlelight, the shadow of a piece of paper taped to the office door. A step closer, and she saw the words: *The door is locked, call the police.* Just that one sentence, and instantly she took a step back and turned toward the kitchen. The note was taped to the door, it was definitely her father's handwriting, and the instruction was simple enough. The door was locked. She should call the police. Yet after two steps she knew she couldn't do it. There was something behind that door, and with a single glance at the note, the whole world had changed. The door was no longer a door. It was a gateway to a future or a nightmare, to the nightmare that lives in the imagination of all children: a life without parents, at an orphanage. No father. No mother. Nothing. A moment earlier she'd been looking forward to her homework, but now she stood in the kitchen and gasped for air, more afraid than she'd ever been.

She peered down the corridor. She couldn't see the note. Maybe it was all something she'd imagined, a dream and nothing more, and she turned on the tap and got the washing-up bowl and bar of soap. Last night's dirty dishes were still in the sink, plates and cutlery and frying pans, and as long as there were chores to do she didn't need to think about the note. She had to do the washing up. Scour plates and rinse pans and wipe glasses. She doesn't remember how long she stood bent over the sink, but when her mother appeared in the doorway her fingers were pruney and pale, and the frying pans gleamed like new.

Ana, is that you? said her mother. Are you standing here in the dark?

Ana looked toward the door down the hall, shivering.

Oh, hey, sweetheart, what's wrong?

Her mother took two steps toward the office. For a second she paused, then turned her head slightly to the left, as though speaking to the wall.

Ana, go to your room.

Ana sobbed and put away the sponge. She went in and sat on the bed, and over the next hour she heard neither the officers nor the sound of the door being kicked in, not the hubbub of the paramedics or the relatives clattering up and down the stairs. She heeded none of it, sitting on her pink bedclothes, with her eyes shut and her fingers so far into her ears that she heard nothing but the slenderest little whine.

What happened, when she finally heard it, and who told her, she doesn't remember. She remembers only these facts:

That he was hanging from a cord tied to the curtain hook.

That he'd burned his thesis and his diaries in a stockpot.

That he'd been kind enough to put a towel over his head.

When I got home from Woodside that evening, when I opened the door to the apartment and found a postcard from Lærke on the mat, when I opened the window, looked across at the apartment on the other side of the street, and watched a woman do the dishes in her kitchen: that was when I realized I'd been thinking about Ana's story all week. From our midnight snack at the diner, when she'd explained about her appendix, through tales of sculpted dunes and her father's suicide, Ana had been trying to tell me something, and although I didn't understand why she had chosen to talk to a shadow of a man like me, I knew there was something at stake.

That evening I scribbled down the story about Ana's father in a notebook, and as I lay between the sheets I thought about his final hours, about the minutes before he hanged himself, the panic or serenity that seized his body as the cord tightened around his neck, and I tossed and turned until the last light was put out across the street. Then I gave up and untangled myself from the sheets, grabbed the computer and called Lærke.

She was sitting on a bus headed out of the city, a bottle of rosé in her bag, which she was planning to drink at a friend's allotment cabin. They'd painted it pink last weekend, she said, and while they were giving the side wall a final coat her friend had told a story about a colleague's housemate, a yoga instructor in her late twenties who copied all the colleague's purchases with OCD-like precision, buying the same shampoo, the same white wine, the same tub of butter. I could hear in Lærke's voice that she was smiling, and I couldn't help grinning either, but there was more, because one day the yoga instructor had apparently forgotten to buy a birthday present for her boyfriend—she'd spent all her cash on pot, or on a birthday present for her pot dealer; either way she was flat broke—but luckily she'd heard you could get a gift voucher if you let them biopsy your groin at the Panum Institute. So that's what she did, and her boyfriend was pleased with the gift voucher, only now she'd lost her job at the gym or yoga studio or whatever it was, because ever since the biopsy she'd had trouble balancing on her left leg and walked with a limp. What that had to do with the cabin I never figured out, because at that moment Lærke laughed and asked why I was calling her so early in the morning.

I couldn't sleep, I said, and explained about my evening with Ana, about the story or riddle of her father's suicide. It made no sense, I said. No matter how hard I tried I couldn't imagine what had made her father so desperate, how he could have abandoned his daughter like that. For a second Lærke's voice disappeared as though she'd hung up the phone, and when I heard it again it was like the frequency had altered or the distance widened.

Don't you think it's kind of weird she's telling you stuff like that?

In what way? I asked. Weird how?

Lærke was silent again; for a second or two there was only the crackling of the line or the muttering of the passengers, or maybe the doors of the bus grunting open and closed.

It's just so personal, she said. I've not got a surprise in store for me, have I?

What do you mean?

I mean, this story. Isn't it more the kind of thing you'd tell boyfriends or lovers or someone like that? Is she trying to get into your pants?

I laughed. Of course she isn't.

Not even a teeny-weeny little bit?

No, not even a teeny-weeny little bit.

Okay. But then promise me there's nothing between you.

You're serious?

Dead serious, said Lærke, and made me promise there was nothing romantic going on, made me swear I'd never leave her for Ana or any other artist or performer or Eastern European more generally, and then she got off the bus and I said I missed her, and she said she loved me, and there were only eleven sleeps before we'd see each other again.

Over the next few days, Ana's story rattled around in my head. In the daytime at the gallery, I pictured the last time Ana had spoken to her father, wondering what he might have meant by humbug, and at my desk at night I made up excuses to see Ana again. I wanted to ask her why he'd hanged himself, what had driven him to that point, but each time I started an email I realized it was impossible. Ana was several years older than me, a promising artist with exhibitions all over Europe, and although she'd treated me like an equal, I couldn't crowd her with my prying questions.

Then, one morning, she called me. Four days after our evening in Woodside, while I was stuffing envelopes at the gallery, I picked up the phone and heard Ana's voice, and beneath her voice a touch of disappointment or pique, or disappointment disguised as pique.

I was going to invite you to a party, she said. But you never call, so I guess you don't want to see me.

No, no, I do, I said. I've actually been thinking about calling for a couple of days.

It's fine, you don't have to call if you don't want to.

But I do want to.

Are you sure?

Yes, I'm sure. I thought we could get a drink sometime?

That's actually why I'm calling. Remember when I told you about my friend Monica?

Yeah, the editor.

It's her birthday tonight. Just a little get-together at a bar, but you can come and say hello if you like?

I'd love to.

Drop by my studio at six, and we'll have a drink before we head to the party.

Sounds good.

Oh, and bring a few examples of your writing. I'm sure Monica would like to see them.

She gave me the address and we said goodbye, and I was left holding the warm phone in my hand, scarcely able to believe my luck. I was going to meet an editor, and for the next few hours I basked in my own fantasies as I stuffed envelopes and went to the post office. Conceited, childish fantasies about the tales Ana had told me, about the short stories that would grow out of them and wax into collections or novels, and about the editor who'd one day take them on. I considered too what I should give Monica. A birthday present that made an impression, showed respect and gratitude, but wasn't too presumptuous. I couldn't think of anything like that, so after I'd mailed the letters I found my brother in his office and asked what kind of gift would make an impression on a woman you didn't know.

A notebook, he said. Always a nice notebook and a bottle of spumante.

A notebook, I said. Isn't that a bit much?

No, people love that shit. You're appealing to her self-image. Here's a woman who's sophisticated. Here's a woman who's full of original thoughts.

I laughed, but my brother wagged his index finger and said an empty notebook was like a mirror, and if there was one thing people liked it was their own lovely mug. He'd given scores of notebooks over the years, and out of them had sprung hours of conversation, exhibitions great and small, sweaty nights in studios squashed under roofs, in bedrooms tucked under courtyards, in open kitchens perched high above Brooklyn Heights. It worked every time, and if you were really bold you could write some pithy observation or a line of poetry on the flyleaf, preferably in Danish, because Americans loved that sort of thing.

Who is it you want to impress? he asked.

An editor, I said, and told him about the friend Ana was going to introduce me to, an editor who might be interested in reading my work, and then my brother got up and pushed his letters and papers aside.

I'll come and buy it with you, he said. I've got a studio visit anyway.

It was a warm afternoon turning into a brittle spring evening with white cauliflower clouds, the fruity scent of floor cleaner in the air and gusts of wind that followed us eastward through the borough. At the bookstore on Court Street we'd chosen a leather-bound book with unlined pages, and now I was striding through Cobble Hill like some hotshot with a bottle of sparkling wine in my hand and a bundle of stories meant for an editor. My brother led the way through the silent streets mottled with magnolia petals, talking about the abandoned factories and warehouses that once had filled the whole city, from Newtown Creek to the Gowanus Canal, the scruffy buildings, ex-playgrounds of Trisha Brown and Laurie Anderson, Walter De Maria and Gordon Matta-Clark, and I smiled and felt enchanted; to think I was actually here, to think I was walking through a city where people cut holes in buildings, danced on rooftops, and filled a whole apartment with earth just because they could, and because the world was so beautiful, the city so glitteringly full of secrets, that it almost made you weep.

When we reached Graham Avenue, I said goodbye to my brother and biked the last mile to the Bushwick address Ana had given me. The street lay in an industrial area not far from the Jefferson L stop, and I biked around the warehouses and ex-factories for ages looking for the entrance, but there were no doors or gates.

The buildings had their backs turned to the street, putting their minds to practical purposes: storing goods and repacking cases. It was a part of town for the dead and the finished, not a tree in sight, no workshops or factories that hummed with life. Now and then a truck roared by, but otherwise I saw not a single person. How Ana could make art in these surroundings I didn't understand, but I'd heard my brother tell me before: Real artists don't need inspiration, or something along those lines; inspiration was for amateurs.

By six thirty I still hadn't found the studio, and as I walked up and down the side streets I grew more and more convinced that Ana had given me a fictitious address. Finally I entered a whole-sale store and asked the way. The man who worked there looked at me like I was speaking some unknown language, and when I repeated the question he waved his hand, escorted me out onto the street and up some stairs, and plonked me into an elevator without a word. It must have been at least sixty or seventy years old, grunting and groaning its way up through the building, and when it stopped with a judder I pulled the door aside and was struck by the aroma of fresh-cut wood. A narrow corridor opened in front of me, a mannequin stuck one leg into the air out of a dumpster, and for a moment I stood still and listened. Two voices in animated discussion. A whistle. A drill, whirring somewhere far away.

Farther down the corridor I found Ana's door. The chipboard was painted entirely white, apart from the number written in pencil, and I took a few seconds to silently screw up my courage. I knocked three times, but no one answered. I tried knocking harder, and this time I heard Ana's voice through the door.

Come in, she yelled. The door's open, just come in.

I don't think I'll ever forget that studio. Light poured in through an enormous bank of windows, ivy crept through a shattered pane, spreading tendrils down the wall, and a furrow ran clear across the concrete floor, where dust and metal shavings lay like sediment from several decades' work. In one corner stood a workbench and the plastic cast of an Afghan hound, in the second was a shelf full of cardboard tubes and video tapes, and in the third I saw Ana. She was sprawled on the sofa, and I caught myself waving. I jerked my hand back instantly, but luckily she hadn't noticed.

Oh, it's so early, she said, struggling upright. Much too early for me right now.

She rubbed her eyes and explained she'd slept over at the studio, only waking when I knocked. She was going to have a wash, she told me, and then we could sit on the roof, watch the sunset, and have a drink. That sounds fine, I said, and so she picked up her clothes and towel and disappeared into the corridor.

While Ana was in the bathroom, I sat down at her desk and did a little rummaging through her stuff. On top lay a notebook full of timetables and almanacs, and underneath a sheaf of articles about a French speleologist, a caver whose name I'd never heard of. At the very bottom, beneath all the other papers, I found a folder full of pictures and curatorial statements and descriptions of her work, which must have been Ana's portfolio, and I opened it and skimmed the pages. Most of the texts and photographs came from Ana's exhibitions, but there were also some drawings and notes, and in a plastic folder I found a crumpled text in strangely broken English. It was a kind of story, but one difficult to read. The verb conjugations were a mess, there were no paragraphs, and the commas were scattered almost haphazardly on the page. I returned to the first line; there was something I didn't quite understand. It couldn't be right, I thought, and as I thumbed through the pages I felt a childlike wonder, turning my mind to the infinity of the universe or remembering that dust was dead skin. And yet. This *was* my own short story I was holding in my hands, the only one I'd published in Denmark, evidently fed through a translation program.

Find anything interesting? asked Ana behind me, and I flew up out of the chair, not having heard her approach.

Yes, yeah, I said, gesturing with the folder. Sorry. Your artworks, they're nice.

Nice? God, I hope not. I mean, I'd rather they were a little ugly, or nasty. A little viciousness about them, you know, a little rage.

Ana paused, struggling with her hoodie. Casting about for something else to say, I put the folder back and picked up a framed picture from the desk, a photo of a young man standing at the prow of a sailboat.

Who's this guy? I asked her.

Ana's head popped out of the sweater.

Oh, that's my ex-fiancé, she said. Come on, let's go up on the roof.

I put the frame back on the table, Ana grabbed mugs and a bottle of whiskey, and we followed the stairs up to the roof as she explained how she met her ex-fiancé in Bergen. She'd just moved to Norway and had no friends—or maybe she did, but not very good ones—and that was when she first met Isak and they fell in love, or thought they fell in love, and moved in together on his boat at Sjøflyhavnen. It was early 2006 or late 2005, Ana couldn't recall, but it was cold, and it rained all the time. They started making art together, the happiest months of Ana's life, but one day she told Isak about the time she'd lived in Morocco, and after that everything withered.

See? said Ana. That's why I'm done with men.

Morocco? I asked. What happened in Morocco?

Trust me, she said. You don't want to know.

Ana filled the mugs, and for a while we sat and stared out over Bushwick, which lay flat and pallid beneath us, all bedbugs and great expectations. As we sat there, I couldn't help but wonder about the machine-translated story. How long had Ana had that lying in her folder? Maybe it wasn't so strange that she'd been curious and tried to read it, but the pages were at the very bottom of the stack, dog-eared, the staples torn out, and something told me it was printed several weeks ago. The thought made me uncomfortable, and I stared at Ana, as if I could force an answer from her with my glare, but she didn't notice it, or didn't care, or pretended she didn't.

Hey, Ana, I said. Remember the short story you read. The one with the appendix?

Mm, she said. What about it?

Well, I was just thinking, how many of my stories have you read? Just the one?

Yeah, the one about the appendix.

Nothing apart from that?

No, just the one. But it was good.

Thanks, that's kind of you.

It's not kind, it's true. You can ask Monica yourself when you see her.

Ana sat up straighter and topped off the mugs, and we clinked them together and were silent for a while. Beneath us the city quieted, garage doors slamming, the roar of the trucks slowly dying down. I looked at the towers across the river, shining on the horizon like a mirage, and out of the corner of my eye I could see Ana huddled beneath her hoodie, swilling the whiskey around in her mug, and I bit my lip and tried to read her pale face.

Ana, I said. There's something I've been wondering. Why are you doing all this for me? Taking me to this birthday thing, introducing me to editors and everything. You barely know me.

She looked at me. For a moment her gaze was distant, as though she'd forgotten who I was and why she was sitting there, but then her eyes lit up, and she smiled.

Because you're sweet, she said. So sweet and young and naïve it almost makes me sad.

Sad?

Yes, sad. Sad because I've never been as young as you. Not even when I was a little girl.

I laughed, but Ana said she was serious.

I was born old, she said, and then she explained that her childhood had somehow slipped between the stitches of her memory, and she told me about the years after her father's suicide, the hundreds of weeks compacted almost into nothing, just a flash or two left behind, vague images and moods, scents, hardly anything tangible. She'd played a lot of chess in those days, but the games she'd played were long forgotten. She liked drawing, but she'd thrown out all her sketchpads. For eight years she'd lived like a sleepwalker, looking without seeing, hearing without listening, forgetting everything, and she'd probably be living that way now, said Ana, if Bogdan Marco hadn't woken her with a question.

She met him at the chess club. Bogdan was eighteen, she said, newly arrived in Drumul Taberei from the southern suburbs of Bucharest, a boy with an easy laugh and downy upper lip, and the first male Ana had met for several years. He was clumsy and plump and not all that cute, but Ana was in her third year at the Central High School for Girls, and Y chromosomes were thin on the ground. How her mother had finagled her into Bucharest's finest secondary school Ana never fully understood, but it felt so alien to her it might have been another planet. Everything she knew from Drumul Taberei, the wide concrete planes and horizontal windows, the straight lines and green, open spaces, everything sensible and planned, was ousted by a world ornamented and closed, by columns in the little garden, cramped nooks with busts and paintings and rows of ancient plane trees, which shielded the school from uninvited eyes. It was an old world full of codes and references unfamiliar to Ana, and every morning she traveled the long route from Drumul Taberei to the city center, dozing on the bus, while her classmates slept in their villas and mansions and luxury apartments, and when Ana finally made it to the Promised School she found a tight-knit clique of girls who'd known each other since they were little. They called her the Bus Princess, they called her the Queen of Drumul Taberei, and although she never had any friends, she did get used to a life of girls and women, of female teachers and lunch ladies, and forgot that she'd once ordered the boys around in the parking lot, forgot, almost, that whole swathes of the population had testicles at all. Her mother's father had died ages ago, her father's father she'd never met, and now that her own father was pushing up daisies and their portrait of the Nation's Father had been archived straight down the garbage chute, Ana forgot hair could grow on a human back, forgot the prickly feel of stubble against cheeks. She forgot what having friends felt like, and when Bogdan Marco entered her life and asked his question, it was like waking up from a long and quiet dream, a blind woman's dream of a peaceful, empty cubicle.

The first time she saw him at the chess club, he was sitting with his nose in a sci-fi novel while the teacher illustrated a pawn storm. The fourth or fifth time he showed up to class, Ana noticed he was reading *Flatland*, and he noticed her noticing, and Ana drew a pentagon she slipped across the table.

Are you into sci-fi? he asked, as they were packing their bags together. I've got some awesome ones at home.

That evening he took her to a burger joint at the new shopping center, and afterward they went back to his house to swap books. Ana tried to suss him out the whole way there, Bogdan, three parts nerd and one part ghetto, and even before she entered his room she'd guessed he had a shoe box of rolling papers and a lump of hash underneath his bed. They shared a joint while sitting on the windowsill, and over the following weeks they watched science-fiction movies together, and when they had money in their pockets they snuck into one of the new bars on Lipscani and made up stories about the students on the dance floor. By Christmas they were best friends, and every evening they talked on the phone until Ana's mother tore the line out of the socket.

Do you think we're made of money? she'd say. Get off your backside and walk over there.

It wasn't just chess and sci-fi they had in common. Bogdan was an ambitious young man, and while the other girls lost their vir-ginity in toilets and tanning booths on Lipscani, Ana sat in the library and did homework with Bogdan. While their classmates were slogging away at sines and cosines, Ana and Bogdan were already busy with vector calculus and binomial simulations, and they felt nothing but contempt for the idiots who got stuck in physics class, mixing up beta minus and gamma decay. As they sat in Ana's room after chess lessons, Bogdan told her about his mother and stepfather, who ignored him like the lint behind the sofa, but it didn't matter, because soon he'd be going to Imperial College, he'd wave goodbye to Bucharest and never look back. In return Ana told him about her father, Ciprian Ivan, chess cham-pion and mathematician, and how she wanted to apply to the Institute for Mathematics and publish all the articles he never got to write.

Can't you stop all that number witching? said Ana's grandma when she saw Ana and Bogdan bent over an equation.

Doesn't the boy get food at home? said Ana's mother, when Bogdan had once again picked the fridge clean.

On the eighth anniversary of her father's death, Ana invited him to Ghencea Cemetery. Every year she paid her father tribute with a little ritual, lighting candles and reading aloud from Euclid and asking God to look after him. Now it was January again, and for the first time she was going to share the day with someone else. They met outside the chess club on the cold, dank day, and Ana wore a dress and tights for the occasion. She'd put on eyeliner, and Bogdan laughed when he saw her.

What's going on, he said, you headed for a street corner?

Ghencea was deserted that day. They walked its empty paths,

their boots sinking into the gravel and squelching through the mud between statues and monuments, until Ana pointed out the grave. Getting down on her haunches, she cleared the leaves and dirt, then lit a candle and read aloud, and Bogdan sang a psalm his mother had taught him. Finally, Ana placed a letter by the head-stone, and for several minutes they stood in silence, watching the grave, while dusk crept up on them.

How did it happen, again? asked Bogdan with a sniff. Why'd he hang himself?

It was an obvious question, but Ana had never thought of it before. Her father had hanged himself, that was a fact chiseled into time, a certitude, like the French Revolution or the twenty-four hours in a day, and she'd never considered there might be a reason. Her mother'd often said it was just something that hap-pened, it wasn't anything her father could help, and Ana had made do with that explanation, but now the words had abruptly wriggled free, atomized between Bogdan's lips.

I don't know, said Ana. It's not like I can ask him.

Bogdan stuck his hands in his pockets.

No, he said. But I was thinking more about what he wrote. Didn't he say anything in the letter?

What letter?

You know, the note.

There wasn't anything like that.

Nah, come on. A note, said Bogdan, and he told her about the hundreds of suicides he'd seen in TV series and movies, razor blades and train tracks and hunting rifles, the method varied, but there was always a letter or a note or a secret message. Maybe it was sitting in a safe-deposit box or written in invisible ink, or once he'd read a novel where a man had carved it into his own chest before swallowing a cyanide ampoule.

Bogdan, said Ana, I think I'd like to go home.

Okay, let's move, he said, giving himself a shake. They walked through the gate, Bogdan jumped onto the bus, and Ana followed the yellow light along the main road, passed by bus after bus, as a fine mizzle fell across the streets, and she thought about what Bogdan had said. Why had he done it? Why had her father left her, and if there was always a note, then why had she never read it? When she finally got home, her grandma was sitting in front of the television and her mother was in the kitchen, doing the dishes.

What have I told you about going to the cemetery? snarled her mother. Next time you'll be grounded.

And her grandma, proudly: You've always been so fond of church.

Ana took off her shoes and hung up her jacket on the peg, put the water on to boil and settled at the little kitchen table. Steam rose from the sink, and with a practiced motion her mother washed a pot clean, then lifted a frying pan out of the basin.

Mom, said Ana, did Dad write a note?

For a moment her mother froze. Then she lowered the pan and turned around.

Why do you ask?

No reason. I just want to know.

For a second she gazed at Ana. Then she nodded, turned back to the sink and picked up the pan again.

Your father wasn't well, sweetheart. And he burned his letters in a stockpot.

That was all her mother would say on the matter, but Ana couldn't forget Bogdan's question. Suddenly she couldn't concentrate in class, she lost her appetite, and she lay sleepless through the night, staring at the bony branches of the plane tree. To cheer her up, her grandma gave her little tokens, even slipping her a silver cross. She tried resolutely to get Ana to come to her Bible group, but to her grandma's chagrin Ana was interested only in the more morbid aspects of the Orthodox Church's liturgy, the burial and mourning, the stuff about eating Jesus's flesh and blood.

At Easter she went to chess camp without Bogdan. Ana pestered him to come too, but Bogdan wouldn't be swayed: He was saving up to study in London. She arrived at camp with her father's chess pieces and two books about chess theory, and every day she played until the squares began to swim before her eyes. Afterward she stood in front of the trophy case and admired the cups inscribed with her father's name: Ciprian Ivan, the Talent from Târgu Jiu, four-time champion at the Drumul Taberei chess club. She wanted to be at least as good as him, she wanted to be the Romanian Judit Polgár, and while the other kids went down to the lake to fish, Ana remained at the cabin, solving chess problems. In the evening, when she couldn't move another piece, she sat in the common room and listened to the older chess players tell stories of long-lost endgames. A few evenings before they were due to go home, the camp leader said to Ana: Your father could have been the greatest chess player in Romania.

Could he? But then why did he stop?

The camp leader sighed, scratching at his beard. Yeah, that's a good question. He left Bucharest for a few years. But I'm not really sure. He wasn't quite the same when he came home.

Ana solved a whole book of chess problems that Easter, and filled two notepads with diary entries. She wrote a lot about her father, questions and guesses, ideas as to why he'd never become the great chess player he'd seemed destined to be. She promised herself she'd ask her mother about it, and when it finally came time to pack her things and head home, she was almost glad. But only almost. On the way to Bucharest she sat with her forehead against the train window, gazing out at the slippery fields, the rainy weather, and when they reached the gray suburbs the camp leader sighed and laid a hand on her shoulder.

I know, I know, he said. If you've got no other pleasures in life, at least you've got the pleasure of coming home and kicking off your shoes.

Back home, she applied for entry to the Institute for Mathematics at the Romanian Academy, sweating for days over the admissions essay. The night before she was due to send it off, she couldn't sleep. She listened to the water streaming through the pipes from the cisterns, stared at the outlines of the treetops, and thought about her father's application to the Institute, the one he'd written when he was young. She'd seen it once, worn and discolored in a scrapbook, and there might be a sentence or two she could borrow. Not wanting to wake anyone, she didn't bother switching on the light, and when she stood in the corridor she paused for a moment. The door to his office was open, and from the corridor she could see the window, the curtains taken down, the moon shining in. It was eight years ago and the curtain hook was gone, the holes from the screws filled in and painted over, the panes and molding around the window replaced, the floors newly varnished. She stepped into the office and the books were still standing; it was still the same desk. But the smell was different, the spots of candlewax gone, the marks on the wall thoroughly scrubbed away, and not the least vestige of her father remained. The thought was so brutal she had to sit down. Time had erased him, the years had come between them and removed the last physical traces, and soon it would dim her memories too, and she would never feel him again. She pressed her hands to her mouth, as crying rolled through her chest and spit slid through her fingers.

Ana, said a voice behind her. Are you crying?

It was her mother, and she laid her arms around her and spoke in a calming voice. There, sweetheart, she said. Calm down, there's nothing to cry about. Leading her into the room, she gave her a blanket and a cup of tea, and they sat together while Ana shook with sobs.

I've lost him, said Ana. He's vanished completely, I can't even remember how he smelled.

That's not true, her mother said. He's still with us somewhere.

No, said Ana. He's just gone, there's nothing left of him. It's been eight years. I've lived almost as long without him as with him, and all those years, it's like—they're thinning him, they're watering him down.

Her mother said nothing. She held Ana and stroked her hair, and slowly Ana calmed down and crumpled in her mother's lap, her face red and puffy.

Mom, she sniveled. Why did he do it?

Sweetheart, your dad, her mother said. And she took a pause, a pause that opened like a trash chute, a trash chute full of Styrofoam and tinfoil, cat litter and plastic bags, and the pause was everything Ana needed to hear. She straightened up and dried her eyes, staring at her mother.

Why did he do it, Mom?

Your dad, he. Well, he was a bit of a pessimist.

A pessimist?

Yes, he was. You know what? I think it's time the two of us went back to bed and got a proper night's sleep.

The next morning Ana went to the library. She ought to be in school, but the missing note rattled around inside her like a fact, or not *like* a fact, because it *was* a fact, and when the librarian opened the doors Ana was the first one to rush in among the shelves. She borrowed books about famous suicides, notes from desperate poets and politicians, and the rest of the day she sat in the reading room and flicked through the volumes. Bogdan was right. There was always a note, and if there wasn't a note, there was at least an obvious explanation. A suicide was no different from the rest of the universe. Nothing happened spontaneously: Everything in this world consisted of cause and effect, an apple tree won't produce a quince or a pear, and people don't emerge from the sea.

Later that afternoon Ana went to the cafeteria behind the post office, bought some soup and sat at a table to leaf through her notes. The conclusion was plain. If all suicides had a cause, then that cause must be deducible. It was all a question of method and thoroughness, like being a good mathematician, all about observation and verifying assumptions, excluding probable but incorrect conclusions and arriving at the truth. The raw data she knew by heart: her father's upbringing in a village in Oltenia, his years at the Institute, his thesis on topology, which came to nothing in the end, and his stockpot of burned letters and diaries. Now it was just about gathering more information, analyzing her data, and if she was rigorous enough she'd arrive at a connection, an order in the chaos of choices and decisions, omissions and imaginings, which altogether constituted a life.

That evening Ana began her investigation. As soon as her mother had gone to bed, she crept into the office and thumbed through her father's books and the Russian dictionary, turning the pages in a hopeless search for handwritten comments in the margins. She hadn't forgotten what the camp leader had said, and all weekend she rummaged through the files in the chest of drawers. She played archaeologist in her father's life, eager to know why he went so early to the grave and wasted his talent. She soon discovered it was no easy task. Her father clearly hadn't been one for documentation, and all she found was a file of correspondence on topology, a single photo album and a pile of unexceptionable postcards.

And the witnesses? Silenced, like in a mafia movie.

I don't know, said her mother, when Ana asked about old pictures or letters. It was twenty years ago, for God's sake, I don't remember.

He was born under an unlucky star, was her grandma's explanation for the suicide, but Ana didn't give up. She asked: But why did he stop playing chess, why did he burn his diaries?

Yeah, and why did the sun rise this morning? said her mother. How should I know?

Since she wasn't getting answers to her questions, she began coming up with hypotheses with which to pester her family. He might have been sick with cancer or Parkinson's, suicide perhaps his final dignified act, saving the family from a humiliating decline. Or he'd got on the wrong side of the Ceauşescu regime, smuggling dissidents over the border, maybe he was a spy, she jabbered, until her mother slapped the newspaper down on the table.

Put down that folder and do your French homework. You've got an exam to think about.

When Ana had read all her father's books without result, she tried to access the old things of his that were stored in the basement, but the key was gone, the janitor took ages cutting a new one, and for the Whitsun weekend Ana's aunts came to visit from the countryside. After they'd eaten, Ana stood lurking in the corridor, and when her aunts walked by she drew them aside and asked why her father had taken his life.

He was too fragile for the big city, said one.

God always takes the best of us first, said the second.

It was his head, it was too big, said the third. He choked on all those clever, clever thoughts.

Ana kept going, working like a scientist. She read her father's letters. She interviewed the neighbors and the local chess players. But did she find cryptic messages in his notes? Did she see patterns in the topological figures he'd left behind? Did she hear rumors of a mysterious past, a secret lover, or at least a secret *câine communitar*, a communal stray he couldn't stop feeding?

Poor Ana. Her father had lived a Teflon life. All she could dig up was guesswork, shots in the dark, and that wasn't how a mathematician worked. Hypotheses bristled in all directions, and by the end of May she was forced to sideline the investigation and concentrate on her exams. When June came she ran rings around all opposition, even correcting her teacher during the physics oral, and at midsummer she climbed the podium three times to shake the headmaster's hand. First for her high-school certificate, second for the mathematics prize, and third for being top of the class. This was Ana's moment of glory: On stage before her oppressors, volleys of applause raining down, she smiled a rare smile. She'd worked hard, and in a flash of euphoria she raised a clenched fist into the air, a nerd power salute, or, who knows, perhaps a gesture to her father.

The Institute's response didn't arrive until July, and it came as a surprise to no one that she got in. The rest of the summer dragged along at an excruciatingly slow pace. Every day Ana knocked on the janitor's door, until finally he got his act together and cut a new key to the basement. Ana spent the final weeks of her vacation rummaging through boxes in the damp storeroom—her father's coat and shoes, his pants and suits—but all she found in the pockets was the silent residue of life, his forty-two years on this earth boiled down to toothpicks and a few coins, flakes of tobacco, crumpled receipts, and a snapped cigarette.

As the beginning of the semester approached, Ana bought a new calculator, cleared a shelf in the office for her compendiums, and at the chess club she played a farewell game with Bogdan. He'd got into Brunel, but only had money for the first semester, he explained. Still, it'd all be fine.

Next summer I'll come home, he said. Then I'll take you back with me to London.

The day before the semester started, Ana's grandma gave her a little icon, a saint, who was supposed to protect her from the devilry of mathematics, and for once her mother didn't grumble about her superstition.

If you've inherited your father's luck, she sighed, you'll probably need it.

And then suddenly Ana was there, for only the second time in her life: at the Institute, where her parents had met, walking the halls where her father lived as a young man. The first months were a rush of enthusiasm, weeks of conversations rich in mathematical jargon, a feast for statisticians, computer scientists, and youthful talents like herself. If she was ever going to make friends, thought Ana, it would be here.

And Ana did eat lunch with the student assistants in the canteen. She joined a topology study group, drank wine, and surfed obscure internet forums with her new classmate Claudia. She went along to a few parties, and one morning she even said hi to a tall, angular guy on the tram, who fixed her with his almost lashless eyes and smiled at her twenty-two stops in a row. Compared to her dead-dull life in high school, Ana's first semester at the Institute was a ball. She did well academically too, flinging herself into assignments and prizewinning projects, and it wasn't more than a month or two before she was the geometry teacher's go-to girl.

Guess we'd better activate Ana, he said, when the other students refused to answer. Ana'll break the strike, yes, *that's* what I call a scab.

Ana was her father's daughter, she took the Institute by storm, and after a few months she was interviewed for an intern position with an algebraic research group, but lost out to a fourth-year. She had all sorts of good and less-good reasons to enjoy the carefree life of a student, but after the initial weeks of euphoria it felt like a shadow had stolen into the Institute. She couldn't put her finger on what it was, this sensation. A kind of eczema, almost, a small but insistent itch that crawled up her left-hand side as she walked through certain parts of the Institute: the lecture hall, the canteen, the east-facing stairs. Ana never said it to her classmates, nor did she tell her mother, and it took a lot of prompting before she'd admit it to me, because of course she didn't believe in nonsense like that. It was a delusion, pure and simple. Not him, not a haunting, nothing but a young woman's imagination, a dream or nightmare, no more than an illusion, when she sat in the lecture hall and saw her father's shadow slip across the floor, when she caught his scent in the corner of the coffee room, or heard the echo of his shambling gait receding down the halls.

In December, after her first exam was over, Ana's maternal aunt, Carmen, arrived from Budapest. She often did at Christmas, but this time she came early. She came to die. Her pancreas, that was the trouble. The doctors had given her six months, and Carmen was divorced and had no children, so Ana had to surrender her room to her aunt and move into the office. At first she didn't think it would be that bad. Ana'd never had much of a relationship with her flaky aunt, but once Carmen was installed in the apartment she filled up all the rooms, and no matter where Ana went she could hear her intolerable Jacques Brel songs, could see her clothes and jewelry flung across chairs and tables. Soon the metallic odor of sickness began to cling to the furniture, bottles of medicine filled first one then two of the shelves in the fridge, and Ana was often kept up late at night by Carmen moaning through the walls.

One Sunday afternoon, Ana noticed Carmen reading *The Tibetan Book of the Dead*, and when Carmen saw Ana scowling over her shoulder she put the book down.

What's wrong with you? said Carmen. You think I'm pathetic, do you?

Oh, no, said Ana, blushing. Not at all.

Carmen said she'd gotten the book from her ex-husband, a Hungarian mathematician she'd met through Ana's father. Her father was no slouch when it came to sums, but he sure as hell wasn't much of a matchmaker. The first six months of marriage had been great, but then the Hungarian had lost interest, and suddenly he couldn't get it up. He'd rather read the paper or have a bite to eat.

A fag, that's what he was, said Carmen. Do you have any idea how much dick I got that year?

Ana shook her head, appalled, clinging to the armrest.

This much, she said, showing with her thumb and forefinger.

It wasn't long before a ritual developed, and aunt and niece spent afternoons together. Ana and Carmen at her sickbed, Ana and Carmen in the kitchen and the bathroom: Carmen in the tub and Ana on the mat beside it. They used to chat for an hour or two every afternoon, discussing the rice-water cure Carmen was currently taking or the time Carmen was Queen of the Night in Mamaia. See these tits, she said, hauling the sorry remnants out of her bra. Once was I could get a king's ransom for these, and now look at them, like two dried peppers.

For the most part it was Carmen who did the talking and Ana who listened, but every now and then Ana screwed up her courage and told her about the erotic stories her classmate Claudia printed out from the web, or about the male students' ham-handed advances at the Institute. It was also around this time that Ana saw the tall guy with the bald eyes from the tram again. One day around Christmas she noticed him at Laptarie, drinking a beer. He was with a girl from the Ploiestis Chess Club, and it was she who introduced them. His name was Daniel, and Ana was invited to sit at their table. She exchanged a few words with him, if you could call it that—it was hard to hear above the music.

The next afternoon she told Carmen about the encounter.

Did he look you in the eye? inquired her aunt anxiously.

Ana shrugged. She couldn't remember.

Next time we'll have to doll you up a little. Carmen touched Ana's chin, turning her head gently toward the lamp. Cover up those craters.

Ana spent New Year's Eve studying for exams. She sat in the office and flicked through the geometry compendium and her father's mathematical dictionary, and when the first rockets exploded above the apartment block she realized it had been nearly a year since her walk through the cemetery with Bogdan. What had she learned about her dad since then? That he was a pessimist, that he was too fragile or too clever. But she was no closer to an explanation. For a moment she ran her finger over the equations, the geometry problem. Then she slammed the book shut and went to see Carmen.

Her aunt lay dozing to the radio, but she smiled when Ana came in.

Happy New Year, said Ana.

Shitty New Year, muttered Carmen.

Ana took her hand.

At least it'll be a short one for me, said Carmen.

You mustn't say that, said Ana, squeezing her hand. On the radio the host was counting down to midnight, outside the skies flashed yellow and red and blue, and for a while they sat in silence, staring at the colors, until Ana wiped her eyes.

Carmen, she sniffed, how well did you know my father?

Your father? Pretty well, I'd say. But mostly when we were young.

What was he like in those days? Was he a pessimist?

A pessimist? Nah, not at all, he was curious, full of enthusiasm. There was nothing that could stop your father.

Carmen handed her a napkin, and Ana blew her nose.

But, Carmen, why do you think he did it, then? If he was happy and full of courage?

Yes, why did he do it? she said, sighing. I don't know. But your mother always says it was the Institute that killed him. Too many theorems, you know. Far too many numbers. Frankly, it wouldn't surprise me. Turns you a bit cracked, that muck.

It was the only lead Ana had to go on. Three days later, when the Institute opened, she was shifting foot to foot in front of the counter at the library before the bleary-eyed librarian had even turned up. Before he had a chance to put down his coffee cup, Ana was in full flow, explaining she was looking for information on her father, that he'd worked at the Institute in the seventies, and that she wanted to see all the files the Institute had on Ciprian Ivan.

Ivan, you say, muttered the librarian. Doesn't ring a bell. But if you're sure he worked here, they must have a file on him at the archive.

Ten minutes later Ana was crossing the street, walking the few hundred yards down the road to the main library, where a guard followed her down to the basement and opened a door. The archive shivered in the light of a lamp or a single fluorescent tube. It smelled sharply of mothballs, I think she said, presumably with yellowing posters on the walls, and behind a desk sat a pinched and scrawny man, his head resting in his hand. With his other hand he flicked through a newspaper, and when Ana said she needed the file on Ciprian Ivan, he nodded without looking up from the pages.

Permission from the Romanian Academy, he said.

Um, well, I'm studying at the Institute for Mathematics, said Ana. Here's my library card.

And your permission slip from the Academy. Where's that?

I don't have one.

Are you sure? Try checking one more time.

Ana sighed, slipping a bill out of her wallet.

Ah, yes, he said. That's the one. Come on, we'll find this Ciprian together.

Ana followed him down the corridor, farther in among the shelves, until the archivist found a cardboard box, and in the cardboard box he found a ring binder, and from the ring binder he took a thin folder.

You know, you're not really allowed to be here, he said, and glanced at his watch. Hey, look at that, it's nearly lunchtime. If I just nip to the canteen, you'll definitely be gone by the time I get back.

Ciprian Ivan's records were brief. It took her no more than ten minutes to read through them. The first document registered his enrollment as a student. There followed a series of grade books, and then a letter with the names of new instructors for the spring semester of 1974. Her father's name was at the top of the list, and farther down she recognized another name: Paul Pintea, his old mathematician friend. The next document was a copy of his employment contract as a research assistant, dated January 1975, and the final document in the folder was an index of employees' addresses and telephone numbers. Under the heading "Research Assistants," she found her dad's information, and on the next line down she noticed the name Paul Pintea again. That was all. Ana rifled through the bits of paper, but there was no diploma or dissertation, not even a letter of dismissal. Like the record of a hologram, she thought as she turned the pages, until she couldn't stand it anymore and put the folder back, hurrying down the corridor and climbing into the winter's cold.

The rest of the day she tried to track down Paul Pintea. She remembered him from when she was little, a straight-backed man with a thunderous laugh, and as she skimmed through the phone books at the library her mind strayed back to the meal at the restaurant nine years earlier. Paul and her father had fought that evening, she remembered, but what it was about she hadn't a clue. Ana racked her brain for a few hours and tried vainly to reach her mother on the phone, but as she walked past a poster for the Transylvanian Conference for Mathematical Didactics in the canteen it suddenly popped into her head: the university at Cluj. She remembered the city from her father's monologues, the city he'd sent his dissertation to, a city full of mathematicians and scientists, but when she looked up Paul Pintea in the Cluj-Napoca phone book she found nothing. The internet offered no answers either, but when she called Babeş-Bolyai University the registrar confirmed that they did indeed employ a professor of mathematics by that name. Then she went into the reading room and tapped Claudia on the shoulder.

Up for a trip to Cluj? whispered Ana.

Cluj, said Claudia. What on earth would we do there?

They didn't have the money for train tickets or a hostel, but Ana made up a story about a study trip, a sister class they were visiting at Babeş-Bolyai, and at the library she printed off two fake invitations on official Institute letterhead. At their respective ends of Bucharest they showed the letters to their mothers. Out came the wallets, and two weeks later, Ana was entering the railway station to meet Claudia.

In her bag she had Paul Pintea's phone number and an old photograph of him with her father. She hadn't called yet, because she wanted to look him in the eye when he told his version of the story. Why this detail was so important she couldn't explain, but she wanted to surprise Paul and ask why her father had taken his life; something told her he held the key to the suicide, and she wanted to cry or fall to her knees and beseech him to tell the truth. Rehearsing her little plan as she walked across the railway station tiles, at the kiosk she nearly bumped into Daniel, the angular man, his eyes so lashless they seemed naked. It made her jump, but Daniel was with a beautiful girl, so Ana simply nodded. Then she hurried onward to the platform, where she found Claudia. They climbed aboard, and from the compartment she saw Daniel getting on the same train, alone.

Claudia grabbed her arm. Seriously, is that him?

Ana nodded. What are the chances? she said. Of all the trains, just think.

That's *got* to be a sign, said Claudia, clapping excitedly. Ooh, you're written in the stars.

Daniel was traveling first class, but he greeted Ana in the dining car. He invited her for a sandwich, and for the next hour they sat there as Romania whizzed by. He told her he was bisexual, he was an artist, he came from Bistriţa, had traveled all through Europe, was twenty-five years old, that his phone number was seven-seven-one-zero-one-nine, and that he liked Max Ernst. He said he'd call Ana when he got back to Bucharest. They could have a cup of tea.

Why do you think he said all that? yelled Ana over the music at a karaoke bar in Cluj that evening.

No idea, yelled Claudia. But my God, he's gorgeous.

The next morning they nursed their hangovers at a café behind the museum. Ana could get nothing down. She excused herself, saying she might as well get it over with, and crossed the square, past the statue and the flock of tourists, through the streets, until she reached the faculty building. She checked the address and photograph one more time, stepped through the first door, and asked the way to Paul Pintea's office. A secretary gave her directions: up the stairs and down the long hallway, first door on the left. Yes, there was Paul's surname on the door, and she knocked hurriedly before she could think twice. A chair creaked behind the door, a drawer was closed and cups shifted around. She heard steps. The door opened.

Paul, or a man who looked like Paul, stared at her. His eyes were the same, but he was fatter and balder, his cheeks slumped toward his chin like they were melting.

Can I help you with something?

Yeah, you're Paul, aren't you? I think you knew my father, Ciprian Ivan.

For a moment he gazed at her. Then his face split into a laugh.

Ah, Ana! God, is that really you? Last time I saw you, you were just a little thing. And now look at you. I mean, those curves, those curves.

He laughed again, waving her into the office and asking what she was doing in Cluj. Ana told him something about a study trip, and he pulled out a chair for her and sat down behind his desk.

Math at the academy, eh? Well, can't say it's all that surprising.

Ana blushed. No, I guess it isn't.

But it's good, said Paul. It's how it should be. If you've got your father's blood in your veins you'll be one hell of a mathematician.

Ana smiled, Paul nodded, and for a moment both were silent. Then she took out her notebook, keen to get to the point, but she felt muffled in the niceties, she didn't know how to say the words. Paul nodded, as though he could hear her thoughts.

Was there anything in particular I can help you with? he said. Or are you just here to say hi? Needless to say, you're always welcome.

Yes, there is something, actually, she said. It's a bit silly, but since I'm in town I thought, well. You were good friends with my dad. Weren't you?

The best, the closest. Like a molecule, you know.

That's what I thought. When my dad—well, when he died, he didn't leave a note. And I thought, since you were friends, maybe you knew something about why he did it?

Paul nodded, his gaze flitting around the room. It leaped from the desk to the bookshelves, and Ana tried in vain to catch his eye.

Ana, he said. Your father was a very talented mathematician. And he loved you very much.

Then he cleared his throat, got to his feet, and took a step away from the desk.

You know what, he said. Why don't we have a cup of coffee? Let's just have a little cup.

Ana nodded, but before she could stand up he was over by her chair, helping her up and bundling her out of the office, grabbing her bag as he went and closing the door behind them. She understood none of what was going on, but Paul was sweating and tugging at his collar like it was a summer's day. In the teachers' lounge Paul filled cups with coffee, found sugar and milk, and when they sat down on the sofa it was like the air leaked out of him, his body sagging like a block of Neapolitan ice cream, melted yet still upright, all soft and airy and made of powdered milk, collapsing onto the sofa.

Well. Yes, Ciprian, he said. Yes, it was certainly an awkward business with your father.

Ana nodded.

The other day, she said, I started thinking about that time at the restaurant in Bucharest. I wasn't very old, but you got into an argument, you and my dad. And I was wondering whether it had something to do with his dissertation.

You mean, what? Did he hang himself because of his dissertation?

Maybe, yes. It was rejected, and my aunt says it was because of the Institute that he did it.

Paul flapped his hand.

Your father was a very ambitious man, no doubt about that. But he never let himself be beaten down. Hang himself on account of some crappy dissertation? Never!

Paul set the coffee cup on the table. He said: No. If you only knew how many blows that man could take. Every single time they knocked him down he picked himself up again. I've no idea where he got it from.

So it wasn't because of the dissertation?

Jesus, no. He was like that boxer, what's his name? The one in the movie?

Paul punched his fists into the air, chuckling to himself, but then his cheeks sank again, and the timbre of his voice seemed to fade.

But, yes, that was then, of course, when we were young. Before I moved to Cluj.

What happened after you moved?

Yes, what happened then. I don't know. We didn't talk for several years. And when I saw him again, well, I'm not sure. He wasn't the person I knew.

Ana nodded. She wanted to ask whether her father had been depressed or sick, whether he was on drugs or sleeping pills, whether he was an agent or spying on the government, but then Paul got up and drew the blinds. Outside the sun had disappeared behind the mountains, a bluish light lay across the parking lot, and a tour bus pulled up. The headlights shone into the lounge, the bus stopped by the curb, the doors opened, and people tumbled out onto the street. Sweaters were taken off and put on, jackets removed from bags, and a flash cut through the twilight.

Ugh, just look at them, Paul said. Damn Hungarians.

Yeah, said Ana. All those tourists.

But what the hell do they want here? That's what I don't get. There's nothing here but misery and squalor.

Two days later, Ana and Claudia took the train home to Bucharest. In the compartment Ana wrote about her meeting with Paul, speculating about her father. She'd read the few remaining letters and postcards, but they told her nothing. She'd asked his friends and family, and now she'd run out of witnesses. As the train put the mountains behind it and trundled onto the Wallachian Plain, she slid the notebook aside and let it go. She stared out of the window at the fields, at the villages that stood like ghosts in the landscape, razed and resurrected through the endless succession of wars and empires that had swept across the country, the farms and the lives that had been lived there, and were forgotten, and of which not even a shadow remained.

Hey, why the long face, said Claudia. Aren't you going to call that Daniel guy?

Yes, said Ana. That's true.

Claudia nodded and took her hand. You know what I think? I think this spring is going to be big.

The fourth time Ana saw Daniel was at his apartment. They drank fruit tea and listened to music, and Daniel's boyfriend was there too. His name was Sorin. He was a few years older, and a very beautiful man. Not in the ordinary sense; or, no, it *was* a classical beauty, but it was also a—what did Ana call it? An inner beauty sounds so dumb. Well, it doesn't matter. It was a lovely day they spent together, Ana, Daniel, and Sorin. It was like they'd known one another for years, and Ana listened as the two men talked about Gide and Blaga and Tournier, and when it was time to leave they gave her *The Glass Bead Game* to take home in her bag.

Back in the apartment Carmen was waiting, and she said: Tell me.

Tell you what?

So, did he fuck you, or what?

Carmen! said Ana, shushing her. Mom can hear you.

But then she talked about Daniel and Sorin anyway, about the literature they'd discussed and the book she'd got in her bag. It might have sounded grand to her student's mind, but Carmen wasn't impressed.

So he's got a boyfriend? she said. A male one?

Yeah, so what?

Maybe you should take a step back?

But did Ana take a step back, when Daniel called the next day and invited her out for a drink? Hardly. She said, Yes thanks, absolutely, I'd love to. She put on her high-heeled shoes and walked alone up Lipscani. Blowing on her fingers to warm them, wrapping her scarf more tightly around her neck. It was Friday evening, and it was happy hour. Ana bumped into drunk people's elbows and hips, she shook as though with cold, and for a moment she hesitated at the door. Then she screwed up her courage and plunged into the cigarette smoke, set a course for the beer taps and caught sight of Daniel through the dark. He hadn't seen her, and for some reason she felt no urge to draw his attention. He stood side-on, his features almost dissolving in the paper lanterns' glow, but then he turned, and his eyes grew big and round, he drummed his fingers on the countertop, and suddenly he was standing in front of her, staring.

We can go back to mine, he said, when he'd ordered two beers.

And when they'd clinked glasses: You can sleep at my place, if you like.

And when he put his empty bottle on the table: I want to make love to you.

Ana looked down at the table, feeling her cheeks grow hot. Then she got up and found a payphone, called home, and said she was staying over at Claudia's. By the time she got back, he'd already paid the bill, and they walked back to his apartment. They took off their clothes and stood there in the middle of the carpet, Ana wishing she could crawl under the covers. She felt somehow like putting on a sweater, or a blanket would be good; it was so cold in the apartment, and no man had ever seen her naked.

I'm freezing, she said.

Daniel nodded and went into the kitchen for vodka and glasses, cut sausages and pickles, and brought a piece of bread.

There's no reason to be nervous, he said, when they were lying in bed. I've tried it loads of times before.

Then they clinked glasses, and he told her she'd be the nineteenth virgin he'd gone to bed with, and that he'd screwed a hundred and eighteen women and ninety-four men. He'd been a prostitute abroad, he said, because he needed the money, but he'd also saved some up. He kept talking, and the more he talked, the more vodka Ana poured down her throat, until at last she got so wrecked that for the next five years she was just as ignorant of the joys of sex as she'd been before she spread her legs for Daniel.

Why don't you stay? said Daniel the next morning, when she woke up. You can move in, if you want.

Ana, fiddling with her underwear and pants, didn't answer. She wanted to go home and have a bath, she wanted to go outside into the numbing air, she wanted clean clothes and something cold to drink. So they kissed goodbye, her tongue sticking to the roof of her mouth, her hair rumpled and greasy, her groin aching, everything smelling of smoke. On the bus she looked out at the Romani and their ragged children, at the homeless people, who'd had no contact with any water but the rain for weeks or months or years.

She thought of Claudia and her other friends, who had boyfriends and had waited for the right one, and she thought of AIDS and genital warts and syphilis, and then the bus stopped at Valea Ialomiței, and Ana plodded past the thrift shop and the dollar store, and everything almost went black. Then she reached Block A41, and when she opened the door to the apartment she was met by a doctor and two nurses, three neighbors, and a sobbing mother.

The doctor had said it was a question of days or weeks, that Carmen wouldn't live to see the spring. That afternoon the apartment was besieged by relatives and neighbors. Housewives milled in the kitchen, bedclothes were scalded in the bathroom, candles lit around the dying woman in the front room. The funerary circus had been set in train, and Ana never got the chance to speak to Carmen properly. Many nights she held her hand while Carmen slipped in and out of a doze, opening her eyes from time to time, fearfully, and asking: Is it now, is it happening?

Ana clumsily stroked Carmen's cheek, not knowing what to say. She told herself it was her duty to sit by Carmen's sickbed, that she could handle it no problem, that it was the least she could do for her aunt. That was what she thought, Ana, but before two nights were out she was a zombie, a good old-fashioned nervous wreck. Did she sleep at night? Did she keep up with lectures? Did she remember to put her name down for the exam? Could she stop herself making long detours to Ghencea to clean her father's gravestone, which by now had grown a slimy layer of moss? No, no, and no. One day she was woken in the cathedral by a giggling band of choirboys, and couldn't remember how she'd gotten there. Another time she went to pay for her lunch at the Institute's canteen, and the zipper on her wallet got stuck. You paying or not? said the lunch lady impatiently, and then Ana got stuck too, casting around in a panic and upturning the tray belonging to the man next to her, spilling coffee all over him.

Hysterical female, he shouted, you're not the only person in the world, you know!

Two days after Carmen perished with a moan, Ana trudged all the way out to Ghencea Cemetery and jumped over the hedge. In the darkness all the graves were alike, and for a while she traipsed from column to column, baffled and chilled to the bone. When she finally found her father's gravestone, she fell to her knees and laid her forehead against the cooling granite. Opening her eyes again, she saw a dog. It came trotting toward her, a scabby little communal stray. Lowering its head, it approached tentatively, snuffling at her shoes. For a delirious moment Ana thought it was a sign, an angel or something. But then she saw two other dogs come creeping out of the dark, and she scrambled up in fear and grabbed a stone. The dogs retreated slightly and Ana leaned against the gravestone, but just as she was about to turn she saw a fourth dog out of the corner of her eye, bony and more tattered than the others, limping out of the bushes, growling.

Go away, yelled Ana, kicking at it. It bared its teeth and drew back, and Ana fought for breath as everything began to spin. Go *away*, she sobbed, but the dogs came closer, their ears down. The tattered dog snapped at her, and when she kicked at it another one got hold of her pant leg. Ana screamed and flailed her arms, throwing her bag at them. The dogs leaped on the bag, tore and ripped at it, and in the confusion of the moment she crawled up onto the plinth. It was barely a meter high, and now the dogs were back, leaping around the grave and barking. They sprang up to reach her, snapping at her legs, their claws scrabbling at the granite, and Ana grabbed the marble cross and clung to it. Feeling something tug her ankle, she gripped the cross with all her strength, screamed, and thrashed her legs, and luckily a sexton heard the commotion. When he saw Ana he came running over, wielding a rake above his head. The dogs turned and barked but then retreated, first slinking backward, then at full speed. When the sexton was done yelling curses after all the goddamn communal strays in Bucharest, he helped Ana down from the grave.

What d'you think you're doing? he said. We're closed, for Christ's sake, you must have a screw loose!

Ana crumpled into a heap beside the stone and sobbed, inconsolable.

Nervously, the sexton twitched his cap. Aw, come on now. Jesus, I didn't mean it like that.

Ana gasped and gulped for air, and the sexton took her arm and walked her through the cemetery. He knocked on the door of the rectory, where the priest had just got back from mass.

What's going on here? asked the priest, who was still in his robes.

This girl, she was attacked by some dogs. I found her up on a stone.

And?

Well, and I found her like this, all unhappy.

The priest looked from the sexton to Ana, and then back again. Is she mute or what, can't the girl speak?

It was my dad, stammered Ana, sniveling. I never got to say goodbye.

The priest sighed. Oh, alright. Fine, just let her come in.

Then Ana was given tea with milk and honey, and she was given a blanket. She sat in the priest's front room, her teeth chattering, thawing out in the warmth of the stove, and suddenly it all came trickling out of her, nine years' guilt seeping into the carpet. God, her father had hanged himself, and she didn't know why. God, her aunt had died, and she'd been out fucking a gay male whore.

The priest nodded. He smoothed his beard. Ana was in the middle of telling him about her mother's silence and her father's burned dissertation when he interrupted.

May I ask you something, he said. Where do you live?

Ana stammered out her address, and the priest brightened.

Ah, Drumul Taberei, I thought you were new. He got to his feet, smiling for the first time. Do you know what I think? I think you should take the bus home and get a bit of shut-eye. Then, in the morning, go down to your own church. This isn't even your district.

Ana sat where she was, staring at the priest.

My district?

Why yes, my dear, you have your own priest in Drumul Taberei. I know him, he's excellent. Come on now. Off we go.

The priest took the blanket and helped Ana to her feet, bustling her out into the scullery. Ana was still confused, and as she put on her shoes the priest stood over her and watched her fumble with the laces. He said: By the way, you shouldn't be wearing those pants.

Ana looked down at her jeans. What's wrong with them?

Proper women don't wear pants. You know that.

But everybody wears pants.

You listen to me. Pants are for men, and anything else is nonsense. It confuses people. You're tempting men into homosexuality. Surely you realize that? Why else do you think we've got so many gays?

For a moment Ana stared at the priest. The dead eyes, the beard speckled with what might be bread crumbs, or maybe the white from a fried egg. Then she felt something she hadn't felt for years, and she pointed at the priest's legs.

Who are you to talk? You're the one in a dress!

That night at the cemetery, something woke in Ana. I'm not sure what you'd call it. A man dreams about a distant cousin, and the next day he learns she died that night. A woman tells a story about a dead sparrow she saw as a child, and a moment later a bird crashes into the windowpane. A girl is surrounded by a pack of dogs, is forced to climb a tombstone, to cling to the cross of her father's grave. It seemed a predestined confluence of symbols, of events: The sexton hardly ever saw dogs in Ghencea, certainly never in packs, and although it was late April and the reading rooms were bulging, Ana sat in her room and stared at her journal, trying to connect the dots and read the contours of the pattern, of the drawing that had to be glimmering somewhere between the lines.

Claudia got worried. She called every evening and asked if Ana was coming to the reading room the next day. And Ana wanted to go, but at breakfast or on the bus she'd begun to sweat, and in the streets around the train station a kind of itch would rise up her neck and tighten around her throat.

It's hay fever, she said, when Claudia asked what was wrong.

She'd come up with excuses, saying she was going to the doctor or the library, that she'd forgotten a meeting with her mother. Her days passed at the market and in the parks, and hours might be spent on the most basic errands. She had to make a sandwich, but had nothing to put in it, then when she got back from the grocer's she had to bake some bread. She gave her bedroom a quick once-over, but since she had the vacuum cleaner running she might as well give the living room a go, and the kitchen needed one too, and the bathroom could do with a proper scrub, while she was at it.

One day she needed new socks, but in the first store they were too expensive, in the second store they were too big, in the third they weren't made of cotton, and when the sun abruptly fell behind the buildings she got breathless, running to the bus without any socks and cursing herself on the journey home. Another day had passed, and sweet fuck all had happened. Another week had passed, and *still* fuck all had happened.

One afternoon she was sitting in Nicolae Iorga Park, the foliage hanging neon green around her, and underneath the plane trees some students from the art school were holding court. She couldn't see Daniel, but she saw Sorin, and he came over and asked how things were going. Ana lied and said things were great, and Sorin showed her a book about Joseph Beuys, and for a while they flicked through the pages, while she interpreted or guessed what the works meant. Sorin was particularly interested in a performance where Beuys had lived in a gallery for three days with a wild coyote, brandishing a cane and playing the triangle while wrapped from head to toe in felt. Ana had never heard of anything so weird, but it was a beautiful image. There was something strangely intriguing about the coyote and dark-felted figure, and Ana told Sorin about the dogs in the cemetery, and how she'd clung to the gravestone.

Isn't it strange? said Ana. Do you think it was a sign?

Sorin shrugged. You think it was a sign? Then it probably was.

Three days later, Ana tried to go back to the Institute. This time she made it all the way through the gate, forcing herself along the corridors and sneaking into the middle of a lecture. In the hall she paused to find Claudia. At first she couldn't see her, but then she caught sight of her in the dusty light, sitting in one of the back rows and scribbling in a notebook. Ana was about to go over, but she stopped for a moment and watched her friend—eyes turned avidly toward the blackboard, tongue greedily licking her lips— and it was then that Ana realized she'd never be a mathematician. In one of those clear moments novels are made of, Ana suddenly understood that she didn't belong at the Institute, that she didn't have math in her bones, that it was worse, in fact: that she was nothing but a little girl with a table-tennis paddle, sitting on a tree stump and waiting for her dad.

Backing out of the lecture hall, gripped by an overwhelming urge to pee, Ana turned and ran along the corridor, and for several hours she roamed the streets, her geometry compendium and book of formulae weighing heavily in her hands. She thought of her father's suicide, of the dogs at his grave, and late that afternoon she reached the bus stop at Militari. She stood there for a while, gazing at a trash can. A communal stray stood on its hind legs, its head buried in the garbage, chewing at a plastic bag, and Ana gave a deep sigh. It hadn't been a sign. It was a random pack of dogs, her father's grave was a granite block, and everything they'd told her at the Institute was lies. The world wasn't systematic or coherent, life didn't consist of cause and effect. Then the bus arrived, the passengers flocked through its doors, and the dog limped away with its spoils.

You getting on? yelled the driver, above the idling motor.

Ana looked up from the trash can. She nodded. Then she dumped her books on top of the discarded newspapers, the wrappers and bottles and cigarette filters headed for the landfills that surround Bucharest, for the smoldering fires that dissolve everything into air or wind or that smoky breeze that blows through the city late at night, and with two shuffling steps she boarded the bus.

That week Ana cleared the decks. She packed up her compendiums and deregistered at the Institute, tearing down her Kasparov poster with no quibbling from her family. Her mother seemed almost relieved, in fact, and her grandma crossed herself and thanked the Virgin Mary.

Deliver us from mathematics, she laughed, and all its misdeeds.

Not long afterward, the matriarchs packed their bags and decamped for the summer cabin. Ana didn't feel like joining them. She preferred to stay in town and hang out with her friends. But one week later, when exams were over and Claudia went to stay with her grandparents in Sighişoara, Ana was bored to tears. She lay in bed and tried to imagine her future, but her thoughts refused to coalesce. She didn't know what she'd be doing after the summer vacation, and to block it out she read novels and took long walks, getting so desperate at last that she defied her mother's warnings and called Bogdan in London. He didn't pick up, and one afternoon she went down to the art school and asked cautiously about Daniel.

Daniel? said Sorin. Haven't seen him in months.

Sorin asked if she'd like to come to an opening, and Ana had nothing better to do. He grabbed his bag and a few beers, and together they trudged over to the UAP, where Ana was introduced to the other art students. Later that evening they went to a bar, and the next day Sorin invited her to lunch. Afterward they sat in the park and spent a whole day dissecting their experiences with Daniel, and bit by bit Ana's summer passed. There were poetry readings with the art-school crew and lectures at the German cultural institute, but mostly they just hung out, and when Sorin disappeared into a car with some guy or other, Ana sat with his friends and tried to decrypt their banter. She knew nothing about art, but slowly a whole new language opened up for her, a nomenclature of theories, practices, and crit sessions, biennials, magazines, and studio visits, artists she'd never heard of and words she'd never used. The art world was just as complex as mathematics. Even more so, in a sense, because its etiquette demanded on the one hand a feverish kind of activism, and on the other a bored disregard; because there were things you had to do but mustn't mention; and because Ana soon found out you couldn't simply ask: So what exactly is social practice, anyway?

That summer she met feminists and deconstructivists, and for the first time in her life she was asked to talk about herself—downright encouraged, in fact. Initially it was unpleasant, but one day Sorin's crit group wanted to hear the whole story about the dunes and the anthill, and afterward one of the teachers came over and asked if she'd considered applying. As they were walking home that afternoon, Sorin asked her if she'd ever want to.

What, apply?

Yeah, man, they're crazy about you.

But I'm not an artist. I'm a mathematician, my whole family are mathematicians. What would I make art about?

I don't know, do like the rest of us. Scratch around in the trauma, dive into the muck.

But Sorin, I've already done that.

Then you'd better dive deeper, get further into the grime. All the way down to your family demons.

Sorin, listen to what I'm telling you. I've already done that. I know *everything* about my dad.

Okay, he said. But what about your mom?

They continued down the bare street, putting trees and alleyways behind them, while Sorin talked about his own mother, her alcoholism and loneliness, which he'd been so ashamed of when he was a boy. Ana said nothing. For as long as Sorin could remember, he said, he'd been a mommy's boy, a shivering homosexual nervous wreck, but what had been a weakness at school was the reverse at the art academy. There it was better to be a reject, a gypsy, or a homosexual; there you fit in if you had a diagnosis, if you were a little unhinged around the edges, a little borderline maybe.

You've got to have chaos inside you to give birth to a dancing star, said Sorin. Know what I mean?

Ana could hardly hear him above the traffic, but she nodded anyway. There were no shadows on the boulevard, and the heat thudded upward from the molten asphalt, but oddly it seemed like Sorin was enjoying the walk. He must have seen Ana growing paler, the patches of sweat expanding beneath her armpits, but he kept on talking about the torturous coddling and smothering attention his mom had put him through, and the smile never left his face. Ana listened until she could cope no longer. Coming to a halt at a bus stop, she said a hasty goodbye and leaped onto the bus. As she was letting herself into the apartment block, she bumped into her mother. Sweetheart, her mother said, what's wrong? What do you mean, said Ana, what could be wrong? I don't know, said her mother. You look like you've seen a ghost.

Ana stared at her. A ghost?

Her mother dropped her gaze. Then she picked up her shopping bag, and as soon as she'd rounded the corner to the market Ana dashed up to the apartment and into her mother's bedroom. In the wardrobe she found the hatbox, the one with her mother's knick-knacks and mementos. Taking it into her own room, she shut the door and braced a chair in front of it, then she leafed through the scrapbook clippings, the envelopes of photos. She saw pictures of her mother at the tile factory's offices, or clad all in white on a terrace in Dorobanti. She found a childhood diary in her mother's handwriting, her old slide rule. It was wrapped in black cloth in a leather case, and Ana took it out and held it in her hand like a scepter. The bright wood was inlaid with a shiny metal, the look of a revelation as the pale instrument emerged from all that darkness. Ana delved down into the hatbox again, and at the bottom she found a plastic folder. It lay buried under a pile of tax returns, and when she opened it her birth certificate tumbled out onto the carpet. She'd never seen it before, and now she picked it up and studied it. It was neatly filled out in bluish cursive and stamped with the emblem of a Ceauşescu ministry, and there was something oddly nostalgic about finding herself in an obsolete document, a registration number in a disused database. Ana was about to jot down that thought when she discovered a second sheet. Years of pressure had stuck it firmly to the back of the birth certificate—a rougher piece of paper, nearly falling apart. It must have been wet at some point, and Ana struggled to tell one word from another. Only when she realized that it was in French could she make out what was written on it: her own name and that of her parents, and a church in Morocco.

That evening they ate dinner with the radio on.

By the way, said Ana, I think I found my birth certificate today. Two different copies.

Ana doesn't remember what her mother answered—it was nothing special—and they washed up and left each other to their own devices. But the final scene from that evening she'll never forget. When she came out of the bathroom, her mother was standing by the window in the streetlamp's glow. She looked pretty, standing there half-turned toward the pane, as though the light were shrouding her, and Ana took a step into the room, then halted. There was something about the way her mother fiddled with the birth certificate between her fingers. She stood like a cold storage on a night when the power's gone out, a creaking, dripping hall of pallet racks, full of boxes thawing.

Ana, she said. There's something I've been meaning to tell you.

III

It was long past midnight when I left Ana's studio. We never did make it to the editor's birthday party, and as I biked home through the silent streets I felt light, emptied of thoughts, even if it had been a strange conclusion to a long and peculiar day. Ana had told me about her time in high school and her brief career as a mathematician, she'd chatted, gotten sidetracked and rambled for hours, but then suddenly she'd gathered the mugs and stood up and told me she had to get back to work. Did she say goodbye before disappearing down the stairs? If she did, I didn't notice. For a while I stayed sitting on the roof, waiting, but when she didn't come back after half an hour I got up and trudged down to the street.

Over the following days I pondered everything that had happened at Ana's studio, and the more I turned it over in my mind, the less I understood it. I'd seen my short story, translated, in Ana's folder, yet she'd denied knowing of it. She'd told me the most intimate details of her life, yet she'd stood up abruptly and left without explanation. None of it made sense. Each action was in conflict with the previous one. I had no idea what she wanted with me, but it didn't disappoint or annoy me. That was probably how it was supposed to be, I thought, that was probably how artists lived, in conflict with themselves and all the world around them. Who needed predictability? Who cared about order and regularity? I had a friend in New York, I had a story to write, and that was all that mattered.

Still, I couldn't help wondering about the translated short story, and on Sunday morning, when I was out on a bike ride, I swung by my brother's place to ask his advice. It was a surprise to find him in. He sounded hoarse over the intercom, and at first I thought I'd woken him up, but upstairs he was sitting at his desk in the apartment, buried in paperwork, his hair damp and freshly washed, his eyes red, although he seemed pleased to see me. As I made omelets, I told him about my evening on Ana's rooftop, and about the short story I'd found in the folder. Now and again he nodded or made a comment, and I asked if he could figure out why Ana was telling me all these personal details.

She probably needs to vent, he said. You know, offload on you.

I nodded—it did seem likely—but why me, of all people, a total stranger she'd barely met? If there were words she had to get off her chest, if she wanted to confess her sins, if she needed to stitch together all the meaninglessness with some kind of thread, some story that made sense of the jumble of events and episodes that constituted her life, then why was I the one hearing it?

Because no one else will listen? said my brother.

Okay, but then what about the story? Why go to all the trouble of finding it online, translating it, and printing it out? What does she want with it?

She's probably just curious, he said, and he asked about Ana's body clock and how things were going with *The Time Traveler*, but as soon as there was food on his plate he fell silent, munching with a vacant look in his eyes. He got up to brew some coffee, and as he waited for the water to boil he told me about a performance artist in the eighties who'd lived for six months in a small cage, totally cut off from the outside world. I didn't understand where he was going with the story, and he kept stammering and hesitating, dropping the thread. Frankly, he didn't look too good.

You got that right, he said. I'm trashed.

He splashed some water on his face and came back with his coffee. He didn't have a dishcloth, and the water dripped down his forehead, cheeks and chin. He said: I slept with three women yesterday. In twenty-four hours. Then he sighed and paused for a moment. No, seventeen hours. What's up with that?

I didn't know what was up, but my brother did, and he told me about the three women, and how fateful the whole thing had seemed. He'd begun in the morning in Ridgewood with the sculptor he was seeing, who was so sweet and so sensitive her eyes misted over whenever she saw a dead pigeon or rat. In the evening he'd had dinner with an art critic, and afterward they'd gone back to her place for a drink. Before long they ended up naked on the floor in front of the wardrobe, which was a bad idea, because the wardrobe had mirrored doors and the critic clearly didn't like seeing her naked body, or maybe it was my brother's naked body she didn't like seeing, but either way she kept wriggling and slithering away from the mirror, which made it impossible to finish.

Later they went out again, but the critic quickly got drunk off her head, and while she danced around with a bunch of people she knew, my brother met an MFA student, an aspiring digital artist at the bar. By that time the critic barely knew which way was up, so my brother went home with the artist, splitting a cab. He'd been too wasted to notice where they were driving, and it wasn't until he was on his knees on her mattress, his penis inside her, that he glanced out of the window and realized where he was: directly opposite the sculptor's apartment. He could see her orange curtains, the dense yellow light from her standing lamp, her long, slender shadow pacing up and down in the window, and for a moment he stopped thrusting and kept still. He'd screwed in a ring. He'd closed the circle. What the fuck was up with that?

Wow, I said, feeling the hair rise on the back of my neck.

I know, right? You get it, man.

My brother gazed at me in satisfaction. Then he went on: It was like being in a nightmare or something, I got totally freaked out. I just wanted to get out of there.

So what did you do?

What did I do? I finished. I pretty much had to.

I nodded and took the last slice of bread. Underneath the table my brother's leg joggled restlessly. It seemed like the story had perked him up.

What do you think it means? I asked.

Don't know. That Ridgewood is full of horny artists?

We laughed a little at that. Then my brother grabbed some beers, and we toasted to artists.

Oh hey, I almost forgot, he said. I've got something planned for us.

Planned?

Yeah, it's not all fixed up yet, but let's meet next week and have a chat. If things go as I hope, it'll be an interesting fall.

Three or four days later I was standing in the arrivals hall at JFK, waiting for Lærke. Her plane was delayed, something about a strike in Paris, and for two long hours I wandered up and down the airport corridors, eating ice cream cones and checking the time, until I lifted my eyes and saw her coming through the sliding doors, her long hair falling obliquely across her forehead and the phosphorous green of the exit sign tinting her pale cheeks. She headed straight for me through the mob of people, let her bags drop, and stood there with her springtime freckles and the look I loved the most, the look of someone hearing a good story they already know, pleased but not surprised, and then she leaned into my chest, all soft and warm and thrumming.

In the cab she told me about the man she'd sat next to on the plane. A man who'd read Saxo Grammaticus for seven hours straight, a man who hadn't stopped to eat, who took *Gesta Danorum* with him to the bathroom, and where did you meet people like that, why didn't we have more friends like him? I didn't know, but I said if she wanted friends like that then she was in the right city, and I praised Greenpoint's piers and Williamsburg, where you could walk twenty blocks without seeing a gray hair, and I talked about the adventures in store for us in the wasteland under the JMZ line, and about Bushwick, which lived a double life, or a life that was two lives, one that shone like MDMA, and one heavy like ketamine. It was our town now, I said, and Lærke put her head on my shoulder and pointed at the skyscrapers glinting on the horizon. Back at the apartment I brought out wine and glasses, and Lærke walked around the place, putting up posters and photos on the walls. Then she took my hand and led me to the bed and unbuttoned my shirt.

You're so handsome when you're not freezing every two seconds, she said, running a hand over my chest. So much better in HD.

Afterward we lay in bed and talked about the first room we shared in Nørrebro, in Copenhagen, and the time we set up dating profiles for a laugh. The site made you take a personality test: which compliment would you rather have, choose the two words that best express your outlook on life, that kind of stuff. It used an algorithm that incorporated psychological, anthropological, and sociological criteria to identify the most suitable partners, and when we were given our matches it turned out we were number one on each other's lists. Thirty-two thousand users on the site, and Lærke and I were each other's top match. It was the most romantic thing that had ever happened to me. We ran down to the corner shop and bought prosecco, and Lærke said she wanted to have our match rating tattooed on her collarbone, and even after she'd fallen asleep I stayed seated at the computer, gazing at our compatibility report, our profiles, which lined up perfectly: She was sensitive–intuitive to just the right degree; I wasn't too focused–observant, and I still have the final lines in my head: *You both prefer flexible surroundings and have no issues with surprises. You don't restrict each other within rigid structures and are open to adventure.*

That weekend I showed Lærke the city. I took her to galleries and a Polish bakery, I showed her the abandoned lot at the tip of Hunter's Point, and on Monday Lærke began her internship at a literary journal while I launched into my final week at the gallery. I'd been hoping to bump into Ana at the closing reception, but although I came early and left late, I didn't see her. The next day, we began to take down the exhibition. I turned up to dismantle the *The Time Traveler*, but one of the technicians told me Ana'd left a note with instructions, and that she wouldn't be coming to help out.

That week I did nothing but work. There were catalogs to pack up, articles to archive, budgets that needed to be balanced, and every day I hung around the office well into the evening, hoping I'd see Ana. But she never came padding down the hallway, her logbook never lay out on a desk, and when my curiosity got the better of me and I poked through the files for information about her, I found nothing but contractors' quotes, technical specifications for DVD players, and endless correspondence with the Romanian Cultural Institute.

Friday at lunchtime we closed the festival office. Once we'd turned the key in the lock, my brother invited the curatorial assistant and the interns to a farewell lunch at a restaurant in Vinegar Hill. He ordered wine and talked about his plans. He was off to Liverpool the very next day, and from there to Helsinki and Copenhagen, to meet with artists and bigwigs in the cultural world, and he'd be gone for a couple of weeks. Then he lifted his glass and I lifted mine, thinking: My apprenticeship's over then, I have to manage in New York on my own.

For the next few days I stayed home writing job applications. Lærke was engrossed in her internship, off to events every night, and after all those hours alone at my desk I was glad of the interruption when Ana phoned one Tuesday afternoon. She apologized for not showing up at the reception, explaining that she'd met an American curator and that they were organizing an exhibition together. She sounded enthusiastic, and we chatted for a while, me telling her about the job hunt and her telling me about the nonvisual installation she was setting up in the gallery. I asked how it was looking, but Ana said she didn't know because she hadn't seen it yet. That was the whole point. Then she stopped talking, and for a while I stopped talking too, and we listened to the traffic or the crackling on the line, or maybe each other's faltering intakes of breath. I remember I pictured Ana standing on the pavement in Woodside or Bushwick, staring out of the corner of her eye with that dreamy or paranoid gaze, clinging to her little red tote bag, when suddenly I couldn't stand the silence any longer and asked why she had called. There was a moment's pause before she answered.

I just wanted to know if you'd come over and give me a hand with the exhibition. If you get a move on you'll be here in time to meet the curator.

Half an hour later I was crossing underneath the BQE. It was one of those evenings where the wind changes, and a warm breeze makes six o'clock feel like midday. My shirt was sticking to my back as I clambered off the bike in front of the gallery. It was on Johnson Avenue, squeezed between a lumberyard and a carpet store, and a cloud of dust drifted across from the cement works on the other side of the street. The door was closed and the shutters were down, and for a moment I thought I'd come too late and Ana was gone. But when I tried the handle, the door opened. Lights were on inside, and in the middle of the room stood Ana, writing in her logbook.

Welcome to our cave, she shouted when she saw me. What do you think?

Not bad, I said. It's a really nice space.

At that moment a woman emerged from the back office, and Ana introduced her as the curator behind the exhibition. I didn't catch how they knew each other, but her name was Irene, and she'd grown up on the other side of town. Ana took my hand and gave me a tour of the gallery: an exhibition space, its floor covered in sheet metal, a toilet, and a back office full of junk. That was it. But the layout wasn't really important, because Ana's installation was called *Timemachine*, and it consisted of a single blacked-out room. And I don't mean blacked-out like an unlit basement or a night in the woods. No, I mean absolute blackness, a total absence of light, one hundred percent pitch-fucking-dark. Ana's idea was that people would live in the room while they worked or slept or danced; it didn't matter so much what they did, just that they lost touch with the rhythms of the day.

Ana herself would be living there for thirty days, to explore how the darkness altered her perception of time, but first a whole series of other artists were going to use the installation. In the first week they had a guy organizing a string of dinner parties in the dark, then a dancer putting on a proprioceptive ballet. I'm not sure how Irene and Ana had persuaded the gallerist to go through with such a dangerous project, but persuaded him they had, and now their problem was blacking out the space.

We bought staple guns and staples, ordinary and nonslip gaffer tape. We bought a rope that we nailed to the wall all around the gallery, so that the audience could follow it around the room and find their way out of the door again. Irene had brought a mattress that we threw into a corner, and we put a plastic tub in the bathroom so the artists could bathe. Ana padded back and forth across the floor, issuing orders to me and Irene. She was full of nervous energy, and kept saying: Is there any guarantee that the sun's going to rise tomorrow? No, there isn't.

Then we wound down the blinds and switched off the electricity, but there was still the problem of the light seeping in around the door, and we had to rig a kind of airlock system with three layers of black cloth before we were able to block it all out. Finally we taped over dozens of tiny fissures where the sun was shining through, while Ana lectured us about photons.

When you heat an object, she said, it emits light, okay? Light is made of photons. Does that mean the photons are already inside the object you're heating?

No, I don't think so.

Right, so they're produced. They're created. Photons don't exist inside atoms. It's creation, see?

I laughed. It was rare to see her so enthusiastic.

Don't you know anything about photons? They're so tiny and adorable and weird. If you let two photons interact with each other, then you separate them and put them on two entirely separate islands, the first photon on Tenerife and the second on La Palma, measuring the one on Tenerife will instantly alter the state of the other. Literally at the same moment, without any delay. Isn't that absurd? It's like they're teleporting back and forth, or time-traveling or something. It shouldn't be possible, but the photons don't care about possibility. They do it anyway.

Like bumblebees, said Irene.

Exactly.

But it doesn't happen naturally, I said. It's only in artificial experiments, isn't it?

Doesn't happen naturally? cried Ana. It's been demonstrated thousands of times—it *is* nature. In fact, quantum mechanics is so well established that it's considered a definition. So if I take two electrons and measure their mass, I'll always get the same result. I can take that for granted. Unlike you. Can I take you for granted? Can I count on you? There's always going to be room for doubt.

I laughed. I don't know about that theory. You could always test it.

No thanks, she said. I'll stick to photons.

We kept working late into the evening, until it couldn't get any darker. Irene ordered pizza, and we ate it blindly. Afterward Irene went home, and we lay on the floor in the blackness, trying to sense different parts of our bodies in space. Ana unpacked her things; she wanted to do a trial run, spending the night in the gallery. I helped her put sheets on the mattress, succeeding only after five or six attempts, and we laughed at our own incompetence. She unpacked her toothbrush and toothpaste, spare clothes and soap, a notebook with a pen on a string. After taking out a screenless music player full of audiobooks, the last thing she removed from the bag was a stopwatch for the blind and visually impaired. When you stopped the watch it spoke the time out loud.

Count to 120, she said, as we sat resting on the mattress.

Why?

Just do it, count to 120. But count it out in seconds—count to two minutes, okay?

I nodded, which was a ridiculous thing to do, all body language thwarted by the darkness.

Okay, I said, as Ana pressed start and I began to count. Trying to fall into a rhythm of one number per second, I counted Mississippis, and I felt pretty confident in my accuracy. I found a pace that fit the beat of the passing seconds, but when I'd counted to 120 and Ana stopped the clock, three minutes and eight seconds had elapsed.

Wow, said Ana. You've only just got here and already your sense of time is slipping. Time flies for you, I guess.

What do you mean?

I mean you lost a third of it. Don't you see?

No, I said. Three minutes is three minutes. I didn't lose anything.

But Ana didn't want to hear that kind of nonsense, so she told me about an underground explorer and scientist called Michel Siffre, who had spent two months in a subterranean cave buried deep beneath a glacier in the Alps. During his experiment, Siffre had lived there alone and cut off, no sunlight, no watch, his only contact with the outside world a cable telephone he used two times a day to speak to his colleagues: once when he woke up and once when he went to bed. The researchers discovered a disturbance in Siffre's perception of time. When they phoned to tell him that two months had passed, that the experiment was over and he could come out of the cave, he had only slept thirty-six times. He thought just over a month had elapsed. Time had gone more quickly than he'd realized.

Something happened in the cave, said Ana. She spoke more quickly than before, the pitch of her voice changing, her tone suddenly urgent, almost agitated. She said: The clock went twice the speed of Siffre's experienced time. He lost half of it. Half. Can you imagine? Nobody knows why the time passed so quickly, but they think it has to do with routine. When your life revolves around routines, your memory can't pin time down. It slips away. After a day or two you forget what you did the day before, and your only points of reference are falling asleep and waking up again. Apart from that there's nothing but darkness, like one long night.

We fell silent. I wanted to talk about something less creepy. Three full minutes had passed as I counted the seconds, but I had only experienced two. What had happened to the other one? It had vanished. I had missed it, letting it slip through my fingers. And suddenly my seventeenth birthday party rushed back to me, when my brother told me I was already halfway through my allotment of perceived time. It depended, of course, on how old I got, he had added, but in terms of averages. In terms of averages, I'd already lived half my experienced time—the years had long since begun to feel shorter, and they would only get more so. Shorter and shorter and shorter and shorter, he had said, and then my mother had told him to shut up. We never spoke of it again, but now and again I caught myself wondering whether time really did shrink as we grew older, if maybe the last six months *had* flown by more quickly. Lærke had even mentioned it the other night—all of a sudden it was summer again, and we didn't know where the spring had gone.

Why are you so interested in time? I asked, to change the subject.

Because I've been time-traveling my whole life, said Ana.

Yeah, right.

No, really. I have.

You've traveled through time. How did you manage that, then?

I wouldn't dare tell you.

You wouldn't dare?

No, it's a sick story. Really appalling—you don't want to hear it.

Come on, it can't be that bad.

It is. So let's talk about something else, okay?

No, I want to hear it.

But if I tell you, you won't want to see me anymore.

I laughed. Don't be ridiculous. Of course I'll still want to see you.

No, you'll just think I'm lying. That I'd have to be sick in the head to come up with something that disgusting.

We were silent a moment, maybe two—it was so dark it made you doubt everything. All I could hear was the throb of my pulse, Ana's breathing, and the rustling sheets beneath us. Then she leaned her head against my shoulder, and suddenly I felt her fingers grazing mine.

I mean it, she said. People get weird when they hear that story.

I tried to laugh, but I could feel the pressure of Ana's hand against mine. I don't know whether it was deliberate, but she let her fingers rest against my skin.

Seriously, I said. Do you think you have supernatural powers, or what?

But Ana insisted. Her time-travel story had already ruined far too many lives, and it would have been better if she'd never told it to anybody. I thought she was joking, of course—how bad could it be? It was just a story, just a handful of words one after another. It wasn't black magic.

Come on, I said, stupidly. I'm sure I can handle it.

Shifting her body, she laid her head in my lap and drew the sheet over herself, and in all honesty I can't remember how she began her story. The darkness in the gallery was so thick that there was nothing to hang my memories on, only the sound of her voice, the feeling of our sweaty hands, the weight of her neck against my thigh. Did she begin with the birth certificate or with her father? That evening it was difficult to tell where one thing finished and another began, but you have to start somewhere, and that somewhere was in Bucharest during the Good Years, at the Institute for Mathematics at the Romanian Academy, the most celebrated, most prestigious institute east of the Carpathians and west of the Black Sea. Not that there was much competition, it must be said—it was probably the only celebrated institute in those parts—but celebrated it was, especially in those days. The days when the Institute's alumni formed the backbone of international mathematics. The days when Solomon Marcus stalked the halls, devising the first mathematical poetics. The days when Alexandra Tulcea was the femme fatale of the natural sciences, married to Saul Bellow, playing the lead in his novels. The golden days, in short, before Ceaușescu shut them down.

It was during those days that Ana's father, Ciprian, traveled to Bucharest from his rural village to take the entrance exam at the Institute, and as he didn't have anywhere else to stay he took up residence in Cișmigiu Gardens. Not the teeming Cișmigiu Gardens they are today, full of juice vendors, street kids, and Romani families. This was the Cișmigiu Gardens of the Good Years, peaceful and magnificent, a park famous for its black swans. It was here that Ciprian settled down on a piece of grass along the fence near the main street, beneath a tree that doesn't stand there anymore. He lay basking on the benches and relaxed, thinking of all the poems and novels he had read about the Gardens—about unfaithful lovers meeting in the shadows of the trees, about men who died tragic deaths among the flowerbeds—and doubtless of the entrance exam too, and of all the beatings he had received when his illiterate father caught him studying: batterings with bare fists, thrashings with sandals, peltings with beetroots, wallopings with half-empty sacks of potatoes.

I have seen only a single cloudy photograph of Ciprian when he first arrived in Bucharest, but I can easily picture him on the day before the entrance exam, washing his face in the fountain and taking the short walk up to the Institute to solve the mathematical problems he'd been practicing, first as the village's model pupil and later as the provincial high school's mathematics prodigy. And I can picture him several weeks later, too, sauntering across the university square, bursting with confidence and nerves, to read his name on the list of those admitted to the course.

Two months later, when lectures began, he said goodbye to Cişmigiu Gardens and took up living at the university. This was Ciprian's golden age, listening to the professors sketch the illustrious history of mathematics in the lecture halls, going days without talking to anyone other than the staff at the Institute's library. Some days brimmed with number theory, others with combinatorics. In the breaks between lectures he discussed algebra or probability theory with his classmates, and when assignments were due he sat up all night long helping his new friend, Paul. Ciprian spent so much time at the Institute that after the first term he knew the building better even than the ancient janitor, who had swept the halls and changed the lightbulbs longer than any of the professors could remember. He could set his watch by the moment at night when the floors creaked and groaned as the day's warmth receded, and could tell exactly which toilet was in use just by holding his ear to the wall and listening to the water as it flushed through the pipes. He even spent his nights at the Institute. When the last few students packed up their books and the library closed, he wandered the halls looking for the darkest nooks and crannies—a deserted corridor, a forgotten office—so he could roll out his blanket for the night.

Ciprian, Paul would yell from the stairwell, so that his voice echoed in the farthest corners of the Institute. Ciprian, come on. You can't just stay shriveling up in here.

Two, three, four times Paul would shout, receiving no answer. Only very occasionally, when his conscience was gnawing at him, would Ciprian get up and go into town with Paul. Most evenings he pretended that he couldn't hear him, not even glancing up from his book, and Paul would grumble when they met in the break room the next day: This is your first year at university, man, it's *hubris* if you're not drinking yourself into a coma every night. I'm just saying. It's not my fault if you end up going three winters without a summer and only getting women with the clap.

Ciprian was clearly not one of those understimulated country bumpkins who'd come to the big city to revel in the noise and the traffic and the tantalizing store windows. Most village kids his age were rushing out to wine bars, hurling themselves into an orgy of booze and cheap floozies, nights when the city blazed with light in every windowpane. But not Ana's father. He would remember those days and nights for the rest of his life, and many years later he told his wife that all he desired was to live as he had lived during his early days in Bucharest: completely immersed in mathematics.

But who knows if that's true?

Though I can't say exactly how long Ciprian's golden age lasted, by the time he'd celebrated his first New Year in Bucharest and the winter's first storms had blanketed the city in a thick layer of snow, Ciprian had found himself crippled with responsibilities.

It didn't happen at a single stroke, but it happened nonetheless. First came the lunch lady's hardworking but slow-witted daughter: Ciprian tutored her three times a week, paid in cigarettes he then resold beneath the trees in Cişmigiu Gardens. Was it a relief to have some cash in his pocket? Certainly it was. It was a relief being able to buy a piece of smoked meat, to go out with Paul without having to rely on charity and freeloading and scraps from the richer students' table. But it took up so much time! It took time teaching the lunch lady's hardworking but slow-witted daughter even the simplest equations, and it took time standing in the park beneath the trees, waiting for customers in the cold. All of it was time he could have used at the library or sitting in the break room talking to the professors, who were always looking for excuses to dodge their wives.

Cigarettes, said Paul. Doesn't the woman know we use money these days? Jesus, you don't even smoke.

He was right. It wasn't much of a deal that Ciprian had going with the lunch lady. For months he weighed the pros and cons, considering just giving up the job. But one day, as he was eating breakfast with the ancient janitor, the conversation turned to the lunch lady, who'd been widowed in her youth and lost most of her family during the war. Her only hope of a respectable old age was her daughter's exams, which would open the door to university and a richer class of men.

This was hardly Ciprian's problem, of course. There were thousands of stories like the lunch lady's, and it wasn't his job to start doling out charity to widows. One might well observe that his tutorship was worth far more than the lousy packs of cigarettes he got in return, and that he had his own family to think of. One might observe these things, and many others besides, but Ciprian had been taught that a promise was a promise, and even though strictly speaking he hadn't *promised* to get the lunch lady's daughter into university, he kept tutoring her, often so late into the night that he would wake up feeling groggy when the janitor came rattling down the hall.

Moreover, the lunch lady's daughter was not his only responsibility. Since moving to the city, Ciprian had been surviving on the potatoes his older sister smuggled out of the family home and sent by train to Bucharest. Sacks of them would arrive each month, and it was no small risk his sister was running. He tried not to think about it, but he knew all too well that his honeymoon in Bucharest would be well and truly over when the stream of potatoes ran dry, that it would probably be sooner rather than later, and that his three sisters were eagerly awaiting a package full of coffee, nylons, and chocolate from Bucharest.

All in all, Ciprian needed a real job. A job where he was paid in cash, not cigarettes or good wishes. So when the Institute's senior librarian—who wasn't as stupid as he looked—remarked one day that, since Ciprian already spent more time at the library than any of the librarians, he might as well make himself useful, he jumped at the chance.

A job at the library: Ciprian's dream. And there were other perks too, because the senior librarian—who really did look appallingly stupid, and thus had never been able to find himself a wife—had plenty of space in the apartment he'd been provided by the Institute, and he offered to rent a room to Ciprian at a very cheap rate. Cheap in monetary terms, that is: In return, Ciprian had to pay with his ears, spending hours at the kitchen table, listening to his landlord tell interminable stories about his twenty-three years as the city librarian in Timișoara, when he'd been one of the driving forces behind modernizing the library system under Gheorghiu-Dej.

And thus Ciprian came to live at the Institute. True, that's exactly what he'd been doing since day one, but now he was living there properly, with his own bed and everything. Gathering his few possessions into his blanket, he moved into the attic room in the senior librarian's apartment, where every evening he could watch Professor Foias sitting in his study on the other side of the alleyway, his head permanently buried in a book.

Shortly before Easter, less than eight months after moving to Bucharest, Ciprian had two jobs, a garrulous landlord, at least one good friend, and a reputation as the most talented student in his class. Was there a woman or two in the mix, perhaps? Our story is silent on that point. But one can imagine. He was, after all, a good-looking man.

In any case, things were going swimmingly for Ciprian. A country boy from Oltenia, not only was he attending lectures at the most prestigious institute in the whole country, but he was also living and working at the university, getting top marks for his assignments, and before long he was able to send home a box of treats to his family. The whole village would be kissing the icon of the Holy Mother, or whomever they were kissing in gratitude

these days, crying hallelujah and thanks, our father in Heaven and
so on.

But it didn't feel all that celebratory to Ciprian. There was
something nagging at him, and that something was time. At first
he thought it was the winter, the short days and long shadows
that the low sun cast along the boulevards, making him feel as if
time were slipping away. But when spring came and the sun crept
higher in the sky, the hours grew no longer. Quite the opposite, in
fact. Ciprian had less and less time to devote to mathematics, and
each passing week he had fewer minutes to study, solve problems,
and work on proofs. Where had it gone, all that time? Soon he
was doing nothing but cataloging books, tutoring the lunch lady's
daughter, selling cigarettes under the trees in Cişmigiu Gardens,
and peeling potatoes as he listened to the senior librarian's melancholy prattle. It was a paradox. Ciprian lived and worked at the
Institute, but even in the village, where there were cattle to drive
and firewood to chop and fields to harrow, he'd had more time for
math.

Every morning it was the same old song.

Ciprian, called the senior librarian as he fried some sausages.
Are you giving us a hand at the library today?

A hand, mumbled Ciprian to himself. Not a whole damn arm.

And when the summer exam results were posted, he saw it in
black and white: It wasn't just a nagging feeling—his grades were
falling.

Ciprian was twenty-three and had only spent a year in Bucharest, but as the summer wore on and the Institute began preparing
for the autumn term, he was already dreaming sentimental dreams

of his first days in the city. The days when time had stretched out before him like the Wallachian Plain, where he'd driven cows across the fields as a boy. Or, in less vulgar terms: He dreamed of better times. Times spent with mathematics, times spent in research. Here one might well pose the famous question: So what? Our hero was living in the Romania of Nicolae Ceaușescu, Danube of Wisdom, Genius of the Carpathians—of course he dreamed of better times. Premature nostalgia seized him whenever he thought back to his early months at the Institute, to the nights curled up on his blanket, leafing through an introduction to topology. All he wanted was the freedom to gorge himself on Cantor sets, the freedom to sit in the reading room until his eyes fell shut. Freedom from the senior librarian's tedious chatter, and from having to send home all the money he'd saved each month. That was what Ciprian dreamed of. The easy college life—bah! Each night he went to bed as far removed from the riddles and wonders of mathematics as he had been when he'd woken up that morning. Every evening he sat in the window and stared with hungry eyes at Professor Foias's study on the other side of the alleyway—so tantalizingly close!—and at dawn, when the Băltărețul wind whistled through the cracks in the wall, he groaned in his sleep.

I imagine that Ciprian could have lived like that for many years, hard at work and dreaming of mathematics. And who knows, maybe in the end that would have been a better life. But it was not to be, for what happened next?

Love, of course. That's what happened.

Maria Serbanescu, a girl so blonde and upright that half of Ciprian's village fell into a swoon as he paraded her through the streets two years later. Ah, whispered the old women, recalling their own youth. Ah, trilled the girls, sitting by the river and fantasizing about life on the other side of the mountains. Ah, sighed the men, hiding in outbuildings or woodsheds, or wherever they chose to hide and sigh about her.

But first: an unfortunate event.

The senior librarian's sister had been ill for many years when, as if that weren't enough, her husband disappeared out of the blue. One afternoon in July he went off to buy melons at the market and—poof—he was gone. Without so much as leaving a note. At first the family thought it was one of those magical Securitate disappearances, but when the man's lover also disappeared and her family began to receive mysterious presents from Italy, it didn't take a genius to put two and two together.

He should be executed, cursed the librarian as he packed up his things. Down on his knees, one bullet to the base of the skull, job done.

So the senior librarian took a leave of absence, traveling to Timişoara to look after his ailing sister and leaving Ciprian alone in the drafty apartment with the large but incomplete collection of German heroic sagas and the smell of black pudding in the wallpaper.

One week later the Institute hired an interim replacement. Ioan Pancu, unmarried, mid-forties, suspiciously suntanned for a librarian. People took to whispering in corners, and what they whispered was that Ioan was a good friend of Nicolae Pleşiţă, a major general in the Securitate. That would also explain how Ioan got away with rolling up in the late afternoon, unwashed and reek-ing of booze, incapable of any work.

This big, Ioan would say, illustrating with his hands how big her ass had been. I imagine he laughed too, the way real scumbags always laugh, wet and braying. Ciprian tried to laugh too, but was there really anything to laugh about? He crept along walls and bookcases, hiding in the farthest recesses of the stacks, doing whatever he could to keep at arm's length from his new boss, until one sluggish summer's afternoon, when everyone and their mother had gone to the coast or to visit family in the mountains, he could no longer dodge the issue. Ioan slammed the library door behind them, turning the key seven times.

You and me, boy, he said. We're going to the bar.

Now, I've never gone for a drink with the good friend of a torture-happy security chief, but I can imagine that it's not a pleasant experience. I can imagine that there are certain topics of conversation one might try to steer clear of, subjects that one might ignore or run away from screaming. I can also imagine Ciprian sitting in the bar, his clammy hands gripping the pint glass, uncertain whether he should laugh or cry—well, not cry, of course, obviously—but either way being well and truly scared out of his wits.

They drank a beer, then they drank a pálinka. And when they were finished, they drank another round.

You look like the sort who could do with a little fun, said Ioan, after they'd downed their third beer. That's exactly what you look like. When did you last get any, eh?

I'm not sure, said Ciprian. It's been a while. I don't know—I haven't had much time.

You fucking kidding me? No time for jazz, at your age? Now I've heard everything. He's had no fucking time for a decent toot on the old horn.

Ciprian picked at the sunflower seeds spread over the table-cloth. Ioan persisted: I'll be damned, a kid of your age. No time, you're telling me?

Yeah, said Ciprian, forcing himself to stop playing with the seeds. Ioan smiled, his gold-topped canine glinting in the summer sunlight. You know what you should do, he said. You should become a student mentor. That's where all the pussy is. All that tasty student ass. Mm, sweet. Ioan puckered his lips into a kiss, making that sign where you connect your thumb and index finger. A perfect circle. Bull's-eye.

What do you reckon? he said. Want to be a mentor?

Ciprian thought it over for a moment. Thought about the senior librarian and the lunch lady and all his other obligations, about the sisters back home in his village. Then he thought about the student mentors who were often promoted to student assistants, and about the student assistants who were first in line when they were doling out research assistantships.

A mentor, said Ciprian with a laugh, giddy with beer and pálinka. Yeah, that might be fun.

And there it was: the fateful decision he would come to curse many years later as he sat, sick with grief, on a slope in the Atlas Mountains. All I ever wanted was mathematics, he would rage. But what did I get? This god-awful nightmare.

Who would have guessed that Ioan Pancu, the laziest lazy-bones in the history of the Institute, would be the one to heave Ciprian out of his mathematical fantasy world and into reality?

No one, probably. What wasn't so difficult to imagine, however, was the love affair that followed in the wake of his decision. I mean, how many men *haven't* met their wives as mentors or tutors or advisors? It was pretty unoriginal, in all honesty. But this was how it happened: Ioan put Ciprian's name on the list of student mentors, and on the first day of term he was assigned a group of first-years. Three boys and one girl, agreeable young people with wet-combed hair who scampered after him down the halls. Here's the reading room. Here are the typewriters. Here's the shortcut to the canteen, but watch out—Professor Marcus can't stand noise in the corridor. This is how the elevators work, this is how you hand in assignments. Over there is the break room. They were heading across the courtyard when he saw her. Ana says that the first thing he noticed were her shoes: high-heeled, smuggled in. Then the dress: white cotton over suntanned knees. The lipstick: risqué. And last the face: delicate, with gray entitled eyes.

Excuse me, but are you a mentor? she asked.

And he nodded, because he was.

Then it's you I'm looking for.

So. It was a perfectly normal way to meet, this first encounter. Just as the months that followed were predictable. A few parties, a cup of coffee in the courtyard. Extra help with homework over breakfast in Cișmigiu Gardens, and long walks through Uranus, Văcărești and other parts of Bucharest, which back then was still the Paris of the East, untouched by the Great Winter Shoemaker's bulldozers, and which Ciprian discovered he barely knew. On paper it was Ciprian who was the mentor, but when they went walking it was Maria who showed him around. She pointed out the buildings her family had built—there's my grandma's home economics school, my uncle's tile factory—and told stories about her father, who was in the air force during the war and had more than once drunk Prince Nicholas under the table. She told him about the forest her family had owned for generations. The forest that had shared the same fate as her uncle's tile factory, nationalized by Ceaușescu.

Whether it was all that upper-class patter that Ciprian fell for we'll never discover, but it was on one of those walks—while stopping to admire her uncle's palace in Dorobanti—that he felt her hand, at least the back of it, graze his own, and realized he was in love.

In love! It wasn't something Ciprian had tried before. In his village back home he'd had a crush on the neighbor's curly-haired daughter, and had been sweet on the Roma girl who washed clothes in the stream. But this was different. This was the genuine article, is what it was, and Ciprian had absolutely no idea what to do. He listened with half an ear as the lunch lady's daughter rattled off her sums, and was unable to contain his impatience when the senior librarian, now returned, launched into one of his monologues. It was suddenly completely impossible to concentrate in the reading room, and he was constantly having to get up and go into the break room or to the toilet, just on the off-chance that he might glimpse Maria.

Maria this, Maria that. Even Paul, who'd been pleased at first to see a little life in his friend's eyes, got tired of hearing how good she was at ice skating, how much she liked chestnuts, and how fond she was of the baby blanket that her grandmother had knitted in the distant past and that she still hid underneath her pillow.

Paul, complaining: Jesus, is there anything you don't know about this girl?

Ciprian had never known anything like it. For as long as he could remember, he'd only been interested in one thing, and that was knowledge. His whole life had been one long struggle to find time for his studies, whether he was leafing through the lexicon he'd hidden in the neighbor's barn, sneaking Euclid's *Elements* with him when he took the cows to pasture, or hiding behind the horses' trough and reading about Archimedes's circles. He'd been pummeled black and blue because of those books, but suddenly his interest in them had evaporated, supplanted by the woman he walked home from the Institute one late afternoon.

Goodbye, said Maria as they stood on the path beneath the cherry tree. See you tomorrow.

Yeah, okay. Goodbye.

You said that already, she laughed.

And it was at that point he lifted his hand to her chin, exactly as Paul had told him to do.

You really are very beautiful, he said.

Maria lowered her gaze. And the trouble with downcast eyes is that it's tough to tell the difference between shyness and rejection. That sort of body language is hard to decipher, so Ciprian just stood there wavering, cupping Maria's head in his hand like some half-witted Hamlet.

Ciprian, she whispered. Just kiss me.

According to Ana that was how it began, in the autumn of 1971. Ciprian, deeply in love as he'd never been before and never would be again. And Maria—well, the story is largely silent on the subject of her feelings. All in all, Ana spoke very little of her mother. I'd heard chapter and verse about her father, but about Maria I knew only the bare facts. She was born in Dorobanti in the early fifties, her father a successful dentist and her mother one of those orthodox women who sits in churches and chapels for hours at a time, pickling in an atmosphere of death and piety and half-burned candles. Maria Serbanescu grew up in a house with a piano and a library, on the surface a bourgeois home like any other, complete with table manners and freshly ironed shirts. But although they never talked about it, and although Maria was too young to understand the details, she could sense the spirit of the age, as they say, the revolutionary tide encroaching on the family. At night, when Maria put her ear to the wall, she could hear her father's drunken ramblings, and when the family took the train down to the coast one summer's day Maria caught sight through the window of her cousin, who'd disappeared under mysterious circumstances the year before.

Cousin Mircea, she shouted eagerly, waving at the disheveled man digging in the muddy canal. Mom, Dad, look! It's Mircea, she shouted, before receiving a clip around the ear, the first and only time her mother ever laid a hand on her.

The point was not lost on Maria. The family might well be up to its neck in shit, but why should she worry about it? Nobody else seemed to. Every week the house hummed with dinner guests, people danced the Lancers in the living room, and Maria's mother, who'd never been west of the Carpathians, switched into French at the slightest opportunity. The family was on a *Titanic* journey, playing until the whole godforsaken ship went down. They laughed and danced and drank, and one might be tempted to say that Maria's childhood was one big party. A pathetic party? Certainly.

But here one must remember that this was the People's Republic of Romania, Ceaușescustan, a land where anyone could end up in a labor camp, where the president had just returned from a starving North Korea and announced that he felt *inspired*.

It can't have been easy growing up in a home whose very existence was under threat. The political forecast promised wall-to-wall Ceaușescu. Did Maria sense her own vulnerability in that outlook? Of course she did. In fact, it might well explain why she threw herself so passionately into the arms of a farmer's son like Ciprian. He couldn't recite Eminescu, he couldn't tell a symphony from a sonata, and all in all he was made of coarser stuff than the doctors' sons Maria had fumbled around with during her high-school days, but she didn't care. She didn't want some flashy man-about-town. No, she wanted to be caressed by trembling fingers, undressed by greedy eyes, idolized so shamelessly that all thought of her family's gloomy future was knocked out of her system.

To begin with, Ciprian was at a loss about how to handle such a woman. He was used to village-caliber girls, and here was a student who read Beckett and played the piano. But instead of sinking into love-struck indecision, he simply went all out, sending her letters and bouquets of flowers, and raving about her beauty every time they went for a walk: Your nose! Your freckles! Your cheeks! He drew portraits of her and collected enough chestnuts for her to swim in, stopped sending money home to the village even, so he could take her to restaurants and the theater, frittering away his cash on gaudy jewelry she stashed away in a drawer somewhere, and which she never in her life once wore.

But he did get something for the money, Ciprian. I don't know whether it was the family's entrepreneurial spirit or what, but Maria didn't waste any time. Less than a week after their first kiss—one afternoon when Ciprian was showing her one of the Institute's hidden basement storerooms—she pulled her panties down around her ankles and ground herself against him until her virginal blood spattered the sheets of logarithmic graph paper.

Ah yes, it was love! And everything Maria knew about love she'd learned from romance novels, or from the stories her melancholy aunt had told her. In stories like those there is always a wealthy earl or doctor, and there is also a nurse or receptionist or whatever, it doesn't really matter—the important thing is that in stories like those they surrender themselves to love. They gorge themselves on love, guzzling it by the vulgar handful, stuffing each other with love until it's sticking out of both ends. Maria had no intention of being outdone by romance novels, so by the time the Nativity Fast rolled around her routine was set in stone: Every morning before lectures she would come to Ciprian's garret, lurking by the bus stop and keeping an eye on the house, then as soon as the senior librarian hurried out of the gate she would wrench open the door and fall into Ciprian's arms.

And we're going to get engaged? she whimpered as he threw her onto the bed. And we're going to get married?

Yes, he gasped. Yes, yes, yes.

And we'll have children? Two boys and a girl, she moaned between thrusts. And we'll have a house, and it'll be our house, and no one else can come in because it's ours, and we'll have a shed in the back garden, and when I've put the children to bed you'll carry me there and you'll fuck me, because it's our shed, and nobody can come inside, because we own it, and it's ours.

That's how she moaned while they made love, and afterward they lay on the rickety bed and whispered stories to each other. Stories about how Ciprian had left the village and slept in the dark corners of the Institute, living off potatoes, all so he could be her mentor. Stories about Maria, who despite her father's pleading and begging had refused to study medicine, because she'd always known in her heart that mathematics had something in store for her, and what it had in store for her was Ciprian. They whispered about all the coincidences and the peculiar twists of fate that had brought them together.

If I hadn't overslept that morning, said Maria, I'd never have got you as a mentor.

And if I hadn't taken a shortcut across the courtyard, said Ciprian, I'd never have run into you.

Day after day they babbled away like that. It must have been unbearable to listen to. They lay chatting in the garret deep into the night, blithely unaware that they were echoing the state radio broadcasts playing in the background, which spun tales of its own—tales about the Genius of the Carpathians, the First Mate of the Nation, who yet again that year had secured a harvest to end all harvests, about the Helmsman of the Revolution, who'd brought electricity and progress to even the darkest recesses of the land.

They got engaged the following summer. And they were married, too, in the spring of 1973. I've seen photographs from back then, and I can just imagine what it was like for the newlyweds during their honeymoon and in the days thereafter. They lived in one of the recently constructed apartment blocks in Drumul Taberei, which wasn't yet the run-down, communal-dog-infested hole it is today. No—this was the town of the future, an idealized microcosm of Ceauşescu's Bucharest as it looked before rationing, before the gas and electricity and heat were shut off. They lived a comfortable life in the block: mathematics every day, chess club on Tuesdays and Thursdays, and on Sundays a plateful of pork and a walk through the park, where the benches were still free of informants and the black swans paddled around in the lake without a care in the world, in no danger of ending up as soup stock or a roast or whatever they were used for when the shit hit the fan.

Ciprian was in his fourth year at the Institute, and he'd gotten a job as a student assistant for the first-years. Even though the job didn't pay much, he was a happy man, or he looked like a happy man: I've seen the photos myself, where he's holding Maria and smiling like an idiot. Okay, so their life wasn't grand, but neither were his roots. He had a job at the Institute, he had an apartment with a bathroom and central heating and warm water in the taps, and when he tumbled out of bed in the morning he could stand on the balcony, smell the coffee his wife was brewing in the kitchen, and stare down at the students plodding toward the university.

You'll be late, called Maria from the kitchen. You'll miss the bus.

Two or three times she would call before Ciprian went into the bathroom, marveling first at the miraculously warm water that cascaded down over his body, and then at the miraculously electric razor that he plugged into the 220-volt socket every day, while he whispered—and, on his bolder days, loudly proclaimed: Let us take this opportunity to remember a deceased physicist.

Ciprian had every reason to be proud, and proud he was. He was proud when he stood in front of the blackboard at the Institute, proud when he took the train home to Oltenia in the summer with a suitcase full of trade beads, proud when his alcoholic father looked the other way as he handed out stockings and chocolate to his family, friends, and neighbors. Most of all, he was proud when he woke up at night and let his fingers glide across Maria's ribs, hips, and small, perfect buttocks. Yes, things were going very well. But as with all stories, things go well until they start going badly, and they started going badly the day Paul turned up with a job advertisement.

It was in September of 1974. Ciprian was sitting in the break room with his fellow student assistant Florin, preparing their next lesson, when Paul leaned over the table.

What's going on, people?

History of Mathematics, said Ciprian. We're taking the class out sailing with Democritus.

Wrong, said Paul, slapping the advertisement down on the table: You're writing job applications.

Two open positions as research assistants, one of them for Professor Foias. It was the moment our hero had been waiting for, ever since that day at the bar with the drunken Ioan Pancu. In fact, in a way he'd been waiting for this moment ever since he arrived in Bucharest, ever since he'd read Pythagoras's famous dictum as a boy, which he later had woven into a doormat: *All Things Are Number*. The time had come to reap what he had sown, to lie in the bed he had made. Ciprian was a favorite with Nicolae Popescu, the Institute's polynomial prodigy, he was popular with his students, and a well-known figure at the Institute—why shouldn't he be able to get the job as research assistant?

And yet. It was Paul who first brought his attention to the problem, one evening as they sat sipping at their beers and staring at a group of Pioneers who were putting up posters for one of the mass gymnastics events that the Great Winter Shoemaker had become so fond of.

Maestro, said Paul, when Ciprian at long last paused for breath during his monologue on the potential of operator theory. If you want that job at the Institute, you'll have to join the Party. Best to get it over with, don't you think?

The Party, said Ciprian, annoyed by the interruption. What's that got to do with anything?

Paul glanced over his shoulder, then nodded toward the Pioneers. Get your head in the game. Have you forgotten where you live? It's got to do with everything.

It wasn't as if Ciprian had any objection in principle to joining the Party. He had simply never considered it. Politics wasn't something he'd grown up with. It was something that happened in cities, a private party. He didn't kid himself that he could understand politicians and their doublespeak, that intricate madness borne of two thousand years of marriage diplomacy and laws of succession, of the murky redrawing of borders by princely houses, of French rolls laced with hemlock and bodies broken on the wheel. And the wars—yes, the wars. Of them most of all. Politics was something he had no part in. And what difference did it make, anyway, whether it was one person or another wearing the presidential pants? In Ciprian's eyes, not much. Make no mistake: Life in the village was hard under Ceaușescu. But life in the village had always been hard—take the dirt road, for instance. For as long as Ciprian could remember, politicians had been promising that the dirt road from the village into Târgu Jiu would be paved. But did it happen during King Mihai's modernizations? Did it happen during Gheorghiu-Dej's six-year plan, or Ceaușescu's reform programs? No, it did not. The road remained just as pitted and gravelly as ever, and still is today, forty years later, despite the EU having paid for it to be paved not once, not twice, but three whole times. No, politics wasn't Ciprian's cup of tea, but if it could make him a research assistant at the Institute, then there was no more to be said: He'd become a Ceaușescu-ite.

Ciprian, a Party member—who would have thought it? Not Maria, that's for sure.

Have you gone completely nuts, she shrieked. My family will wash their hands of me!

It was their first real fight. She kept it up for days, yammering on and on about the family forest Ceaușescu's hooligans had seized, about her uncle who had slaved away his whole life only to have everything he owned snatched away from him in one fell swoop, and about her cousin Mircea who had come back from the labor camp with shattered nerves.

They only gave him flour and water! she squawked. People died of diarrhea!

After the initial bursts of fury were over, Ciprian decided to go down to the Party offices. Impatient, and convinced that Maria's anger would soon pass, he picked up registration papers and a copy of his birth certificate. Ostensibly wanting to read up a little on the rules, he was, I think, planning to apply in secret. And that would have been an excellent solution, had Ciprian not been careless enough to leave the half-completed registration form in his briefcase.

Tsk, you say. One shouldn't go poking through other people's personal things.

Sure, but try telling that to a suspicious spouse. Maria had sniffed out that registration form before you could say *you're getting warmer*. Enterprising as always, she threw both briefcase and papers into a large stockpot, poured kerosene over it and set the whole thing alight, so that Ciprian woke to the sound of the upstairs neighbor yelling *fire! fire! fire!* Forty minutes later they were sitting in the local police station, obliged to explain what papers they'd been in such a hurry to destroy. Love letters! Maria declared. Love letters from his *curvă*! Lucky for them that her anger was so convincing. The Securitate soon let them go.

A few days later, Ciprian sent in his job application to the Institute—without a Party membership number. Maria thawed somewhat when she saw him sitting on the balcony, looking like a man who'd just returned from a week-long bender: exhausted, dark blotches beneath his eyes, and a stare that cut clear through the block and the city and everyone who lived there. She tried to cheer him up by cooking his favorites, and organized a trip to her family's summer cabin near Constanța as a kind of penance. It was a peace offering, a glimpse into the dream Maria couldn't give up. A dream of diplomats on terraces, of women with diamonds and pearls in their hair. She pictured masked balls at the casino, sailboats with royal playboys, and all the champagne you could pour down your throat. And if Ciprian's best days were those he spent living in the dark corners of the Institute, then Maria's best days were those they spent together in Constanța. When she visits the town today, its grotty beach supposedly still reminds her of Ciprian running his fingers through her hair, and of the breeze from the Black Sea that dried the sweat, the semen, on their bellies.

They were a married couple on holiday, and that was how they behaved: taking drives up and down the coast, buying turbot and shrimp at the docks. It was the first time Maria had had the summer cabin to herself, and she made the most of it. She wore white dresses and invited family friends to dinner, doling out canapés on cocktail sticks and her uncle's illicit booze. And when the guests had gone home, she and Ciprian made love in every room in the house—and in the garden shed, of course—until they collapsed on the terrace in exhaustion.

We did the right thing, she said one evening as she lay in his arms. Don't you think?

What do you mean?

With the Party. We don't need those idiots, do we?

Mm, he said, nuzzling at her neck.

We have each other, don't we? And we have our integrity.

Yes, he said, stupidly. They can't take that away from us.

They lay like that on the terrace, lapping up each other's words, reassuring each other that they were something special. There's still some justice in the world, said Maria. Of course you'll get that job. And even if you don't, who cares? You'll get another chance. The world isn't going to turn its back on talent.

The problem, however, was that it did.

When they returned from Constanța, not only had Ciprian been passed over for the assistantships, but they had gone to none other than his best friends. Florin had swiped the job with Professor Foias, bragging that he hadn't even gone for an interview. The professor had simply handed him a contract. Paul, on the other hand, had been interviewed. Twice, in fact. But nobody had told Ciprian. When he heard the news, they were sitting in the break room playing chess. Ciprian didn't know what to do with himself. He continued with his move, sliding a pawn forward. Said, Congratulations, that's great. It completely knocked the wind out of him. He hated Florin for going on about Hilbert cubes and peer reviews, hated Paul for stealing the job—for having a job at all. Ciprian could understand how Florin was making a career at the Institute: He was, after all, the best algebraist in his year. But Paul, a research assistant? How the hell had that happened? Paul, who spent more time at the bar than in the reading room. Paul, who knew more girls down at the nursing school than researchers at the Institute. A layabout, a good-for-nothing, a *pierde-vară* without parallel. How's the new job, then—much of a challenge? asked Ciprian sarcastically. Maestro, it's fantastic, answered Paul. The craziest Abelian categories, chimed in Florin. It was enough to throw Ciprian for a loop: He lost the game, put his books under his arm, and fled the Institute. Back home, he poured himself a pálinka and worked off his anger by thrashing the bust of Maria's grandmother with a newspaper.

Fucking bitch, he screamed. Who's washing whose hands now?

He swung the newspaper so hard that the bust fell over, chipping the living-room floor, which they'd spent half the summer varnishing. Ciprian collapsed into an armchair.

Jesus Christ, he said. I'm such a loser.

That night in bed he complained to Maria. I knew it, he said. I knew I should have joined.

She sighed. Never mind, sweetheart. You can try again next year.

He spent a week in coffee shops with cigarettes and pálinka, in rainy pedestrian overpasses, in the bus station's crimson foyer.

And when Maria woke up at night to the sound of the radio in the living room, she could see him in the light of the streetlamp, his hand on his neck and a bottle on the coffee table's tiled surface. The whole thing came to a head one evening when the researchers and their assistants were invited to an anniversary dinner at the Institute to celebrate the founding of the Academy. Maria and Ciprian were kindly obliged to stay home. They were eating their soup and listening to the radio news broadcast when Ciprian suddenly let the soup spoon fall from his hand.

You realize what we could have eaten tonight, if you hadn't burned my registration forms? You do realize, right?

You know what? said Maria. Give it a rest. It's so petty.

Petty?

Honestly, yes. Maybe Florin and Paul were just better than you. Have you thought about that?

But apparently Ciprian had not, because with a single flick of his wrist he flung the bowl against the wall, so that the porcelain smashed and the carpet smelled of chicken stock for years afterward. Now you better be careful, he said with a quivering forefinger and everything.

Soon things flared up yet again, when they were at the parade with all its flag-waving and choral-singing. They stood in the cold and watched the Pioneers dance around in formation, cheering the Blue Motorway eighteen times. They heard speeches and saw balloons take flight. Maria was able to keep the mask from slipping, but as soon as they were back at the apartment she began to vent her rage.

What on earth are they thinking? she fumed as Ciprian collapsed on the sofa, sighing, to the sound of his wife's rant.

And the neighbors' children, she said. Why they send them along to this Ceauşescu rubbish is beyond me. Sheep like that, they've got mush for brains. Selling their children to the lowest bidder. It's madness, I'm telling you. If it were my kids they could forget it. They could just forget all about it. There's *no way*.

She flung the window open. Can you hear me down there? You're getting nothing out of me!

Oh, shut up, mumbled Ciprian.

But Maria kept going. And what about my uncle? Is he supposed to watch his own grandchildren running around in Pioneers uniforms? Is it any wonder his nerves are shot? They paid him a visit only last Sunday—the same people who stole his factory. What do you say to that? Ransacking his home, as if they hadn't already taken everything. They know quite well there's nothing more to confiscate. They've known that for many, many years. I mean, they're exactly the same people who fired him from his own company. His own company! And do you think they could figure out how to run it, the idiots? They're thick as two short planks. They couldn't tell their asses from their elbows without written instructions!

For God's sake, just get over it! said Ciprian.

What?

If your uncle hadn't been so goddamn pigheaded he could have kept his stupid job.

My uncle?

Yes, your uncle. Ciprian got up, taking a pálinka bottle out of the sideboard. If he hadn't been so fucking stubborn and refused to join the Party, they would have found a solution. They would have made a deal.

A deal, said Maria, and did she laugh contemptuously? I think she did. A deal, did you say? With those bunglers?

Yes, said Ciprian, shutting the sideboard door. A deal, a compromise. Ever heard of that? It's what people do when they weren't born with a silver spoon in their mouth.

By and by, however, things calmed down. Everyday routine took hold, as it generally does, with its endless series of bus journeys and runny noses, dirty laundry and chess-club gossip. By the time winter laid its flabby hand over Bucharest, one might even have thought that the row was dead and buried, and that things were going splendidly, thank you very much. You might have thought so if you were Maria's mother, or the neighbor coming to visit with a basket of chestnuts. But trouble lurked beneath the surface like the cockroaches they couldn't get rid of, which kept poking their antennas out of the plugholes well into November.

Ciprian still saw Paul and Florin now and then, discussing the latest mathematical journals or Bobby Fischer's dominance at the world championships. But it wasn't the same as before. Ciprian would politely decline when they invited him for a beer or a cigarette in the break room. Instead he would go home and take out books, problem sets, and notepads, sending Maria to dinner parties by herself while he remained at his desk. Am I married to a monk now, or what? she sighed. And at night, when the formulae began to swim together on the paper in front of him, he plodded out to the little hill behind the bus stop, at the point where the apartment blocks gave way to fields. When he held his head at a certain angle, the view was uncluttered by cars or electricity pylons, and all trace of the city was wiped away.

• • •

It was shortly after the new year that the story took a new turn. When the dean of the Institute told him the news, Ciprian got up out of his chair so quickly he banged his knee against the desk. He shook the dean's hand—thank you, thank you, thank you so very much!—and hobbled out of the office, forgetting both his briefcase and jacket in his haste. Here it was at last: his chance, his harvest of righteousness, justice being done. Okay, so perhaps it wasn't exactly what he'd imagined, but it was a research position nonetheless. Pausing on the landing, he gazed at the portraits of the professors and pictured his future: the untangling of topological problems, the proofs and the theorems, promotions and a corner office, the lectern at mathematical conferences.

When Maria returned from the reading room he'd bought wine and turbot, and an elaborate bouquet of lilies was waiting on the kitchen table.

Oh my goodness, what are we celebrating? she asked.

My new job as a research assistant, he said.

There was a moment's disbelief, and then she squealed and threw her arms around him. That evening they smoked and drank like kings, and as they lay in bed later, high on wine and sex, Maria said: It doesn't get better than this, does it?

Nope, he said, and nearly believed it. He blew smoke at her nipple, the right one—the bumpy, raisin-like one he secretly preferred.

What did you say the professor was called, again?

Elena, he said. After all, it was her first name, although nobody ever used it.

Elena. I don't know her, said Maria, running her fingers through his chest hair. Maybe you could invite her for dinner? Might be nice. Then we can meet each other.

Ciprian wriggled free of her arm and sat up in bed. We'll have to see about that, he said, stubbing out his cigarette.

Fine, she said. It was only a suggestion.

One week later Ciprian put on his best suit and stood outside the third-floor office, his hands shaking as he waited. She hadn't arrived yet, but out of the window he saw a white cabriolet enter the parking lot, a rumored gift from the Shah. She swung long legs onto the asphalt, all red jeans and a spotted silk shirt, while a dark-colored Dacia with tinted windows pulled up. Suddenly she was standing in front of him, smiling: Elena Zoia Ceaușescu, the Great Winter Shoemaker's youngest offspring, and only daughter.

You must be Ciprian? she said, stretching out her hand. I've heard very good things about you.

Thank you, Miss Ceaușescu, he said, and had to stop himself from bowing. It's a great honor.

Please, call me Zoia, she said with a smile. We're not at a gala.

Sure enough, the dictator's jet-setting daughter was a mathematician. While Papa Nicolae was busy handling the crisis in Czechoslovakia, Zoia had sneakily done a PhD in mathematics, and having received top marks the whole way through, the obvious next step was to continue down the path of academia. Before the age of twenty-eight, Zoia Ceaușescu—greatly to her father's chagrin—had written her first dissertation and taken up residence in one of the Institute's corner offices.

It can't have been an easy situation for the venerable leaders of the Institute. On the one hand the president would prefer Zoia's career to be curbed, so that the girl could find something sensibly proletarian to do. But on the other hand she was Ceaușescu's daughter, and who was going to risk getting their fingers burned by giving her the sack? So Zoia kept getting promoted, and her research kept getting funded.

Had she earned it? Was Zoia a good mathematician? Nobody really knows. Ciprian hardly knew, even though he was her assistant. Like everybody else at the Institute, he was afraid to read her articles and dissertations, terrified that her work would be awful and that he would accidentally snigger or wrinkle his nose, or in some other way betray his rancor over her success. Several of the mathematicians who still remember Zoia say that she was a real siren, an A-list minx who seduced scores of men in a haze of champagne and cigarettes and lived the high life on a never-ending tour of Europe. But others say she was a girl with her heart in the right place, a white lamb in a flock of black sheep, and that mathematics was her way of hiding from her family's monstrosity.

I don't know who to believe, but I do know that Ciprian was Zoia's assistant, and that he sat in the room outside her office writing drafts, sending letters, and studying vector space. Farmer's son and president's daughter—think what they would have said back home in the village! Would the local paper in Târgu Jiu write a profile of him? Would he be invited to the yearly banquet at the hunting club? Thus ran Ciprian's thoughts as he sat bent over Banach spaces, as he strutted down the corridors with correspondence under his arm, and as he swung around on the landing, heading up, up, up to the research offices.

And what about Maria—did she know that her husband was pulling the wool over her eyes? Did she realize that Ciprian was working for a Ceaușescu? She must have. I mean, obviously the Institute was trying to be discreet about Zoia, but Maria wasn't stupid. She had eyes in her head, and ears as well. But for one reason or another she chose to ignore it. Maybe she was so afraid of the Ceaușescus that she didn't dare form their name with her lips. Or maybe she was so hurt by Ciprian's duplicity that she fell silent, muted by broken promises. Who knows? Maybe she chose to turn a blind eye, like one of those wives who knows that her husband is running around after the secretary, but keeps her mouth shut for the sake of her children and a quiet life, or so that she doesn't have to put up with having the pig between her own legs.

In any case, Ciprian's career as a lady-in-waiting was short-lived. His tenure as a researcher came to an abrupt end one April morning when he found the Institute's door locked and a note clipped to the gate. How does a dictator put his unruly daughter back in her place? This is how:

In accordance with the Presidential Decree and with immediate effect, the National Council for Science and Education has closed the Institute for Mathematics at the Romanian Academy.

The Great Winter Shoemaker, never known for his elegant solutions and sick to death of arguing with his daughter, had simply shut down the Institute. So there! That'd teach her.

Ciprian read the note that spring morning as the rain dripped down the paper. It must be a mistake, he thought, sitting down on the steps to wait. Out of the boulevards streamed pupils, assistants, and professors, one by one coming up the stairs and reading the note, one by one drifting down again and gathering silently by the bus stop. His whole life in Bucharest passed by him that day: the ancient janitor, the senior librarian, Professor Foias, the lunch lady and her daughter. They nodded to him but he barely noticed, sitting there on the stone steps, his glasses fogged up and his jacket soaked through, a dim look in his eye. He sat with his hands resting lifelessly on his thighs, thinking of Paul and Florin, who had come by that same morning. Taciturn, they had stood over him with their cardboard boxes and said that they'd been transferred to Babeş-Bolyai in Cluj. Ciprian had brightened, saying, Hey, that doesn't sound too bad. He had missed the point, letting it pass unregistered. So which department are we transferring to? he had asked. The Institute for Numerical Analysis, Florin had answered. Only, we don't know about you guys, added Paul. It was at that moment that the small hope still miraculously clinging on somewhere beneath Ciprian's headache relinquished its hold and vaporized into the drizzle. But what about Zoia? he had asked, dismally. Isn't she also going to Cluj? Florin had stared at his cardboard box, while Paul scuffed his shoe along the step.

Sorry, maestro. I don't think she is.

It would be misleading to say that he took it well. It would be a lie, in fact. He took it neither with a stiff upper lip nor with his dignity intact. Instead he bought a bottle of pálinka and emptied it in big gulps as he staggered through Cişmigiu Gardens, kicking at the pigeons. At last he collapsed in the mud underneath a chestnut tree, eventually being woken by Paul, who had been looking for him for hours.

Fuck off, mumbled Ciprian.

Come on, you can't lie here. Let's get you home.

Fuck off, he shouted. Just fuck off!

When he finally came home, late the following evening, Maria was sitting in the office and talking to her mother on the telephone.

Ciprian stomped right past her and yanked the telephone plug out of the wall, tearing books down from the shelves and knocking over the bookcases. What an uproar! Notepads were ripped to pieces. The writing table was flipped upside down. Nothing could stop him, until the neighbor showed up and put him in a leg lock.

Fuck off, he screamed until he was hoarse. Why don't you all just fuck off!

Maria ran home and hid at her parents' house, only returning a week later. She had thought that things would proceed as usual: a few days of cigarettes and pálinka, and then back to work. But this time things were different. Ciprian had locked the door to the office, and had no intention of opening it again. Maria knew things were bad when Ciprian didn't even want to touch topology. She had never seen him like that before: chain-smoking on the sofa, staring at the rhombuses in the carpet. Even in his darkest hour he had never given up mathematics, but now he shouted and slammed the living-room door at the slightest mention of a number.

Paul visited before he left for Cluj.

It'll be alright, he said. You'll think of something.

What? answered Ciprian. The Institute was my life.

That's not true, said Paul. You'll cope, there are lots of institutes in the world. It'll sort itself out. He continued trotting out platitudes while Maria made dinner: roast turbot and Ciprian's favorite white wine. Shouldn't we go away? she asked, when Paul had gone home. Shall we go to Constanţa for a few days? Just a few days. You and me and nobody else.

But Ciprian prodded at the fish, then put down the fork and stared out at the buildings. I'm finished with Constanţa, he said. I'm finished with all of it.

The next day he shambled across to the bar and slumped over a glass, downing first one pálinka then another. He turned the glass upside down and bodily collapsed—head, hands, pelvis—and at the bottom, two black shoes. And when, after three months, he awoke to the scent of a new season, he took his coat off the peg and went into the town, joining the queue behind the job center's ashen blinds.

And so it was that the most talented mathematician of his generation, according to Ana, ended up as a high-school teacher. For what can you do when your Institute closes and you haven't even been awarded your degree? You settle. You take what you can get, and what Ciprian could get was a post at Drumul Taberei Technical High School—and in Maria's case, a measly job as a schoolteacher.

Broken dreams, yet again. I don't know how they got over it. But get over it they did: a year or so after the Institute was closed, the stream of family photographs reappears, and the first postcards from Constanța are dated Christmas 1976. Slowly they took heart, and began studying mathematics again. It must have taken a while, but I've been told that Maria and Ciprian behaved like a reasonably well-adjusted married couple when the earthquake hit Bucharest in 1977, even having enough energy to aid in the rescue operation. Ciprian reportedly helped by shifting rubble in the center of town, while Maria took an evening shift at the soup kitchen. Perhaps it was exactly what they needed, an earthquake, to remind them that although their lives hadn't panned out exactly as they'd hoped, there were many people worse off than they were. A failed career or two was nothing to get in a flap about. At least they had jobs and food on the table, and they also had their health. A few months after the earthquake, Ciprian finished the first draft of an article on topological proofs. There was still a long way to go, but at least he had something to show his colleagues. At the soup kitchen, Maria had met two young women with whom she began to organize French dinners and culinary classes, and all in all things were looking up. Even their sex life was improving. And although that was, of course, excellent news, the problem was that Maria was an exceptionally fertile woman. During their four years as a married couple, Maria had been pregnant three times, and gradually that took its toll.

Contraception, you might think, how hard could it be?

Pretty hard, apparently. There was no such thing as pills, and since the Great Winter Shoemaker had forbidden any type of condom, femidom, coil, or diaphragm in his efforts to support the Mothers of the Nation—who got a washing machine for the fifth birth and a Dacia for the tenth—they had to resort to *coitus reservatus*, navigating the precipices of orgasmic brinkmanship. Maria and Ciprian were clearly not masters of that particular art, which was unfortunate, because in his eagerness to swell the Romanian population Ceaușescu had outlawed abortion, and Maria didn't know whether she could cope with another trip to the back-alley clinic. Her uncle had a doctor friend who carried out illegal abortions with gloves and sterilized equipment and a decent grip on things, so she was luckier than most. Luckier than Ciprian's older sister, for instance, whose single abortion had been undertaken by the local wise woman with a knitting needle, and who now would wait in vain to be a Mother of the Nation, if indeed she'd ever been waiting for that.

Poor Maria. In her darkest hours after the procedures, she remembered her Sunday visits to the clinic: the hospital gown, the doctor's jovial assurances that it was a lovely uterus, hers, as pretty as a Grise Bonne pear. Maria thought the doctor was mistaken. Her uterus wasn't as pretty as a pear. Her uterus was a dark, throbbing mucus factory nestled deep inside her, a relentless spewer of pus and blood. No, Maria wasn't at all sure she could manage another abortion. Nor was she sure she wanted a baby. Could she really bring a child into this world? A world where friends and neighbors suddenly vanished and no one asked questions, where children spent their summer holidays at parades for a bird-brained shoemaker?

Maria still remembered what her aunt had said: that a wife's duty was to spread her legs and service her husband, and that she had only herself to blame if he ran around chasing other women or going to whorehouses, bringing back dirt and filth to their marriage bed. Men weren't made of stone, and who could begrudge him a fling or two if his wife was overly stingy? So Maria tried to think back to their first summer in Constanța and whatever she remembered of those deep, wet kisses, or of masculine hands wrapped around her neck, maybe. But they couldn't drown out the clinic and the village knitting needle, or the thousands of uterine scrapings being rinsed into drains every day, and before long Maria could barely kiss her husband without breaking into a sweat.

To avoid Ciprian's advances she chose a new kind of contraception, turning to the method most warmly recommended by the Orthodox and Roman Catholic and many other churches: abstinence. Every night she went to bed before him, pretending to be asleep when he laid his hands on her buttocks, and every morning she crept out of bed before he woke. And when she couldn't dodge him any longer, or her conscience had backed her into a corner, they made love briefly and awkwardly, always finishing in her mouth.

It was no way to live. It was a disgrace, is what it was, and their friends and neighbors were astonished. There were whispers at the greengrocer's and gossip in the parking lot. Maria was twenty-five years old, and it was no secret that the Great Winter Shoemaker had introduced a tax on infertility, so that any married couple still without children by the wife's twenty-fifth birthday was fined twenty percent of their income. The situation could easily have ended in divorce. According to Ana it was Miron, the balding bus driver from the chess club, who saved their marriage.

In those days in 1978, Ciprian was something of a phenomenon at the Drumul Taberei Chess Club. Every Tuesday and Thursday, and every other Saturday during the season, Ciprian dropped by the club and put his opponents in their place. Miron was also in the chess club, and the two men enjoyed sharing a beer and playing a game. Without much progress, it might seem—after the first three years, the score was 128–0–0 in Ciprian's favor—but Ciprian took his club champion's title seriously, and felt it was his duty to teach a man like Miron a thing or two about the wonders of the game.

It came as a surprise, therefore, when the scales gradually began to tip. It started with a fifty-move draw one wet Thursday evening.

Soon, however, their games were ending in technical draws, and before long Miron was noting down his first victory over the club champion. All the other chess players, from the fifteen-year-old electrician's apprentice who had yet to celebrate his first victory to the rheumatic joiner who could hardly lift the pieces, stopped their games and gathered around the table so they could see it with their own eyes. If the balding bus driver could defeat Ciprian, they whispered to each other, then maybe they could too.

Miron didn't let success go to his head. Although he was undeniably a bus driver, and although his bald spot had expanded beyond the point where one could reasonably call it a spot, he wasn't completely stupid, and he had heard Ciprian and Maria's neighbors gossiping on his bus routes around Drumul Taberei. He had no trouble putting two and two together, and he could guess why Ciprian was suddenly off his game.

Listen, is something wrong or what? asked Miron during the Saturday tournament, when Ciprian lost in the second round.

Ciprian shrugged and poured a pálinka.

Between you and me, whispered Miron, if it's your wife there's something wrong with, you should take her to the doctor. That's what I did last time she wasn't up for it. And let me tell you, it worked.

Ciprian wasn't the type to listen to just anybody. And he certainly wasn't the type to listen to balding bus drivers. But it couldn't hurt to ask an expert for advice, so the following Monday Ciprian set off toward the clinic. The doctor? you might be wondering. What good is that supposed to do? But here one must remember that in Romania in those days there was no such thing as couples therapy, and there was also no such thing as online health forums or sex advice columns in the weekly magazines. No, in those days people listened to the clever man in the white coat, and in this case he said, You go home and relax, and I'll ring your wife for a chat. You'll see—everything will be alright.

The following afternoon, Ciprian could already tell something was different. When he opened the door to the apartment he was met by Maria, who cuddled up to him and burrowed her nose into his neck. She took his hand and led him into the bedroom, taking off his pullover. His shirt, pants, socks, and her dress followed. And after they had made love—or whatever you'd call it—she whispered to him with tears in her eyes, I'm sorry, sweetheart, I'm sorry. I didn't know things were so bad.

It was almost too much. But what do you expect with a doctor like that? It's giving him myalgia, he'd said over the telephone. Spasms in his back and nervous complaints. Are you trying to kill him? Because it'll go straight to the heart, you know. It'll end in water on the lungs. A heart attack.

There had been no sex education at Maria's school—it had been done away with by, yeah, guess who—and she had never so much as opened a medical dictionary or an anatomy textbook in her life. On the contrary, she had grown up in a home full of petticoats and hymnals and icons of the Virgin Mary on the bookcases, and as a twelve-year-old she had been frightened out of her wits to find bloodstains in her underwear. Maria was almost illiterate when it came to human reproduction, having heard not a whisper about the birds and the bees and all that. But she loved her husband, and if the doctor asked her to spread her legs for him, then of course she'd fling them open.

And thus their sex life was reinvigorated. Hurray for the Ro-

manian healthcare system! And hurray for Ciprian too. Our hero
had kept his marital vows during his enforced celibacy. He had
remained faithful to Maria, and yet it was as if desire had fer-
mented within him, becoming stronger and bitterer, taking on a
life of its own. Every day at school he could feel it roiling inside
him, and as he climbed the stairwell in the afternoon each step
set it fizzing in his chest. There was a pricking in his fingertips
when he saw her by the kitchen sink or on the balcony hanging
up laundry, and when Maria spread her legs for Ciprian that day,
she didn't know what she was unleashing. A storm of passion
hailed down on her, and in the following weeks he took her over
the ottoman in the living room, filleted her on the kitchen table,
and mashed her thoroughly whenever he woke at night feeling
thirsty. He ground into her at all hours of the day, and after two
months Maria was lying on the bathroom floor and vomiting as
the neighbor held back her hair.

Someone's got a bun in the oven! the woman laughed.

No, I don't, grunted Maria, spit dangling from her chin. It's
something I ate.

Nonsense, you're knocked up. Don't you think I can tell?

It must be the peanuts I can't stomach, said Maria. Interesting theory, I guess. But it wasn't true. Their jar of pickled green
peppers was emptied at breakneck speed, and as soon as it had
been devoured she rounded on the jar of red ones. Suddenly she
could eat a whole jar in a week, and her mood fluctuated like
one of Ciprian's graphs when he was calculating amplitudes or
angular frequencies. After a few months she could no longer
convince herself that it was down to muggy weather or an acid–
base imbalance, so once again she went to see her uncle's doctor

friend, and he once again confirmed that her uterus was as pretty as a Grise Bonne pear, and that it was also carrying a child.

When Maria left the doctor that day, turning down Drumul Taberei's curving boulevard, it was as if something shifted in her body. That might sound facile, but it was how Ana told it. Something shifted in her mother's body, and suddenly a uterus wasn't something she *had* but something that consumed her. As the city's gray housing blocks flew past on the other side of the windowpane, Maria laid a hand on her belly in wonder, smiling for the first time that superior smile that would stay plastered on her face for the next few months. Why she had suddenly changed her mind I never discovered, but she wasn't even nervous when she told Ciprian the news. They lay on the living-room floor, looking out onto the snow-covered balcony while Ciprian caressed her stomach.

I think he'll be a ballet dancer, said Maria. I can almost feel him dancing around inside.

Ciprian snorted. A ballet dancer? What kind of fairy shit is that? He'll be a mathematician.

He most certainly will not.

A mathematician, said Ciprian. Think about it—with our two brains he'll be unstoppable.

Seven months later, shortly after midnight between the ninth and tenth of October, the midwife registered Ana's arrival in the annals of Romanian history. It was a difficult birth, and at the precise moment that the baby slid out of Maria, nobody had an eye on the clock, so the midwife handed the birth certificate to Ciprian and asked which date he preferred.

Will your daughter be a day older or a day younger? she grinned.

Ciprian didn't hesitate.

She was born on October 10, 1979, he said. 10101979, it's a prime number. Just listen to it—isn't it lovely?

Ana always went on about that little anecdote, that she'd traveled in time from her first day on earth. I think I laughed the first time I heard it, and it was only much later—after *Timemachine* was over and many months after we parted ways—that I began to see the symbolism, or whatever you want to call it. The pattern, the prophecy, the premonition of a whole life's lot.

As it was told to me, the period after Ana's birth was the last happy time in Maria and Ciprian's marriage. Life, in its tiny new incarnation, made itself felt in all its strength, overcoming Maria's daydreams and Ciprian's melancholy. The new parents went around in a haze of affection and hormones and baby talk, forgetting all their troubles and concerns, and every afternoon Maria's family came by with food and freshly laundered clothes. Her mother sewed little outfits and her uncle ordered a crib from a carpenter. There seemed to be no end to the celebrations: the party when the little family came home from the hospital, the christening two weeks later, the gifts after the baby's first month, then her second. And on the Epiphany holiday Maria and Ciprian took the train out to the village to present the marvelous child, so that Ciprian's sisters gushed in chorus and even his aging father couldn't prevent a slight twitch of the lips.

Look how she's waggling her arms! they said. Oh, and now she's smiling just like her mother. Look at Ana rolling around, look at Ana biting the *Disquisitiones Arithmeticae*, look at her funny paper hat. Look at her. Look at her now. And now. Look at her all the time. Oh yes, they were joyful days indeed.

So what was it that marked the beginning of the end for the little family's happiness? By now it can't be much of a surprise. Mathematics, of course.

Since the Institute's closure, theorems and set theory and topological space had slipped out of Ciprian's days, diluted by fathering and paper grading. It was as if his life had come to taste—well, what would he have called it? A trifle bland, a little on the unsalted side. Of course, mathematics hadn't completely disappeared—all things are, after all, number. But by this point Ciprian had been slaving away at the Technical High School for nearly five years, and although he did teach mathematics, it wasn't high-school math he dreamed of.

And was Maria any better off? No, not really. For four years she'd worked as a primary-school teacher, her days filled with runny noses and blank stares and the occasional pair of pee-soaked pants. Not exactly what she'd imagined when she enrolled at the Institute. But unlike her husband she had no long-held dream that had to be torn up by the roots and replanted in a flowerbed much too small for it. When it came right down to it, it wasn't all that hard for Maria to accept how things stood. And once her life was filled with Ana's childish laughter, her first smiles and steps, Maria soon forgot all her scholarly ambition and settled down at the school.

It helped too that the headmaster was an engaging sort of fellow. As a Hungarian, it was a minor miracle he had climbed that far up in the system. He must have had sharp elbows, the good headmaster, and a soft spot for Maria too. Rumor had it that in his heyday the Hungarian had made it all the way up to the highest offices in the Council of Education, but that he'd been dismissed in one of the anti-Hungarian purges. He harbored a grudge against the government, and it was whispered that he led a ring of smugglers who helped people defect. But who knows whether that's true? All I know is that the headmaster was a real gentleman, the kind of man who didn't treat his teachers like faceless employees. A man of the old school, who kissed hands and pulled out chairs and slipped little notes into Maria's pigeon-hole. *Enjoy your vacation!* or *Break a leg with the exams!* The Hungarian headmaster, as the social studies teacher was fond of pointing out, was like an ideal nation-state, hard on the outside but soft on the inside, and if anyone found him treacly or overly forward it wasn't Maria.

She and the Hungarian had gotten into the habit of drinking tea together after work on Fridays, when they would sit with their Turkish tea glasses clinking in their saucers, talking about Steiner and Piaget's theories and, later, about Liszt's Piano Sonata in B minor, which the headmaster had struggled with so much as a boy. Did more than tea drinking go on inside that office? I don't think so, but who is to say? In any case, one overcast day in June Maria entered the headmaster's office to find him deep in thought, hunched over a letter on his desk.

Ah, he said, when he noticed her standing in the doorway. Maria, sit down, sit down.

And so she did, waiting for the headmaster to pour the tea.

Maria, he said. I was just thinking—you've been at the school for some time now, haven't you? And it's no secret that you don't get much of a challenge. That's a shame, don't you think? I mean, you took exams at the Institute, speak fluent French. What are you even doing here?

Maria stared at her boss in wonder. Was this some kind of test?

Tell me, said the headmaster. Are you trying to keep the other teachers down?

No, stammered Maria indignantly. Of course not.

Well then. Why on earth aren't you working at a high school, or a university?

Well—I mean, I don't know.

You shouldn't sell yourself short, said the headmaster, wagging his index finger. The world is full of opportunity. Are we agreed? They were agreed. Good, he said, and slid the letter over to her side of the table. I think we should arrange for you to take this job abroad.

A job in Morocco. Or, more precisely, a job at the Lycée Sidi El Hassan Lyoussi in Sefrou. *That* Maria had not seen coming.

It was a curious circumstance, one largely forgotten by historians, that more than a few Romanians were sent to Morocco under Ceaușescu. The Great Oak of the Carpathians was a good friend and close ally of King Hassan II, and as part of their alliance they frequently swapped gifts and favors. In those days the Romanians were famous for their technical aptitude, and those were the sort of people who ended up in Morocco: irrigation engineers, aviation specialists, miscellaneous academics. The king must have sent one or two things the other way—weapons or chemicals, who knows, dates perhaps—but in 1979 it was mathematicians that he needed. It had occurred to the king that Morocco had a great mathematical tradition—oh yes, Arabic numerals—and he decreed it should be reinvigorated. He wanted to bolster training at Morocco's universities and high schools, planning eventually to send a team to the world mathematics championships. But you can't just snap your fingers and redress two hundred years of academic sloppiness, so King Hassan turned for help to Ceauşescu, who was more than happy to send a small army of mathematicians.

In all honesty, Maria didn't know what to do. She paced the apartment biting her nails, sat absorbed in thought, and heard neither the water boil nor Ciprian come in through the front door.

Maria, he said. What's going on?

On the one hand it was a flattering offer, a chance to kick-start her nonexistent career and see something of the world—and who knew, maybe even to cut and run for the West?—but on the other, it was a four-year contract in a foreign land without any friends or family. And the Hungarian headmaster couldn't promise he'd be able to get a job for Ciprian, so what was he supposed to do with himself?

Not that it worried Ciprian. Euphoric at the thought of Morocco, he immediately heaved the atlas down from the shelf and the pálinka bottle out of the cupboard, dancing around the living room with Ana in his arms until she squealed in delight. He had never much liked his job at the high school, and anyway, he thought, how bad could it be to live life shaded by palm trees and unpestered by parents, in-laws, friends, or close acquaintances, a life where he'd finally have enough time to finish that article on topological proofs he'd been fiddling with for years?

Over the next few days they chewed it over, taking long walks in the park and writing lists of pros and cons. And after they put Ana to bed in the evenings, Ciprian talked about everything that lay in store for them: the palaces and oases, the cities like labyrinths and the caravans that sailed over the crested waves of the Sahara. He talked about the Berbers and the Tuareg people stained deep blue, about the narrow streets that wound through the medina and the thousand smells of the spices at the bazaar, about the tanner's leather, the minaret's songs, and the workshops' coppery ring, but it was of little use in calming Maria's fears. It was as if something inside her head was pressing or pricking; I imagine it like one of those shards you get under your skin—after breaking a glass, for instance—which wanders around in your body until suddenly and very painfully it presses outward through your skin. In any case, Maria lay awake at night with an ache in her head, trying to understand what kind of strange doubt was forcing its way to the surface. She lost her appetite, her breasts stopped producing milk, and after a few days in that state she was at her wits' end. She asked her friends for advice and even turned to a priest, but he refused to council her on such worldly matters.

In the end it was her family's reaction that spurred her into going. When she told them about the job offer, her mother ran wailing into the chapel and lit a candle for her grandchild's soul while her father and uncle tried to dissuade her—the latter diplomatically, the former less so.

Maria Serbanescu, he shouted. You're not going anywhere, I can promise you that.

They listed the dangers of the Maghreb: the diseases, the age-old culture of thievery, the assaults and robberies and general state of banditry, the time-honored sport of bride kidnapping, and also: they raised cats for food. A desert is no place to raise a child, her mother wailed, but if they thought they could frighten Maria with lies and racist scaremongering, they didn't know her very well. While previously she had hesitated, suddenly she was busy procuring visas and airplane tickets, getting their furniture put in storage and subletting their apartment. She'd show them, she would. As if she couldn't look after her own daughter! What did they take her for—some sort of child, some slattern? Two months before they left, Maria received a letter from her parents in which they begged her to stay in Romania, and one month before they left, Ciprian's childless older sister showed up on their doorstep unannounced, offering to take care of little Ana while they were away.

Maria wouldn't hear of it.

What were they thinking? she raged once Ciprian's sister had dozed off on the sofa. I'm not a bad mother!

They're hicks, said Ciprian. Just ignore them.

Maria sighed, leaning over the crib and whispering to Ana.

There you are, sweetie. You want to come to Morocco with Mommy and Daddy, don't you? Does our little mouse want to go on an adventure? And Ciprian put his hands on his wife's hips and said, Just the three of us. We'll be happy anywhere.

One might say that they ignored the warning signs. That they turned their backs on all the frantically ringing alarm bells. But there's much one might say from this vantage point, thirty-five years after the fact. Back then the indications probably weren't as clear, and when Ana read Ciprian's letters many years later, it didn't seem that he had noticed any cause for concern. While Maria fussed over the details of the journey, over stamps and visas and a house in Sefrou, Ciprian did what he did best: disappeared further and further into topologies and mathematics, into dreams of al-Khwarizmi and al-Battānī and all the legendary scholars of the caliphate, into picturing the dry desert climate, so unusually well suited to mathematical thought. He felt as if the greater part of him were already in Sefrou, sitting in a café and waiting for his corporeal shell to catch up with him. It was as if he could see his failed life in Bucharest volatilizing before his very eyes. All of a sudden he could walk through Cişmigiu Gardens or pause in front of the Institute without being plagued by a single disappointing memory. He could smoke a cigarette by the bus stop and look right through the apartment blocks of Drumul Taberei as if they were greenhouses creaking in the wind, and when Maria, outraged, showed him the front page of *Scînteia* with Ceauşescu's plans to tear down the whole of central Bucharest, he felt not the least twinge of sadness, only a vague sense of justice: It was a fitting end for this accursed city.

When spring came, Maria said goodbye to her class and Ciprian gave a valedictory speech at the chess club. Then one May morning they called for a cab, and took their bags and child to the airport.

Ciprian's three sisters met them at Otopeni. They had come all the way from the village in the hope that Maria and Ciprian would reconsider and leave Ana in their care.

Oh, we're going to miss you so much, said Ciprian's childless sister.

Funny, laughed Ciprian. We're not going to miss Bucharest one bit.

They cried and hugged and pinched Ana's cheeks until they must have gone numb. Take care, sobbed the sisters, and may God be with you. And then it was time to show their papers from the Council of Education and Research and answer questions at passport control. And then: Ana crying when the jet engines started up, Maria rocking her to no avail, a shot of cognac in her milk somewhere over the Mediterranean. In the car from Casablanca, surrounded by dust and strange desert plants, their hair fluttered in the salty breeze. To the west was the ocean's unending blue. Ciprian's hand on the seat found Maria's as the words welled up in his chest: Just look at what we've achieved, us two against the world—we did it, Maria! But he knew nothing then of loneliness, of cold nights in the Atlas Mountains. As yet he was unconscious of his own abilities, not knowing he could bend time and numbers, could rewrite a whole life.

That first night, they slept at the Centre Pédagogique in Rabat. It was a Friday, and they sat on the collapsed mattress listening to the sounds from the mosque. The next morning, while Maria ventured her first rusty sentences in French and Ana toddled around pulling at the palm trees, Ciprian skimmed over the newspaper's curling letters and sipped at the first Pepsi of his life. All in all it was very exotic. And it got no less exotic when they reached Sefrou with its donkeys and sunken city walls, fez-wearing men and all the horseshoe-shaped archways you could wish for. They had three days of Orientalist near-idyll before Monday came and Maria started at the high school. Ciprian got back to work too. Of a sort. He wandered around trying to find the café he had dreamed about, the café where he would solve the riddles of topology and drink tea with intellectuals in the inner courtyard. Such was his plan. Ciprian wanted to find that café, because if you're going to do groundbreaking research, you can't sit just anywhere. You can't sit at home in the living room with Ana's diapers hanging from the ceiling to dry. You can't sit under fluorescent lighting in a gray library, or in the dank air of the tenement courtyard. Elbow room, that's the ticket. And if on top of that you can find a comfortable chair or a decent view—over the desert, for example, lying all empty and monochrome and ready to be filled with new ideas—then that won't hurt either. A good working environment, that was what Ciprian was after. And he took his time finding it. There wasn't any rush. He ambled throughout the city, trying out bars and cafés one by one, but in each case the radio was blasting some sports program, or it was too dark to study, or all the other customers sat and stared at him like some sort of performing monkey.

Oh well, no matter. So it would be something other than a café that inspired our hero to mathematical greatness. Ciprian experimented with various routines, going directly from his bed to the desk in the living room or taking a brisk morning walk along the city walls before settling down to the day's work. For a whole week he even tried taking the bus all the way into Fès so he could work in the university reading room, but little came of his efforts. His run-up took too long. Every day hours went by before he got going. Washing, shaving, breakfasting, a trip to the post office. And there was always something to sort out. Ana had to be dropped off with the nanny, letters had to be answered, money had to be sent or received. Then when he finally sat down to his calculations, often late into the afternoon, he was hungry again and had to go out and get food. And how the time flew! For no sooner had he bolted his lunch than his blood sugar plummeted and his eyelids drooped, so that there was nothing to be done but get up and find a cup of coffee. It was the caffeine high that usually gave him enough energy to scrawl a few figures in his notebook before the sun fell behind the city walls and the melancholy, golden light of early evening set in, and it occurred to him that he had barely said a word to another human being.

So what? he tried telling himself. He'd given the postmaster a nod, the neighbor a *salam aleikum*, the constable a *bonsoir*. And anyway, what did he want with people? They had always been an inconvenience. Now it was just him and mathematics—did he really need anything other than that? Obviously. Whether Ciprian admitted it or not the loneliness gnawed at him, and he usually ended up collecting Ana early from the nanny or going home to the apartment to wait for Maria. And thus he passed his days, while at night he would wake with a start and sit up in bed: Now! Now was the time to get cracking. In the darkest hours of the night he would sit at his desk in his pajama bottoms, staring at the notepad that lay exasperatingly empty before him.

Oh, how human. All Ciprian had prayed and begged for his whole life was time, and now that he finally had it, it had become a burden. Did he drink more than was advisable? Did he go back to bed after Maria had left for work and sleep for an extra hour? Did he masturbate more than once a day? Did he spend hours reading the chess section in *L'Opinion*, poring over every detail of the world championship in Riga, even though, truth be told, it was one of the most boring championships in ages? Of all the silly things one can spend time on, Ciprian spent time on the silliest, and it frustrated him—it frustrated him terribly. He felt trapped by his own bad habits, every day an intolerable, humdrum treadmill, a vicious cycle of self-loathing and remorse and enough feelings of inferiority for a whole army.

And then—and then. Just one short month after they arrived in Sefrou, Ciprian came home from the post office and opened the cupboard for a little swig of something, a break from the endless stream of mint tea. But what was this? An empty jar of peppers? And not two days later: another one. I think we've heard this song before.

Strange things began happening to Maria. Suddenly she could smell what everyone on the street was making for dinner, and when the biology teacher complimented her skirt one morning she broke down crying and had to spend the rest of the day sniveling under the bedclothes back home. I'm astonished that they didn't act sooner. Maria and Ciprian, I mean. There's a lot one might say about them, but idiots they were not. They must have seen the signs, read the writing on the wall. So why didn't they do anything? I have no idea. But it had been a tough year—life as new parents, a new country and everything that came with it, the visa applications, apartment hunting, language barriers, changing routines—and it's possible, I guess, to miss a pregnancy under those circumstances. I don't know whether it was down to stress or denial, but when Maria finally went to the doctor she was six months along.

Over the next few weeks Maria gazed in astonishment at her body. For half a year there'd been no visible developments, but when it did at last begin to show, it happened quickly. In three weeks her belly swelled to the size of a melon, her breasts expanded, and Ciprian fell into one of his notorious fits of rage.

You've got to be joking, he screamed. What the hell were you thinking?

On the casualty list: the Venetian vase they'd been given as a wedding present, three plates, and a refrigerator door kicked so full of dents that from then on it gave a creaky whine whenever anyone opened it. During those weeks Ciprian went sulking and grumbling around the town, sitting in hotel bars and complaining to anybody who would hear him. Pregnant again! Six months along! But his problems met with little understanding. When the hotel bartender heard about Maria's unexpected condition, he immediately cracked out the Pernod, on the house.

My friend, he said. God is with you!

But that wasn't how Ciprian saw it. He did not feel blessed. Cheated and deceived, more like—led well and truly up the garden path. Why hadn't Maria told him that she wasn't menstruating? How would they afford another child? And what about their family at home in Romania—oh God, what would they say? That evening he drank himself into a stupor, a feat not easily accomplished in a place like Sefrou. He lurched through the ancient city's narrow streets, maundering on in hotel bars until he was thrown out. Blind drunk, he stumbled down the boulevards, supporting himself against the wall the whole way home, where he collapsed in exhaustion on the living-room floor.

He must have eaten something vile that night, because he woke the next morning to a painful spasm in his gut. He just about made it to the toilet before spewing whatever it was back up, and spent the next few weeks shuttling back and forth between the bathroom and the bed. It dribbled out of him in watery rivulets, and the doctor had to be summoned to mix salt-and sugar-water and to advise about antibiotics and fiber-rich foods. At night Ciprian sighed through feverish dreams, and during the day he lay feebly in the heat, waving away the flies. His cheeks sunken, hips and ribs protruding beneath his skin, he had to be force-fed soup and bathed by Maria with a cloth and washing-up bowl. Only gradually did his condition improve. After three long weeks in bed he was able to take a few first steps outside the apartment, but was obliged to remain within a conservative striking distance from the toilet or risk the humiliation of shitting by the side of the road. And just when he thought that the worst was over, having eaten for the first time two meals in a single day, he was seized by stomach cramps so dire that they sent him straight back to bed, palely rocking himself in the fetal position.

That night Maria kept watch by his bed as Ciprian whimpered, calling down curses upon the heads of all the unhygienic Arabs in the world. He clutched his stomach and buried his face in the damp sheets. Falling in and out of an unquiet sleep, he muttered incoherently as he tossed and turned all night. When he woke, the sun was shining in through the window and Ana was squatting down before him on her small, chubby legs. She swayed gently back and forth, holding a drawing in front of her, then flailed her arms and lifted it above her head. It daddy, she shouted into space. It daddy!

Maria, he murmured, Maria, look.

But she was already by his side. Shh, she said, her voice breaking and everything. Look, your daughter. She can talk.

There wasn't much else Ciprian would remember from the months he lay exhausted in bed. The stabbing pain in his stomach, the feeling of the toilet paper he used to dab his rear end, the square of sunlight that crept from the bedside table across the headboard to the wardrobe against the far wall. He lost all sense of time. All sense of everything, really. Never leaving the house, he forgot there was a life outside full of responsibilities and arrangements and things to organize. Forgot that Maria had a job, a small daughter, a sick husband, and a pregnant belly to think about.

So you're in your seventh month? asked the neighbor's wife one day as she helped Maria with the laundry.

Yes, said Maria.

Then you should be taking it easy.

But did she heed that advice? Of course she didn't. She made no effort to slow down, still lugging groceries and bags of rice home from the market, still tutoring disheartened mathematics students and still washing Ciprian's nether regions as he muttered away to himself, lost in feverish nightmares. Maria, working around the clock. Maria, barely sleeping during those months. Was that perhaps the reason she didn't tell her parents about the baby? International phone calls were outlawed, mail from overseas was monitored and censored and often lost, but still. If she knew she'd reached her seventh or eighth month, why didn't she tell her family? Was it shame, or a guilty conscience over having dragged her family to this alien, poverty-stricken country?

We'll never know the reason, but one day in the late autumn Ciprian got up from his sickbed and began to walk through Sefrou again. It was the end of October, and Maria had been invited to a banquet at the Université Al Quaraouiyine. It was Saturday, October 31, 1981, to be exact. Ciprian was sitting outside a café, adjusting his watch. What is it again? asked the Algerian businessman next to him. Spring forward, fall back, so we put the clocks back again? And Ciprian nodded, Yes, that's more or less how it was. I've never understood it, said the Algerian. With the time, I mean. Daylight savings and leap years and all that. Don't know much about the earth's orbit either, where it is and how it works. Ciprian smiled and turned the hands on his watch, explaining to the Algerian about atomic time and astronomical time, about how the earth took not three hundred and sixty-five days to travel around the sun but three hundred and sixty-five days, plus five hours, forty-eight minutes, and forty-six seconds, and about the leap days that made up for lost time every fourth year.

He was only too pleased to explain. Pleased, and proud to think we could play with time like that, deciphering the planets and their tilts and rotations, their elliptical orbits; it was wonderful we had a system that took it all into account. The Algerian listened and nodded with interest as Ciprian tapped demonstratively at his watch. That's how we deal with it, he said. That's how easily it's done. Time—we can always rely on it. It moves forward, from the past to the present to the future, never going back again. Well, not exactly: Sometimes—at very high speeds or at very, very tiny sub-atomic levels—it does. But that doesn't matter, it's not what we're talking about here. It's of no significance for you and me and our everyday lives.

Hold on a minute, what kind of nonsense was that? Time could go backward? The Algerian wanted to hear more. He ordered another round of tea, and a plate of biscuits too. And Ciprian was happy to tell him. He was bursting with things to say; the world was so rich and large, and it felt so nice to sit out in the sun. There was so much to understand about curved space-time and all the mysterious things quantum physicists were discovering in laboratories around the world.

At home in the apartment, Maria was pottering around and

trying on dresses. A representative of the Université Al Quaraoui-yine had called that morning: They were aware it was very short notice, but a Romanian professor had fallen ill and sent his regrets. Was Maria interested in taking his place at the banquet as a representative of the exchange program? She was indeed. Very interested. So now she was busy putting on makeup and shaving her legs and writing a speech—she had a hundred and one things to do. And where had Ciprian got to? He had promised to come home at four o'clock to look after Ana. She glanced at the clock above the fridge: twenty past four and still no Ciprian. Maria ground her teeth. It was completely impossible to write a speech with Ana bouncing around in the living room, but she tried anyway. Distracting Ana with some wooden blocks, she tiptoed over to the writing desk with her pen and paper. She got as far as jotting down a few thoughts in the notebook—an amusing little play on words, if she did say so herself—but no further. Ana had begun to wail. First came little gasping sobs, and Maria sank her shoulders as if she could hide from the tears or will them into silence. To no avail. By now Ana was howling, bawling so loudly it was unbearable. Maria sighed. What is it, sweetheart? But she noticed soon enough. Ana was in the middle of the room, writhing around in a tantrum. She had diarrhea all the way down one leg; it dripped out of her shorts, leaving long smears on the floor. Oh for God's sake, muttered Maria. This was the last thing she needed. And where the hell was Ciprian? She had to take off her dress so that it wouldn't get dirty. Then she sat in the bathroom and comforted her daughter, struggling with the washtub and her swollen belly, which kept getting in the way. She had just managed to strip off Ana's diaper, find the right temperature and rinse her down when the telephone rang. Maria straightened up, thinking, Who on earth can that be? Oh, just let it ring, Maria, it's just a stupid phone call. Let it ring so we can have a happy ending, escape all this misery. But no. Maria *had* to straighten up. She had to look over her shoulder, God help us, she had a ball to go to, she had a speech to write, a dress to pick out. How did they do things in Morocco? Was her lipstick too red? Should she put lipstick on at all? And what about her shoes—the pointy ones or the heels or the ones in patent leather? And the slit down the back of the dress, was that alright? There, the telephone was jangling again. It might be someone from the university. Perhaps it was the Romanian consul? Maria had already gotten to her feet. Ana lay in the bathtub and water gushed from the tap and Maria could almost see the telephone shaking—no, trembling—with excitement and information. She walked through the living room with bare breasts. She had often thought they should put up curtains, but somehow they'd never gotten around to it, because there was so much to do and so little time, but at that moment she felt annoyed about it, now that she could see the neighbor at the kitchen sink on the other side of the courtyard, and now that the telephone was ringing as she reached out and felt the cold receiver in her hand.

Hello, she said.

Out on the street, Ciprian was ambling slowly home. He was in no rush. He still had ten minutes before the clock struck four and the weather was lovely. Not too warm, with a nice breeze, he thought, stopping in front of the building. There was still enough time for a cigarette, and he drew out a packet. Lighting up, he glanced around. On the other side of the street, a man was installing new windows in his basement. Ciprian was all warmed up after his conversation with the Algerian. His French was so fluent today that he was in the mood to go over and say hello. They were virtually neighbors, after all, he and the man. So he did. He went over and said hello, asking whether he could help with anything. And might he offer a cigarette? The man said thank you. It's the outer pane, he said. It's the outer panes that are the problem. You can have as many inner panes as you like. Twenty, thirty inner panes. But if the outer one leaks, the water pisses right in. Ruins everything. Ciprian nodded and sucked on his cigarette. He knew nothing about windows. But it was probably true—it sounded right. Ciprian could well imagine that outer panes were important. And it was good that there were people who knew about such things. Division of labor, he thought, and that was when he heard the scream. A scream like nothing he'd ever heard before. A— what do you call it? A primal scream, I suppose, but that sounds so idiotic. A scream of terror, a mortal scream? Not that either. No, I don't know. I give up. I don't know what you'd call a scream like that, if you'd call it anything. But this was what happened. Ciprian was standing there in the street with his cigarette when he heard it: Maria, screaming for their dead daughter.

It's at this point that the story gets a little—how to put it? Murky. How much of what follows is Ana's imagination and how much is absolutely true I can't say. Then again, the same goes for the whole tale. I guess you can't ever pinpoint a moment and say: That was how it happened. It would be nice if we could, but we all know that the truth is a closed chapter, the truth is of the past. So what can we say? We can say that Ana sensed and experienced a series of phenomena that shaped her understanding of events. That we can say.

But that's not saying very much.

We can say: For two days they mourned over the tiny corpse, not leaving the house. And on the third day Maria went into labor. She lay half-naked on the bed and whimpered, falling in and out of consciousness. Her water broke, slopping around her and absorbing into the mattress. Ciprian tried to take her to the hospital. Come on, he said. Come on, sweetheart, or something will go wrong. But Maria understood only part of what he said. Something had already gone wrong, horribly wrong, a long time ago.

My baby, she gasped when he tried to lift her from the bed. My baby, don't touch her.

She flapped her arms and legs, scratching and biting with the crazed violence of instinct. Ciprian would have to change tactics. But what now? He might have been scientifically minded, but he didn't know much about childbirth. He was familiar with the basics, of course, having witnessed scores of births back in the village. There was something about boiling water, that much he knew. But what exactly was he supposed to do with it? The best course of action would have been to call a doctor, or at least a midwife. But that wasn't what Ciprian did. Bringing sheets and blankets from the wardrobe, he laid them on the bed, wrapping them warmly around Maria and dabbing her forehead with a cold cloth as he tried to soothe her with the nursery rhyme they had sung to Ana. Maria groaned and whimpered, her eyes rolled, she screamed and babbled incomprehensibly, fighting her unborn child with all her strength. It was a long, long night. But by late morning, hormones and instinct took over, life's imperatives pulsed through her veins, and with a jerk she tore off Ciprian's clutching hands, got out of bed and crawled onto the floor. Squatting down, bellowing as their second daughter came into the world: born in two pushes, she was swaddled in towels, and laid on Maria's breast to dream of all the things newborns dream of.

In the days after the birth, Ciprian often stood watching over them in the doorframe. Maria and the newborn, breastfeeding happily. He kept his distance, an uneasy fear spreading within him as he thought of Ana lying in the bathtub muffled in sheets, feeling that it wasn't real. No doctor had taken her pulse, no official had filled out a death certificate. Ana couldn't possibly be dead: it couldn't be true that a child could die so easily, so completely without echo or consequence and without being noticed by a single soul. If she were really dead, his sisters would ring, they would hear from Maria's mother. Yes—if she were really dead, someone would have done something. Surely? You couldn't leave a dead child lying in a bathtub without repercussions, it just couldn't be true. The world didn't work like that.

And yet it did, of course. The child was as dead as a child can be, and deep down Ciprian knew he had to act. Knew it was up to him to handle the corpse and the neighbors, who had begun knocking on the door and bringing gifts, Maria's screams and the newborn's cries having sliced through the walls. Ciprian kept them at arm's length with excuses: It was a difficult birth, mother and child needed to rest, he said, playing the culture card by explaining that in Romania a mother and child lay in bed for a week, that it was tradition. He bought a little time, enough to pace around in circles in the living room, to spit up bile in the kitchen sink. He couldn't be in the house with all its strange smells and sounds, instead he sat in the tenement courtyard, speaking Romanian to himself.

We have to go to the authorities, he said. That's obvious. But what good will that do? he added a moment later. This fucking shithole—he was shouting now— What do they care if our daughter is dead? He tried to pull himself together, wanting to be pragmatic. Okay, first things first, then second things second. Loudly he said to himself, This isn't the end of the world. He himself had had two younger siblings who had succumbed before the age of two: a boy and a girl. One died in childbirth and the other was struck down by some kind of illness. Or was he imagining it? Suddenly he wasn't sure, overwhelmed by a powerful urge to write home and ask. The post office was right around the corner, after all—he was only a telegram away from the mountains of his homeland, which all at once he missed so much that his head began to swim. No, he didn't want to think about Oltenia. First: problem-solving. He went inside to get a notebook and paper, drawing up a table. First a Plan A, then a Plan B. A Plan C was also necessary, as anything systematic always came in threes. Duck, duck, goose. Rock, paper, scissors. Always in threes—or fours. He had only just started when he heard crying from the bedroom, and tried to concentrate on the promising schematic in his book instead of the worrying sounds from the other room.

There you go, said Maria. There you go, Ana. You're a hungry little one, aren't you?

Ciprian knew he had to do something. But what? His diarrhea was back, but he didn't dare use the bathroom where the corpse lay, shitting instead in a bucket in the broom cupboard as the flies buzzed around inside. He sat sweat-soaked in the living room watching Maria, who flitted silently around the apartment, look-ing after the baby, changing diapers and bedclothes, cooking rice and peas, washing up. Who knows what would have happened if Maria's headmaster hadn't phoned. They had gone stark mad in those rooms.

Ah, you must be the man of the house, said the headmaster when Ciprian finally pulled himself together enough to pick up the receiver.

Yes, that's me, said Ciprian, apologizing for his wife's absence on her behalf. You must understand, she's just had a baby.

I know, I know, said the headmaster, who had already guessed how the land lay. He congratulated them both and instructed Maria to take it easy. Take three weeks, get her strength back, and was it a boy or a girl and Masha'Allah and all that.

It was precisely what Ciprian needed to kick him into gear: a deadline.

That night he didn't sleep, nor did he sleep the next. He sat up flicking through maps and bus timetables and tourist brochures for Morocco's national parks. And in the late afternoon on the third day he sneaked out of the house, taking a bus to Fès then another from the Place de la Résistance to Immouzzer. He sat with his sports bag between his legs, looking out of the window at the mountains as they vanished into the dusk. From the bus station he wandered among the stalls in the souk, mixing with the tradesmen, then continued along the main street and up the steps to the old church, hewn into the rock, surrounded by trees. Darkness had fallen, he tried the handle but it was locked, so he sat for an hour before the gate: Ciprian, never known for his piety, with his hands folded in prayer for his daughter's soul. Then he hoisted his bag and trudged into the woods, brushing cobwebs from his face and bits of twig from his hair. He walked like that until the trees thinned out, up over the ridge of the hill and down the other side, reaching at last a clump of bushes and trees where he took up his trowel and dug a grave.

For a week they lived like ghosts in the apartment in Sefrou. The rooms were no longer theirs, sorrow written in every corner. Silently they padded across the floors—and was it then that they hatched it, the story that would shape Ana's life? I don't know, for good reason: Ana was just a baby girl, she can't remember a word. But I don't think it was some grand plan. No, I think it was a manner or a tone, a language that grew out of the circumstances, casual and—well, you wouldn't call it natural. Organic, perhaps. Maria went around with the newborn close to her breast. She went to the laundry room and the market, and at night she writhed and twisted in nightmares. Her laugh had gone, her smile was rare. She nodded glumly to the neighbors, stood patiently in the queue at the baker's, stroked children's hair.

And Ciprian? He bribed a doctor in Fès and went to Maria's headmaster, talking about complications and postpartum depression, and got her an indefinite leave of absence from the school. Every morning he crept out of the building, past the housewives by the washing line who whispered in secret, out into the dry wind that swept in from the desert, that barren, treeless plain before him. He missed Oltenia like he'd never missed anything before. The woods and the fields and the cows' heavy stench, their rolling gait as they returned home from the mountains in the afternoon, their udders full of milk. The mountains—that was what he wanted. The feeling of the landscape enfolding him and wrapping him up, tucking him in between banks of fog in spring or the winter's reassuring layers of powdery snow.

When Maria came home one day from a walk with the baby, he was waiting for her, solemn, on the sofa.

Come here, he said, patting the cushion with the palm of his hand. But she didn't come, and didn't sit down. She went over to the sideboard and continued going about her shrill business, so he got up and put his arm around her. My darling, he said, and tried to talk to her about the dead child. But she jerked her shoulders free, shaking off her firstborn with a blink of her eyes and a twitch of her left cheek. She opened the drawer. Goodness, she said, we've run out of dishcloths. She tried to edge past Ciprian into the utility room, but he wouldn't let her pass. Taking her arm, he said, Maria, we need to leave this place.

He had expected her to protest, or at least to ignore him. But she simply lowered her gaze and nodded.

Alright, we can do that, she said, as if he were suggesting a walk in the woods or a trip to the beach. Wriggling out of his hands, she went into the kitchen and put some water on to boil for a load of laundry.

Ciprian was still trying to understand it all when they stood at the bus station four days later.

We could just go home, he said, as the bus pulled up.

Maria said nothing, adjusting the baby's woolly hat, which had slipped down over her eyes, four sizes too big.

Maria, we could just go home. Home to Romania.

At that moment the bus stopped in front of them and out milled the passengers, bundled up in windbreakers and blankets and scarves. The sun had yet to rise, and a biting wind swept in from the north, bringing the sand with it. He could feel his stomach roll, his guts contract; he had held such great hopes for this country. But what had it given him? Dust in his eyes and a daughter buried in the desolate earth.

Let's sit at the back, said Maria, as Ciprian maneuvered their baggage on board. Through the back window they caught a last glimpse of Sefrou: the tradesmen's discolored awnings, the wooden crates crammed with pulpy fruit. The bus climbed up into the mountains, glass rattling in the window frames, the vibrations from the engine rocking the passengers to sleep. Ciprian leaned against the window and studied his daughter. She had the same pointed chin as the one he had buried, and it struck him that age was a relative quantity. Yes, there we have him: a man shaped almost like the father Ana will get to know. He is thirty-two years old and the first lines are emerging on his face, a crease appearing on his left cheek. His eyes still shine behind their glasses, but there is a drooping twist to his lips that only rarely fades. He still believes mathematics has something to offer him, unaware that he will spend four years toiling in this wasteland, and that there's nothing waiting for him in Romania but a populace in disarray, a rejected thesis, and an early grave.

When Ciprian woke, the bus had stopped by a shack. Passengers smoked cigarettes, stretched their legs. Two boys sold sweets from a kiosk. A man on the seat in front of him had turned toward Maria, pointing at the baby in her lap.

Such a cute little girl, said the man. How old is the little beast?

Two, said Maria, lifting the knitted cap so the child could open her eyes. We've just celebrated her birthday. Isn't that right, sweetheart?

But Ana didn't answer, of course. She turned her head and squinted. It was early morning, and the sun was peeping over the Atlas Mountains.

IV

Normally several days could go by without me giving a thought to Ana, but after she told me her story, she colored my life like a filter. I could no longer ignore the clock on the microwave, which I'd forgotten to switch to daylight savings. When I went up the stairs, I caught myself counting the seconds, and before long just looking at my watch became a worrying experience. I couldn't help noticing that although I'd probably never had more time to myself, it was like time was shrinking around me. More and more often I glanced up from the computer and realized it was already eight or nine, and a few evenings after Ana told me her story, I went down to the pier to watch the sunset, only to discover that the streets were already dark.

That night as I lay in bed, Ana's story filled my thoughts. The blinds were drawn, no lights were burning, and as I stared into the dark it was Ana's parents I saw, and all the moments they'd erased. The trowel cut into the soil, the child wrapped in thick towels, a cold hand against the soft fabric, all of it contrived away. I couldn't comprehend how they could do something so terrible, and after lying awake for an hour I unwound myself from Lærke's arms and switched on the computer. Hunting around online, I trawled through forums about the People's Republic of Romania to find a loose thread in Ana's story, but all the facts fit. Ceauşescu's daughter really had been a mathematician, and the Institute for Mathematics really had been closed down by the president in 1975. There had been a Romanian exchange program with Morocco, and on an antiquated website I found a travel diary by a mathematician stationed in Rabat who mentioned a Sefrou-based female colleague in his entries. I could scarcely believe it, but all the details held water, and it worried me. If Ana actually had been brought up as her own sister, if her parents had done something so awful, then why had she told me? Maybe she had been right in keeping the story to herself, and I shouldn't have pressured her to tell me. All that talk about the story being appalling, sick, ruining lives even, did she really mean it, or was it an act meant to goad me on and make me interested? I didn't understand, and it scared me, but it also made me curious, and when I went back to bed I puzzled over what was going on.

The next day was a Saturday. I'd barely shut my eyes all night, but that afternoon I took Lærke all the way up to the Bronx Zoo anyway. I'd promised to show her a coati, and today was the day, tired or not, lugging a picnic basket and wine and everything. The sky was blue and endless, ice-cream trucks jingled like Pied Pipers through the streets, and as we sat in front of the flamingos and drank out of thermos mugs, Lærke told me about last

Thursday, which she'd spent with one of her new colleagues, a
man who wrote grant applications for the journal. The colleague
came from a provincial town in the Midwest, a town haunted by
meth labs and the moldering dreams of high-school athletes, and
in this town he'd grown up with his twin sister, who'd blazed
a trail out of the womb and entered the world fifteen minutes
before him. Their whole childhood, it was the same story. His
sister was the first to walk; she could read several months before him; it was she who chose their friends and decided their
games; and because she wanted to be a ballet dancer, he did too.
At thirteen they were dancing at the local ballet school, and later
they studied modern dance, and naturally they were each other's
dance partner at the provincial college's sequined recitals. Quite
a story, said Lærke—a pair of dancing twins from a town where
the fog was thick with polychlorinated biphenyls, where the wind
gasped around the vacuum factory's abandoned halls and rip-
pled the lake where mutated fungi multiplied—and maybe it was
because they were twins that they were invited to audition for
a corps de ballet in Chicago, a corps that called them back for a
second audition, and while they trained and dreamed of shining
marley floors in theaters across the world, the sister made a jump
and landed badly, twisting her knee, tearing the meniscus or the
ligament clear across, and in that one jump her career was over.
Of course, they didn't know that at the time, said Lærke, because
at the auditions he danced for both of them, while she sat by the
mirrors and stared into his eyes during the exercises, her dark
eyes fixed like lodestars through the développés and arabesques,
her gaze reaching for his collar and guiding him through the
dance, a gaze that was more like a cord or a noose, and the ballet

master wanted to accept them both, but only once the sister's knee was healed, so she went back to the provincial town to recover, while he began the training at once. Oh, but how cold and lonely it is in the big city without your twin—or how cold and lonely it *was*, for soon the company was setting off through California and Texas, and the sun beat down on Florida and the Carolinas, and in DC the cherry trees blossomed, while his sister went through physical and chiropractic therapy, methods both Mensendieck and Feldenkrais, and the gaps between her emails widened, splitting into gorges or chasms, until at last they stopped entirely, and then one evening there was a knock on his dressing-room door: a European agent, taken by his turnout or his port de bras or those tremulous dark eyes of his maybe. How her dancing colleague was able to drop his contract and head straight for Europe Lærke wasn't entirely sure, but before long he was dancing on stages in Hessen and Baden-Württemberg, Moravia and Cisleithania, and the applause came thundering down as they toured through the Middle East and crossed back over the Atlantic, until finally they reached his home state, where he hadn't been for several years. That evening his twin sister had to work a late-night shift and couldn't come to the performance, so they nervously agreed by phone to meet the next day. It might have been nerves, in fact, that took him to a bar with his fellow dancers after the performance, and at the bar he bumped into three friends from high school, boys who now were men, or men who still were boys, Lærke couldn't remember which way around, and they took him on their crawl through the town, surging from bar to bar toward the suburbs, till late at night they reached a club near the outskirts of town, a strip club populated exclusively by men, by hollering, raucous groups of men like the group of which he was a part, but which now dissolved into the bar, his old friends vanishing or sinking into the night—or perhaps he couldn't see them through the disco smoke and alcohol—when suddenly a spotlight appeared with a flash and a silence fell across the audience, and he looked up from his shot of tequila or whiskey to see his own body emerge out of the dark: his own legs coiled around the pole, buttocks slowly lowered toward the edge of the stage, thighs spread, dollar bills pressing against thong; and through the blinking flare of the stroboscopic lights he saw her eyes, his sister's dark eyes boring through the night, as though their lives and fortunes were a zero-sum game, all his luck countered by her humiliation and decline, as though they could never rise out of the muck, the two of them, because for each step one of them took toward the surface, the other sank deeper down. Then the colleague's voice had broken, and Lærke had ordered another round of drinks, and she'd told him about her own past in the sticks, about her dad's handball club and her mom's obsession with radon and mold, the imaginary mold that crept behind the ceilings and the bathroom tiles and deep down into the bronchial tubes, and they'd talked about school gyms and walks down country roads in the early morning, as the sun rose above the corn or the rapeseed, beech or buckeye, on the way home from parties, and then they'd caught a cab to a club and danced all night like you dance in lost provincial towns.

How'd he end up as a grant writer? I asked.

Something about his knee. Some injury or other.

Like his sister?

Yeah, isn't that insane? Always like his sister's shadow.

Exactly the same thing with Ana, I said.

What is? said Lærke, pouring more wine into our cups, and as the flamingoes quarreled with the ducks over their pink-pigmented feed I told the story to Lærke: how one sister was buried among the hills while the other prattled, swamped in a two-year-old's loose clothing; how one sister was like the echo of the other; and how Ana's parents had conceived an idea so strong it took corporeal shape and gained life in the world of reality, living beyond their consciousness, like a boat tugged loose from its moorings, a ship without a crew drifting across the ocean, its windows frosted with salt, its hold gapingly empty, a can of soda rolling back and forth across the icy deck, its only cargo, pitching through the waves.

Yeah, alright, said Lærke, enough with the metaphors.

But seriously, I said, how could they *do* it?

Lærke just shrugged, like it was possible to shake the story off. She didn't believe it—the story couldn't possibly be true—but then I told her about all the evidence, about Ana's father, who'd hanged himself, about the appendectomy that nearly cost Ana her life. I mentioned the photograph at home on the bookcase, the one where Ana was a whole head shorter than her classmates, and maybe I got carried away, because Lærke didn't say much, and later she went to the bathroom, or I thought she went to the bathroom, and it was a while before I realized she was gone. When I finally stood up, I found her in the tropical house outside the coati enclosure.

Just look at them, she said. Aren't they the cutest things you've ever seen?

Lærke showed me how she'd once fed a wild coati a piece of pineapple, describing the dainty way it held the food in its small, furry paws, and I crouched down to see the animals better. They were inquisitive little beasts. One of them came right up to the glass to study me, sniffing at the pane with its long snout. Lærke looked at us with a smile.

Hey, it looks like you.

I stared at the animal. It had started licking something, its tongue buried in a brownish slop.

What? No, it doesn't.

It totally does. Just look at it.

Lærke took a step backward to compare us better: It was something about the pointed nose, she said, something about the self-satisfied smile. On our way out of the tropical house we passed through the nocturnal animals area, and as we sauntered among the glass enclosures of bullfrogs and opossums and flying foxes, I couldn't help thinking about Michel Siffre, the speleologist, and I told Lærke about his last great experiment. In the early seventies NASA got interested in his experiences underneath the glacier, having heard about the peculiar results. They wanted to investigate human beings' internal clocks, to get to the bottom of our perception of time, so in 1972 they lowered him deep into a cave in Texas. For six months Siffre lived in the cave with electrodes and cables hooked up to his brain, living without daylight, without clocks, cut off from external time and seasons. For half a year he lived exclusively according to his body clock—each day he got up when he woke, each day he went to bed when he was tired—and he kept a record of his silent days in a logbook. He explored the cave, listened to records, and read books by the light of a lamp. It was a uniform life, a regular life, and the logbook entries that described his days were roughly the same length. Each day he completed approximately the same tasks, each day felt more or less the same;

but the researchers on the surface could see the distortions. One night he slept thirty-three hours at a stretch. Another night just two. Some of his days were fifty-two hours long, others only six, but when Siffre read his diary he couldn't tell the difference. He'd perceived the days as absolutely uniform, as if they were the same length.

So what? asked Lærke.

So what? Just imagine if you could bend time like that. Imagine you could be awake for six hours but feel like you'd lived a whole day. Life would feel a lot longer.

Bullshit. You'd still be living the same amount of time.

On paper, yes. But it's the feeling that matters.

Lærke said nothing. She turned toward the exit.

Don't you see what I mean? I said. That's what makes Ana's work so strong. You think it's about science, but really it's feelings she's exploring. Feelings manipulated by science, or science distorted by feelings. It's feelings, see?

Yeah, said Lærke, opening the door onto daylight. You don't need to tell me that.

Not long afterward, I began writing a short story about a girl who's her own sister. I changed none of the details, just filled in the gaps. The librarian's spare room, where the girl's father lived as a young man. Two infatuated mathematicians in a shed behind a summer cabin, a bus lurching up the Atlas Mountains. I saw it very clearly. Her mother walking through the living room, impelled toward the phone, her sister's arms splashing in the water. The girl many years later, reading a note on the door to her father's office. I'd never been so full of a story, never felt another person's life rush so clearly through my body, and for the next few days I set my alarm clock early so I could write in peace and quiet, before Lærke woke. In the early light of dawn I made a cup of coffee, and sat quietly at my desk, writing about the girl, uplifted by the epic mood that sometimes gripped me when I heard about other people's lives, the places they'd been, the people they'd met, the possibilities their choices opened up, and for a moment I felt like *I* could lead a life as rich and complex, if only I would listen closely.

Four days after our trip to the zoo, I was walking through the gilded columns of the Brooklyn Public Library when Ana called. By that time it was probably six or seven days since I'd seen her, my short story about the two sisters was in full flow, and I was on my way to the library to track down books on topology and algebra. I was brimming with questions about Zoia Ceaușescu and the Institute for Mathematics, but I didn't get a chance to ask them, because when I picked up the phone I could hear the disappointment in Ana's voice.

So I was right, then, she said. I should never have told you that story. Now you don't want to see me anymore.

What are you talking about? Of course I do.

Then why haven't you called? It's been a week, and I haven't heard anything.

I'm sorry, Ana, it's just that I've been pretty busy. My girlfriend's just flown into town.

Oh yeah, your Danish girl. Right.

Then she told me about the preparations for *Timemachine*, her performance, which was beginning in a week. At first she'd been looking forward to moving in, spending nights at the gallery to get used to the dark, but the past few nights had been full of nightmares and daydreams and hallucinations, there were scratch marks all over her body, and last night she'd been convinced that the blankets were wet, because there was no light to separate sleep from consciousness. It was impossible to tell if she was asleep or awake, and she'd groped around on the mattress for hours, clawing at her arms to make sure she was still there, still breathing in that abysmal anti-light. All she was sure of was the feel of skin pressing against her fingernails, pain emanating from her forearms, sensation her only bulwark against everything that might creep out of the darkness, imagination all there was to fill it.

Look, Ana, I said. Are you sure this exhibition is a good idea?

Of course. It's just a been a weird couple of days.

Weird how?

Well, it's like my brain's on playback. When I can't see anything, it starts broadcasting reruns. Old memories, conversations, TV shows I thought I'd forgotten.

Then she reeled off a series of memories that had come to mind in the dark: the heroine in a Russian cartoon she'd once seen; the names of the hens they'd kept in the bathtub during the lean years in Bucharest; an incident in the nineties when the family cabin was overrun by a swarm of grasshoppers. She'd been ten or twelve at the time, the air had hummed with insects, and every day she followed the grasshoppers around the house. She wanted to find out whether they were really as lazy as Aesop said in his fable, so she followed them through the woods and far across the fields, watched them gnaw the ears of wheat and mate unthinkingly, and decided Aesop's story had done a number on their image. They were no lazier than other insects. They didn't play the violin all

summer long. One day she followed a grasshopper that was be-
having strangely. She found it at the edge of the road and tracked
it across the field as it hopped along without pausing to rest, leaping among rows of sunflowers toward the pond. But instead of
stopping at the water's edge like the other grasshoppers, it hopped
straight into the water. It didn't swim. It didn't even try to get out.
It just lay on the surface, utterly still, its head beneath the water,
as though it had lost courage or the will to live, a dejected little
insect. She'd not thought about it since, but as she lay there in the
dark the suicidal grasshopper had popped into her head, along
with an article she'd read in a science magazine a few years back.
The article was about a hairworm, a parasite that infects praying
mantises and grasshoppers through drinking water, and lives in
their stomachs. When the hairworm is sexually mature, it no longer needs its host. All it needs is an aquatic environment where it
can mate. So it spreads its genes through the grasshopper's nervous system, infecting its brain and changing its nature, ordering
the insect to plunge headfirst into water, making it drown itself.
Then, once the grasshopper has committed suicide, the hairworm
crawls out of its guts, abandons the corpse and swims out into the
water to lay its eggs, and a new cycle can begin.

Jesus, Ana, I said. That's the kind of stuff you think about?

I can't help it, she said. It just happens.

But are you sure it's a good idea, all this darkness? It doesn't
sound very nice.

Nice. What do you think this is, a picnic in the woods?

But you shouldn't be all alone in the dark. Isn't anybody going
to come and visit?

Sure they will.

Are you okay, though? Are you sure you can handle it?

Of course I can handle it. It's a performance. It's supposed to be difficult.

But thirty days in the dark. Sounds kind of dangerous.

Are you even listening? That's the whole point.

Yeah, okay, fair enough. I guess you know what you're doing.

Of course I know what I'm doing. Everything's fine, I'm doing great. It'll all be alright.

Well, okay, if you say so.

I'll let you know if I feel like company, okay?

Okay. Just look after yourself in there.

How many times do I have to say it? There's nothing to look after.

Then she hung up, and it was only as I entered the shelves of books on geometry and set theory that I realized how nervous I was on Ana's behalf. For one thing, I was sure she was lying about her emotional state. She'd spoken briskly and with confidence, but all my senses told me she was afraid, and was trying to reach out to me in her own proud way. There was something shrill and clenched behind those tough words, something quivering behind her teeth. Until our conversation that day I'd thought of *Time-machine* as an innocent performance, some silly little game, but all of a sudden the piece reminded me of some mad professor's experiment. There was something alchemical about it, the way Ana was trying to break down time, seeking desperately to forge a situation where its rules were lifted, like she was some medieval enchanter. Barricading herself into a dark room for several weeks—wasn't that a kind of self-harm? Wasn't it a cry for help? Of course it was. Ana had roped herself into a kamikaze project, and why had she called me and told me about her nightmares if not because she was afraid and needed help?

That afternoon at the library I googled *Timemachine*'s curator, and when I found Irene's email address I wrote her immediately, explaining my concerns. Irene answered promptly to say that Ana knew what she was doing, that she'd be fine, but that I should definitely let her know if she was feeling ill. It was a tactful way of saying that she didn't take me seriously and couldn't care less about my worries, and frankly, who could blame her? I was just a young intern with no experience with performance art, and no matter what I said Irene would never listen to my warnings.

For a while I tried to forget about *Timemachine* and went back to my books, but all I could think about were prisoners in hoods and blindfolds, hostages hidden in dark attics, children in cells buried deep under basements, and Ana, scratching her arms until they bled. I couldn't leave her in the lurch when she clearly needed help, but Ana and Irene would never take my advice. So what could I do? I mulled it over for a few hours, imagining Ana alone in the dark on her mattress, and at last I had an idea. If I could prove that *Timemachine* was harmful to Ana, if I could find scientific evidence that the project wasn't ethically defensible, then Irene might listen to me and call a halt to this insane experiment. That was my plan, and over the following hours I shuttled to and fro between the bookshelves and the yellowish, discolored computers, sourcing collections of articles on sensory deprivation, on psychopathy in isolated prisoners, on cognitive disturbances among crew members on submarines. As I read psychiatric journals about the traumatizing effects of solitude and darkness, I edged further out onto the scientific fringe. I skimmed dissertations on chronobiology, dissertations on temporal perception, and when the librarian flicked the lights on and off for the third time, I was the only one left in the reading room.

That evening as we lay in bed, I told Lærke about a psychology experiment I'd read about, conducted at McGill in the 1950s. They'd had the idea to test how people would react if all their senses were cut off, so at the beginning of the experiment the test subjects were given dark goggles and earmuffs and had cardboard tubes tied around their hands so they couldn't feel anything. With all their senses shut down, the subjects were alone with their thoughts, and after a few hours they began to hallucinate. Small pinpricks of light, at first, and simple geometric shapes, but soon the hallucinations became more complex. They saw repeated abstract patterns that appeared as if papered onto a wall, rows of yellow men in black hats, and finally they saw whole scenes or ceremonies—a procession of squirrels marching along with sacks over their shoulders, prehistoric animals rambling through the jungle—and no matter how hard the test subjects tried, they couldn't stop the visions. One man saw nothing but dogs. Another only spectacles. Several of them heard voices, one saw the sun rise over a church to the sound of clanging bells, another felt like he was getting electric shocks, and a third that his arm was being pelted with shots from a miniature spaceship hovering around him. After two days nearly all the test subjects were worn thin, and the researchers had to abandon the experiment.

It was an unexpected outcome, and at McGill the psychologists debated what had happened. One group of researchers claimed the brain created meaning where there was none. When there was nothing to see or hear, when next to no signals were coming from the nervous system and all was darkened chaos, the brain began to piece the scraps into a reality of sorts. Evidently that was how consciousness worked. It found patterns where there were no patterns, spun sense out of shadow, and soon conjured a reality of illusions, a universe of the imagination, a little world all its own. It was a dizzying thought, and I lay with my arms around Lærke and tried to work out how much of our own reality was a reflection of the true, physical world and how much was invented by our imagination. Every single day our senses absorbed millions of sounds and sights and scents, but how could we distinguish between these genuine signals and the tales our minds scripted out of them? It was an exhausting question. I grew tired at the thought, and I guess Lærke felt the same way. As I talked her breathing grew slower, her body somehow heavier, and when I was sure she was asleep I pulled my arm from her grip and sat down at my desk.

That night I read a research paper about fear and paranoia among prisoners in solitary confinement, then I skimmed a dissertation about hallucinations among long-haul pilots, getting more anxious all the while. A woman whose father had hanged himself, who'd grown up in a home atrophied into misery and shame and hand-rolled cigarettes—was that a woman who should be living alone in a dark room for several weeks? No, it was madness. It was only a question of time before Ana lost her mind, and I swore I'd do whatever I could to get her out of *Timemachine* with her wits intact.

Early the next morning I wrote a long email to Ana and Irene, laying out my concerns. I attached summaries of articles and dissertations, and spent the rest of the day telling Lærke about the problems with *Timemachine*. But my misgivings didn't stop Ana, of course, and on Friday evening she opened the show. I arrived late to the blacked-out opening, and for a few minutes I stood under cover of darkness, listening to Ana's voice. From the entrance I could hear her introducing her guests to each other, the sound of laughter and cheerful voices. It was like people spoke more freely in the dark. The white noise of age and appearance was switched off and the tone sharpened, all small-talk about jobs and art projects sieved out. A woman was talking about a dream or a fantasy that had tormented her as a child, a nightmare about fumbling down the corridor in her grandmother's basement, while around the corner crept the night or the dark, and when she went back up the stairs it followed her like a shadow. Or, no, like an imaginary friend, she said, and as a joint was passed around, an Australian began to wheeze frantically for air and said he had to go outside for a minute. There was nothing else I could do. The exhibition had already taken on a life of its own, and I walked farther into the room, navigating like a bat by the echo of Ana's voice, and when I reached her I laid a hand on her shoulder and wished her luck with the show.

Thanks, she said. See how well we set it up? They're tiny little beasts, those photons, they get in everywhere, but it really is dark in here.

Have any critics been to take a look?

Yeah, there were a couple, I think.

Awesome, Ana, congratulations. By the way, my brother said he'd try and drop in later.

Oh yeah?

Yes, he really likes your work.

You sure about that?

Of course. Why else would he invite you to his exhibitions?

To fill his quota of Eastern Europeans.

What, did he say that?

Ana said nothing, but I pictured her shrugging or smiling a private smile.

Oh, you're kidding, I said.

Maybe. But you shouldn't believe everything that man says.

What do you mean by that?

I mean, if I believed everything he said we wouldn't be standing here.

Why not?

Because he said you were bad company.

What? That *I* was bad company?

Yep. You.

What exactly did he say?

Are you sure you want to know?

Yeah, of course I do.

Well, okay, said Ana, and she told me about the lunch meeting my brother had invited her to. Evidently he wanted to get in touch with a Romanian conceptual painter, an ancient woman with a studio in Bucharest, and once they'd finished their salads or quiches or sandwiches, he asked Ana whether she knew the woman. Ana didn't, but her friend Sorin did, and after taking down Sorin's email address my brother ordered coffee and dessert, and that was when he said he was a little worried about me and Ana. I don't know what you've been telling my brother, he said with a smile, but he talks about nothing but time travel and mathematicians and Ceaușescu. And then Ana nodded or shrugged, or maybe just stared at him with dead Eastern European eyes, and he said: My little brother . . . well, he tends to develop these fascinations with people. You should take care. He'll just end up burning his fingers, and yours in the bargain. Ana didn't understand a word of this, so she asked him what he meant, and so my brother explained that she shouldn't let herself be flattered by my attention. Right now you're probably intriguing and exotic, he said, but remember to look out for yourself. My brother'll want a taste of you, he'll want to hear about your experiences—basically he wants stories he can tell his little friends—but his attention, well, that's a fickle thing.

What? I said, laughing. This had to be a weird kind of Romanian joke.

I thought it was strange too, said Ana. But he wasn't completely off the mark.

What's that supposed to mean?

Well, there's a touch of the vampire about you. Don't you think? You like sucking stories out of me. All my exotic stories.

What are you talking about? It's not like that.

Oh, come on. If you're being completely honest, isn't that what it's about? Tasting a woman with a bit of mystery, an artist like the ones your brother fucks. You're like your brother, aren't you? Like a slightly subpar replica of your brother.

I didn't know what to say, and suddenly my face felt hot. Through the dark I tried to make out her eyes, but there was nothing to see, and for a moment both of us were silent. Around us the guests were talking loudly, out on the street a truck roared by, and I felt like telling her she shouldn't smear my brother like that, behind his back; or maybe I should have flounced out, done all the stuff you're supposed to do in a dramatic scene, but I kept standing there, dithering and lightheaded.

Hey, I'm just teasing, she said, putting her hand on my shoulder.

Yeah, yeah, of course. I'm just going to get a beer.

She said okay and patted me on the back, a peculiar gesture, like I was a pony or a dog, and I blundered over toward the sound of beer cans being opened. For a while I stood at the drinks table, listening to conversations, peering into the dark, and wondering if I ought to leave. I didn't owe Ana anything; I could vanish out into the city without looking back and never speak to her again, but who was I trying to fool? I'd been in New York five months, and Ana was the only person I knew apart from Lærke and my brother. She might be toying with me, but I couldn't just cut her out of my life. I was already too deep into her story, I couldn't put it down without knowing the ending, and so I drained my beer and took a final lap around the room. I greeted Irene's voice and said a nice goodbye to Ana, and then I followed the woozy Australian out of the gallery, and for five minutes, until his girlfriend arrived and calmed him down, I watched him walking in circles and muttering to himself, confused and afraid.

A few days after *Timemachine* opened, my brother called. He'd just got back from his trip around Europe, and he asked if we could meet at one of the new galleries that appeared and reappeared like stubble on Ridgewood's chin. His plans for the fall were now in place, he said. There was a photo exhibition someone'd recommended, we could check that out, and then we could discuss projects and ideas.

When I arrived at the gallery that evening he still hadn't shown up, and I wove through the jam-packed room and looked at the photographs. The work was by an American photographer. Every surface in the gallery was papered with images of naked young people, and the room hummed with an intense, almost cultish atmosphere. Young people were everywhere, drinking beer and chatting to other young people, while from walls and ceilings even more young people stared down at us. There was something self-consumptively orgiastic about it, and I settled by the window and looked at the clouds that were puffing up outside, heavy and black.

While I kept an eye out for my brother, I thought about what he'd said to Ana. Or, who knows, maybe he didn't say it, because why would he warn Ana against me? It didn't seem credible. We'd always been honest with each other, and we'd never fought, not since I was eight, anyway, and forbidden to enter his room. What would he get out of betraying me like that? No, I couldn't make it fit; but one of them was hiding something. Either Ana was lying or my brother was making a fool of me, but I had no proof one way or the other, only gestures, guesswork, and secondhand tales, so that evening I decided to forget about it and never bring it up again.

Still, I noticed a hesitation in my voice when my brother walked through the door ten minutes later, did a lap of the gallery, and flung his arms out at the photographs.

Decor, he said. Adornment, empty calories.

Looks pretty good, though. Don't you think?

It's pictures of beautiful young people. Of course it looks good. But where the hell's he going with it?

I had no idea, but my brother did, and he said there was nothing at stake in this exhibition, that it was ornamentation and retinal art, a game for wealthy people's idiot kids. He said the photographer's only concern was what rich people wanted in their living rooms, what rich people wanted in their holiday homes, and that the last thing the world needed was more pictures of naked pretty people. I could see that, of course—he did have a point—and I asked him what, then, made a good piece of art. Was it was better, for instance, when Ana lived by another calendar or stayed in the dark for weeks on end?

Better, he said. Better relative to what? It's not a competition.

He went on to explain that it wasn't a matter of good or bad art. It was a matter of asking the right questions, of broadening the horizons of the possible, and when I asked him what that meant he steered me into a corner of the gallery and showed me a picture on his phone. It looked like a pile of burned wood, maybe the charred remnants of a building, and as we stood beneath the lurid spot lighting he told me about the art festival he'd visited in Finland.

He'd flown up there to meet the committee—they wanted him to curate a few pieces for the fall festival—but at first he'd been a bit leery of the idea. The budget was microscopic, there was barely any press coverage, and the festival took place in a small town in eastern Finland. After the meeting he'd wandered through the town's shuttered mall, past businesses long since closed or maybe never opened, through the arcade behind the grill bar, where men drank beers and boys kicked moped tires, and all the while he'd been thinking that this was a town for rednecks and alcoholics and overweight mothers, a town deserted by six o'clock, not a thinking human being in sight, and the only sound the wind, howling through the streets.

That evening at the railway hotel he got drunk from the minibar. The town gave him the creeps, and he decided to meet the festival director the next day and turn down the job. That was the plan, and that's what would have happened, if he hadn't passed a charred wooden sculpture at the harbor the next morning. It was a strange colossus of a statue, standing sootily on the waterfront, at least three meters high, a kind of totem pole or moai or monolith of burned wood, its twisted face casting a grim shadow over the lake.

Christ, who'd made something so ugly? he had thought, and over coffee he asked the festival director the same question. For a moment she adjusted her glasses, then she laughed a nervous laugh, a laugh more like a coughing fit, and explained that a few years ago she'd blown her entire budget on the largest, vilest sculpture she could find. After several months' search, she tracked down what she was looking for at a handicrafts market in Dakar: a gigantic copy of a ceremonial figure from the Mambilla Plateau in Nigeria, or from the Donga Valley in Cameroon, or maybe just from the workshop behind the bus station in Dakar, she never learned which. That summer they transported the statue north and unveiled it at the waterfront, and afterward the festival employees split into two groups, both of which went undercover in the local community. One group set up a society in honor of the artwork, organizing sing-alongs and flea markets and barbecues on the promenade in front of the wooden effigy, and anytime they got the chance they sang the statue's praises. They talked about the importance of a landmark and the value of having a meeting point for local youth, about the tourists the monument would attract and the prestige the town on the other side of the water was missing out on. Meanwhile the second group did all they could to spread a feeling of hatred and bitterness and envy. They wrote letters to the editor. They whispered in corners at bars and pubs: Why's that miserable sculpture on the best square in town, what's a Negro statue doing up here in the north, why should we waste our hard-earned taxes on an ugly wooden man nobody likes? Before the summer was out, the town had split into two rival factions, and the mayor was obliged to explain himself in the press. In the fall the statue was vandalized with graffiti, a few weeks later a Somali man was attacked on his way home from the train station, and four days before New Year a group of unknown culprits poured gasoline over the statue and set it on fire, nearly burning the Sailing Association's clubhouse to the ground.

Wow, I said. That's one dangerous sculpture.

Batshit crazy. But you see what I mean, right? There's something at stake. It's not just a naked photo or a shitty bronze statue at a roundabout.

And what happened then?

Yes, what happened then? Then I agreed to curate the show for them.

You're kidding, I said, and laughed. So now you're spending several months in some one-horse town in Finland?

My brother shrugged. Yeah, well, it is what it is. If you want to win, you've got to put something on the line.

Later that evening we went to a restaurant underneath the grimy tracks of the JMZ line. My brother led me over to a table by the window, and as we read the menu he told me about the work he was thinking about putting on in Finland, the turnip field he wanted to plant in the town's disused athletics stadium, the climbing plant he wanted to grow over two enormous silos. He was going to bring the plant from a Mayan ruin in Belize, and in five hundred years' time, when it covered both silos, the green cylinders would soar up over the houses and cranes. It was an immensely slow work.

Vines, you know? he said. I've always had this thing with vines.

I nodded. I didn't remember him having a thing for vines, but it was a nice image. Green silos reflected in the lake, two twin towers that grew unperturbed out of the centuries.

We've got to work with slowness, he said. That's where we're headed. Getting nature involved, sort of.

I agreed. That sounded right, that stuff about nature and slowness, and he told me about the time he'd sailed up a river in Guatemala when he was on 2C-I. Vines had grown along the river, their tendrils wriggled deep into the underbrush, more tendrils crawling between those tendrils, which led in turn to other tendrils, and before he knew it he'd fallen into a trance or a doze, and he was hovering far above the river, sensing the forest or the mangrove swamp or whatever it was. I tried to picture it, but got stuck on the mangrove swamp. I didn't have a clue what one looked like, and suddenly he got up and said: Listen, I've got an idea.

Then he went over to the bar and bought beer, and when he came back he wanted to hear my plans for the next month or two. When I said that grad school started in September, that I was looking for a job and writing a few short stories about Ana, he hauled out his bag and told me he'd been invited to an important biennale in Spain.

Congrats, I said, that's awesome.

Taking a folder out of the bag, he told me the biennale was one of the biggest art events in the world, an exhibition he simply couldn't refuse, but if he was going to get things ready in time for

October he'd have to skip the festival in Finland. And that was a problem, because he'd already signed the contract, the Finns were counting on him, there were directors of foundations and major cultural figures from across Northern Europe on the board, and if he canceled on them his reputation would be permanently ruined.

So I can't get out of Finland, he said. But I can't miss out on the biennale either.

But, then what are you going to do? You can't be in two places at once.

No, and that's why I was thinking *you* could go to Finland.

Me?

Yeah, as my assistant. Go shake up those Finnish hayseeds a little.

While you're in Spain, you mean?

Exactly, it's just two months. You'll handle it no problem.

Then he showed me a map of the disused stadium. The local council had already approved the planting of turnips on the athletics track, he explained, the piece had been conceptualized down to the smallest detail, and now it just had to be planned and organized, the soil plowed and seeds sown. Wouldn't it be a cool experience, since I didn't have anything else to do that fall?

But I *have* got stuff to do, I said. I've got loads to do.

Sure, but not here, in the city. You can easily study from over there, can't you?

Well, yeah, but I'm also writing something for Ana.

Listen. I know it's not the greatest job in the world, but if you do this, I promise you there'll be better opportunities down the road. I promise you.

Can't you just hire an assistant?

If I had the money, I would. But there's no money in this crappy little festival. That's the problem.

So it's unpaid?

There's a small allowance. But fuck money, it's about doing something together. As brothers. Wouldn't it be cool to make art together?

But two unpaid months in Finland, I said. That's a tall order.

He leaned across the table and said he knew how I worked, he trusted my judgment, he'd love to have me as his understudy, and wasn't this a totally unique chance, an experience we'd remember all our lives and one day tell our children, and then he put down the bottle and stared into my eyes.

I know it's a lot to ask. But I really need your help. Won't you do this for me?

I nodded, and he smiled, and I turned away and gazed through the window. Outside the rain had begun to fall. People were crowding underneath the awnings, and a small, dark-haired woman looked at me through the glass. For a second I thought it was Ana, and at that moment I suddenly realized what she'd meant. My brother opened the folder, taking out the contract and the budget specs, and it was like the space compressed. The dented tin ceiling, the scarred brick, the hiss of the espresso machine, all of it curled tightly around me, and I felt the urge to get out of there, away from this version of myself, the me that acted like a shadow or a dog, like a lapdog whose only talent lay in mimicking its owner's mood, who lived off the scraps from his table and trotted up wagging its tail each time he called. Even that analogy wasn't quite accurate, because at least a dog had its instincts and its urges, beneath the tame surface. No, it was worse. I was more like a hologram of my brother's being, his ideas and experiences copied onto an airy, flickering image, a projection without mass or weight at all.

So, what do you say? he asked. Do we have a deal?

No, I said, straightening up. No, we don't.

What? he said, gazing at me in astonishment, as if he didn't speak my language. What's the problem?

I don't want to go to Finland. I've got so much stuff to sort out here.

Fine, yeah, but can't you—for a moment he paused, his eyes sliding across my face. Really, do you mean it? Are you sure?

It won't work. I'm sorry, but not this time.

He looked at me, then scratched his neck.

Okay, well, it's up to you, of course. But think it over. Promise me you'll think it over one more time.

A few days passed, and then he called again. I was in the middle of a job application, and I was going to ask whether the festival could give me a recommendation letter, but I never got that far, because my brother had an offer for me.

We'll split my fee from Spain, he said. What do you say? Let's do this thing together.

Do what together? That field in Finland?

Yeah, man. I've been mulling it over, and I think it should stay in the family. I'd rather lose a bit of cash than give the job to some art student in Helsinki. Look, just think about it for a minute. We'll be creating a whole stadium together. In fucking Finland. When's that ever going to happen again?

Then he said something about the power of art to shape whole cities, landscapes, about Joseph Beuys's seven thousand oaks in Kassel, about Francis Alÿs, who moved a whole mountain in Peru, and now it was our turn to do something together, to leave our mark as brothers, and, sure, it was only a two-bit show in Finland, but it might be the start of something big.

Don't you get how much this means for me, he said. It's my whole career on the line.

Yes, but I really can't help you. I don't have time.

But can't you make time? Seriously, I'll pay you.

Look, how many times do I have to say it? I don't want to go plow some field in Finland.

For a second or two he was silent. Then his voice crackled down the line.

Okay, fine. Just forget it.

Then he hung up and I sat there for a moment, listening to the tone, before going over to the sink and getting a glass of water. I tried to settle back at the desk and pick up where'd left off, but the sentence I'd begun was swimming incomprehensibly onscreen, and suddenly it struck me how unpleasant our conversation had been. When I thought about it, I realized I'd heard tension in my brother's voice, and despite his enthusiastic patter about all the things we'd do together, I'd sensed impatience beneath the cheery chatter, as though he were straining not to lose his cool and start yelling down the phone. It was like he didn't fully believe his own words, and while I paced restlessly around the room, my mind turned to his exhibitions, to earlier works in back rooms and disused apartment blocks, installations in white cube galleries, all the projects and festivals I'd helped with since my teenage years.

I'd planted trees and cleared weeds, scrubbed exhibition rooms clean, played chauffeur and attendant, errand boy and bartender, and although there was no shortage of interns in the art world, I knew he'd never find another one like me. An assistant who never asked questions. An assistant who never backed out. Was it possible he'd tried to scare Ana away so he could have me to himself? So he didn't have to share me?

I didn't want to believe it. I didn't want to think so badly of my brother, and I got up and changed into shorts and went for a run to shake off the idea. By the riverbank the clouds hung low and ill at ease above the city. The clammy heat settled around my neck, and although I ran so fast the summer air burned my lungs, I couldn't give my thoughts the slip. The hours I'd sat in doorways at his exhibitions, the chipboard sheets I'd lugged up stairs, the grant applications I'd written in his name; all of it passed through my head.

I couldn't keep living as his shadow, I told myself. It was time I stepped up and found my own place in the world. But how? As I jogged along the waterside, I racked my brains. I imagined cities I could move to, jobs I could apply for. I thought of my short story about the appendix and the things Ana'd encouraged me to write; perhaps they were the solution. That magazine editor had been interested in reading them, and if I could get a few stories published, if I could get an editor in New York, it would prove I could manage on my own. That was the idea I landed on as I stopped, out of breath on the Pulaski Bridge. A desperate idea, a naïve idea? Absolutely. But an idea that gave me something to work with nonetheless, and as I walked down the stairs toward Greenpoint, I promised myself I'd work harder than ever before.

I'd dedicate myself to Ana's stories, I'd write at least eight hours a day, and I wouldn't stop until I reached the edge of the story, the rift where Ana's life collapsed into fantasy.

By dawn the next morning I was already at my desk. Lærke got up at seven thirty, we had breakfast, and as soon as she'd gone to work I sat back down at the computer and wrote on. A couple of times I wondered what Ana would say if she knew I was copying her stories, if she'd feel betrayed or abused, or if a stack of such tales was exactly what she wanted. But I didn't waste much time on those questions. My thoughts soon drifted on, condensing rapidly into a story about a girl who was her own sister, into the two years of the girl's life that didn't exist but were the center of her world: a two-year void on which her family turned, like a galaxy revolves around a black hole, and suddenly the sun had set, and Lærke was home, and I was still trapped in the cold blue light of the screen.

Over the next few days I remembered all kinds of details from Ana's anecdotes. Sometimes I'd be standing in the bathroom; other times I was mid-conversation with Lærke when a story came crashing into my mind, and my gaze faltered, and my answers grew light and fluffy. On those days I forgot to eat, I forgot to drink, because there was always another sentence to include, always a piece of dialogue to add, and the one thing that made me relax was sitting at the keyboard, writing Ana's stories. As soon as I got up and left the apartment, I longed to be back at the screen. At the coffee shop or in the park, with Lærke's hand in mine, I pictured the scenes I was going to write: a man setting his watch, a girl's hand dissolved in soapy water, the reek of paper burning in a stockpot. When I couldn't stand it any longer, I asked Lærke, Shall we go home?, and as soon as she'd gone to bed I took out my stories and flicked through the pages.

I kept going like that for a week or so. I wrote from morning till evening, and I was making progress, or I believed I was making progress, and one night, as I lay in bed and waited for sleep, I had the hopeless idea of writing the story from the dead sister's perspective. Because the narrator was dead, the voice wouldn't move through time like normal people did. No, the narrator would be outside of linear time, she'd live in time like a landscape—a landscape where all moments existed side by side and nothing was ever in the past. It was an original idea, I thought, stupidly, or at least an unoriginal idea that might bind the short stories together. As soon as the library opened the next morning, I rushed from shelf to shelf, borrowing books about block time and eternalism, articles about tenseless languages and tertiary tenses, future indefinite and pre-future tense, and dissertations on tribes with uncommon perceptions of time.

That evening, as we were barbecuing on the roof, I told Lærke about my dead narrator idea and about an article I'd read, a dissertation about the Aymara people from the Andes, whose conception of time was apparently the reverse of most cultures'. In their language, time wasn't a space consciousness moved through, like a line drawn from the past through the present and into the future. Instead, they saw consciousness as a fixed point. They imagined humanity standing still in the present, the past ahead and the future approaching from behind. Like a man who stands at the center of time's space and braces himself against the gale, his eyes riveted on the past and the winds of the future blowing at his back.

Later we lay in bed and talked about the Hopi tribe and the linguistic debate about their ancestral language that had been raging for years. One group of researchers insisted that the Hopi had no grammatical forms or constructions or phrases that referred to what other people called time, and thus couldn't conceive of it as we did: as a continuum through which everything else in the universe flows. What they *did* think about time the researchers never fully established, and I tried to imagine a world where past and future didn't exist, but it was impossible, I couldn't see it, and then Lærke rolled over and said I should try imagining a world where the alarm clock went off at seven.

Days passed, summer sank over the city, and although I couldn't write like a Hopi, and even less like a girl who was dead, I convinced myself I was gradually producing short stories worth reading. The desk bulged with notes, the floor swam in discarded drafts, and one Wednesday morning I sent an email to Ana's editor friend with the manuscript attached. Even after I'd sent the stories, I continued reading about the unreality of time and the temporality of consciousness, checking my email again and again. But the editor didn't respond, and ten days later I sent another email. That night I fidgeted beneath my desk lamp, leafing through the stories, making corrections and additions, striking out words and changing sentences, until suddenly Lærke was standing behind me, her hair tangled and her eyes drowsy, staring at me and holding the computer's power cord.

Oops, she said, pulling out the plug. Must be a power cut.

Then she dragged me back to bed, but I couldn't escape Ana's stories so easily. I saw them everywhere, and the following night I woke from a nightmare. It was a dream about a sink or a pipe or a radiator that had sprung a leak, and in the dream I roamed around a pitch-dark gallery, trying to find the source, but of course I couldn't find it, and the water rose and rose, reaching first my navel, then my shoulders and chin. It was a predictable, clichéd nightmare, but a nightmare all the same, and I woke up with a cry.

I still hadn't shaken off the dream the next morning, when I was waiting for the train and happened to overhear a conversation. Two men were discussing a colleague who was originally from Rwanda but had been adopted by an American family. One of the men had been invited to the woman's twenty-seventh birthday, but a few days before the party the woman had canceled it without explanation. He was puzzled, because the woman had been talking about the party for weeks, and when he saw her some time later he asked what happened. Apparently, in the process of setting up life insurance, the woman had contacted the adoption agency to get a copy of her birth certificate, but when it arrived a few days before the party, she discovered to her horror that the orphanage had lied on the forms and pretended she was three years younger than she was. Presumably it had been easier to get a four-year-old adopted than a strapping seven-year-old. Thus, in a single blow, the woman was no longer an emerging talent in her mid-twenties but an unmarried thirty-year-old without children or a permanent job, neither engaged nor pregnant, and death had crept three years closer.

That night the nightmares returned. I don't remember how long they lasted. Three or four nights, maybe a week, and then one morning Lærke came back from her run later than usual.

It was hot out, and her face was covered in sweat, her hair wet and her cheeks red. I was sitting at my desk, rewriting one of the short stories, when she came right over and stood so close that the sweat dripped onto the keyboard, and when I looked up her jaw was tense and her eyes narrow and dark. She said: What is it with those stories?

What, Ana's stories?

Yes, those. We haven't seen each other for months, and you're still spending ten times as long on them as you do with me.

She wiped the sweat from her brow, her gaze sweeping over the sheets of paper.

And when I read what you're writing—how Ana feels about her dad, what Ana's thinking about this or that—I feel like I'm all alone. When was the last time you asked me how I was? You don't care. You don't think about how I'm feeling, or if I like coming home to a boyfriend who's never here.

Lærke, I said, of course I think about you.

No, you don't. You're gone. I don't know you anymore. When I wake up in the morning, you're sitting at the screen. When I get home from work, you're still sitting here. I've got to creep into my own home, it's like living with a stranger. How do you think that feels? How do you think it feels to be forgotten by your own boyfriend?

She kept on like that for a while, and I listened silently as she told me she couldn't reach me anymore, that I was living in a fantasy, that I didn't react even when she spent whole nights dancing with a stranger, that I'd left her for another woman, in mind or body, same difference. She'd traveled thousands of miles to build a new life with me in New York. She'd left her family and her friends and everyone she loved in Copenhagen, and I'd just casually turned my back, pushed her away to focus on a story, to hear another anecdote or polish a piece of writing, and even when I promised to improve, even when I swore I'd get my act together and be a better boyfriend, even when I reminded her of the good times we'd had, our first room in Copenhagen, the time we hitch-hiked to Hamburg, Lærke already knew it was over. I could see it in her face. It was like she'd known the whole time, like she was suddenly struck by a thought long forgotten, and despite three years of living and dreaming, of fighting and sleeping together, it only took two nights to tear the whole thing up. For two nights we talked until the sun rose, and as we sat on benches and fumbled with the shreds of our relationship, I could see the scene from the outside. Two sad people on a bench, a woman leaving a man. When the sun rose on the third day, I could see the outline of the man left behind. A man so self-absorbed he lavished care and attention on the characters in a story but forgot the living, breathing woman in the bed next to him. A man kidding himself that he could render the nuances of a human life when he didn't even notice the person who needed him the most. A man so false and empty he milked the sorrows of a whole family and used them to fertilize his writing. A mosquito man who lived off the suffering of others, a human tick who sucked the tragedy out of the people around him, a boy with so infinitely little to offer that even his self-critical metaphors were clichés; that was the little boy I saw on the bench.

Two nights and three days, that was all it took, and on the third morning Lærke packed her things and carried her suitcase down the stairs. A quick hug on the sidewalk, then the driver put her suitcase in the trunk, and I caught a last glimpse of Lærke's freckles through the window before she drove off. For several minutes I stood gazing after the car, until it vanished around the corner. Then I went up to the apartment and sat on the floor and looked around me. The pictures and posters had been taken down, bits of tape left dangling from the brickwork, nothing but magnets remained on the fridge, the last rays of light were cast against the bare wall, and suddenly I was exhausted, far too weary to switch on a lamp.

I lay on my back and thought about the first time I saw Lærke, one dark-blue night in a backyard in Copenhagen, and how I'd never wake up next to her again. Five months earlier we'd left our apartment and taken the metro to the airport, chatting about all the new things that awaited us in New York, and now I was lying on the floor without her. How had it happened? I wondered, but I was too tired to answer. I shut my eyes, and I don't know if I fell asleep, but when I opened them again the last light of day had disappeared, and for a few seconds I didn't know where I was. My gaze flitted across the empty walls, and through the gloom I saw a photo on the shelf, a girl in a school uniform, with a stiff stare and tight lips. It was Ana, and she was smiling like a hairworm.

It's easy to imagine what happened next. I could tell you about the endless nights, about the begging texts and desperate calls, but why wallow in it? For several days I saw no one; I didn't even speak to the clerk at the bodega. I never heard from the editor at the literary magazine. One by one my job applications were rejected, and when I lay in bed at night and tried to picture the next months of my life, no images would come, as if my thoughts were Polaroids that stayed dark and shiny no matter how long I waved them in the air. The only thing that helped in those days, strangely, was the heat wave that settled over the city. The tortured looks of the passengers on the subway platforms, the sweat stains on the waitresses' shirts, the cab drivers fanning themselves with news-papers, the whir of air conditioners, like a membrane around my mind, ten million flapping, rotating blades, humming all through the city. When the cloudburst finally came and the heat lifted, I took a long bike ride. The city was mirrored in the puddles and overflowing drains; it was like the streets had gained an extra di-mension, like the buildings and lampposts stretched both up and down, and I biked aimlessly through neighborhoods I had never been to before and have never visited since, and by evening I was standing in the light drizzle of a cement works' sprinklers, star-ing at Ana's gallery. I hadn't given it a thought since Lærke left, but now it suddenly occurred to me that Ana was still in there. The idea seemed ridiculous. It felt like ages since Ana had begun her performance, like another era, another season, at least, and all that time she'd been in the dark. I leaned the bike against a wall and checked my watch. It was a little after ten on Sunday evening, and the gallery must have closed hours earlier, but I went up to the door anyway. The place looked abandoned. The shutters were rolled down and there were scraps of a poster hanging from the wall, but as I leaned forward to read the opening times I saw a note glued to the mailbox. *Ana Ivan's performance of* Timemachine *is open 24 hours*, it said. *Entry is at your own risk. The gallery cannot be held responsible for any injuries that may occur.* I turned the handle and stepped into the dark.

Although the sun had long since set, it still felt like sinking into a cave. I shut the door behind me and drew the first black cloth gingerly aside, then the second, then the third, and the room grew chillier and very still, smelling earthy or damp, like wet towels left too long in a heap, and I had to stop for a moment and get used to the dark.

Ana, I shouted. Are you there?

For a second or two I heard nothing, then there was a crackle or a rustle, and I paused and tried to place the sound. I thought I could hear a voice, very faint, barely more than a hushed whisper, and it took a few seconds before I could tell one word from the next. I couldn't be sure, but it sounded like Ana was rambling to herself. One moment in English, the next in Romanian, as if she were amputating sentences and reconfiguring them into new and mutilated shapes.

Ana, I called again. Where are you?

There was no answer, only a dusty whir, a muted mutter or two. Her voice seemed to come from somewhere distant, as though she'd just woken up or was still asleep, but as I listened I could hear she was saying something about the inhabitants of Samoa. Something about how they'd lost a whole day of their lives—Friday, December 30, I caught among the words—when the country's time zone shifted west of the International Date Line. I couldn't tell if she was speaking to somebody or preaching into the darkness, and I found the rope on the wall and took my first blind steps. There was something weirdly tantalizing about having your eyes open without being able to see, and I held my arm out in front of me.

Are you okay, Ana? Where are you?

Over here, I heard from the other end of the room. Come on, I'm lying over here.

I switched direction toward the voice and took another couple of steps, my shoes dragging along the floor. The walk felt like an eternity, the gallery incomprehensibly huge without my sight, but at last I stubbed my toe against the mattress, and Ana said: Hi. What are you doing here?

I was just passing by the gallery. So I thought I'd drop in. You know, see if you were okay.

Right.

And are you?

Yeah, fine. Given the circumstances.

Given the circumstances?

Yeah, given the circumstances.

We were silent a moment. I got the sense we weren't alone, and peered over my shoulder, out into the endless dark.

Is it just the two of us? I asked. Or do you have visitors?

I don't think so. Nobody but you.

So who were you talking to?

Myself. It's nice to hear my voice.

Yeah?

Yeah, it is. When I hear my voice ringing against the walls, it's like I know I'm here. I know it's not all in my head.

I wasn't sure what to say, so I settled down on the mattress. For a while we sat together in silence. The air in the gallery was strangely heavy, as though it had been pooling for years, and I could hear Ana biting her nails. I wanted to say something, maybe lighten the mood a little, but I couldn't think of anything. Now and again Ana murmured something incomprehensible, and I could sense her scratching or scraping her arm. This wasn't good, I thought, and tried not to think of Michel Siffre, who got so lonely in his Texas cave that he spent a whole week catching a mouse to keep him company. When he squashed the mouse by accident with a saucepan, he was seized by a grief so deep it took him several years to recover. His wife left him, he suffered from suicidal thoughts. I felt my stomach pucker. Ana risked losing her wits— perhaps already had—and I wanted to fill the dark with words, with something warm and kind and everyday, so I said: By the way, I'm writing a new short story for you.

That's sweet of you. Any good?

I hope so, I said, and I told her about the story and my experiment with the timeless narrator. Ana listened, in concern or with interest; it was nice talking with somebody again. It must have been at least a week since my last real conversation, and before I knew it I was telling her about the festival in Finland, about the job applications that were turned down. One word led to the next, and soon I was talking about Lærke, who'd left me, and the apartment I couldn't afford by myself, and when I finally finished my monologue I heard Ana slide herself up against the wall.

You know what? she said. I think it's best you go home.

She didn't say it in an accusatory way; it was neutral, like she was asking me to open the window or put the kettle on.

Why? I said. What have I done?

You haven't done anything. I just think you should leave.

But why?

Because I ruin the people around me, okay? And now I'm ruining you.

Ruin? What are you talking about?

Look at me. It's like I'm a sickness, some virus or bacteria. People get sick with me, don't you get it? Don't you get what I'm saying? Just go away.

Maybe she was right. I should've gone, but at that moment it was impossible. I could hear the tears prowling in her voice, the sound of nails on skin, and I couldn't leave her in the dark like that.

Hey Ana, I said, putting my hand on her shoulder. Nobody's sick.

Yes, they are, she said, as the first sob went through her. Somebody's always sick, and it's always me that infects them.

It's alright, calm down. Everything's fine.

No, it's not fine, she sobbed. I ruined my fiancé, I ruined my dad, and now I've ruined you.

Hey, easy now, I said, pulling her nearer, and she crumpled onto my chest. I felt the tears dripping onto my shirt, heard her stuttering crying, wiped the tears and snot from her face with my sleeve, and Ana said nobody ever listened to her warnings. It's just a story, they'd say, how dangerous can it be, and before I could fish a napkin out of my pocket Ana had begun to tell me about her fiancé. I could hear it in her voice, long before she mentioned his name. It wasn't the voice she used when she spoke about chess or art; or it was, but with something gone from it. This was a softer Ana, a tentative, more faltering Ana, and her speech was flat and simple, utterly without sarcasm or irony, like a child with something thrilling to tell. She explained about Isak's drawings and doodles, the concrete sculptures that snaked through the

workshop, their engagement, their time travels, about the whole
strange tragedy or farce, which started with an anecdote at a Bucharest café.

It was on Strada Covaci, said Ana, in 2005, and the rain beat
against the panes, but inside she was sitting on the sofa, listening
to Claudia's story. It was a dark day, she remembered, late October
or early November, and the rainwater dripped from Claudia's hair.
They were both wet and cold, but Claudia beamed as she talked
about her application to Pierre and Marie Curie University, how it
was a miracle they'd let her in and given her a full scholarship for
two semesters.

Paris, squealed Claudia, her cheeks pink with enthusiasm. Ana,
I'm going to Paris to study.

God, said Ana, when they'd finished celebrating. I didn't know
you got such good grades.

Claudia laughed. It had nothing to do with being talented, that
wasn't how it happened at all. It was just about seizing your opportunity. This was the Era of Eastern Enlargement, and if you were
a poor, starving Romanian, you practically had to duck to avoid
getting smacked in the head with bags of EU money.

Anybody can do it, said Claudia. Just write something about
Ceaușescu in your application. Just say you're an orphan.

That afternoon Ana went home like a sleepwalker. Crammed
between passengers on the bus, feeling someone's hand grope her
ass, she thought: Would I miss the communal strays and the male
chauvinists? The eternal traffic jams, the mildewed teachers at the
Academy, and their ceaseless Iron Curtainry? From the bus stop
she took a detour to avoid the glue sniffers' alley, and as she walked
across the sludgy lawns behind Block A41, she kicked at the trash

and listened to *What Have You Done for Me Lately*. But the question was really: What has Bucharest ever done for anybody?

Back at the apartment her mother was rinsing peppers while her grandma snored moistly in the living room, and in a joyless flash-forward Ana saw spinsterhood before her. Taking her father's old atlas, she barricaded herself in her room. She couldn't remember living anywhere other than Drumul Taberei, and since her infant years in Morocco she'd never been farther afield than Budapest, so moving was a scary thought. But if she could travel through time, she told herself, then she could certainly travel through Europe. Choosing Norway was more or less an accident. She came up with a list of all the art schools in Europe from A to Z, and simply started applying. One rejection from Amsterdam, and then: jackpot.

Bergen? exclaimed her mother, holding the acceptance letter. Ana just smiled. She knew nothing about the place.

The letter said she'd been accepted for the semester beginning in August, but Ana had never gotten anything for nothing, and she'd anticipated a bigger bureaucratic hassle like the one from the Romanian Cultural Institute. But no. One wave of her hand, and she was allowed to have her cake and eat it. More cake than she could shake a stick at, in fact, plus a dorm room, a full stipend, and a cleaning job at the university. She got whatever she pointed at, and I don't think Ana's astonishment could be underestimated when she found herself on Nygårdsgaten one bright summer's night, health insurance card in her hand, watching trashed Norwegian teenagers reel by.

·   ·   ·

That first month in Bergen, Ana lived by herself. During the day she was at class or in the cutting room, in late afternoon she washed the floors, and in the evening she called Claudia or sat in her dorm room and studied video art. Ever since hearing the story about her dead sister, Ana had become obsessed with her camera, studying Final Cut and making an entry in her video diary each evening. She felt a strange urge to document herself. She hung stills from Chantal Akerman's 16mm films on her dormroom walls, learned Rosler's and Grigorescu's work back to front, browsed the art school's entire video catalog, and Ana and Isak could have slid past each other easily if she hadn't been invited to a lecture by her dormmate.

At first she politely declined, because the dormmate in question was suffering through a chronic dry spell, and his gaze flitted so rapidly among his peers' breasts that Ana had never seen the color of his eyes. Two days after the first rebuff, he asked again, and Ana still said no, but the third time she said no he must have misunderstood her, because the next day he'd bought them tickets. Ana could have stayed home, of course, pretending she was sick, but the lecture sounded appealing enough. Having figured out that Ana was interested in science, the dormmate had bought tickets to a talk on quantum cryptography, and thus one Tuesday evening they entered the auditorium together.

It was an American physicist giving the lecture, and Ana took notes while her dormmate yawned his way through it. Afterward there was a Q&A. The moderator had barely opened discussion to the floor before a man requested the microphone, launching into the type of question that's really an accusation, his hands busy knitting a half-finished sweater bunched up in his lap. The guy knew his terminology, and during the American's response he obstinately shook his head, grinning the occasional mocking grin, the faint clatter of the knitting pins resounding through the auditorium. Ana couldn't help smiling. She didn't know what the guy reminded her of, but it was something different from the polished college kids. It was refreshing to find a little disorder in this pedantically clean town, and before they went back to the dormitory she watched him vanish into the streets, knitting still in hand.

The next time Ana saw him, it was Christmastime. She'd gone into town with Jorunn, a new friend from the academy. They sat at the bar, because a bar is the only place in Norway you can meet a man. That's what Jorunn always said, though Ana'd never met any men there. It was always Jorunn who caught their attention. And sure enough, in five minutes flat, there were two guys from the business school standing next to Jorunn, flirting. Ana had to sit there politely and spit in her beer, playing with her cash and folding a napkin, and that was when she noticed him. Sitting at the end of the bar, with a draft beer in front of him. He looked indescribably sad. Clean-shaven, wearing a crumpled shirt, he had a cross hanging from a chain around his neck, and for a while Ana tried to catch his eye. It wasn't easy, because he was staring at a tea light, but then Ana took two coins and a slice of lemon and arranged them on the bar so they looked like a smiley face. At first he didn't see it, gazing into the light, but then Ana slid the coins and lemon closer, and finally he glanced up, a little afraid to start with, but when he saw the smiley face, he laughed.

His name was Isak Bringedal. He had blond hair and sharp, skeletal cheekbones, he'd studied at the art school, and he built installations out of concrete, cast bathrooms and living rooms, fillings of the negative space in apartment block stairwells, that sort of thing. Ana told him she'd seen him get his teeth into the American physicist at the lecture, and he nodded and pointed at the candle.

It's the photons, he said. They teleport. That's why so many strange things are happening.

Strange things?

Exactly, he said, and explained about photons, the way they interacted at long distances with no delay whatsoever, nor any intervening force. They had to be in touch through some godlike energy, he said, because the photons' behavior was nuts. Either they were present everywhere at once, or they traveled through time. And that made Ana smile. She felt an instant fondness for the photons, which ignored the common sense of causality and place, or whatever you wanted to call it, and traveled through time—it was nice to think that even elementary particles were unstable.

What else do they do, these photons? asked Ana, but she never got an answer, because Isak had begun to cough. He thumped his chest, saying: Ugh, for Christ's sake, it's those fucking smokers. Come on, shall we get some fresh air?

So they wrapped themselves up in jackets and hats and scarves, and as they walked toward the art school he told her about a game he'd played once as a boy, when a Ouija board had predicted that his big sister would get juvenile arthritis. At Ana's studio they shared two beers, then Isak shrugged his coat back on and Ana watched him vanish into the dark.

That night Ana had a nightmare about her father. She woke up all sticky with sweat, and the same thing happened a few nights running. She thought it must be the upcoming crit that was stressing her out, and who knows, maybe that's all it was. She was presenting her latest video piece, and two minutes before the session began, Isak came creeping into the classroom. He crept the way larvae and caterpillars creep, first one half of his body, then, with a jerk, the second. He used to be a tutor at the school, and still dropped by to check out the new students. This time he wore glasses and a blazer too short in the arms, but the cross still hung around his neck. Ana waved at him and he smiled back, and for some reason it made her relax a little.

After the seminar they played chess, and Isak told her about his own crit sessions, about the students who'd sneered at his studio approach, and about the professors who'd been so scared of treading on their own toes they hadn't dared say a word, sitting like gurus at the head of the table and letting their pupils talk bullshit.

You shouldn't listen to their crap, said Isak. Critiques are the Devil's own invention.

You think so? said Ana, putting Isak in check. Isn't it kind of healthy to reflect on why you're doing what you're doing?

Isak shook his head, and with a flick of his hand he knocked Ana's queen off the board.

Hey, stop it, said Ana, but Isak hit a pawn, then slapped a knight so hard it leaped onto the floor.

What the hell are you doing? said Ana.

No, fuck my intentions, he said. It's not the thought that counts. You see?

For a moment she looked at him, confused. Then he laughed.

Yeah Ana, you get it. Come on, let's go.

So they trudged into his workshop and ate Elvis sandwiches, and the week after that they met several times to play chess. Say what you like about Isak, but you never got bored in his company. She taught him the Spanish Opening, and he taught her about block time, which neither went nor passed, and about photons, which had no rest mass and predated even the Big Bang. Whole nights they'd sit like that, mentally heavy petting, and then one day, when Ana dropped by the workshop, she found Isak lounging on the sofa in his dad's old rabbit fur, strumming a guitar. When he caught sight of Ana, he sat up with a jerk.

Keep your jacket on, he said, pointing at her. *Now* we're going to show them what I've got.

As they headed into town, Isak explained that he was sick of all that concrete sculpture bullshit. He was going to play guitar. She would see, he was the best in all of Vestlandet.

We'll be like Sonny and Cher, he said excitedly. Ike and Tina?

Ana laughed. Like John and Yoko?

No, not them, he said immediately. For God's sake, anyone but them.

And then they reached the main square, and Isak launched into *Wonderwall*, which must have been the only song he knew, because he bawled *Wonderwall* all day long, while Ana ran around with a hat and took donations, and afterward they went to a burger bar, and Isak put the hat on the counter and bought all the burgers that were ready.

Three days later, Ana invited herself to lunch on Isak's boat. It was moored at the quay in Sjøflyhavnen, and although she couldn't see him anywhere she recognized the name on the boat and climbed aboard. Below deck it reeked like an after-hours bar, and Isak was sitting on a plank bed, drawing on a cigarette. Ana crabwalked over to him and waved the smoke away.

What are you doing? she said. I thought you didn't smoke.

What are you talking about? he said, gazing at her in surprise. I've always smoked.

He gave Ana a shove, so Ana shoved him back, and they kept shoving each other until they lay naked and moaning on the plank bed, and this time Ana remembered every single touch, and many hours later, as she walked wearily back to the dorm, she didn't feel a single spot of shame. On the contrary. She stopped at the harbor and watched the birds flirting in the air and a gull dragging a pizza box along the pier, and she thought about the time her dad had rescued a pigeon from a paper bag, and for a moment it felt true: Maybe Isak and the block-time physicists were right, maybe there was no before or now or after, maybe all times existed side by side, and nothing was ever over; and then the pizza bird jabbered up into the sky with a squawk of victory that made Ana's body tingle.

The next morning the sun streamed through her window, and a gull sat peeking in from the frame. It had a yellow beak and bright round eyes, and Ana smiled and checked her phone, but Isak hadn't texted. So she went into the bathroom and got the giggles over Isak, who'd asked her to talk dirty in Romanian and told her that his cock was five point seven inches long, and that he averaged three hundred thrusts before he came. All told she was getting one hundred forty-three feet of cock per fuck, which was disappointing, wouldn't she say? They hadn't even screwed the distance from the boat to the ice-cream kiosk.

She didn't hear from Isak the next day either, and Ana made a deal with herself that she was only allowed to check her phone twice a day. She did as her father had taught her, sublimating until she was blue in the face, burying herself in her work at the art-school reading room. As she walked through Bergen she did like the CIA and blasted Van Halen's *Panama* so loudly through the headphones that it was completely impossible to think, and, in the late evening, when she couldn't repress him any longer, she walked past Isak's workshop and watched at a distance as he danced around the cement mixer like an alchemist, until the butterflies in her stomach made her sick.

She only spoke to two people about Isak. The first was Claudia, and over a crackly internet connection they discussed Ana's next move.

Doesn't matter what you do, laughed Claudia. You're head over heels.

She told Jorunn too, one evening on the ferry from Askøy. They'd been visiting Jorunn's family, and Ana hadn't intended to say anything. They stood on the deck, watching the sunset in a wind so bitingly cold that Ana had to wrap her scarf around her face, and suddenly the words came, like her worries were squeezing them out of her larynx.

Could you date an artist? asked Ana, and added a little anecdote about a mutual friend who'd fallen in love with two painters, two conceptual artists, and one photographer, but who'd been flagrantly dumped by all of them, because that kind of man only loved himself, and had no morals at all.

Lol, said Jorunn. Artist or accountant or baker, makes no difference, as long as he's got a dick.

But then Jorunn's smile had gone rigid, and a silence had fallen over her.

But you've got to stay away from the weirdos, she said. You don't want to end up with some fucked-up pedophile.

Ana nodded. But what if you do fall in love with a weirdo?

Jorunn hunched over a cigarette, and when she'd lit it she said: Then I guess there's not much to be done.

But what would you do?

I don't know, OD on him maybe? Get so much of his pervy cock I was fed up with it.

Not the best advice that's ever been given, but Ana couldn't come up with a better idea. She was too shy to knock on Isak's door, and she didn't dare ask him out, so she used an old art-ists' trick and texted him, explaining that she was working on a video project and needed his help. For the first couple of hours she didn't hear from him, but in the evening, when Ana's phone had phantom-vibrated for the tenth time, he finally texted: *Sure and ice cream after? It's on me*

They agreed to meet at Isak's. Ana had no video project, of course, but she did have a camera, and she set it up on the table in front of him and gave him a piece of paper.

This is in Romanian?

Yes, I'd like you to read it aloud.

She told him the piece explored the experience of living in a foreign language, and Isak nodded, and then he stammered his way through the text: *Eu, cel mai frumos băiat de pe pământ te iau să-mi prietenă, iubită, mamă a copiilor mei și soție a mea*, and so on. It was a marriage vow, and without realizing it, sitting in front of the camera, Isak promised to love and honor her, for better and for worse, in times of good art and times of bad art, to comfort and encourage her, and to take her as a friend and lover and the mother of his children, from this day forward to be her fiancé.

Was that good enough? he asked, glancing up.

Ana nodded, barely able to speak. She was fighting the lump in her throat, the light that fell askew through the dirty panes, and Isak, who looked exactly like Peter Pan. She spent that night on Isak's boat, and the next in his apartment. She dropped by Sjøfly-havnen with tea and stopped bothering to study, living off Maria cookies and spring water and semen, and lost so much weight she had to punch a new hole in her belt. She bought a toothbrush, and moved so much of her clothing to his apartment that by early April she'd de facto moved in. Together they visited his grandma in Sandnes, went to services at St. Mary's Church, and when the college organized a study trip to Galicia, Isak bought a ticket and went with them.

Are you sure you want to come? said Ana. You don't have to.

Of course I do, said Isak. I've got to look after my little girl.

I'll never forget it, said Ana to her video diary, the day before they set off: *my little girl*. And the look in Isak's eyes. The look of a person in love.

The art school had an exchange agreement with the Facultade de Bellas Artes in Pontevedra, and Ana'd never been to Spain before. She'd been looking forward to it for weeks. She'd had enough of Norway's cold and wind and darkness, of winter gnawing at her bones, but when the plane broke through the clouds, the rain was still beating heavily against the wings.

It's probably just a shower, said Isak.

But it wasn't. The rain fell at evening and at night, it fell against the windowpanes in the hotel's breakfast room, and Isak wouldn't put up with it. He wouldn't sit in the hotel and rot, he said, they were only in Galicia once. Then he disappeared into the town. That day Ana was on an excursion with the art-school group, and when she got back she found Isak under a sunshade with a beer.

What's up, baby, he said, swinging a car key around his finger. Where do you want to cruise?

He'd rented a little convertible, and for three days they traced dying villages and deserted resorts, brownfields of a forgotten landscape. Ana had been so high on love for the last two months that she'd fallen drastically behind on her work, and now the semester was nearly over, and they were ransacking Galicia like two vandals, sifting for a story they could use to brew art. They found old farmsteads and a tumbledown industrial estate, drove up hill and down dale—but did Ana make a single video recording? She sensed the highways stretching deep into the continent, the quiver of the mossy forest roads, and she leaned her head against the car seat and took Isak's hand, staring at the hamlets and the Galician rain that seethed in front of her, impossible to capture with her camera. What was she doing with art, anyway? She had her eyes and her ears and her mouth, she had herself and Isak, and the entirety of Europe open before them, a Europe of cities to discover and places to drive, and afternoons so long and soft they seemed to liquefy.

On their fourth day in Galicia, the rain finally stopped. The sun parted the clouds, and the last puddle had scarcely evaporated before the air was full of insects and the towns swelled with girls' bared legs. Isak immediately made a beeline for a nature reserve. He wanted to catch butterflies; he'd bought a net and everything. He wanted to catch the spring, he said, and Ana just wanted to come along. From the parking lot they ran down the mountainside, the day clear and the valley green in front of them, and Ana said: Look, you can see all the way to Portugal! Isak caught a yellow butterfly and one with dots, and before they let them go they whispered messages for the butterflies to carry up to God. Ana sent a greeting to her father and Isak asked for world peace, or maybe some chips, and when they reached an overhanging rock, he flung the net down. He pulled off Ana's dress, she dealt with her underwear, and they stood naked, holding each other, pointing down at the river that snaked through the valley. He traced her beauty spots with his finger, and Ana gulped the air. Oh, it was like getting over a bad cold: To think there were so many scents, such radiant warmth on her skin; and then he thrust into her, and she collapsed onto all fours.

Later, as they sat in the car, she said: Isak. I think that was the happiest hour of my life.

He turned his head. What did you say?

On the mountain. The last hour, I think it was the loveliest of my life.

He reached for her hand and gave it a squeeze, looking into her eyes until he had to glance back at the road.

What do you reckon? he said. Want to get it back?

Get it back? said Ana, and at that moment he pulled over and spun the wheel around. What are you doing, she said with a laugh, and Isak smiled and put his foot down, taking the next exit and speeding down toward the river.

Come on, he said, when they'd parked at the side of the road. Kicking the door open, he tumbled out of the car. Come on, Ana, it's this way. He grabbed her hand and pulled her over to the bridge, the river to Portugal. Come on, get a move on, he laughed, leaping onto the pedestrian crossing. The metal rumbled as they

ran, the water gleaming beneath them through the mesh, and Isak
drummed his fingers against the latticework.

This is a magical bridge, he shouted breathlessly. Can you feel
it? We're traveling through time.

And Ana gasped for air; yes, she could feel it. The vibrations of
the bridge, thrumming all down her fingers and arms and everywhere else, into the roots of her hair, and the river streaming
beneath them, as it had done for thousands of years and would do
long after all borders and time zones had been forgotten. When
they reached the disused custom house on the other side of the
bridge, Isak put his arm around her and pointed at the clock: one
hour earlier than five minutes before.

That afternoon they walked up the slope to Valenças, bought
T-shirts with the Portuguese flag and messed around on the city's
useless fort, which had been conquered first by the barbarians
and later by the Arabs, then by armies from León and Asturias
and Napoleon's troops—oh yes, the French, even them. It was a
sad, pathetic fort, and Isak laughed at it so long he got a stomach
cramp, and as they walked back across the bridge to Spain, Ana
stopped and looked at the river, which ran lazy and golden beneath them.

Isak, she said. Did you know I've time-traveled before?

She'd promised her mother never to tell about the gap in her
life, but she was standing on a bridge that was a time warp where
everything shone, and before she knew it, the words were bub-
bling over, and she was telling him about a fall day in Morocco,
when her father had set his watch and her mother had run for the
phone, and the water had gushed into the bathtub. Isak listened

and nodded. For the first time, the story slithered outside the Ivan family. As the gnats came forth in the dusk, Ana whispered about the silence between her parents, about her father's suicide, about her dead sister, who in a sense was she herself, and as the last light faded from the bridge Isak dried her eyes and didn't understand what was happening or what it would lead to, or how the story was already sidling through the cracks in his mind.

Five weeks after the Portugal trip, Ana was on a plane to Bucharest. She was going home for the summer; it had been a strange time. Isak had worked constantly on an exhibition in Stavanger, and he'd been staying at his grandmother's farm outside Sandnes in order to be closer to the museum. Ana had been busy too. Her semester project was due in late June, and she was doing a whole series of Norwegians reading promises in Romanian.

They only saw each other twice.

The first time was on Isak's grandma's birthday, a weekend full of toasts and dinner guests so polite Ana thought she'd shrivel up. Isak's entire Lutheran family had gathered at a community center outside Sandnes, so the young lovers had to steal their kisses between the inquiries of curious uncles and questions about Dracula and Ceaușescu and whether it was really true that a beer in Romania was cheaper than a bottle of water. When they finally had a moment to themselves, Isak spoke only about the exhibition, about the concrete, which wouldn't take shape.

They're torturing me with all their rules, he said. I can't work like this.

The second time was three days before Ana had to leave for

Bucharest. She'd been to a final critique and got so much praise it was almost embarrassing. At the thesis exhibition she'd met a curator from Prague who asked for her card, and it was in that mood that Ana arrived in Stavanger. Sunburned, her nails painted cornflower blue, she stood on the platform and hummed, astonished by the long summer days, the fresh, cool air, the passengers on the platform, so practically clad in windbreakers and hiking boots, when on a bench along the wall she caught sight of Isak. He hadn't seen her, and when she sat next to him he looked up, pale and disheveled, a cold sore blooming on his lip.

Baby, is that you? he said, smiling. I'd forgotten how cute and tiny you are.

There were only ten days left before Isak's exhibition opened, and he spent all his days at the museum, where he broke up concrete and poured out cement in a Sisyphean process that Ana rapidly gave up trying to understand. She lay on the floor and chattered about everything they should do when he came to Bucharest—the places he should see, the food he should taste—and when she got tired of fantasizing she prepared lunches and snacks, read aloud from the paper, and watched Isak shovel cement.

Ana had been hoping for a romantic gala ball of a weekend, but if she'd thought they were going to be counting shooting stars in the park or kissing until the sun rose, she was very much mistaken. Isak hoarded every minute for his exhibition, tight-fisted even with his seconds; and late at night Ana would wake to find him sitting at the edge of the bed, scribbling a sketch, muttering to himself.

On the morning of the day she was due to leave, they found the time for goodbye sex, and afterward they lay in bed and cuddled.

Sorry I've been so preoccupied, said Isak. It's this stupid exhibition, it's psyching me out.

Ana smiled, stroking his nose down to his cheek. It's okay, she said. We'll be in Bucharest soon, and then we'll have nothing but time to waste.

Fourteen hours and two stopovers later, she could just make out the runway at Otopeni, split and asphalt-patched. When the wheels hit the ground, the passengers clapped and hollered, and in the arrivals hall Ana had to search for half an hour before she found Maria among the swarm of weeping mothers and returning sons, their nylon bags bulging with migrant-worker loot. Ana cried too, but her mother shook her head.

Skin and bone, she sighed, feeling Ana's ribs. Nothing but skin and bone.

In the cab they drove past the dam and Casa Scânteii, which hung as usual like two teenagers in the cityscape, clumsy and oversized. Yet something about the city felt different, and for the first time in her life, Ana noticed the stubbornness, the engineered, unbending river and rule-straight motorway, all the direct lines that insisted on crossing through the city. She remembered Bucharest as a slovenly, chaotic place—she'd warned Isak about street hustlers and lunatic drivers—but she saw now the rational madness, the practical apartment blocks, the six-lane boulevard, the pedestrian underpasses placed at rigidly regular intervals.

God, said Ana. Has it always been like this?

No, sighed Maria. Not when we lived in the villa at Dorobanti.

And then the cab turned into the labyrinth of Drumul Taberei, and Ana rolled down the window and smelled the linden trees and the exhaust and the sweetish, summery scent of garbage. She hadn't been home for a whole year, and was looking forward to seeing what had changed.

The short answer? Fuck all.

The same stringy communal strays barked them welcome in the parking lot, and from the neighbors' windows came the same old soap-opera tune. Outside the corner store, the same old soaks sat on the same old plastic chairs, and the shopkeeper still hadn't forgotten the good times under Ceaușescu, when the whole neighborhood had buttered him up with baked goods and flattery, trying to get their hands on the next scoop of coffee. Up in the apartment, her grandma was snoring the same wet snore, and when Ana met Sorin at the café behind the Academy, he was just as frustrated by the city's lazy and unfaithful men as he had been when Ana left.

Keep going, Sorin, she said with a laugh. I love it when you're angry.

There was something reassuring about the way Bucharest hadn't changed, the way her friends acted like they'd seen her yesterday. She went to the cemetery with her mother, to mass with her grandmother, and in the evening she worked on her videos in her old room, which was exactly as she'd left it, with last summer's newspapers slung across the bedside table.

Ten days after her arrival, Ana stepped inside the café at Strada Covaci to meet Claudia. At first she didn't recognize her, but then she noticed the woman sitting in the corner, her hair twice as long as before, wrapped in a scarf, a cigarette dangling loosely from her lips. She'd swapped practical jeans and sneakers for a long dress, and she didn't wear a bra. Somehow she looked light and porous, sitting there in the lamp's white cone of light, and then she turned, smiled, and brushed back her hair.

Hey, Ana, look at you, she laughed. You haven't changed a bit.

That summer they took long walks through the city, turning every stone of their new lives. Ana chatted about Isak's sculptures and the curator from Prague, while Claudia talked about the Congolese theater director she'd dated in Paris, and about her professor, who'd raised the question of a PhD. They sat in parks and laughed at their ill-starred, incompetent Romanian compatriots, and Claudia took Ana's hand and told her that Bogdan, her childhood friend, had drowned in Vama Veche. When they cut him open at the autopsy they found three ampoules of heroin in his rectum, and rumor had it he was part of a smuggling ring from Transnistria, though that part of the story couldn't be confirmed.

It's odd, sighed Ana, after they'd toasted to Bogdan. There aren't many witnesses to my childhood left.

Congratulations, said Claudia. Now you can just make it up.

Three days later, Claudia left to visit her grandparents in Sighişoara, and that afternoon Isak arrived from Norway. Ana put on her best dress, wrapped a scarf around her hair, and drove to the airport with a cardboard sign that said *Johnny Depp*. The expectant women sighed with disappointment when they saw it was just Isak who came shambling out of the terminal, but Ana had tears in her eyes, and she kissed him so long a policeman yelled, Get a room. Isak looked worn but relieved, and when she asked about his exhibition, he waved his hand.

Fuck that shit, he said. We're here now.

He was sweating, patches spreading underneath his arms, and in the cab he kept quiet while Ana held his hand. In Drumul Taberei she introduced him to her mother and grandmother as a classmate from Norway and showed him the parking lot and her old school, the chess club and her favorite communal dog, and when evening came she made up the bed in the guest room, her father's old office.

Aren't I sleeping with you? asked Isak, and Ana shushed him.

Hey, this isn't Scandinavia. We've got rules here.

Ana's mother still believed Ana was a virgin—or at least Ana believed she believed it—so Isak had to play along with the comedy and sleep in the spare room. If this had been a romance novel, Ana might have snuck in there at night, wet and warm and whispering, while the family was sleeping. But it didn't work like that, and they sat either side of the dinner table on their best behavior, without even playing footsie, and in the evening they lay in their respective beds with their hands folded demurely over the covers. They didn't even manage to sneak a quick fuck while Maria was out shopping, because her grandmother hovered over them like a drone, and after three days in Bucharest Ana was so tired of playing secret lovers that she suggested a visit to Claudia in Sighișoara.

Then you can meet my second favorite person in the world, said Ana, kissing him.

Isak nodded and wiped the sweat off his brow, and when Ana thought about it later she realized he'd never actually agreed to come. He hadn't said no either. He'd said: I guess we could do that. He'd said: That's probably not a bad idea. He didn't commit one way or the other, but early the next morning Ana hauled him out of bed, and one hour later they were sitting on the train, puffing through the suburbs. She laid her head on his shoulder, glad to be alone, but when she put her hand on the bulge in his pants, he pushed it away and twisted his crucifix around his finger.

Hey, he said. Easy now.

They chugged through forests and villages, through fields that had once been Europe's grain store, but Isak didn't notice. He dozed and murmured in his sleep, twitching his leg from time to time, and it irritated Ana. Why was he being such a wet blanket? Why wasn't he interested in her country? She woke him once or twice to show him a magnificent view or steal a kiss, and Isak took her hand and gave her a smile.

Hey, relax, Ana, just chill.

Then he kissed her forehead and Ana smiled. He was heading over the edge, and he didn't know it or he didn't care, or he hid it so well that Ana didn't notice. When the train pulled into the platform the sun was high in the sky, which was dotted here and there with clouds. The scent of resin and cinnamon hung in the station, and behind the building were the jutting church spires. Claudia stood waiting for them in the shade, and when they got off the train she came to meet them. She kissed Ana and asked about their trip, but when she tried to kiss Isak on the cheek he pulled back like he'd gotten an electric shock.

Ana, be careful, he said. There's something wrong with her.

Ana laughed, thinking it was a bad joke, and she took Isak's hand and smiled.

So, she said. Shall we go home and unpack?

But Isak wanted none of it.

No, he said, taking a few steps back. She's evil, that one.

Ana gazed in astonishment at Isak, who was pointing at her best friend.

Just try and act normal, she said. Come on, for Christ's sake, let's go.

But Isak wasn't going anywhere. Well, that's not quite true: He was going away from the devil woman and back to Bucharest, and without another word he rolled their suitcases toward the ticket office.

What's going on? asked Claudia.

No idea, said Ana, and she marched after Isak to ask whether he'd gone completely off his rocker. What the hell was he thinking? What kind of a way was that to treat her friend?

Have you lost it, said Ana. Is it because she's dark, or what? Are you racist?

Isak shook his head, rummaging through his bag while drops of sweat trickled from his brow.

Okay, tried Ana diplomatically. What if we just each lunch? And if you still don't like her, we'll take the first train home.

I'm not eating with her, said Isak. It's her energy, can't you feel it? I can see her face, for God's sake.

What about her face, snapped Ana, scowling down the platform to where Claudia stood and gaped at them. Then Isak grabbed her arm.

Please, he said. I can feel it. She wants nothing good for us.

So there Ana was: her fiancé on one side, her best friend on the other. If she could do it again, she'd sit Isak down on a bench and deal with it calmly, but Ana couldn't take any more bullshit. She was exhausted after the long train journey. She was hungry and sweaty and sick of Isak carrying on. First it was the exhibition stressing him out, now all of a sudden he could sense some monster inside Claudia—no, wait, her *energy*—and if it wasn't one thing it was another. Why didn't he just pull himself together and man up, said Ana, the words grating between her teeth, and then she said, Fine, then. Just buy your stupid ticket.

Done.

They never saw the citadel or the clock tower, nor did they see Vlad the Impaler's childhood home. All they saw in Sighișoara were the station building and Claudia, who vanished through the gates in such a huff she wouldn't speak to Ana for weeks. And so they rocked back across Romania for the second time that day, Isak rubbing his cross between his fingers, Ana buried sullenly in a book. The sun went down behind the mountains, and by the time Ana woke from a nap it had gotten dark. They were cutting through a narrow valley, not a light visible beyond the window-panes, and in front of her Isak's seat was empty.

Ana knew at once that something was wrong. She sat up with a start: the compartment was preternaturally silent, only the creak-ing of tracks to be heard along the corridors. First she checked the dining car, then five identical compartments, and just as she was on the verge of panic she caught sight of him in the aisle, holding his bag as though he were getting off at the next stop.

Jesus, Isak, she said. I thought something had happened.

And perhaps it had, because when he turned his head and Ana looked into his face, it was wholly rigid and white, the pupils black and contracted.

Ana, he said. We can't sleep together anymore.

What—what are you talking about?

Ana. You're just a little girl.

A little girl?

Yes, and I've touched you. And that's not okay.

Yeah, I know you've touched me, she laughed. Now come on back inside, you loon.

No, no, he said calmly. Listen, it's alright. I know what I've done. When we get to Bucharest, we'll go to the police station and I'll turn myself in.

Don't be ridiculous, said Ana, pulling him into the compartment and shoving him onto the seat. For a moment they looked each other in the eyes, and then he rummaged in his bag again, drew out a notebook and began to scribble. Small, shapeless letters. That much Ana could see, although she didn't understand the Norwegian words on the paper. He filled the page so densely that even the margin was covered, and she was astonished. Usually Isak only drew, and she should have asked what he was writing, but she said nothing. She was too weary to speak another word. Finally the train reached the city limits, and Ana packed books and jackets into her bag and stood at the compartment door and looked at him. Coming? she asked, but Isak didn't answer. He put down his notebook and gazed out at the city lights, his eyes lit with the central station's neon—red, purple, blue—and the glow of a thought it was impossible to follow.

That was it. That was their big summer in Romania, and four days later they were sitting on a plane to Norway. When they landed in Flesland, Isak kissed her goodbye—he had to make the train to Stavanger—and Ana was left alone, watching her suitcase trundle around the carousel. She didn't hear from him for a week. She had the key to his boat, but it sat so low in the water, bumping against its mooring, that she couldn't read or work. When she couldn't stand it any longer, she went home to Jorunn and rang the bell.

So, what now? said Jorunn, when Ana had told her about their summer. Think you should pack your stuff and get out?

Get out?

Yeah, he doesn't sound very well.

Oh, no, said Ana, drawing up her legs beneath her. He's just going through a rough patch.

A few days later, Isak returned to Bergen. His T-shirt was laundered and his beard shaved; he looked fresh, and as he folded out a chart on the kitchen table he explained his new project. The whole thing was already planned and arranged. He just had to sort out the practical side, and then he'd sail his boat up to a little settlement in Nordland, right where the Arctic Circle cuts through the coast.

Nordland, said Ana. What on earth do you want there?

I've had it with Bergen, he said. These people, they can't think for themselves.

That week Isak began to ready the boat. The motor hadn't been used in years, so he hunted up spare parts and cleaned off rust and dirt, giving the hull a coat of paint. Jorunn began to get worried. She hovered over Ana and chaperoned her to the studio, and over the weekend she dragged her to her family's summer cottage. At first Ana didn't want to go, but Jorunn insisted, so they drove north to the family cabin and sat in the little front room with the doors open to the lake, talking about art and drinking boxed wine and laughing themselves into fits at the dragon tattoo Jorunn's ex-boyfriend had just gotten in the middle of his back.

You'll see, said Jorunn, as they were lying in their sleeping bags. Booze and art and cigarettes. You'll soon be back on track.

Ana smiled. She didn't want to seem ungrateful.

But Jorunn, she said. There isn't anything wrong.

Oh, come on, Ana, wake up. Isak's not well.

But Ana didn't want to hear it. Isak was stressed, she explained, he was a sensitive guy, and the exhibition had taken a toll. If they didn't stick together when times were tough, then what was the point of being together? Driveling on into the darkness, Ana just kept going: Think how much that exhibition meant to him, she said. You'd be upset too, wouldn't you?

For two days Ana prattled about Isak. Poor Jorunn, God knows how she put up with it. On Monday they packed the car and drove home to Bergen, and when Ana crawled down into the boat, she found Isak bent over a tub of crawling crabs he'd fished out of the harbor.

Baby, take a look at that, he said, kissing her cheek. We've got everything we need right here in the fjord.

What, crabs?

Yes, crabs. What do we need with all this crap? he said, flinging out his arm as though to encompass the harbor and the city, the shops and their wares, the highways full of cars, the families on their way to Oslo or Denmark and the rest of Europe, to the whole putrid continent that lay beyond.

That evening they sucked out the crabs' claws, and later they drank tea and played chess and talked about the Northern Lights and indoor cats and friends who were long dead, but when night came, when Ana was flushed with rum toddies and Isak's hand resting so close to her leg, he put down the mug and shook his head.

Think about it, Ana. You were just a little girl.

When?

When I molested you.

For a second she looked at him to see if he was joking. Then she leaned back on the bed and sighed.

Isak, for Christ's sake, I'm twenty-seven years old.

Don't give me that, he said, waving his hand. I know what I've done.

But you haven't done anything, she said, getting to her feet. Rummaging through her bag, she took out her student card.

Look, she said, slapping it down on the coffee table. It says right there. I just finished art school. Do you think they'd let me go to art school if I were a child?

But Isak resolutely shook his head. It's wrong, he said. You told me that yourself. You're much younger than it says.

Christ, said Ana. If you won't believe me, let's go to the police. Isn't that what you wanted? Let's do it.

For a moment he hesitated, then he stood up.

Okay, he said. But it has to be the Stavanger police. I don't give a shit about the corrupt pigs in Bergen.

Early the next morning they packed up the car and drove to Stavanger. Six long hours over bridges and into tunnels, through a landscape so incredibly beautiful that Ana couldn't comprehend it. The fog that hung above the hills actually existed. The green fields wedged among the rocks, the shadows that wandered over the fjord—all of it was real, yet the whole situation was so absurd she was experiencing it at arm's length, as if she were standing outside and watching herself in a comedy or farce, lost in the vaudevillian bowels of someone else's dream, and then they turned off the main road and drove through the town and parked outside Stavanger's gray lump of a police station.

So, what can I help you with? asked the officer behind the counter.

My name is Isak Bringedal, he said. And I'd like to turn myself in.

Well, now, said the officer. I see.

It's because I've slept with a minor. Her.

Isak pointed at Ana, and for a moment the officer was quiet. Only his gray mustache twitched a little, and he leaned back slightly in his chair, looking from Isak to Ana and back again. Then he cleared his throat.

Right, well. We'd better take a look at this. If you'll just wait here, someone'll come and get you.

Before long they were led into an office, where a policeman sat behind a desk and Ana and Isak sat in upholstered chairs. Isak stated his date of birth and address, and then he told the man about Ana, the underage Romanian girl he'd slept with. Ana couldn't believe her eyes or ears or senses in general. If this had been Romania, he'd have been chucked into a cell and his family milked for bribes, but the officer just nodded and took notes, adding a follow-up question or two, and finally he asked Ana whether he could see her passport. He inspected it carefully and ran it through a machine, then he typed a few lines and nodded in thought.

Have a look at this, said the officer, turning to Isak. He pointed at the watermark. I can see this is a real passport. And it says right here she was born in 1979.

Isak looked at the passport skeptically, but before he could speak, the officer continued: And this was consensual sex, or was there any coercion?

Consensual, said Ana.

Yes, consensual, said Isak. But it was with a minor. You understand that, don't you?

The officer nodded, typed a little more on his keyboard and printed out a form, which he filled out. Then he slid it across the table.

Now, you listen to me, said the officer. You did the right thing, coming down here so we could get this straightened out. But there's no doubt about it. Miss Ivan is not a minor.

He reached for his pen, scribbling the date and his signature, and Ana had never seen anyone look as relieved as Isak when the officer stamped the form three times. His face lit up, and as they sat in the car in the parking lot, it was like his smile softened, like the muscles in his cheeks relaxed. When Ana asked if he was okay he leaned over the dashboard, hugging the wheel and gasping for air, then sat back in his seat and laughed until he shuddered.

Oh, Ana, he laughed. They said it themselves. They've just said it. I haven't done a thing.

He sat and roared with laughter, and Ana laughed too, and when he could breathe again he started the motor, and they drove to the ice-cream stand and bought the most outrageous cone Ana had ever set eyes on. It had chocolate and strawberry, vanilla and pistachio, soft serve, and a marshmallowy topping, and when they couldn't cram any more down they drove along the fjord to Sandnes, high on sugar and forgiveness. It was a soft afternoon, Isak's hand rested on her leg, warm but not clammy, and Ana was so full and hot and drowsy that the sensations came pouring in. Her sluice gates were open, unobstructed by thought, and they sat for a while in silence, gazing through the windows at the shadows that reached down the hills, the gulls that circled the harbor, the light that grew deeper and deeper, but as they drove around the hill, a wind crept through the pane, and Isak turned to her, his lips tensed and pale.

You knew him, didn't you?

Ana looked at him.

The officer, he said. You knew the officer. Do you really think I'm that stupid?

She turned toward the window, smelling the wind and the dampness of the coming fall.

It was an actor, he said. Say it was an actor.

Isak, no, she whispered. No more.

I saw the way you looked at him.

Isak, no.

Okay, I may not be a great artist, he snarled, but I'm not a fucking idiot.

That evening Ana checked into a hostel. She didn't want to stay at Isak's grandma's. She lay in bed and cried quietly, but so ceaselessly that the girl in the top bunk hopped down and sat beside the bed.

Hey, she said. It'll be alright.

No, sniveled Ana. It doesn't matter. Everyone I love is ruined.

The next morning Ana drifted around in Stavanger, unsure of where to go. She didn't have the keys to the apartment in Bergen, and she didn't want to call Jorunn and admit she'd been right. On her third day in town, she went to an internet café and found an email from Isak.

Ana, I think I've fallen apart a bit. I can't bear everything I've done. I feel pretty wretched, but I think I'm on my way back up to the surface. On the other hand, it's nice to be down here at the bottom. I can see all the people up there on the surface, swimming around in the sun, and I know I'm at the bottom, so I can't get any farther down. I'm stable, I'm stuck in the mud. And no matter what— people, intelligent, with two brains, trying to stick their tongues into each other's holes? You've got to admit, it sounds perverse.

Was that good or bad? Ana didn't know, but she decided to see for herself. Boarding the local bus to Sandnes, she asked the driver to let her know when to get off for Isak's grandmother's farm. She sat at the back with her bag on her lap, staring out of the window at the bus station and the town disappearing behind them. She rested her forehead against the glass and dozed off to the rhythm of the engine, and she didn't wake until the bus driver yelled that this was her stop. Getting up in a muddle, she grabbed her stuff, the bus exhaled and drove away, and she was left alone on the asphalt, blinking in the light reflected from the driveway, where a police car was parked on the gravel.

You're the girlfriend? said the officer, as she approached. Maybe it's best if you come with me.

This is everything they knew: The previous evening, Isak had drunk a whole bottle of whiskey and gone into Stavanger. Several witnesses had seen him rambling around the town, and at two in the morning he'd lumbered onto the bridge. What he wanted there was impossible to tell, but there wasn't much traffic on a weekday night like that, and nobody noticed him climbing over the fence and onto the platform where the steel cables were secured. He stood there for an hour, staring down at the ferries and boats sailing past him below, until suddenly he wasn't any longer. He might have jumped, he might have stumbled. The evidence was ambiguous. It was too dark on the platform for the cameras to catch much detail, but the police report concluded an overwhelming likelihood of suicide.

And so, just as abruptly as Isak had entered Ana's life one winter's evening eighteen months earlier, he disappeared again. Ana wasn't even invited to the funeral. His family made it clear she wasn't welcome, and the following nights she slept on Jorunn's sofa. During the day, while Jorunn was at work, she sat in the window and stared at the gulls, and in the evening she walked along the harbor and cried until her face felt dissolved. Her body changed. Her breasts and hips deflated, her eye sockets darkened, her cheeks swelled from crying. She'd sit in St. Mary's Church, whispering about why she hadn't sent Isak to the doctor, why she hadn't called his family, a psychiatrist, the police. Somebody. She hadn't realized anything was wrong, she tried to tell herself, but soon she was cast into doubt, and asked family and friends if the whole thing was her fault.

Jorunn shook her head. You can't conjure up psychoses. Who do you think you are, she grinned, a witch or something?

Ana's mother wasn't so sure. Isak probably had a predisposition, she reasoned, but something had to push the poor boy over the edge, and maybe Ana's time-travel story had been the final shove.

So it *was* my fault? sobbed Ana down the phone.

I'm not saying that. But what you don't know can't drive you crazy.

For several months Ana remained in Bergen, wondering whether to stay and find a job. But, frankly—what was there to keep her? Isak was dead, Jorunn was starting a teaching job in Oslo, and as soon as the first cold blew down from the mountains, she bought a ticket to Bucharest. It's there we find her next: back in her old room in Drumul Taberei.

So, what now? asked Maria, as they sat at the dinner table that first evening. Maybe a Romanian next time?

No, I'm done with men, said Ana, smoothing the tablecloth.

From now on I'm going to live like a prime number. Wild and unbroken and only divisible by myself.

Ana's grandma had passed away that fall, leaving mother and daughter alone in the apartment once more. During the day they went to the market. They shopped and cooked. In the evening they watched television and drank tea. Now and again, Ana walked up the hill behind the bus stop and gazed out across the blocks, which were bound to be her home forever now. She felt infinitely tired, and certain that her life was over. Sure, there would be events—mealtimes, movies at the cinema, days of sun and days of rain—but she'd never be alive again. And so the days passed silently, short, muffled weeks huddling to form a muted, vacuous year. Ana and her mother cleaned and cooked; they'd made a pact. Ana never asked about Morocco, about those two years and the sister she'd never met. Maria never asked about Isak and her time in Norway, and even when she saw Ana's work, full of video clips and photographs and a whole saga about Isak's library card, she just nodded and said: Looks good, Ana. Genuinely.

Instead of talking about all the tragedies, Maria talked about the Good Years: about the tile factory and her family's confiscated forest, about her own father, the famous dentist, and about the villa at Dorobanti, where she'd seen her parents dance the Lancers macabre on the night the Securitate's dark Dacias came gliding up the driveway.

On Ciprian's birthday, Ana borrowed a dress from her mother, and together they drove into town for dinner. On the way they passed the Institute, and Ana asked the driver to stop for a moment. She hadn't been there for nearly seven years, and I've seen the sad picture they took that day: two widows in old frocks, wan and mistrustful, each with a dry smile on her lips. At the restaurant they drank two bottles of wine, and when they were mid-dessert Maria drew a gift from her bag. It was a shabby old book, its spine held together with tape, and Maria tapped the cover heavily.

I think your dad would have wanted you to have this.

Ana opened it at once. It was Euclid's *Elements*, its pages thoroughly scrawled with Ciprian's notes and commentary, his drawings in a childish hand. In the middle was a photograph of a girl, no more than a year old, and when she got home she put it in a frame and hung it above her desk. Over the next few months her art began to change. Her work filled with formulae and number theory, science crept into her videos, and gradually she formed her practice. She studied the philosophy of time, became obsessed with calendars and clocks and the resonant frequency of caesium-133, and every evening she tried to capture time by keeping a logbook. She read Henri Bergson and J.M.E. McTaggart and several shelves' worth of quantum physics, and on the rare occasions she held exhibitions, it wasn't at galleries downtown but at studios and exhibition spaces belonging to friends and acquaintances abroad. She was part of a show in Prague, of another in Vienna, and one fall she had a residency in Villa Waldberta with Ciprian Mureşan, who was representing Romania at the Venice Biennial the following spring. But as soon as she got home again, she barricaded herself in her old room and kept herself aloof from the Bucharest art scene. She kept house and washed clothes, cooked food and went shopping, occasionally meeting a friend from art school.

Ana, they said. Why didn't you come to the opening? Why are you wasting your talent?

One year became three. In the parks, the chestnuts dropped from the trees and sprouted anew; in the city center, scaffolding rose and was abandoned; and one day Ana was sitting in a café on Strada Covaci, trying to find a title for a piece she was exhibiting in New York. She was hunched over the form they'd sent her, filling out the title of the work, her name and birthday, when a tap on the windowpane made her turn. Outside it had begun to rain. She saw the drops fall diagonally against the glass, saw them gather into glistening patches in the headlamps' beams, and for a moment she pictured the rain falling over Bucharest. She pictured it pattering down on Cişmigiu Gardens and gathering in dark puddles on the Institute's roof, whipping against the gables in Drumul Taberei and onward to the dunes by the sea. Pictured the droplets seeming to hover in the dark between the shops and the townhouses on the other side of the street, between the long boulevards of the apartment blocks and all the lives that were lived there, and then she lifted her pen and filled out the title, name, and birthday. She called the work *The Time Traveler*, her name was Ana Ivan, and she was twenty-eight and thirty years old.

This was the story Ana told me in the blacked-out gallery, and in the stillness that followed her words I imagined Isak lurching on the edge of the metal bridge, at once living and dead, existing in two states at the same time, like an electron in superposition. For a long while I waited for the next anecdote, but no more came. A quiet sniff, a rustle as she pressed against the sheet: That was all. I listened to Ana's breathing as it seemed to grow weaker, her inhalations shallower and shallower, and I don't know how long I

lay on the mattress, whether I fell asleep, but through the blackness I saw or dreamed about a coin, a silver or cupronickel coin,
rasping against the toe of a shoe. Perhaps it was the closeted air in
the gallery, but it felt like my head and fingers were buzzing—my
tongue and lips dry, my whole body longing for fresh air—and
when I sat up on the mattress, Ana was no longer by my side. For
a few minutes I groped around for her, calling her name, but she
wasn't there, or she wasn't answering, and at last I got to my feet
and stumbled out of the gallery.

Outside, it was still dark. I unlocked my bike and trundled
home through the deserted streets. The puddles had nearly evaporated, the cicadas hissed from the trees in the park, and when I got
back to the apartment I felt drained, used. I pulled off my shoes
and clothes, and the last thing I did before crawling into bed was
plug my dead phone in to charge. From the bed I saw the screen
light up, and before I fell asleep I noticed the time was just past
twelve, but perhaps that was just a guess or a dream.

When I woke up again, it was nearly sunrise. The first yellow
light of dawn seeped between the buildings, the street was still
free of dog walkers, not a single yoga mat was in sight, and when
I switched on the computer and checked my email I discovered it
was early Tuesday morning. For a moment I stared at the screen.
Then I checked a few news sites, and sure enough: It had been
more than thirty hours since I'd stepped inside Ana's installation.
Either I'd spent more than twenty-four hours in the gallery, or I'd
slept that long in bed, or I'd mixed up the days and thought Monday was Sunday when I opened the gallery door. None of those
explanations made sense, and for a while I sat on the windowsill
and tried to work out how it all fit together: Ana's stories, my re-

tellings, Isak Bringedal's sad, short life. Down on the street, the traffic was beginning to swell. From my window I could see the trees, the leaves rippling in the wind, the flowers, or what was left of them, lying brown and sludgy in their beds, and then I opened a document and wrote down Ana's latest stories. I tried to think about Isak. Tried to imagine him in his apartment in Bergen, functional and anonymous, as I pictured it, on the top floor of a red apartment block, smoking or maybe sitting on the sofa, while Ana told a story. I tried to picture Isak Bringedal, on the couch or maybe on a bridge, listening to Ana, and then my head began to ache. Then my hands began to tremble and I shut my eyes. There was something disturbing about Isak's story that had escaped my attention, but I couldn't put my finger on what exactly. Isak sat on the couch with a cigarette, or he stood on the bridge in the dusk while Ana talked, and I sat at the window while my gaze wandered over the desk, the walls, the floors, the bits of furniture; but no matter where I looked there was something I didn't want to see. Lærke's towel hanging from the doorknob on the wardrobe, the silly pink one from the dollar store, the only thing she'd left behind, like a residue of her being. On the floor by the mattress were business cards from my brother's festival and a map of the stadium in Finland, and on the desk: stacks of Ana's stories, notes about her life. It felt as though I had a name on the tip of my tongue, some thought or memory that kept slithering away. Then, before it came to me, I got up and walked through the single small room of the apartment, saddled with the objects that until recently had constituted the basis of my whole life, without looking at them or bumping into them, a maneuver that required the grace of a ballet dancer. I picked up the phone and called Ana, listening to the drone of the ringing until it collapsed into voice mail, and when she didn't pick up on my third try, I headed for the gallery.

Johnson Avenue looked like an abandoned construction site or battlefield. The road potholed or cratered, a smell of something rotting, the gallery shrouded in a cloud of dust. When I tried the door it was locked, the note about *Timemachine* no longer attached to the mailbox, but down the block the loading doors were open and two men emerged from the gallery carrying a crate. The shutters seemed to have been opened, the electricity switched on, and when I peeked inside the gallery I noticed the rope around the room had been removed, the black cloth was gone, and everything was steeped in a sharp, tawdry light.

Can I help you? one of the men said, wiping sweat from his nose.

Yes, I'm looking for Ana Ivan. The artist.

I don't know, man, no Ana around here.

She was doing the performance. In the dark. Do you know when she ended it?

Nah, we only just got here.

What about the gallerist, is he around?

Sorry, we're just installing the show. I think you're going to have to call his assistant.

But is he here?

I dunno. You better call the assistant.

I looked over his shoulder for any sight of the gallerist, or maybe of Ana or Irene, but all I saw were the white walls, the floor of metal sheets coruscating under the fluorescent lamps, a single wooden crate marooned in the center of that enormous room. I thanked the art handler and got on my bike again and rode to

Ana's studio, soft asphalt sticking to the tires. On the top floor the heat was suffocating. This time there were no sounds of activity, no smell of fresh-cut wood. No one opened when I knocked on the studio's chipboard door, the rooftop was deserted, and even the dumpsters had been emptied. The whole building seemed to be abandoned, evacuated in the face of an impending demolition, and I hurried down the stairs, afraid of getting stuck in the ancient elevator. I went home, exhausted from the humid air, and after calling Ana's voicemail and sending her another email, I sat on the windowsill with my computer in my lap and watched the first of thousands of office workers returning from the city looking drained or sapped or wrung dry of dreams, eyes fixed on their phones as they dissipated through the streets.

When I woke up the next day it was almost noon. I was still dressed, and on the pillow next to me the computer showed some amateur documentary about the Ganzfeld effect, the browser lost in a vortex of online videos. As I took a cold shower I thought about my night in the blackened gallery, searching for any clues as to why Ana didn't answer my calls, if I might have said or done something wrong. Then I dressed and sat down by the fan, browsing through the library books on sensory deprivation, trying not to call Ana to listen to the ringing bleating like an echo of my last unanswered call. Late in the afternoon, when I couldn't stand it any longer, I called Irene's number, and when she didn't answer, I found her website, found her office address, found my keys and my wallet, and went down the stairs.

Across the river the sun was still above the towers, hovering like a kind of mirage. Or not the sun, but what appeared to be the sun, because it was one of those days when the light glitters in the windowpanes, or the reflections glitter, and the sun seems to emerge where it isn't. I moved slowly through the translucent neighborhoods along the waterfront, without quite understanding what I wanted. Everything that made up Ana she'd placed in my hands: her stories, her secrets, her experiments, for a moment even her body, while she herself vanished into darkness. But what was I supposed to do with all of it? Maybe I was hoping Irene could answer that question, or maybe I was just hoping for someone to talk to. In any case, I made a beeline for her building.

I'd imagined an office either like Ana's studio, a raw and industrial workshop, or someplace sterile like a clinic or a gallery, white, and full of simple sharp-cornered furniture. The reality landed somewhere between my imaginary poles: a coworking space on the third floor of an unremarkable building furnished with desks and office chairs, wall-to-wall carpet, a vending machine, and a water cooler. An intern showed me Irene's empty cubicle, and I unfolded a chair and waited under the droning light of the fluorescent tubes. No, lighting doesn't drone, I thought; maybe there was a printer or an air conditioner humming through the landscape of the office, a landscape that must once have been stately and simple, but which now was overgrown with decades of architectonic excrescence. Oak windowsills peeped out beneath plastic paneling, the ceiling had been lowered dramatically, and all the carpet and walls and ceiling tiles were gray. And not the kind of gray that radiated order and quiet; no, the gray of a derelict tower block, and the block had been under siege. Then the main door opened, and I saw Irene's torso glide toward me, her legs concealed by the row of cubicles.

What's up? she said. I heard you were in here.

She looked at me with surprised suspicion or maybe amused boredom, as though she'd just discovered waiting on her desk a gift or cupcake she didn't want. Then she dropped her bag on the floor and started rummaging through it, telling me about a call she was waiting for, that the phone might ring at any moment, and all the while a smile was glued to her lips.

And what about you? she said, as she dug out her notebook and phone charger, her tissues and keys. How's it going with those stories?

The ones I sent in, you mean? I never heard back.

Well, whatever. What matters is we got them written down. They don't need to be masterpieces.

Then she sat in her chair and leaned back, cradling her phone in her lap.

What's up? she said again.

Ana, I said. I don't know, I don't think she's doing very well. I went to see her, but she isn't at her studio or at the gallery, and she isn't returning my calls.

Of course she's not at the gallery. The show is over, Irene said, glancing at her phone, and when she didn't add anything else, I tried to explain Ana's mangled speech, full of lost Romanian words, and I repeated what she'd said: that she felt like a virus or a curse, that she ruined the people around her. I said she'd cried and asked me to leave, then told me about Isak anyway. Irene smiled. I wasn't sure if it was something on her phone or if it was me who'd amused her, so I told her about Ana's story, about the two years her parents had invented, and about what the story had cost: Ciprian's suicide, Isak's madness, my own disturbed months.

Maybe there's something to it, I said, and I told her about the hours I'd followed Ana into the dark, the days and nights I'd spent writing down her stories, how for each word of Ana's I'd repeated, the further away I'd slid from all that was real and tangible, from my girlfriend and my brother and my university studies, and while I talked the humming in the office pressed in around us, like the sound compacted into a single pulsing point, a point that disturbingly seemed to be Irene's lap, and I told her how I'd pushed Lærke away, that I had even turned my back on my own brother, that all I had left now were the stacks of Ana's memories and imaginings, memories that weren't even my own, until suddenly a new whine opened between Irene's legs, a whine that turned out to be a ringtone, and then Irene got to her feet with a sweeping, apologetic hand gesture, picked up the phone, and stalked out of the office.

Dusk was falling, or something like it. I don't know how long I waited for Irene, but when she returned the direct light of day had vanished from the office, and the gray surfaces beneath the desks were sinking into black.

Funny, that, said Irene, sitting down and pointing at the phone. My friend. It was kind of like what you were saying.

What was?

Do you know my friend Anastasia?

Sounds familiar, I said, afraid it was a name I ought to know, an artist Irene was about to school me on. But it wasn't an artist she had in mind; it was just a friend, an academic with a PhD in French Creole who'd been dating a classical musician for a few years. Irene had met them a handful of times and they were a beautiful couple, the linguist and the wind instrumentalist, but then one spring or summer's day the linguist was on her way home from a conference when she got an email. An email from her oboist. Yeah, we all know where this is going. He'd met someone or it couldn't go on or he didn't love her anymore, Irene couldn't remember. But he was moving on. For a while the poor French Creolist tried her best to win him back. She sent desperate texts, but he soon changed his number. She showed up at his apartment late at night, but a new tenant soon answered her buzz. That's when she realized she barely knew any of the oboist's friends, and he wasn't on good terms with his family, or pretended not to be, who knows, she never met them. In any case, all the linguist could do to calm her nerves was stalk him on social media. Poring over his photos, she soon discovered another woman, an expat Ukrainian architect or city planner who showed up in the periphery of the oboist's posts with alarming frequency. Soon, sure enough, the Ukrainian started liking the same pictures as he did, she started commenting on his posts, and one night, staggering home after a few drinks too many, the linguist could no longer hold back her rage. She sent the oboist a message or a tirade, demanding to know who this Ukrainian architect was. The result being, of course, that the oboist blocked her, leaving her with no recourse but to carefully construct a new, fake profile. Not that it took that much care. A bland and neutral name, a handful of photos downloaded from some random profile—that was all, really. And armed with this new avatar, the expert in Bourbonnais Creole started adding and following the draftsmen and architects and resort developers in the Ukrainian's circles, started adding the Ukrainian's ex-coworkers and college classmates, and finally, after a few weeks, began following the Ukrainian herself. It's not like she was proud of it, Irene said. The linguist had trouble sleeping back then, and the pills didn't work, so she just kept at it all night long, sifting through hundreds or maybe thousands of posts with the strangest ideas racing through her mind, until one night or morning she saw a video sent by the Ukrainian architect from an aquarium in some seaside town or neighborhood, and could have sworn she heard the voice of her oboist in the background. His face wasn't in the picture, and as far as she knew the oboist never went to the coast, but for a second she *did* hear his laughter, and then the image dissolved and she was plunged back into the fluorescent night of her basement bedroom.

Do you see what I'm talking about? Irene said.

Yeah. She stalked her ex.

Well, yes. But she also descended into fiction.

The linguist did?

Right, said Irene, although back then the linguist didn't think about it in those terms. She just scrolled through the newsfeed of her fictional profile, and one night she saw a photo posted of the oboist or his doppelgänger having dinner with a group of architects at a restaurant in Brighton Beach. Trawling through the photos and videos tagged there, she noticed another picture of the Ukrainian architect sipping wine with a man by her side, a man with a back like her oboist, and that same night she got on the southbound Q train. For an insomniac, it wasn't such a bad ride. As soon as they emerged from the tunnel at Prospect Park they barreled down the elevated tracks, the city glimmering on the horizon, her mind in some half-conscious stupor, until the doors pulled open and the ocean breeze wafted in, and when she shifted in her seat she saw a glimpse of the architect's maimed face and Astroland grotesquely silhouetted through the darkness. Most nights she'd sit at the bar in the seaside restaurant, staring at the dinner parties until a waiter stirred her and she'd go freshen up in the salty or deep-fried or sticky-sweet breeze of the boardwalk. That's where she met the other Ukrainians. They were underemployed adjuncts, PhDs like herself, Anastasia and Vadim and their crew. They wrote high-school admission essays for the children of Chinese industrialists, carving out a business writing like aspirational twelve-year-olds, that's how they made a living. Not a very glamorous living, let's be honest, but a living nonetheless, like amoebae persisting in the cavities of a tooth, in the rotten molar of some great and terrifying predator. Now, Irene wouldn't say they became friends overnight, the Ukrainians and the linguist, but one evening they did show her where to get the best pirozhki in Brighton Beach, and there were moments when the linguist felt happy listening to Anastasia's ramblings, or sitting around in bars pouring water into their glasses so the waiters wouldn't foist another drink on them. It was still the summer break, after all, and the French Creolist still couldn't sleep at night, so to pass the time she started picking up Ukrainian. She was not a linguist for nothing, and to build her vocabulary Anastasia took her to the warehouse parties in Ridgewood where she DJ'ed on the weekends, to after-hours clubs in Bed-Stuy, and to late-morning drug sessions in moldy bungalows in Sheepshead Bay, the two of them sinking farther and farther south through the borough, until, eventually, they arrived in Brighton Beach, where Anastasia retreated to her cramped apartment and the linguist went back to the restaurant, thinking or maybe whispering: I know you're here, you can't hide forever. But evidently the oboist could, because she never did see his face again, except one night as she sat on the Q train passing through Midwood, the wild parrots probably screeching in the background, and on the seat next to her she sensed a shape, a tender presence she remembered, and slowly she turned around and saw his face, or a face just like it, a sleeping face that morphed into the face of Anastasia, as if the whole thing were a telenovela with an endless list of actors all playing the same parts, and that's when Anastasia opened her eyes, and that's when the linguist took her hand, and that's when she put her head in her lap and fell, finally, asleep.

Irene cast down her eyes. In her lap the phone was vibrating, and I could have asked what happened then, I could have asked what she meant or was insinuating by the story, but instead I just sat mutely and stared at Irene's half-illuminated face, watching her pastel-painted nails dance across the screen.

That's it, she said, looking up.

She fell asleep?

Yup. A happy ending, she said, and at that moment or the one right after it the lights in the office went out. We'd been sitting still for too long, but neither of us waved our arms, and neither of us clapped our hands. For a few seconds we sat gazing at each other in the darkness, or in the cone of light that fell through the pane like a searchlight from the office on the other side of the street. I think I could see Irene's teeth brighten into a smile, and I thought: Is she calling me an insomniac stalker? Is it me that's the jilted lover? Is she just full of shit? Then Irene flicked her hand and the lights came back on, and she picked up her keys and phone and grabbed her handbag off the floor, so there could be no mistaking that it was time to go. As I got up, Irene said something I couldn't hear.

Sorry, I said. What?

Don't worry, she'll let you know when she's ready.

Ready for what, I thought, as Irene accompanied me to the door. When I'd walked a few steps down the stairs, I turned around. Irene was still standing in the doorframe staring at me, a smile on her lips and the phone glowing in her hand. Talk soon, she said, and then she shut the door.

That evening I tried again to write about Isak. I tried to conjure him on the bridge in the dusk, listening to Ana's story, wearing a Portuguese T-shirt two sizes too small and the smile of someone teetering between curiosity and dread, a thought already gestating behind the synapses and sodium-potassium pumps, behind the forehead soon to be crushed against the waters of Stavanger harbor, a forehead to weep for, as I tried to imagine it. A little after midnight, the one remaining light across the street was switched off, but I went back to my computer as though summoned by the words Ana had spoken, words that I repeated deep into the night like some mournful incantation. The sun rose over Brooklyn. And then again, any number of times, while I tried to transcribe what Ana had told me, sitting at my computer or standing by the sink, watching myself from the outside: a young man bent over his desk in the dusty glow of a lamp, poor, lonely, sleepless, obviously lost in illusions. Irene was right. The show was over. The curators and critics had paid their visits, the reviews were already published, the collectors had groped their way through the darkness, and somewhere Ana was probably constructing a new piece. It was all done, rent was coming up, I didn't have the money, and the only food around was granola and coffee, so much coffee that my hand shook and the pen skittered over the paper like it was transmitting in Morse code: What are you doing? Get out of there, go home to Denmark, forget all about Ana and her deranged boyfriend, forget all about that woman and her experiments nourished on anti-light, on anti-matter and non-time, on two years that never happened. And I stared at the text again, and I tried to picture Isak on the bridge, but I couldn't or I didn't want to, and then I shut down the computer and grabbed a plastic bag from under the sink. The apartment was a mess. The desk was flooded with papers and folders and dirty glasses, the floor stacked with books and plates and unwashed clothes. Unfurling the bag, I took note-books down from shelves, gathered the short stories and articles, crumpled up drafts and the photograph of Ana, and I threw it all into the bag, and the next morning I returned my books on the perception of time to the library.

It was mid-August. I'd run out of ideas—out of money too—and although I knew I should give up the apartment, forget Ana's story, and get on with my life, I couldn't pull myself together. Something told me the story wasn't over, and reluctant as I was to get fur-ther entangled in Ana's fantasies, I still hoped for a last goodbye, a conclusion or a resolution, or maybe just proof that the past few months weren't sheer manipulation.

At the end of August came the phone call I was waiting for. It was early morning, not later than six or seven, when the garbage men were still busy on the street, and I fumbled for my phone, half asleep. Lighting up the screen was Irene's number, and before I could think twice my hand had picked up the phone and my finger had touched the screen, and my voice had said hello.

Did I wake you? said Irene.

Yeah, you did, actually.

Sorry, I know it's early. But I was wondering if you had time for a quick meeting today.

Today? Yeah, I'm sure we can sort something out. What's it about?

It's about Ana. There's a bakery in Woodside, not far from her apartment. Shall we meet there, say ten o'clock?

Sure.

Good, I'll send you the address.

It was already a hot, oppressive day when I biked north a few hours later. The whole route up the back of the city, behind the crooked pipes of the refinery, across the Greenpoint Avenue Bridge, over the barges loaded with slag, past the glinting heaps of scrap metal and the containers, rusty and full of stagnant rain, I tried to guess what Irene might want to tell me about Ana. There'd been something oddly mechanical about her voice on the phone, like she'd had to concentrate to breathe and shape air into words, but every time a thought arose I didn't dare follow it through to the end. Finally I reached the shops of Roosevelt Avenue, crouched under the elevated tracks of the 7 train, and caught sight of a Chinese bakery between the terraced houses. When I stepped through the doorway, I couldn't see Irene anywhere. Ordering coffee, I sat by the window and listened to a traffic cop, who was standing in the shadow of the awning and speaking loudly into his phone. When it was twenty past ten, I ordered another coffee and began to drum my fingers against the table, increasingly nervous that Irene wouldn't show up. At ten thirty I called her, but she didn't pick up, and when I tried Ana's phone a voice said the number I'd dialed was no longer in service. I sat there for another fifteen minutes before I paid the bill, and I was just gathering my stuff when a dark-haired girl came walking into the bakery. She was small and short, not more than eleven or twelve years old. She glanced around, then, catching my eye, made a beeline for me.

Excuse me, she said. Are you waiting for Ana Ivan?

Yeah, in a way. I was going to meet her colleague.

Okay, here. I'm supposed to give you this.

Thanks, I said, as she handed me a shiny white plastic bag.

Then she smiled and nodded, and before I could ask what had become of Ana and Irene, she turned and made for the exit. For a moment I considered running after her, but then my eyes fell to the bag and the black notebook inside, and I recognized it immediately. It was Ana's logbook. I remembered the frayed spine, her name in silver felt-tip, and I lifted the book out of the bag and turned it over in my hand. When I opened the first page, an odd sensation prickled at my neck. A feeling that someone was looking at me, like I was in the middle of a performance or a show, and I turned and peered around, but the bakery was completely empty, even the traffic cop had left, and so I closed the book and got to my feet. One last glance over my shoulder, then I stepped out into the street and ducked beneath a taco cart's tarpaulin, heavy with rainwater and dark with soot, and walked south in the striped shadows of the railway ties.

That day I followed the Newtown Creek down through Brooklyn to its stale source in Bushwick. When I reached Morgan Avenue, I sat at a coffee shop, called my landlord, and gave notice. Through the window I could see the warehouses and metal fences of the industrial park, figures flickering across the warm asphalt like holograms, and when it began to get dark I stood up and walked the last half mile to my brother's building. For a few minutes I circled the entrance, then I squared up in the gateway and pressed the button next to his name. Silence for a second or two. Then the gate buzzed and I trudged upstairs, and when he saw me from the doorway his eyes shone with surprise.

What the hell, he said, smiling. You look like shit.

Over two beers we chatted about the biennale in Spain, about Lærke, who'd left, about Ana's phone number, which was disconnected, and then he opened his computer and let me listen in as he fired his assistant in Helsinki. He grabbed his pot and tobacco and rolling papers, and when he'd lit a joint he leaned back on the sofa with a smile.

It's good to have you back, he said. Now it's the two of us against the fucking Finns.

Yeah, I said. It's just us now.

A few weeks later I packed up my scant possessions. The mattress I threw onto the street, the lamp and dresser I sold online. The books I gathered into a pile, ready for a thrift shop, and when I'd packed my final suitcase I paused at the kitchen sink and glanced around me. There wasn't much left of my life. Piece by piece it had disappeared: one less girlfriend, one less friend, soon one less city, until all that remained from the past six months was a fraying notebook. From the sink I could see it in the pile. Several times I'd tried to throw it out, but now it was in front of me I couldn't take my eyes off it. The shiny black surface, the worn white spine. I tried to resist, but after a minute or two I put down the dishcloth and picked it up. For a moment I let my hand glide across the cover, then I opened the book and leafed through the pages.

ACKNOWLEDGMENTS

This book wouldn't have existed without Cristina David and her constant mingling of fact with fiction.

Special thanks to Anna Will for her relentless drive in animating this novel; and to Geoff Shandler and Chloe Moffett for believing in what she brought to life.

Thank you to Caroline Waight for her rigorousness, craft, and patience; and to Jenny Thor for her vision and perseverance in bringing this book to just the right readers.

Thank you to readers Maria Marqvard, Oline Møller Wissing, Martin Rosengaard, Janne Breinholt Bak, Stinne Lender, Szilvia Molnar, Minna Haddar, and Claire Stephanic for their helpful suggestions.

Thank you to James Hannaham, Maxim Loskutoff, Clarinda Mac Low, Jakab Orsos, Emily Witt, and Cathrin Wirtz for opening up America.

Thank you to the curators and artists who responded to endless queries: Marian Ivan, Yvonne Bialek, Alexandra Croitoru, Dana Kopel, Florin Bobu, Livia Pancu; and to the tranzit.ro/ residency in Iaşi.

Grateful acknowledgment to the Danish Arts Foundation for generous support; and to Candace and Doug Loskutoff for hospitality.

Finally, my deepest gratitude to my parents, my brother, Louise, and Magnus for their love, patience, and belief.

About the author

2 Meet Mikkel Rosengaard

About the book

3 Behind the Book
13 Questions for Discussion

Read on

17 "Papaala, Me'ekamui,
Vectorgold"—A short story

Insights,
Interviews
& More . . .

Meet
Mikkel Rosengaard

© Caitlan Hickey

MIKKEL ROSENGAARD is a three-time recipient of the Danish Arts Foundation's Literary Fellowship. His fiction has been published in five languages and his nonfiction has appeared in the *Architectural Review*, *Bomb Magazine*, *Guernica*, PBS's *ART21 Magazine*, and many other publications. He grew up in Elsinore, Denmark, and now lives in New York City. ∽

A Conversation Between Julie Buntin and Mikkel Rosengaard

In Julie Buntin's bestselling debut novel, *Marlena*, a librarian tells the story of a passionate high-school friendship that spirals into drug abuse. In Mikkel Rosengaard's debut, *The Invention of Ana*, first published in Denmark in 2016, an intern tells the story of an unlikely friendship with an uncompromising artist who retreats into a blacked-out gallery. Both novels are told by naïve narrators who fall into friendships with dominant and seductive characters. And both novels explore the dangers of losing yourself in another person's story.

Buntin and Rosengaard first met in the fall of 2010, and they are both transports to New York City from the rural Midwest and from Denmark, respectively. As they slugged through post-recession literary New York, they attended the same readings and shared the same group of writer friends, often equally enamored of the seductive characters around them. For the U.S. launch of *The Invention of Ana*, Buntin interviewed Rosengaard about crafting vague but compelling narrators, being seduced by another person's story—and by the mirages of New York. ▶

A Conversation Between Julie Buntin and Mikkel Rosengaard *(continued)*

Julie Buntin: *The Invention of Ana* is one of those magical books that will mean something different to everyone. It can be read like a story about an unlikely friendship. It's also about communist Romania, time perception, visual art, and about what it means to disappear in a narrative, and how dangerous and intoxicating it can be to lose yourself to someone else's story. Out of all these layers, what was the thing that drew you in and made you write this book?

Mikkel Rosengaard: The idea that got me started was to write a story of seduction. But where instead of boy meets girl, it would be an anecdote that was the Don Juan character. The novel would follow this one story as it traveled from person to person, seducing everyone it meets along the way. When I started writing the book back in 2010, Knausgaard had just published *My Struggle* in Scandinavia, and there was this autofiction mania going on. All the papers and literature magazines were full of essays where Knausgaard and the other autofictionists were claiming that society was drowning in fabricated stories. That we were all suffocating on stories told by advertisement, social media, political campaigns, TV, films, and so on, and that we had to rid ourselves from these manipulative narratives by writing something more authentic. And of course, I could understand their disgust. I too was feeling frustrated with the political campaigns and social media feeds and advertorials and so on, all these manipulative stories clamoring for attention all around us. But I found it strangely reactionary and nostalgic, to think that we would go back to a more authentic and honest mode of telling stories. I felt that, if we really wanted to explore and understand our contemporary moment, we had to *through* fabricated and manipulative narratives. All the storytelling we are all marinating in today, none of it is going to go away. We can't just turn our back on it. So with this book, I wanted to do the opposite of autofiction. I wanted to write a novel that was all about stories being manipulative. A novel about a story so manipulating, that it not only changed a person's life, but changed a physical aspect of reality.

Julie Buntin: Yes, I find it interesting how this book is almost anti-autofiction. I thought it was really refreshing how the book resists those ideas of authenticity. It's popular right now to say reality is the most interesting thing, or that this is the age of reality in fiction. And this book is so *not* autofiction. It deals with fiction and narrative on every page, both in terms of plot but also in how it's written and structured. The novel is narrated by this unnamed intern who gets obsessed with an artist, Ana, who is telling these stories about her life that ▶

swamp the novel and take over his life. I wonder—why did you choose to have it narrated by someone else and not through Ana?

Mikkel Rosengaard: If the book was just about getting Ana's story across to the reader, then having Ana narrate her own story would be the natural choice. But to me, the whole point of the book was showing the power of a storytelling and how a story can thwart and mold and shape reality. And in order to show how this story contaminates all these layers of the Ivan family's lives, it had to be narrated by someone who was not part of Ana's family. Someone who had a larger perspective. Or else it would just be Ana's story. It wouldn't be a story about stories. Or about how narratives can pass from person to person. Because this book is just as much about what it means to listen to a story.

Julie Buntin: Yes, the novel asks some really interesting questions about what it means to hear and tell somebody else's story. At one point, Ana calls the narrator a vampire, accusing him of sucking out her exotic stories. The novel doesn't offer a clear answer but I'm curious, what do you think as a writer? Do you think it's okay to tell a story that is not your own?

Mikkel Rosengaard: It's a really difficult question. Especially when you are telling a story from a culture that is not your own. Who owns a story? Is it the person who experienced it? I don't have a straight answer, but I think a story always has a life of its own. A story is never static. It is continuously passed on, it is retold, it changes shape, it goes in and out of people's lives. And that shape-shifting process has always interested me. How we make up stories and then those stories go on to shape both the person telling and the one listening.

Julie Buntin: Your narrator describes himself as "a shadow of a man." And I think that is a hard move as a writer, to create a narrator who is compelling *despite* himself. Because even if the narrator is a shadow of a man, you have to make the reader feel compelled by the narrator's story too. You can't get the reader to care unless they really feel connected to the narrator's journey. Otherwise, the whole novel falls apart.

Mikkel Rosengaard: Exactly, it is a very difficult move. I spent a very long time trying to get the balance right. It actually took me years. But I feel like it's an important area to explore, this kind of weak or uncompelling narrator. The voice of the naïve or enthusiastic follower, this kind of minion or yes-man who tags along and loses himself in a stronger person's fictional world, that voice seems very ripe for exploration. Especially when you look at our ▶

A Conversation Between Julie Buntin and Mikkel Rosengaard *(continued)*

political landscape today. I imagine you went through some of the trouble making an uncompelling narrator work, because you are doing that same balancing act in *Marlena*. Where your narrator is telling the story of her friend Marlena. And Marlena's story is much darker and more complex and compelling than the narrator's own.

Julie Buntin: Yes, and getting it right was hard. An easy cop-out to make the intern more interesting, would have been to make Ana and the narrator have a relationship. But you didn't. The narrator lives with his Danish girlfriend when he becomes obsessed with Ana's stories. And instead of creating a romantic relationship, the act of storytelling is the center of the book. The story is the seducer, not Ana. As a writer, I thought, Mikkel's defying expectations here in a way that's really interesting.

Mikkel Rosengaard: It was crucial to me that Ana and the narrator did *not* have a romantic relationship. But the curious thing is, no matter what you do as a writer, if you introduce a man and a woman in an intimate situation, the reader will automatically assume that something romantic is brewing. This is one of my favorite things as a writer, playing with these archetypes. If you put a boy and a girl together, then you barely have to do any work as a writer.

The reader will assume that now they are going to fall in love. Even if you are actively planting clues that this romance is *not* happening. As a writer, that sets you free. While the reader is busy filling out the gaps of the love story, you can create an entirely different kind of narrative. And when the reader accepts that is not a story of romance, hopefully this alternative narrative will come as a pleasant surprise.

Julie Buntin: *The Invention of Ana* is also a novel about ideas. I learned a lot of things as I read this book. For example, the NASA experiments about living underground for six months, which I had a nightmare about the other night. There are all these ideas about sensory deprivation, philosophy of time, perception. How were you able to fit all these ideas in with the plot and the emotional lives of the characters?

Mikkel Rosengaard: The story at the center of the book—the story that seduces everyone it meets, the Don Juan story—is a story about a Daylight Savings switchover that goes wrong and has all kinds of consequences for the Ivan family. And since the central story in the novel was about time and time perception, I started reading up on the philosophy of time. What struck me early on in this research was a theory of time called *block time* or *eternalism*. This theory believes that time should ▶

not be understood as a flow but more like a landscape that is continuously expanding. For example, right now we are sitting in Brooklyn, but just because our consciousnesses are here, that doesn't mean that Manhattan or Copenhagen or Jupiter has stopped existing. And the same goes for time. Just because your consciousness is right here in 2018, that doesn't mean that 1985 or last Friday no longer exists. All moments exists at once: your four-year-old birthday party and your first kiss, Saturday's tequila shots and Sunday's hangover, too. It all exists simultaneously and the past is never over. I remember very clearly the night I read that theory—it was late, midnight or one in the morning, and the moment I grasped the vastness of that idea, I grabbed my coat and raced down to the bar where my girlfriend was working. She had just finished her shift and was dancing with some friends, and I remember standing on the dance floor yelling above the music, crying, trying to explain that nothing was ever over, and that every kiss we shared and everything we ever did together would last forever. It was the most romantic thing I had ever read.

Julie Buntin: And that moment is happening right now.

Mikkel Rosengaard: Exactly! And in the novel, I wanted Ana to live according to that theory of time, the block-time universe. Which is of course impossible, but I wanted that idea of time to inform the way Ana lived her life. Without retorting to sci-fi or fantasy. I mean, it's not impossible to fully grasp the idea that the past and present is happening simultaneously. Our minds simply can't comprehend it. But I wanted to at least try and imbue the book with this ethereal idea without the book ever leaving our normal, pedestrian, everyday kind of physics.

Julie Buntin: Another thing I admired is how the novel is also a really beautiful love letter to Brooklyn. And I guess I'm curious—you are not from here, so I wonder about your relationship to this city and what Brooklyn means to you as a writer and for this book.

Mikkel Rosengaard: New York is a place that lives off this one deeply seductive story. The story about making it in the city, about becoming someone under the big lights, that whole "Empire State of Mind" thing. Whenever I go back to Copenhagen, I'm always struck by how often I see that story projected, even all the way over there in Scandinavia. You'll see some model running between yellow cabs in a TV commercial, a fashion shoot set in Chinatown, all kinds of advertisement using the Manhattan skyline or the fire escapes. And since *The Invention of Ana* is a novel about storytelling, it made sense to me that the book should be set in this mirage of a city, this place that feeds off seductive storytelling. And since the story of New York is almost entirely a story about Manhattan, I thought it would be interesting to have the characters live and work in Brooklyn. Because this is the reality for most young artists today. Nobody can afford Manhattan anymore, it's a domain for the one percent. So in the novel, the characters never make it into Manhattan. They are spending all their time in Brooklyn and Queens, and Manhattan only exists as this shimmering, shiny island in the horizon, as a story that is pulling them in. I think a lot of people can relate to that story. You are from the rural Midwest. I'm from a provincial town in Denmark. We both came here because of the story of New York. In that way, the city is the biggest Don Juan character. It seduced both of us. It's seducing millions every day. ◠

Questions for Discussion

1. The novel tells the story of Ana, her parents' lives during the Ceauşescu dictatorship, and the two surplus years in Ana's life, but the novel is narrated by a man who doesn't play any role in the Ivan family and who isn't even Romanian. What is the effect of having an outsider tell the story? What does the narrator and his fascination with Ana add to the book?

2. Before Ana tells the narrator about her sister, Ana says that her *"time-travel story had already ruined far too many lives, and it would have been better if she'd never told it to anybody."* Why do you think Ana tells her stories to the narrator? What does the narrator represent to Ana that she needs or can use?

3. Throughout the novel, there are no quotation marks to indicate dialogue. What is the effect of this seamless blending of Ana's spoken words and the narrator's recounting of the events? How would the novel have been different if Rosengaard had provided quotation marks to indicate spoken dialogue?

4. Ana and her father play a game where they connect random dots ▶

on paper to construct a picture.
What does this game tell us about
how Ana understands the events of
her life? How is this game connected
to how she tells her stories? Why
do you think Ciprian whispers
"Humbug, humbug" when they
play the game?

5. The narrator becomes deeply
fascinated with Ana's story, yet
nothing romantic happens between
them. Despite spending many nights
together, they never fall in love or try
to seduce each other romantically.
Could Ana's storytelling be seen
as a kind of seduction? What could
Rosengaard be trying to say by
making Ana's story the Don Juan
character of the novel?

6. When Ana's parents first fall in
love *"they lay chatting in the garret
deep into the night, blithely unaware
that they were echoing the state radio
broadcasts playing in the background,
which spun tales of its own."* What is
the effect of juxtaposing Ceaușescu's
authoritarian propaganda with the
sweet-talk of two lovers?

7. After the death of her fiancée,
Ana says she is *"going to live like a
prime number. Wild and unbroken
and only divisible by myself."* What
does she mean by that? How is living
"like a prime number" different
from the way Ciprian lived a life
of mathematics? Could the Ivan

family's obsession with mathematics be seen as method of creating order in a chaotic existence?

8. Ana deals with many losses— her father's suicide, the death of her fiancé—but in spite of adversity she manages to live a fulfilling, creative life. How do the other characters in the novel deal with loss and adversity? For instance, Ciprian losing his mathematical career, Isak messing up his museum exhibition, Maria and Ciprian losing their firstborn. Why do you think Maria and Ana survive their loses, while Ciprian and Isak break down? How do Ana and Maria use storytelling to cope with loss?

9. Why do you think the relationship between Lærke and the narrator ends? Is it the narrator's fault— is he too absent? Is it Lærke's fault— is she too demanding? Is it Ana's fault—is she too intrusive?

10. The narrator characterizes himself as *"a shadow of a man"* and *"a mosquito man [living] off the suffering of others."* Do you agree with these characterizations? Is the narrator taking advantage of Ana and her stories? Or is it Ana and the older brother who are taking advantage of the narrator?

11. Toward the end of the book, a curator asks the narrator to come to a bakery where he receives Ana's ▶

logbook. When he picks it up he feels *"that someone was looking at me, like I was in the middle of a performance or a show."* Why do you think he feels this way? Later, when he tries to throw the logbook out, he cannot bring himself to get rid of it. Why do you think it so difficult for him to let go? Is the logbook the beginning of something new for him?

12. In Adolfo Bioy Casares's novel *The Invention of Morel* (1940), a nameless fugitive falls in love with a woman he later discovers to be just a hologram. The fugitive realizes that the inventor of a holographic machine, Mr. Morel, has captured the woman's actions with his machine in order to reproduce reality and loop her actions for all eternity. Why do you think Rosengaard chose the title *The Invention of Ana*? Who could be re-creating and looping reality in *The Invention of Ana*? And would Ana be the inventor or the one being invented—or both?

13. The narrator becomes euphoric when he starts writing Ana's stories. What does this tell us about him? Does he feel alive only when he imagines he is living out a story? Is this a common trait in today's society—do we only live through the stories we tell, perform, and imagine? ◠

Papaala, Me'ekamui, Vectorgold

A short story by Mikkel Rosengaard

Translated by Caroline Waight
First published in Stonecutter Journal, *2018*

I

These days, whenever the credit card terminal gives a beep or a wire transfer pops up on my phone, I can't help but think of the twin kingdoms of Me'ekamui and Papaala and their sovereign ruler, King David Peii II, doing battle with the global financial world among servers and computers deep in the Melanesian jungle. I first heard the king's name last year from Julia W., a PhD student in German literature at NYU, who had stumbled across the story in one of the academic journals where she and her colleagues deposit their research.

That winter's evening I'd been skyping with Julia while she was on a research trip to Berlin, and we'd lost all sense of time and place in a discussion about the Bitcoins her boyfriend had started mining. Darkness had fallen in her apartment, and her contours twitched through the twilight, disintegrating and reassembling in the radio waves or electromagnetic pulses, while Julia explained that there was something diabolical about Bitcoins, ▶

because they defied reality. Like nightmares, they existed only in our imagination, degenerate and warped, all bonds cut to the world of the real.

And the money in your bank account, that's a figment of the imagination too, said Julia, explaining that throughout human history money had always been based on valuable *objects*. First people exchanged goods, then they bartered in gold and silver coins, and even after the governments of the world began to print paper money the notes could always be exchanged for gold. For half a century the Federal Reserve had defined one dollar as 1/35th of an

ounce of gold, and since all other currencies could be converted into dollars, all the world's money rested ultimately on a bed of gold—a system known as the gold standard. So far so good. Until, forty-six years ago, a shift occurred.

Our symbols rebelled, said Julia. They broke off. They began to slip their bonds to the physical world.

In the 1960s, when the post-war economic boom had come to an end and Western economies were beginning to stagnate, the American government realized that it would soon lack the money to pay its bills. Either spending had to be cut or money had to be printed. Cuts weren't an option in the middle of a nuclear arms race and the Vietnam War, but neither could they simply print new money at will, not while every dollar had to be convertible into gold. In 1971 Richard Nixon charted a radical new course. In a televised speech to the nation, the president declared he was going to uncouple the dollar from gold and leave everybody's money resting on— well, on nothing.

It was an experiment the likes of which the world had never seen. If a dollar could no longer be converted into gold, then what was it worth? Overnight, money was no longer tied to the physical world. It was based solely on our *conception* of value.

There's something perverse about it, said Julia. Our money has wrenched free of reality; it's like Santa. It's only worth something as long as we believe in it.

I objected that a dollar had plenty of value, as long as there was a demand for it, but Julia had no time for that sort of nearsighted twaddle. I had to see things from the broader perspective: it was as though the word *tree* had relaxed its grip on poplars and firs, referring no longer to oak, birch, or alder but merely pointing back toward itself in an eternally self-referential circle, like a snake devouring its own tail.

Julia sent me a few graphs, explaining that since the Nixon shock, the Fed and the other banks had introduced 3.7 *trillion* new dollars into circulation. 3,700 billion dollars, in other words, invented out of thin air—but how did we know all that money was worth anything if it wasn't tied to the physical world? It was an illusion, a sleight of ▸

hand—and was it coincidence, Julia
wanted to know, that 1971 just so
happened to be the point at which
income inequality began to explode?
Across all the centuries money had been
tied to precious metal, productivity and
the hourly wage had gone hand in hand.
When a worker produced more per hour,
she was paid more for her time. But the
moment currencies were set adrift and
money was tied solely to a notional
value, the hourly wage stagnated, even
as productivity continued to skyrocket.

You see that graph? said Julia. No
economists can explain what's going on.
How could they? They don't even know
what a dollar *is*.

In 1976 the Federal Reserve removed
all reference to gold from its definition of
the dollar, and since then no definition
has existed. Ditto for the euro and the
yen and the pound and so on: either the
central banks have no definition, or they
define their currency in relation to other
currencies, like the Danish krone, your
teeny little country's copy-cat currency,
said Julia, which is fixed as one 7.46038th
of a euro, basically a fiction defined by
a fiction; and then I asked Julia to back
up a little and tell me how she got into
all this monetary stuff. Apparently her
interest had been spurred by a piece
of writing she'd stumbled across while
researching German colonial history
in the Pacific Ocean, an article that
discussed a new gold standard taking
shape in the kingdom of Papaala.

I'd never heard of this kingdom,

and as Julia continued her monologue about the quantity theory of money, I googled it and was presented with a few Tumblr profiles and a fashion blog— no sovereign realm in sight. Adding *kingdom* and *gold standard* turned up a spa resort in the Caribbean and a branch of the Jehovah's Witnesses, but there was nothing about Papaala. Julia, annoyed by the interruption, tried various spellings—Papala, Papalaa, with and without *Pacific Ocean*—but without success. Before we logged off— it was getting late in Berlin—she insisted that the country she was thinking of was an island realm somewhere in the Bismarck Archipelago. All right, all right, I said, and wished her good night, imagining that the kingdom originated in some film or TV series, and that in Julia's head it had got tangled up with all the financial theories she was dabbling with. Before I switched off the computer, I scanned the Pacific Ocean using Google's virtual globe, and the familiarity of the countries reassured me that imagination and reality must have coalesced in Julia's mind.

The next morning she emailed me from the library of the Ethnological Museum. She was looking at the article on the screen in front of her, in an issue of *Governance and Development in Melanesia*. Sure, a journal pretty far out on the academic fringe, as she freely admitted, but there it was in black and white: The Royal Kingdom of Papaala, ▶

Papaala, Me'ekamui, Vectorgold *(continued)*

a pseudo-state at the southern tip of Bougainville, itself an autonomous Cyprus-sized island in eastern Papua New Guinea. I told Julia I'd love to read the article, and soon a PDF materialized in my inbox.

The article described a financial movement aimed at wresting first Bougainville, then the rest of the world's developing countries, free from the global banking system. The idea was simple enough: the movement wanted to create a virtual blockchain currency, Vectorgold, which like Bitcoins could be freely traded online without any interference from the banks. But whereas dollars and pesos and Bitcoins are based solely on trust, Vectorgold could be exchanged for real, physical gold at any time. The new currency was supposed to ensure stability and sustainability: money would once again be grounded in the physically tangible, not on castles in the air, and soon all the debt-ridden nations of the world would switch to the new currency, casting off the serfdom imposed by the banks and sending a big fat fuck you to the financial vultures in London, Frankfurt, and New York.

The first part of the text sounded legitimate enough, but as I continued to read I couldn't help noticing the language grow hazy, the phrasing cryptic. The article mentioned *two* semi-fictitious states, Papaala and Me'ekamui, where the global financial revolution had begun, but whether the states had any real power, whether they governed an actual population, was only vaguely and equivocally described. I underlined, for instance, that *Papaala presents itself as the financial bedrock of a new state*, and—more cryptically still—*Me'ekamui is the hardware, Papaala is the software; Me'ekamui is the body, Papaala is the spirit*.

Later that week Julia sent me her login for NYU's servers, and with access to all the world's academic journals I delved deep into Bougainville's history. It seemed the kingdom of Me'ekamui had emerged as the result of a bloody conflict over gold: tons and tons of gold. For in the middle of Bougainville's verdant central ridge is an abyss, and through the pit of its maw runs one of the world's richest gold and copper veins, Panguna, which contains metal reserves valuing more than 50 billion dollars. Since the 1930s, gold, silver, copper, and uranium had been dug out of Panguna, while its riches were syphoned into the pockets of the Australian mining corporation Rio Tinto and the government of Papua New Guinea in Port Moresby. But perhaps they dug too greedily and too deep, because the fish in the rivers started to vanish, the women gave birth to malformed children, and within a few years the island's flying foxes had gone extinct.

Local engineer Francis Ona, who was employed by the mining corporation and had seen the environmental damage ▶

Papaala, Me'ekamui, Vectorgold *(continued)*

with his own eyes, demanded action, and the corporation agreed to appoint a committee to investigate the effects of mining on the island's fauna and freshwater. But when their report concluded that the water in the river was sparkling pure and that the flying foxes had all died of a virus, Ona marched out of Panguna. When he returned, it was with a rebel army. The mine was sabotaged, the power cut, and when the Papua New Guinean government sent in a squad of riot police, Ona's ecological militia began murdering foreign consultants at Panguna. The corporation and police withdrew, the airport was burned to the ground, and from his mine Francis Ona proclaimed the island the autonomous state of Me'ekamui.

One man's freedom fighter, another man's terrorist group, and the government and Rio Tinto, not inclined to give up one of the world's richest mines, soon countered with a military invasion. The island was plunged into a brutal civil war. Villages went up in smoke, civilians were executed, and up to 15,000 people died, but even after the government hired a band of ex-apartheid mercenaries, even after Francis Ona died of malaria in 2004, the army of invaders could not prise the gold mine out of Me'ekamui's grip.

On that much the articles were in agreement, but how all this avarice and misery was connected to the global

money markets I had no clue. And
what about that other pseudo-state,
Papaala; what about the virtual gold-
backed currency? Julia asked around
at the university, but to no avail, and
even after questioning a German
anthropologist who specialized in
Melanesia she returned with the same
answer: nobody had heard of Papaala
or Vectorgold.

II

Six months later, on a sluggish day in
August when my boss was on vacation
and my colleagues were absorbed in
their Snapchats, dating sites, and
wedding registries, my friend Chloe
messaged to ask whether I had time to
read something for her. It was rare for
Chloe to ask a favor. As a child during
the dot-com bubble, she'd seen her father
invest the family's entire savings in a
company that, with Whoopi Goldberg
as standard-bearer, sold online gift
cards, and it was in the ruins of this
now-bankrupt chimera that Chloe had
grown up. The family was forced to
sell the house, Chloe had to share a
room with her teenage brother, Gabe,
and after their parents' divorce their
dad went to live with a neo-Pentecostal
community in Panama. Their college
fund ransacked, Chloe and Gabe worked
in soap factories and bicycle repair shops
as they drudged their way through the
cheapest schools in the Midwest, but ▶

despite their budget degrees they'd both landed excellent jobs: Chloe as a senior executive at a charitable foundation and Gabe as head of digital development at an investment bank in Singapore.

Or such had been the case until recently, anyway, because that day Chloe told me that her brother had quit his job and sold his apartment to launch a fintech start-up with a group of Japanese and Australian investors. It all sounded exciting enough in theory, but there was something about the company's prospectus that Chloe didn't like. The language was somehow both woolly and overwrought, like the evangelical mumbo-jumbo their dad was always pushing, and before we logged off I promised I'd take a look at the document.

On the train home from work I scrolled through the PDF, and when I read the title I felt an odd prickling sensation wash over me, a kind of dizziness I'd rather not go into here, because this is a story about Me'ekamui, Papaala, and Vectorgold, and not about my nerves. Beneath the title *Vectorgold*, the prospectus set forth the idea of a virtual currency that could be exchanged at any time for physical gold, and at the bottom of the page I noticed an orange logo and a signature: the First International Bank of Papaala, in association with King David Pei II. I could barely believe what I was reading. Six months earlier I'd stumbled across the rumor of a fictitious kingdom and a dubious financial revolution, and now I was staring at a document signed by the king of a country that didn't exist, all of it articulate, professionally presented, and without the least trace of irony.

Who was this king, now materialized and taking shape in reality? That evening I googled his name and was directed to the far reaches of the internet: a Mormon investment blog, a forum f or Australian neo-colonialists, a self-published book about the rebel army of Me'ekamui. The motley assortment of websites didn't agree on much. That the king's civilian name was Noah Musingku, that he was behind a pyramid scheme in Port Moresby in the 1990s, that he'd hightailed it straight from this scam into Me'ekamui, and that Francis Ona had bestowed upon Musingku his own sub-kingdom, dubbing it Papaala—so far they were in agreement. That King Pei II almost never left his jungle palace, that he spent his silent days on the internet, that he had renamed the calendar months after precious metals and wore a nine-pound crown of solid gold—several websites mentioned that, too. But where the Australian writers referred to Noah Musingku as a charismatic swindler, the humbugging leader of a cargo cult, another handful of bloggers described King Pei II as a pioneer and freedom fighter seeking to jailbreak the island from the gilded prison of the financial world.

Clearly Chloe had good reason to worry about her brother. But I had no ▶

idea what I should write to her. What,
from among this jumble of pseudo-states
and gold mines, offshore companies and
eco-warriors, pyramid schemes and
digital currencies, was true? One
question was blindingly obvious. If
Gabe, King Pei II, and their Australian
and Japanese partners were about to
found a cryptocurrency tied to the gold
standard, then where were they getting
all the gold? Well, the Panguna mine, of
course. But the mine had been dormant
for three decades, and besides, how were
they going to acquire excavators,
hydraulic shovels, and smelting facilities?
How would they lure technicians and
engineers to a fictive state nobody
recognized?

The answer appeared in the form of a
forwarded e-mail three weeks later.
Chloe had been sitting in a coffee shop
when Gabe skyped her from Singapore
airport. He was on his way to Port
Moresby, where he would travel onward
to Bougainville or Me'ekamui or Paalapa
or whatever the island was called these
days, and Chloe had asked him whether
this whole venture was really a good
idea, because how would they ever get all
that gold out of the mine? For an hour
Gabe had babbled on about the digital
gold standard, about how the gold atom
was a child of the stars, created only
through the cosmic collisions of
supernovas, while Chloe listened and
sipped nervously at her coffee, more and
more coffee, until her hand shook and
the teaspoon tapped against the table as

though transmitting in Morse code: wake up, Gabe, come on, go home and forget all about Papaala and its fantasy king, its sovereign fed on virtual currency and quasi-law, on a land that doesn't exist. Chloe got no answer that day at the airport, but three days later she received an e-mail. Gabe can have the last word. Here is his e-mail, in my condensed, lightly edited version.

C,

   Have you ever heard of Yap? It's a teeny little island in the Pacific. Jungle, beach, the works. There are no precious metals out there, and in ancient times they used coconuts, pearls, that sort of thing as money. Then, more than a thousand years ago, sailors from Yap arrived at an island many nautical miles away, and when they went ashore they saw limestone for the first time. Out of the rocks they hewed round blocks as large as mill wheels and sailed them back to Yap, where the inhabitants were like people everywhere else—fascinated by all things new and beautiful and rare. Soon the enormous stones became a precious commodity, and the sailors set out to fetch more. A hunk of limestone could be swapped for a house, it could function as a daughter's dowry; but of course there was one problem. The stones were heavy, troublesome, and costly to move. Nobody knows how the practice began, but soon the stone money transformed from something concrete to something deeply abstract. A fisherman ▶

exchanged a stone with a carpenter, but the stone itself didn't move. It remained standing where it had always stood, but everybody in the village knew that it was now the carpenter who owned it.

In fact, the stone didn't even need to be on Yap. One day several hundred years ago, a barge was on its way to Yap with a newly cut stone when a wave capsized it. The stone sank. Reaching the shore, the sailors told their story, and the village decided the stone had value despite it lying at the bottom of the sea. And today, generations later, there's still a family that owns the stone, even though no one has seen it for hundreds of years.

So where will the gold come from, you ask?

We already have the gold. It's under the mountain; it exists even though nobody has touched it. Why should we dig it out? We have test excavations, we have geological maps, we have fifty years of polluted rivers as proof. We all know the vein of gold exists. And that's all we need.

But it's just a fantasy! you say. It's Dad deluding himself all over again!

It's a mountain, Chloe. It's a ridge full of metals. I've literally set foot on it. In fact, I have my feet planted on it at this very moment. I can feel the grass between my toes, and from where I'm sitting I can see the treetops stretching down the slope. Far beneath me the coastline opens up, the green hills pass into the turquoise sea, and isn't that more real than the numbers in your bank account? The profiles you follow? The stories you read on your

phone? If you don't believe me, come out
and see for yourself. The waterfalls, the
palms swaying in the breeze. Just come,
leave the others to their tiny screens, their
stock-market bubbles, their online lives.
It's not dangerous, Chloe, you can even
bring your phone. We have Wi-Fi, for
Christ's sake. You can sit right here and
look at your screen. You can sit here on
a mountain full of gold and stare at it,
as all that is solid melts into air. ∽